FAIL DEADLY

John Baird Rogers

Mayfield – Napolitani #3

For Beverly, ever my inspiration
and for Geoffrey, Edward, and James,
who repay my pride with decency and love.

Fail-deadly: a concept in nuclear military strategy that encourages deterrence by guaranteeing an immediate, automatic, and overwhelming response to an attack, even if there is no one to trigger such retaliation.

Fail-deadly: The opposite of fail-safe.

Fail-deadly: A hand grenade with the pin pulled.

FAIL DEADLY

Mayfield-Napolitani #3

CHAPTER ONE

INSIDE A GREEN metal-sided shack several miles east of Lake Okeechobee, D'Quan Brown fidgeted as the last two minutes ticked down toward the handshake of HelioCorp's Solar Field One with the US power grid's Eastern Interconnection.

"Deke, aren't you supposed to say something profound about now?"

D'Quan gave a lopsided grin to the comedian on the feed from headquarters.

"How about . . . a small step for solar power and a big-ass jump for your stock option."

Appreciative laughter. They'd all get a big bump when this new technology hit the market and HelioCorp went public.

D'Quan threw the switch that would allow the load leveling software to handshake with the grid. An intruder—a few kilobytes of computer code—saw its opportunity, altered a check digit, and tagged along like a caboose on the leveling instruction. Inside the firewall, it separated itself from the other code and hid in an electronic trash bin.

It was very cool that the engineers had chosen D'Quan to throw the switch on maybe the biggest solar energy project of the year. He deserved it—those weeks working to set up the hundred-football-field array of panels in the Florida summer sun, myriad insects feasting on him, those weeks away from sweet Maria and the kids—now, his proud work coming to fruition.

At T minus ten seconds, the computer countdown started.

The intruder set its self-destruct function for a half-second after attachment.

At two seconds, D'Quan drew in a breath. *Show time.*

At zero, he closed the switch.

The intruder dove into the flow of instructions.

Several milliseconds later, a sound like the sizzle of meat slapped on a hot griddle filled the shack. Two employees standing a hundred feet away felt the prickle that lightning-struck survivors talk about.

Inside the shack, the sizzle took a half-second to climb the audio curve to a scream. It was the last sound D'Quan Brown heard.

CHAPTER TWO

Joe Mayfield cracked the window of the Subaru, letting the thick Florida air rush in. Pine scent, sweetness, and a hint of rot and regeneration. Real Florida air. Not the dry, conditioned stuff he'd left back in Boca Raton, with its glass-and-steel office towers, manicured shrubbery, and gated communities.

He'd charged the car's batteries in Ocala. Now he cleared the commercial clutter on the western edge of the city, and the autopilot headed the car north toward Panacea, the river, the peace and quiet. Mississippi John Hurt played on the car's sound system, singing about Avalon, his hometown. A long weekend with Weezy was coming, Joe's reward for the three months of fourteen-hour days preparing HelioCorp for its initial public offering.

Joe's implant bleeped the HelioCorp tone. He blew out a puff of irritation. It had taken three hours for someone to discover they just had to override his message privacy shield and call. What could it be? Another investment bank demanded to be added to the list of sponsors? Some junior lawyer found a typo in the offering memorandum? Or maybe Kapoor just wanted to chew a chunk off his butt.

Ignore it.

One of the pleasures of this trip was to get away from HelioCorp and its CEO, Brianna Kapoor. The closer the attachment of HelioCorp's solar technology to the Eastern US power grid approached, the more Kapoor's rising tension had magnified her normal irritability. Everyone in the small office felt like they were sitting a few feet away from a high-voltage power line, hair on end, waiting for a paralyzing jolt.

But the main pleasure of getting away was to be with Weezy. The question he needed to ask her had occupied more and more of his mind as the date approached. He pictured paddling on the Wakulla River with her. Maybe that would be the best place to ask. No, better, Ochlockonee Point, looking over the Gulf. Or maybe under the live oak over a takeout dinner from Pelican's Roost.

It wasn't that the long-distance relationship wasn't working: it was that love had crept up on them. She'd said she'd stay a while that day in the canoe three years ago. They had been tentative then—she a loner by nature, his emotions still raw from losing Cynthia to cancer. Weezy was the smartest person he'd ever met—quirky, funny, always exciting to be with. And beautiful. But she was in Bethesda; he was in Florida. She was unlikely to want to move from her job as a tracker at the IAC, America's national firewall, and Panacea felt like home to him. Still, maybe their love would wash the problem away.

Joe's implant bleeped the HelioCorp tone again. He glanced at the console. This time, the call was marked Urgent. Of course. He sighed and tapped the car's video. Kapoor's face filled the screen, the wide-angle lens making her nose seem huge.

"Mayfield, get your ass back here!"

"Why? What happened?"

"You don't see news feeds?"

"No."

"We threw the switch, and it blew up."

"You threw the switch? What switch?"

"You having trouble hearing?"

Joe's mind spun. Attachment to the Eastern Interconnect was scheduled in ten days, a week after he got back to Boca.

"Were you testing the handshake software? It was fine yesterday. No reason to—"

"We decided to go early."

"You mean full connection?"

"No reason not to." Her tone was defensive.

"Good God, Brianna, there's every reason not to. Do you not understand that we are locked into a pattern because of the stock offering? Quiet Period ... that ring a bell?" He realized he was nearly shouting but kept on. "You want to sink your company all by yourself?"

"What? I'm going to upset a bunch of stuffy Ivy League trust fund babies?"

"No. You're going to upset the Securities Exchange Commission, and they are more than capable of shutting the offering down."

Joe rubbed his temple, sick at heart. All that work. "What happened?"

"We threw the friggin' switch. Just like the test yesterday," she said, voice brittle. "The interface software opened a portal through the IAC firewall to the Interconnect. Our power should have flowed into the grid. Should be cool. Should put us ahead of the game. But it blew up. Literally. The full force of the grid came back through the control shack. Took out the substation, destroyed the hardware, and"—her voice quavered—"D'Quan Brown was in the shack, running the junction board."

"Is he—"

"He died. It's a goddamn disaster."

Joe let out a long breath. He remembered Deke joking around with the programmers the other day—easy-going, light-hearted, talking about his kids.

He hung his head, rage fighting with shock over D'Quan and disappointment over his plans ruined. Kapoor stared out of the monitor, waiting for him to say something. "Okay. I'm coming back. Don't talk to anyone outside the company."

Kapoor's eyes slid away from Joe's, and the video signal blipped out.

Joe tapped the brake to disengage the autopilot. He pulled to the side of the road, leaned forward, head in his hands.

"Goddamn you, Kapoor," he slammed the heel of his hand into the steering wheel. How could she be so smart in some ways but so clueless in others? Finally, he exhaled and tapped the console.

"Call Weezy." D'Quan Brown dead and HelioCorp's plans up in smoke. The beautiful weekend, his plans up in smoke, too. He mashed the music off. John Hurt's sweet song was an accusation, too hard to bear.

"Joe, what the hell's going on?"

Weezy appeared on the car's screen, chestnut hair mussed as usual, mouth a thin line, jaw set.

"Weezy, Kapoor just called, and there's a problem—"

"A problem? No, Joe. A problem is something out of an algebra book. This is a friggin' catastrophe."

"HelioCorp? You know about HelioCorp?"

"That fancy implant of yours doesn't keep you up to speed? Of course I mean HelioCorp. Your client has been all over the media. Doesn't she talk to you before—"

"What happened?"

"She apparently scheduled a news conference for later, but a blogger got to her first. She did one of those foam-at-the-mouth diatribes you say are her trademark. She's accusing the IAC of being responsible for the failure of HelioCorp's connection to the power grid."

"Was it? Could it be a firewall glitch? I mean, I know the IAC is hard to pass through by design. Maybe . . ."

"None the system sees. Anyway . . ." Resignation replaced anger in Weezy's eyes. "World's sticking its ugly snout in our love life again."

ON THE RIDE back to Boca, Joe let his fury distill into the speech he would give Kapoor. For the first half of the trip, he let his anger pour out. For the last half, the diatribe modulated into questions: What about building trust with the outside world? Doing what you promise? Being responsible to your employees?

He arrived in Boca after dark. The building's curved glass wall flashed his headlights back at him as he pulled into the HelioCorp parking lot. The first floor was dark but for a couple of offices. HelioCorp occupied the second floor, all windows brightly lit. Joe stepped into the humid night, his glasses fogging, and wished he was parking on the gravel in front of his single-wide trailer in Panacea instead.

He waved his keycard at the door and climbed the circular stairs to the reception area. At the top of the stairs, he heard Kapoor's voice. He couldn't make out the words, but the staccato delivery and tone made her anger clear. He followed the sound toward the far corner of the building. The door to the large conference room was cracked open. Words took shape as he approached.

"Maybe? What do you mean, *maybe*? Was the backflush software in place or wasn't it?"

Joe pushed the door open. The six members of the company's programming group sat at the table. Five of them stared at the tabletop. Brianna Kapoor, a five-foot-two combination of brilliance and pugnaciousness stuffed into a too-small business suit, stood at the end. She leaned toward them, fists planted on the table.

Kapoor's laser-like stare bore into David, a young programmer, who looked ill. Kapoor glanced at Joe, her stare more intimidating, if that was possible. "Where the hell have you been?"

"I turned back as soon as we talked."

"And stopped for a goddamn five-course dinner on the way," she said.

"An accident near Titusville."

"Bullshit!" Kapoor shook her head in disgust. "Sit," she said. Joe worked his way to the back of the room and leaned against the wall, arms crossed.

Kapoor let out a little huff of irritation and said, "For your benefit, we were speaking of the interface between us and the IAC. Since the failure, our programming staff has inspected every line of code in that program and concluded . . ." Kapoor leaned forward, refocused on David. "You were . . . *just saying?*" Her voice became a cruel imitation of his.

"Uh, that the back-flush protection couldn't have been active for—"

"Holy shit." Kapoor rolled her eyes upwards as if conferring with some unseen presence, then turned to the man and said softly, "Of course the back-flush wasn't on."

She stretched her mouth to a grimace. "You're no use here. Get out."

David slumped. The man next to him, Bartek Krol, the company's senior programmer, put his hand on the young man's forearm.

"Stay."

Then he turned to Kapoor. "It would not be wise to send David away. He wrote part of the interface that may have been compromised." His Slavic accent softened the first syllable of the name. The others were silent, as if they had seen an explosion and were waiting for the sound and shock wave.

"Well, *Bar*-teck, if we can't afford to lose *Dah*-vit, then we don't need you, right?"

"It is foolish to treat good employees with disrespect. David was stating the obvious, and—"

"Out!"

"—you will never get the solution by—"

The shockwave hit.

"OUT!"

"As you wish." Krol's nostrils flared. He rose from his chair. "You shout 'out,' and I wish to be out." He gave a slight bow to his colleagues and one to Joe. "I have enjoyed working with you." Turning to Brianna Kapoor, he gave her a half smile but no bow and left the room.

The room seemed to deflate, much like the aftermath of an explosion. Kapoor was silent for a moment, then with a shake of her head, turned her attention to Joe.

"So, mister hotshot finance guy who once managed to hack the IAC, what is it? Your friends found a way to mess up our project, or was it some hacker?"

"Brianna, I have no idea what's going on except what I've heard on the news."

"It's Dr. Kapoor." But she seemed to cool slightly. "What do you think really happened?"

"I have no idea."

"How about your little IAC chickie? Think she knows?"

Rage nearly overtook Joe. The trip to Panacea gone because of Kapoor's selfishness and stupidity, HelioCorp's best programmer quit, and now the diminution of Weezy in front of the group. Joe's fixed glare at Kapoor wiped the smirk off her face.

"Louise Napolitani is nobody's chickie. You know that." He paused to let his silence chastise Kapoor. Weezy became Joe's "chickie" to Kapoor after someone circulated a profile of her titled *Ultra Hacker Gives the IAC the Edge.* Joe had been angry the first time she said it, confronted her the second time. She snarked at him about being hypersensitive but hadn't used it since.

"Or maybe she did it." Kapoor nodded in agreement with herself. "You might have mentioned we're short on cash. A temporary problem, engineered by—what did the *Journal* call her, 'the ultra-hacker'? Maybe a little help from her would let your Wall Street friends swoop in and pick us up for a song. Maybe—"

"No," Joe said with a single shake of his head. No one seemed to breathe.

Kapoor sat down slowly.

Joe waited for another explosion. But Kapoor scanned the other five faces and said, "You know what you have to do. Go to the last backup of the interface before the crash. I want every line scrubbed. Find out what happened!"

No one moved.

"That means now."

Chairs scraped as people stood.

"Mayfield, stay with me."

Joe stayed standing as the others filed out.

"Close it," she said to the guy Krol had protected, who flinched, then closed the door behind him as he left.

"So, your friend Napolitani can't be the person who hacked us, right?" Kapoor smiled as if she was about to pull a rabbit out of her hat. "Then you won't be surprised that she's going to be assigned to solve our problem."

"No, they wouldn't do that. She's a tracker, not an expert in power systems, and—"

"Ahh, but Joe, the IAC is a governmental body." She gave Joe a tight smile and leaned toward him. "The governor is good fishin' buddies with the vice president." She paused for Joe to digest her meaning. "I expect that little chickie of yours is going to be working on this problem by tomorrow."

She gave Joe a huff of triumph and turned to leave.

"Stay with me," Joe said.

Kapoor did an about-face, hand on the door handle, incredulous.

"What?"

"Damn it, Kapoor. Blow your fuse, hose down the people who can help you, but leave Napolitani alone." He paused, watching a sneer forming on Kapoor's face. He continued, "I don't know what caused the problem, but don't make it worse than you already have. You need the support of the people here and people on the outside who admire what you have done. Letting your best programmer quit was foolish. Flaming on the IAC was—"

"Are you telling me what I can and cannot do?" Her lips quivered in barely contained anger.

"Yes, I am. I'm telling you what any advisor who has your best interests at heart—"

"You're forgetting you're just here to get us financed. If you can't do that, why am I paying you?" She leaned toward

Joe, breathing hard. "And don't give me your bullshit about good advice. I know the finance vultures think you're God's gift to business management. And you've wormed your way into the hearts and minds of my employees with your smarmy—"

"Hold on. HelioCorp has a real problem, the kind you should use your brilliance to solve. Ditch the theatrics and work the damn problem. Do that, and I'll stick with you until HelioCorp is back on track. Then I'm leaving."

Joe stopped, shocked at words he hadn't seen coming.

Kapoor, still at the door, now seemed to be using the handle for support.

CHAPTER THREE

WEEZY, HALF AWAKE, felt a soft presence on her face. Joe? Panacea? Jumbled images of morning sun, slow lovemaking, coffee, pancakes. A woodpecker pounding. No, a jackhammer? Wait, no jackhammers in Panacea.

The vision dissolved. The jackhammer was a damp nose-in-the-ear nuzzle-purr. Bethesda, not Panacea. Sappho the cat was in stage one wakeup mode.

Weezy sat up, yawned, and squinted at the clock. 6:40. The alarm was set for seven o'clock. She burrowed back under the covers. She almost succeeded in dozing, but Sappho moved into stage two, which involved walking across her bladder. Weezy reached out of her cocoon and shut off the alarm, got up and stumped into the bathroom. Waking slowly, she peered into the mirror, ran her fingers through her hair, and brushed her teeth. No shower this morning. Then she continued to the kitchen, said "three cups" to the coffee maker, opened a can of Feline Delight for Sappho. Back to the bedroom to her pile of T-shirts and shorts. She found a combination that seemed okay, paired it with yellow socks and Nikes.

Her e-pad noted the weather in Bethesda was normal. The ride to work would be pleasant, but she would sweat on the return trip. The unused ticket to Tallahassee popped up. She sighed. It had been too long without Joe. She wasn't sure whether it was love, but it sure wasn't bad and she wanted more of it. She rolled over last night's conversation. Frustrating, because what Joe had been able to say made little sense. Power surging back at HelioCorp when everything had worked fine the day before? The firewall itself would have nothing to do with a problem like that. The news feed on her e-pad had several articles about the incident, the promise of HelioCorp's solar technology, and Kapoor's career—but nothing to explain the accident.

She rode her bicycle to work from her apartment above the garage of a lovely older Bethesda home. The trip was three miles along curving, tree-lined roads. By the time she entered the IAC bullpen, her boss, Keith Sanders, was in his glass-walled office. It occupied a corner of the half football-field-size space that was the nerve center of the Trackers unit of the InterAgency Channel. The open area held thirty cubicles, each with a desk encircled by several monitors.

A man Weezy recognized as a manager from the utility grid group was in Sanders's office, not quite yelling, hands planted on Sanders's desk. Sanders was leaning back, looking intimidated. Must be something about HelioCorp. Weezy was tempted to insert herself but decided she wouldn't do anything until someone asked. The problem, as far as she could put it together from Joe's scanty details, had nothing to do with her job.

Weezy went through her morning routine. First, she checked the hit list of active hack attempts on a big electronic display on the wall across from Sanders' office. Next, she read the overnight dump from Revelator, a program she'd started writing at MIT. It scanned the many portals into the IAC, identifying attempts to breach the firewall that protected the national data system. Nothing special this morning, but Weezy kept busy, attention jumping from monitor to monitor. She noticed but did not focus on traffic going in and out of Sanders' office.

She was concentrating on a hacker from Indonesia . . . nope, Vietnam . . . who was trying to get into an online broker's clearing system when Madeline Hollingsworth appeared in her peripheral vision. Maddie led the OddBalls, Weezy's best tracking team. She looked like the southern belle she was raised to be and had the sinuous curves that made it hard for most guys to keep their eyes on her face. Looks were deceiving. She was the best mathematician at the IAC and did not suffer fools lightly. The OddBalls called her Mad Dog, meant as a compliment.

"Seems like Keith's having quite a morning," Maddie said.

"Probably that HelioCorp problem." Weezy concentrated on monitor four, waiting for her tracking data on the Vietnamese hacker to finish sending to Enforcement.

"People in and out ever since I got in," Maddie said. "Now, two serious ones doing the power walk. Must be up from DC."

Weezy disengaged from monitor four. Sure enough, several people jammed Keith Sanders' office, all seemingly talking at him. Looking a little hopeless, Keith gestured for Weezy to come to his office. Keith had never just gestured before.

Maddie chuckled. "Guess he needs the SWAT team."

Weezy pushed back her chair and navigated through the workstations, now having the attention of most of the floor.

Keith stood as Weezy entered his office. "Louise, we need your help on a problem that came up yesterday."

The people crowded around Keith's desk turned toward Weezy. "*This* is the genius tracker you were talking about?" expressions made her wish she had at least combed her hair or skipped the yellow socks. Maddie had counseled her after the last such incident, a magazine interview, that 115 pounds stretched over five-feet-eight, the big eyes, and the uncombed chestnut hair made her look like a runway model down on her luck. Also ten years younger than she was. Not like a person who graduated *summa* from MIT in Operations Research. And most of the people staring at her were DC staffers wearing suits.

Introductions circled the room. The IAC Director, two people from the power grid group, two from systems, a woman she knew vaguely as a PR person, and a stocky man whose face resembled a bulldog and whose attitude said Alpha Male.

After twenty minutes of several members of the group chewing over the HelioCorp problem, Weezy knew little more than she had learned from Joe the evening before. Everyone was being overly deferential to Alpha Male, who had a proper name, Granston Harmon, and a business card, which he handed to Weezy. The card needed three lines to list his full title as an assistant to the vice president for cybersecurity, among other things.

"You."

Weezy realized Harmon was pointing at her.

"Napolitani. Everybody says you're the best tracker."

She shrugged and watched her boss cringe.

"Is this a system hack?"

"I have no idea," Weezy said. "Could be. Or it might be a one-off glitch, or their software, or little green men—"

Harmon turned to the group. "We're finished here."

Weezy turned toward the door. "Stay with us," Harmon said. The rest of the group filed out, leaving Keith, Weezy, Harmon, and a short, blond guy she hadn't noticed before who wore a navy blue suit, white shirt, and a rep stripe tie.

Weezy stayed standing, at the ready, stifling her nervousness.

Harmon looked around the room, stared for a moment at Keith, who began to rise from his chair. But he apparently decided to go informal and perched one leg on Keith's desk instead.

"So, you work with hackers, right?"

"Not so much with as against," Weezy said, wondering where the conversation was going.

"This HelioCorp problem may be a problem in the firewall," Harmon said, "or it may be caused by a hacker. Everyone agrees that if it's a hack, you are most likely to figure it out." He cleared his throat. "I am assigning you to work on this problem full time. But that does raise a dilemma. Both IAC security and the NSA say that if it was a hack, and if I had to bet who breached the IAC, you would be in the top five. Maybe the top one."

Harmon stared at her for a moment, then thrust his arm out toward his assistant.

"The document."

The assistant produced a blue-backed document, which Harmon slipped across Keith's desktop. Turning to Keith, he said, "This enjoins Ms. Napolitani from internet activity for thirty days, except as required for her work. It will be renewed at my discretion. You are responsible for her adherence to the spirit and the letter of it. You will report progress in solving this problem to my assistant daily."

Keith gaped, reminding Weezy of an unfortunate cod on ice in her father's Boston fish market.

Then, not waiting for confirmation, Harmon turned to Weezy, "You will also note that your security clearance has been reduced. The document allows the government to surveil your electronic activity, and you can rest assured we will do so."

He stood, gave Weezy a cold smile, and said, "I expect you will devote your considerable talent to finding the breach in our firewall and repairing it." With that, he marched out the door, his assistant trailing.

KEITH PICKED UP the blueback gingerly, as if it might explode, and began reading. Weezy stood, irritation overlaid with anxiety. What the hell were they doing? Telling her to work but taking her tools away? Keith flipped a page, then back, then forward, concentration deepening lines on his brow. Finally, still staring at the document, he said, "You need to read pages four through six very carefully. You'd be best advised to do nothing at all on the net unless it's at work." He looked up, handed the blueback to Weezy. "And let me know when you do go on the net."

"So you're giving me time off?" Weezy said, hearing anger

she didn't bother to hide. "Because I'm not going to be doing much but making paper airplanes without the 'net. This is the dumbest damn—"

"Louise, listen to me. This is the first time a person who reports to VPOTUS has come here, right here to the bullpen, in person. This is very important, at least in Harmon's mind. The natural reflex of a bureaucrat faced with an unknown situation is to shut everything down and figure out what the downsides are. That's what Harmon's doing. We need to roll with it. Play by his rules until the spasm passes."

"Downsides?"

"You know more about hackers and how they work than anyone. You spend your free time with the most accomplished hackers in the world. If this is a hack, chances are you know the hacker or at least know of them." He slid the blueback across his desk to Weezy. "He sees you as both his biggest opportunity and his riskiest downside."

"Yeah, I get it. Bulldog thinks I might be that hacker."

Keith sat back, interlaced fingers supporting his chin, and nodded.

Weezy left Keith's office, the blueback crushed in her grip. She briefed Maddie and the Oddballs and learned that the IAC lawyers were bickering with the HelioCorp lawyers about if, when and how to open a video channel to allow her to meet with HelioCorp and work the problem.

She read the blueback once, then again, growing angrier and angrier. Harmon wasn't just taking her tools away, he was tearing at her reputation. She should be at the plate, hitting the ball into the bleachers.

Harmon's blueback put her on the bench.

CHAPTER FOUR

By afternoon, the government lawyers had drafted a coordination agreement between IAC and HelioCorp. A video link between Bethesda and Boca Raton went live. Weezy called Joe and asked him to be in the room to introduce her. "I've been fending off reporters and the financial press all morning," he said, tight lines around his mouth. "Give me five, then make the connection."

Weezy was on the verge of spilling her guts, then thought about Harmon's promise to surveil her electronic activity. This was not the time or place to do it. She said only, "Harmon has restricted my internet access, and I'm probably being monitored."

"What? That jerkwad—"

"Let's get this conference going, then talk tonight," she said.

Joe sighed. "Sure. Five minutes." His video went dead.

Weezy got a coffee, took a seat at her workstation, exhaled, and opened the link.

The feed showed a utilitarian conference room with an off-white wall marred by use, a long, chrome-legged table with composite top extending toward the front of the room, and stackable metal-legged chairs with molded plastic seats. On the wall facing the camera, a whiteboard was full of lists and diagrams. Five people were seated at the table, which held a collection of coffee cups and water bottles. A trash basket in one corner overflowed with crumpled fast food wrappers, reminding Weezy of IAC all-nighters spent with her team. Joe stood in foreground, only his left shoulder in her view, apparently in the midst of describing the IAC and Weezy.

"... She is the leader of a group of trackers who are responsible for protecting the IAC from internet intrusions, and—"

"We know," an angular young man spat out, then glanced at the monitor and saw Weezy. Someone chuckled.

"—in any case," Joe continued. "Napolitani is their best problem-solver, and—"

"Uhh, Joe, looks like she's joined."

The group looked remarkably alert, considering they had probably not had much sleep. Weezy saw a range of emotions from indifferent through aloof to angry. Not a great way to start a project. She wished she was in the room rather than on a video feed.

Weezy introduced herself and listed out what the IAC team had done to address the problem. She learned that the five people were HelioCorp's whole programming team and asked for a review of the problem from their end.

Jenna, the de facto leader of the group according to Joe, began. "The grid blew back a huge power surge that melted our control cables and caused the main switching panel to explode." She threw the words at Weezy as an accusation, then paused, staring down at the table. "D'Quan was standing in front of the panel," she said in a softer voice.

She cleared her throat and continued, pulling on strands of hair that had escaped from her dark blonde ponytail. "We've eliminated the obvious hardware issues. The optical cable connecting us to the IAC firewall has not been breached, but the connection to the Eastern Interconnect was rejected. When the power surged back, the back-flush protection didn't cut it off like it should have."

"Have you made changes to the software, any of it, since the IAC certified it?" Weezy asked.

"Of course not," Jenna said, her nostrils flaring. "Once it's certified, we can't change it."

"And their expert doesn't know that?" Andrej, the angular

guy, said to the tabletop. Jenna stared at him until he looked up, gave an exasperated shake, and continued, "We tested it three days ago, and it worked fine."

"But something had to cause the failure," Weezy said, "and my colleagues in Bethesda can't see anything unusual on the IAC side."

Andrej snorted. "So now we start the ass-covering, right?"

Weezy paused, struggling not to go into Dumbass mode. "No, we figure out what we're missing." She rolled her trackball to focus the room's camera on the white board. A list running down the left side had two dozen physical attributes, things like *optical cable scrub* and *control box overload.* The center held software questions. On the right side, a heading titled *Cause* had no entries.

"Good, I see you've started. And you have scrubbed the code?"

"Triple-scrubbed," Andrej said, his tone drawing another irritated look from Jenna.

"Hmmm. Any chance D'Quan could have made a mistake? Hit the wrong button?"

"No," Jenna said. "We saw the correct start sequence here at headquarters."

"Okay. My team here in Bethesda has checked most of the things we know might go wrong with the firewall, and they'll keep on it. But assuming for a moment that the firewall wasn't at fault, and your code is unchanged from the version that was certified and worked in testing, it's either a random glitch we've never seen before, or someone was able to put in an instruction that subsequently self-destructed, leaving no trace."

"That'd be nearly impossible," Andrej said, with a slight shake of his head. "System logs every keystroke."

Weezy thought for a moment, then said, "But a clever programmer could do it. And if done well, there would be no trace of it or its action."

Jenna broke in. "Maybe one of your hacker friends. I don't think anyone here has the chops to do that . . . maybe

Makayla, but none of the rest of us."

Heads swiveled to Makayla. She was already shaking her head. "No. Only Bartek, and he's—" she stopped, eyes widening. "The video. That would be the only way to catch something like that."

"Video?"

"Everything in the programming bay is recorded," Makayla said.

Weezy, confused, said, "I've never seen a programming operation with video surveillance."

Makayla shrugged. "It's some sort of business reason, at least that's what Kapoor says."

Joe jumped in. "If she patented HelioCorp's solar panels, the inverter design, and the management software, then the technology would become public knowledge. Any one of a dozen well-funded companies would find ways to copy her ideas with minor variations, and the legal battles would begin. And China would rip off the stuff they want." He shrugged. "The other option is to keep everything secret. Of course, following that approach means she either has to trust her employees—"

"Yeah, right." Only Andrej said it, but from the grimaces and chuckles, the others agreed.

"—or keep a tight lid on everything HelioCorp does."

"Thus, the video surveillance," Weezy said.

"Right."

"You have to review that video," Weezy said to groans from the group.

"To keep the job to a minimum, I'd work backwards from the day everything crashed," she continued. "If I were doing an insertion, I wouldn't want that deviant code to be in place any longer than it had to be, because it would be visible until the moment it was activated. Someone might stumble on it."

"Who's going to do it?" Andrej again. "I mean, we're all suspects, right?"

"How about Joe?" Weezy said.

"Yeah, I suppose he could do it," Jenna said. Heads nodded.

Weezy smiled at the semi-visible Joe. "Sounds like you win the prize."

By four o'clock, the HelioCorp group had eliminated several possible causes of the backflush problem, and the OddBalls had exhausted their ideas as to how the firewall might have failed. Weezy sent a message to Joe to call later, put the crumpled blueback in her backpack, signed out of the bullpen, and went through the side entrance to the bike rack.

Her Bianchi gave her a shot of pleasure. The elegant bike was solid and graceful at the same time, and its signature celeste blue color made it stand out. She had been advised to get a cheaper model for regular use but refused to give up the pleasure of riding it. She performed the ballet of undoing and securing the cable lock and de-activating the electronic sentry. She mounted the machine and glided toward the bike path that paralleled the access road.

A rotund man in a hard hat with a camera attached to the top stepped out from behind a pillar and into her path.

Weezy slammed on her brakes. "Watch where—"

A red light on the camera pulsed.

"I see the big guns have assigned the big gun to the Helio-Corp fiasco," he said. "I understand there's cabinet-level involvement. Comment?"

"Nope." Weezy said, pushing the bike forward. The guy juked sideways and held out a microphone. His white shirt and tie contrasted with wrinkled shorts, spindly calves and dirty running shoes.

"You working for HelioCorp now? Trying to fix the mess IAC has made of Kapoor's technology?"

"I'm working for the IAC, trying to define the problem," Weezy said, stopping short of the guy's shoes and planting a foot on the ground. "I don't know much more about the problem than you broke yesterday, Brad. It looks like this was a one-off event, and I believe HelioCorp is optimistic they will be able to restart soon."

The guy stepped back.

She continued, "Brad the NanoWiz, right? I read your feed."

Astonishment shone on his face. "You read ... NanoWiz?"

Weezy flashed him a half-smile. "Yeah, Brad. You're only wrong about a third of the time. You've followed HelioCorp for almost a year, right? 'It's either the next big leap forward or a beautifully designed hoax.' Isn't that what you said?"

Brad had begun to blush. "Uhh, yeah. But that was before the bench test showed thirty-four percent improvement—"

"As far as I can tell," Weezy said, "you're an honest guy who knows a lot about technology. I have no axe to grind here, and I know little to nothing about the problem as yet. Let me look at the situation, and I may become your friend on this issue. But don't push me, and don't misquote me."

Brad stepped back. He tapped the camera and the red LED above the lens went out.

He held a card out to Weezy. "An interview with you would help reassure the markets."

"Sure," Weezy said. She took the card and slipped it into her pocket, then retook her seat and continued toward the bike path. "As long as you quote me honestly," she said over her shoulder.

SAPPHO GREETED WEEZY at the apartment door with a list of complaints and needs. Ordinarily, Weezy would have kicked off her shoes, made a cup of tea, and relaxed into her recliner. After a suitable period of feline indifference, Sappho would have jumped into her lap. But this was not an ordinary day.

Weezy was still boiling over Harmon, the blueback, and his cavalier invasion of her privacy.

She made the cup of tea, then dug out the scanner she'd used to find the bug last time somebody had been interested in her home life. She walked the apartment, testing for audio and video signals.

She found nothing transmitting. They'd probably camp on to her phone signal and any Wi-Fi connection she used, but at least they weren't bugging her house.

She plopped back into the recliner, pulled Harmon's blueback out of her pack, and read it again. All internet activity, it said. Except work related, and only at work. A vague prohibition against contacting "nongovernmental internet operatives, deep web/dark net operators, and internet associations." Pages four through six laid out the consequences of not observing the restrictions, and they were dire: suspension, loss of security clearance, firing, prosecution under several espionage statutes.

She sighed, sipped from the cup of tea, now tepid, and called Joe.

He was in his office at work. Of course.

"The meeting went well," he said. "You did a great job. Quite an accomplishment, considering the general feeling around HelioCorp that IAC's incompetence has kneecapped us. So tell me what that stuffed-shirt loser Harmon did to you."

"Joe—" She saw Joe's fury and felt herself winding tighter and tighter. Hard enough to bear alone, but—

"And, yes," he continued "I remember you told me our privacy is being violated in the interest of so-called National Security, and—"

"Joe, I'm pissed, too, but Granston Harmon, the Assistant to the Vice President of the United States for Internal Affairs, Cybersecurity, and a couple of other things, is nervous or scared or just plain pissed, and he can make my life miserable, so let's talk over what to do next. I mean, short of scrambling all of Harmon's emails."

That drew a chuckle, and she saw Joe relax.

Sappho trotted toward her chair, preparing to jump up. She stopped mid stride, her nose questioning, switched directions, and jumped to the chair across from Weezy. She circled a couple of times, gave Weezy an accusing look, and finally settled. Weezy realized her jaw was tight, painful.

"They've ordered me off the internet."

"You said. Why would they do that?"

"My hacker reputation, apparently. They probably think I might know the hacker, or maybe I'm the hacker who pulled this off."

"That's crazy. You're their best hope of figuring this out before it turns into a national story about a failure of the IAC, and you need Olegarten to do your work."

"You're right, at least about the Olegarten part. But I bet they're going to shut the case down and take the blame. They'll call it a 'glitch that won't be repeated' using some national security excuse not to tell the media any details."

Joe sat back, rubbed his forehead as if he had a headache.

"They did understand that it was you that broke the biggest medical scam anyone can remember—"

"You, too, Joe."

"Yeah, but mainly you taking things into your own hands when IAC management tried to cover the MedRecord hack. You saved hundreds of lives. They do remember that, don't they?"

"Sure. That's probably the reason for the injunction. We broke the MedRecord case by doing an end-run on the IAC suits. Made them look bad. That's what they remember."

"They can't be so dense as to think you can't get around some vague admonition to stay off the net."

"I thought about that too," Weezy said. "But now he's warned me. Anything that comes out about this that he doesn't like"—she snapped her fingers—"that 'IAC tracker Louise Napolitani'—she's going to be the problem."

Weezy sat back in her chair. Why did they choose her to fix this problem, anyway? Maybe she wasn't a fallback, but part of a plan.

Sappho stood, stretched, jumped down from her perch, then up to Weezy, purring.

Joe's brow knit. "With you off the net, how the hell are they going to figure out whether there's a hacker lurking out on the dark net, waiting to strike again?"

"Just what I called to discuss." She stroked Sappho. "I think I know how the HelioCorp crash happened. You need to watch that videotape."

CHAPTER FIVE

WEEZY WAS ROLLING the Bianchi out of the garage next morning when a blue sedan pulled into the drive.

A young man in a suit and tie emerged. He had smooth, adolescent features interrupted by a scar next to his right eye. Short blond hair exposed creeping baldness. He looked as if someone had told him to look serious and he was having a hard time figuring out how.

"Ms. Napolitani?"

"Yes."

He flipped open a wallet which displayed a credential. "Homeland Security. Come with me, please."

"What for?"

Weezy leaned toward the open wallet. Sure enough, Homeland Security.

"I am here to escort you to a meeting in Washington."

"I need to call my boss," Weezy said.

"Your office is informed."

Weezy pulled her e-pad from a pocket in her cargo shorts.

The guy's look changed from firm-but-friendly to bored irritation.

"Call Keith Sanders," she said to the e-pad, locking eyes with the kid. One of his eyelids drooped, or was he squinting at her?

The call bounced from Bethesda headquarters. A second ring, then Sanders, wearing a shirt with an unbuttoned collar, smoothing over a cowlick that refused to cooperate. It was the least formal Weezy had ever seen him.

"Louise, where are you?"

"In my yard, getting ready to ride to work, standing in front of a guy that says he's from Homeland Security."

"He is, Louise. You need to meet with the Assistant to the Vice President." His voice capitalized the title.

"About what?"

"There's been bad publicity about HelioCorp. That's all I can say."

Weezy signed off, opened the car's back door, shrugged off her backpack, and said to the kid, "Okay. Let's go."

The ride to Washington was mostly silent. The freeway gave way to a matrix of streets, occasional views of the Capitol and the Mall and finally a stolid, gray building. The car drove to an underground entryway, where two gray-suited men waited.

"Thanks for the ride and scintillating conversation," Weezy said as she got out.

The agent cracked a smile.

She reached into the car for her backpack.

"You can leave that," he said.

"There is confidential material—"

"Okay, have it your way."

Weezy gave him a long, sour look and shouldered the backpack. One of the gray-suited men had come away from his station at the door.

"Follow me."

The escort directed her through a double door and down a long corridor. Beige walls and concrete floor gave way to a carpeted area with a desk and a uniformed guard in front of a mahogany door. The guard stood as they approached. He pointed to a table next to the desk. "Backpack."

Weezy shrugged off the pack. He extracted several electronic devices from side pockets. One brow raised slightly at the red lace bra she'd forgotten to take out after she and Joe had to cancel their Panacea weekend; otherwise, he wore no expression.

The guard placed her backup e-pad, headphones and a

plastic container of data cubes into a boxy device. A brief whirr was followed by a row of LEDs flashing sequentially and finally a click. Apparently satisfied, he put them back in the pack along with her bra.

"Scan," he said, indicating the retinal scanner next to the door.

Weezy leaned forward and felt more then saw the brief light of the scan.

The door clicked open. "Enter, please," her escort said. "We'll go to the third door on the right."

The door opened into a room with a central table, chairs, a mirror that was likely two-way and bare walls. Deep blue carpet and leather chairs did not disguise the room's purpose.

Weezy's guide asked if she needed anything.

"A bottle of water."

The guide stepped out of the room and returned almost immediately with the water. He added as he turned to leave, "This shouldn't take too long."

Weezy opened the water, drank a few sips, re-screwed the cap.

She tried deep breathing to relax.

The door swung open, and the same short, blond guy she'd seen at IAC headquarters entered, again wearing a navy blue suit, white shirt and a rep stripe tie. He was followed by Granston Harmon, who still looked like a bulldog. One who had eaten some rancid meat.

Blond guy took a seat in the corner away from the table. Bulldog sat down across from Weezy. "You spoke yesterday with a person who styles himself NanoWiz, right?"

"Yes. Brad ambushed me as I left the building."

"So, you're giving confidential information to some pip-squeak internet blogger. Did you read the document I gave you and not understand the instruction to keep this confidential?"

"I read it, and I understood."

"But you went ahead and gave an interview to a blogger.

You told him HelioCorp's problem was likely a one-off event. You also said there might be some outside entity that has hacked into the IAC."

"No, I did not tell him that. He pulled that one out of his—"

"He reported that it was a one-off event. He said you didn't deny—"

Weezy exhaled. "—out of thin air."

Bulldog gestured to the guy in the corner, who punched at an e-pad, then handed it over.

The NanoWiz logo filled the screen, then a close-up of Brad.

"This afternoon, I spoke with Louise Napolitani. For those of you who don't know, Napolitani is reputed to be the IAC's best tracker. She has been working on HelioCorp's failed attempt to connect their solar field to the Eastern Interconnect. The company has refused to comment. Well, except . . ."

The camera cut to Brianna Kapoor screaming and zoomed in on her red face, spittle flying as she denounced the IAC.

Brad's face returned. "Here's what Napolitani said."

Weezy appeared, saying, "It looks like this was a one-off event." The rest was cut off and Brad appeared on the screen again.

"Napolitani also noted they think it wasn't a glitch in the IAC."

His face drew close to the camera.

"So what is it? If it's not a glitch, is it a successful hack? Napolitani should know. Or . . ." Brad tilted his head as if realizing an answer that had been there all along. "Maybe Napolitani's elite hacker friends know what happened."

Harmon snapped the video off and leaned toward Weezy.

"Has IAC been hacked?"

"It's possible," Weezy said. "HelioCorp thinks it may have been an internal breach, but there might have been outside interference, as well."

"What about you? What's your estimate?" He seemed to be looking for an answer he already knew. "Maybe your hacker friends at that dark net site . . . what's it called?" He snapped his fingers.

"Olegarten, sir," the blue-suited assistant said. "It's a chat room hiding behind a defunct manufacturer's website, which—"

"Maybe these Olegarten people figured out how to get into the IAC? Maybe with a little help from their friend?"

Weezy tried to keep her face calm. A bead of sweat ran between her breasts. Not surprising that the NSA knew about Olegarten, but—

Bulldog sat back. "What is it, twenty, maybe twenty-five hackers. If anybody could do it—"

Weezy's anger surprised her. She was talking, practically shouting, before she had a chance to tame her answer. "Olegarten covers the government's ass when they're too stupid, too lazy, or too self-serving to protect their fellow Americans. The bad stuff might happen a hell of a lot more often if Olegarten wasn't there."

She drew a breath. Harmon smirking now. The fine tailoring, the power tie, the card that took three lines to lay out his title. This guy was never going to understand Olegarten.

Harmon leaned forward, elbows on the table, and folded his hands under his chin. "Like every self-serving hacker, right? Assange and WikiLeaks, all the others that followed. Truth and beauty? But really, notoriety, money." He sat back in his chair, a smile forming. "Word has it that the Volkov conspiracy was destroyed by one of your Olegarten people. But the money disappeared. So, was that protecting Russians from 'bad stuff,' or was it plain larceny?"

The accusation should have infuriated Weezy. She hadn't heard of Volkov, but it might be true. Olegarten had its own rules. Money and information were generally fair game. What a court of law would consider stealing was a gray area for Olegarten . . . "necessary financing" if extracted from others' ill-gotten gains, such as Volkov. Freedom, particularly in speech and ideas, was paramount. Big organizations, be they government or corporate, were suspect.

"Olegarten has never disclosed critical information," she said. "We don't take anyone who does that. If your dudes figured out Olegarten, they understand that."

"Of course." The right side of Harmon's mouth stretched into a knowing half-grin. "This Mayfield, the one you collaborated with in the MedRecords issue, he's the head of finance at HelioCorp." His eyebrows rose. "And you and he are, uhhh, close, are you not?"

"We are."

"So we have a brilliant IAC tracker who knows perhaps more than anyone else about hacking technique, works with a group that can and does steal vast sums of money, plus the man with insider information about a soon-to-be sensationally valuable company."

A convenient conspiracy theory. How nice. How neat. So easy to use it as the broom to sweep this whole mess under the rug. And both she and Joe with it.

Harmon nodded to his assistant. The man stood, cracked the door, and said, "We're ready."

Two blue-uniformed officers, a male and a female, entered. They looked like regular cops, except for the DHS logo on their sleeves.

"Ms. Napolitani, you violated the directive I gave you yesterday," Harmon said. "As a result, I am putting you under house arrest by order of Judge Cheryl Alvarado of the Cybersurveillance Court." The female officer produced a powder blue device that looked like a shackle.

Harmon slipped a document across the table. "This warrant is based on the risk you pose to national security. It restricts your movement to an area that covers your home and your IAC office and the path you travel to work. You will see the map on your e-pad when we return it to you. You will wear a monitoring device. This device will send your movements and biometric data to Homeland Security continuously. If you violate the terms of the warrant, you will be taken into federal custody."

The officer stepped forward, opening the device.

"Put your right foot on the chair," she said.

Weezy left both feet on the floor.

"Give me my e-pad." She wasn't sure who she was going to call. In the movies and videos, the bad guy always called his lawyer. She didn't have one.

"Of course." Harmon nodded toward Weezy's backpack. His assistant, flustered, rummaged through its contents. The assistant found the device, looked relieved, and handed it to Harmon.

"Let me help you," Harmon said. "Before you embarrass yourself, call Keith Sanders."

Weezy took the pad, did the retina scan to activate it, and called Keith.

"Keith, I am late today because—"

"Yes, I know, Louise." He was sitting stiffly. "I have been informed that you are under house arrest."

"How is this even remotely legal?"

His tone changed to stuffed-shirt formal. "I believe they have an order based on the threat to national security."

"By order of the Cybersurveillance Court. Yes, I got that part. What does IAC think about that?"

Keith stuttered, "I . . . umm . . . the CSC is pretty much the last word, Louise. Not much we can do."

She exhaled, stared at the tabletop as seconds ticked by., thinking *didn't take him long to cut me loose*. Fear overcame her anger. She had no friends to help her. This was not an intellectual exercise where she could win by thinking faster than everybody else.

She lifted her right foot to the chair.

THE SAME DRIVER was waiting when Weezy came to the end of the long corridor and entered the parking lot. The device rapped her ankle as she got in the car and made her feel clumsy. Besides, it was embarrassing. She'd worn shorts to go to work, and the thing was as obvious as a blinking neon sign.

When they approached Bethesda, Weezy said to the driver, "Take me home."

"Uhh, I was directed to take you to the IAC facility."

She flipped open her e-pad, suddenly near tears.

"Call Keith Sanders."

The call connected, caught Keith in a Five Guys, burger on a tray, mustard and onions, as usual.

"Louise. I'm so sorry about this uhh, situation. We're pulling for you, and—"

"Keith, I'm going home for the rest of the day. Maybe tomorrow."

"Umm, I understand taking some time, but it's important for us to work this HelioCorp issue and for you to make it clear that you are with us on this."

"You think a great way to motivate me to solve an important problem is to humiliate me in front of the whole world? See this?" She angled her e-pad to show her ankle and the monitor. Then pulled it back close to her face. "I'm under arrest, man. I'm not going into the bullpen wearing this thing."

She sat back in the seat, suddenly embarrassed at having shared her humiliation with the driver. "If you want my help, I need to work from home, and I need my internet privileges back."

Keith drew a long breath. In the background, music played, and diners chatted.

"Louise, the reason you're under house arrest is because Harmon is concerned about your contacts on the internet, so internet use from home isn't going to happen. Go home for the rest of the day, then let's talk in my office tomorrow morning."

Weezy was about to tell him what to do with his burger but paused, swallowed the snark. "Gotta go. I'll be in tomorrow."

The driver had been watching her in the rearview mirror. "Take me home," she said. He nodded and redirected the car.

It took twenty minutes to get to Weezy's apartment, during which the driver cleared his throat several times, seeming about to speak, glanced at Weezy in the rearview, and said nothing. Part way there, a text from Joe popped up. "Interesting news" was all it said.

As soon as the car stopped in her driveway, she had the car door open and was out, dragging her backpack behind her. She slammed the door hard enough to make the driver flinch. She pounded up the stairs to her apartment two at a time, almost tripping because of the ankle monitor. Inside, she tossed her backpack on a kitchen chair, ripped her e-pad out of her pocket, and collapsed into her recliner.

"Call Joe."

He answered on the first ring. When he saw Weezy, he raised his eyebrows in a look of concern. He read her so well, even on a small video screen. Part of her anger and frustration drained away. "So tell me and the others no doubt listening your interesting news."

Joe perked up. "Your advice about the video was brilliant, and Bartek Krol was unlucky."

"Unlucky?"

"Yeah. He put something into the software just the day before the crash. The handshake was scheduled eleven days in the future, so he probably thought there'd be low risk of anyone looking back that far on the video. He was a little careless when he erased five minutes. Then Kapoor jumped the schedule, so the little glitch came up right away when I started working backward. No wonder he chose to quit the night of the backflush disaster."

"So there was inside help. That would explain the backflush, but—"

Joe nodded, "Yes, I know where you're going. The team agrees that there must be an outside operator involved to have pulled this off, unless it's an IAC blunder. They sent a note to Homeland late last night and briefed them this morning. Homeland seemed skeptical, but they're sending someone over to talk to me this afternoon. It's a relief we're making some progress." He grinned and said, "So, what's your interesting news?"

"This," Weezy said, and angled the e-pad toward her ankle.

"Huh? What's that? Hope it's not a new fashion statement."

Snappy repartee stuck in Weezy's throat, somewhere between a chuckle and a sob. After a moment, she said, "I'm under house arrest. Seems as if the new theory, put together following the logic of walks-like a-duck, quacks, so the hell with her rights, is that I am the most likely source of Helio-Corp's problems. Oh, and you are a fellow traveler. That person showing up this afternoon may have one of these for you, too."

Joe massaged his forehead with one hand. "What kind of people are running this country?"

"The kind who cover their asses first, think second," Weezy said. "Anyway, I'm too damn upset to go into work, so I'm staying home with tea, Sappho, and maybe oblivion in a mystery novel." She tried briefly to imagine a lazy afternoon. *Right.*

"In the meantime," she said, "keep your hopes up it was that IAC glitch everyone would like to believe in. That'll get the problem solved, the Assistant to the VP happy, Kapoor off the IAC's back, and this monitor off my ankle."

"In other words," Joe said, "pray for Murphy's Law to have made something go wrong—"

"—instead of something sinister and intentional," Weezy said and gave Joe a half smile. "Sorry. Gotta stop finishing your sentences."

CHAPTER SIX

"Finished the cash projection, Joe."

Joe had just finished an impromptu conference call with a potential investor and was passing the treasurer's office.

He stopped, went back to her doorway, leaned on the frame. "How many days?"

"Twenty-three, not including extra expenses for restarting the demo." Joe saw fear on her face. She had been an early employee, moving from somewhere up north. A single mom if Joe remembered right. Pictures of kids were grouped around her diploma and a couple of professional certifications on her office wall. A plant, some kind of bromeliad, was dying in the corner. Her dark hair was pulled back in a bun, and her eyes, magnified by round, tortoise shell glasses, were serious.

"A lot of people are nervous, Joe," she said. "I mean, HelioCorp looked like a once in a lifetime chance to do something important. We all want this to succeed, but Boca is not exactly a Mecca of high-tech . . ." Her voice trailed off. A weight descended on Joe. He had been brought in as a consultant, but he had become part of the HelioCorp family. All these brilliant, hopeful people. Families uprooted, houses sold, friends left behind, all for this marvelous idea that might be about to die.

"Like you said, HelioCorp is important," Joe said. "One failed connection won't sink the company." Sure, they'd get other jobs, he thought. But to a thirty-something single woman with two kids, a mortgage, and a job that allowed no social life, HelioCorp's precarious position had to be terrifying. He thought of his sister, losing her job in the same year she got divorced from a husband who just couldn't stop drinking. How her life went from comfortable to bare survival and made her into a bitter husk of her former self.

"It'll be tight, but we'll make it through this," he said, projecting a confidence he didn't feel, hoping he wasn't lying.

"MAYFIELD!" KAPOOR'S VOICE froze the programming bay, where Joe was conferring with Jenna.

"Mayfield, come with me." This time a normal voice, and she added, "Please."

Joe followed her to her office. What had started as a modern, utilitarian space with a nice view of the retention pond behind the building had become a cave. Messy stalagmites of papers and magazines reached toward the ceiling. The lovely walnut of Kapoor's cluttered desk was marred by gray rings from past coffee cups.

Kapoor navigated around the stacks to her desk. The over-size chair and Kapoor's short stature led an office wag to christen her "the seated Vishnu." Kapoor would have fired the man if she had known; still, now it was impossible to enter her office without being reminded of the Hindu deity.

"Sit," she said, waving to the one mostly empty chair. Joe moved several journals to a fairly stable-looking stack and sat.

"Huey, Dewey and Louie called," she said, referring to HelioCorp's three major investors. "All are positive and confident that we will 'work this problem out.' " Her nostrils flared, and she exhaled sharply. "Each of them gave me some bullshit about how their board feared sending good money after bad. But each had gone to bat for us. Then each offered to 'help us out' at ridiculous terms."

"Not surprising," Joe said. "The sharks smell blood in the water. We have to prepare for giving up more of the company."

"Easy for you to say. That 'we' you're talking about is

mostly me. Besides, I also got a call from Donel McTavish. He said his earlier offer stands, 'despite the bad news.' "

Joe's eyebrows shot up. "Mac? Really? I thought he'd want a bigger bite."

Kapoor's sniff reminded Joe of her opinion of finance people in general, Joe sometimes, and venture capitalists always. "He wants you to go up to West Virginia and talk about a 'significant partnership' with United Energy."

"I bet McTavish will want more ownership."

"Not gonna happen," Kapoor said. "Nothing's changed, except the IAC screwed up. He was drooling while we talked. Get me an offer I can accept."

"I'll do the best I can, but he knows the ten million he offered before the crash is now a life or death issue for us. It's him or no restart, Brianna."

DONEL MCTAVISH RENFRO, "Mac" to most of the world, leaned toward the men's room mirror. He ran a comb through his hair, which was a bit long for his board's taste, and straightened the Windsor knot in his tie.

HelioCorp should jump at the ten million he had offered seven months ago, before they got grandiose ideas from the New York investment bank that proposed a public offering which would bring fifty times more. Mac knew HelioCorp's cash balance, a side benefit of the confidentiality agreement that gave him access to the company's financial information. The ten million would get them through a restart. They'd need more, lots more, but right now they were probably feeling like they'd been hit in the nose . . . blinding pain, tears, and trying to figure what to do next.

He had met Joe Mayfield only once, after Kapoor blew off his offer and the HelioCorp's board installed Mayfield to lead the public offering from inside. Mac liked him immediately, even after Kapoor spurned the offer. Joe was a bright guy who didn't continually remind you of how smart he was, but who understood both the logic and human dynamics of the deal right away. He was relieved Kapoor had agreed to have Mayfield represent HelioCorp in the investment he expected United Energy Ventures to propose.

His implant tapped him; Mayfield had arrived at reception. Mac washed his hands, fished a towel out of the basket next to the basin, squared his shoulders, and put on a smile.

CHAPTER SEVEN

Joe's text had surprised Weezy. He was going to West Virginia to see United Energy. She was elated to hear he would detour on the way back to Boca to see her.

"How long?" she texted back.

"Just the day and evening. Can't take the nose off the grindstone for too long."

He had arrived at IAC in the afternoon, full of good spirits, after a visit to United Energy headquarters. "Just like traveling back into the nineteenth century," he said. "Impressive old building, stodgy old guys—all cousins—on the board. But I like Mac Renfro, and he is excited about HelioCorp. And"—his eyes twinkled—"it gave me a chance to swing through Bethesda and see my sweet, ankle-bracelet-wearing, mad-as-a-boiled-owl, sweetheart."

He'd found a nice, quiet restaurant near the IAC complex and within Weezy's range of movement. They sat at a bay window table looking west across a green space filled with flowers.

"Good choice," Weezy said after the server lit a candle and took their wine order.

Joe had a way of looking at her, drinking her in, that made her beautiful. Not feel beautiful. Be beautiful. A rush of warmth flushed her cheeks, and she realized how much she had missed that feeling and how let down she had felt when they had to cancel Panacea. It had been too long.

The server appeared with two glasses of wine and took their order for fried shrimp and baked flounder. When he had left, Weezy said, "Tell me about your meeting with Mac."

"He offered just enough venture money to get the project up and running. He wanted more rights for shares when the company goes public, but nothing more now. Given our situation, most vulture capitalists would ask for double or triple ownership. Either he's a poor bargainer or a true believer."

Weezy gave him a half-skeptical squint. "In other words, he wants something he's not telling you about."

"You might be right," Joe said with a half grin. "But I have the sense that he's trying to prove to the world that he's a heavy hitter. Maybe he wants to be sure we give him the nod so he'll be the new smart guy on the block. Maybe he wants to come onto the board."

The server returned with dinner, refilled wine glasses. They were silent for a bit, enjoying the food and the view.

"I'm looking forward to this assignment being over," Joe said. "In fact, I'd be happy with pretty much anything like a normal life."

"Lovely thought," Weezy said, flashing him a smile. "Utter bullshit, of course, but lovely thought."

"What?" Joe stopped, a bite of flounder halfway to his mouth.

"What I mean," Weezy said, "is HelioCorp is going to be successful. Kapoor's board is going to tell her to hire you—"

"I doubt that they would consider—"

"And Kapoor is going to jump on that like a dog on a bone."

"As soon as she's funded, she'll find some hotshot New York—"

"Joe, I know you're blind, 'cause you go all googly-eyed over me. But are you deaf and dumb, too? Kapoor wants your financial, management and human talents even more than she lusts over your manly body. Which is to say, a whole lot."

"I don't know about—"

"Second," Weezy gestured with her fork, "You hold onto that 'ordinary guy' thing as sort of a mental insignia. With all we've been through . . . you've been through, losing Cynthia,

Phoenix . . ."

"You're right." He shrugged. "After all that, you find you're a different person." He grinned. Weezy raised an eyebrow.

"I was thinking," he said, "about paddling down the Wakulla with you after Phoenix. I wanted to find another job like the one I'd been fired from." He chuckled. "Remember? You damn near capsized us when you whipped around to tell me, vehemently, that I no longer had any right to call myself an ordinary guy. For that, I owe you much more than a 'thank you.' "

Weezy exhaled. "Damn, I wish we were in Panacea."

She gazed out over the fading sunset. "I like that idea of a normal life. I wish we could be together more, but I'm afraid you'll always be in one place and I'll be in another."

"Glad you brought that up," Joe said. "There is a solution, you know."

"Like what?" Weezy said as she dipped a shrimp in cocktail sauce.

"Like marry me."

"You mean . . .?"

Joe reached across the table and opened his hands. Weezy put down the shrimp, resisted the urge to wipe a spot of sauce off her fingers, and gave him her hands.

"Yes. Louise Napolitani, will you marry me?"

Her heart stopped in its tracks for a moment, then revved.

"I . . . uhh . . ." Would he want her to quit IAC? Move to Panacea? Would he quit his job to be near her?

Why were her hands shaking? Why were his so warm?

Would she ever be able to replace Cynthia, perfect in his mind's eye?

Why was her body saying, "I will, yes, I will, I will, I will?"

"I . . . I love you . . . and I have to think about it."

She saw shock in his eyes. He had expected her to say yes. He let her hands go, pulled his back. His pain cut her like a hot knife. Why had she lacked the courage to say *Yes*?

"Is it about your job? I know you love your work."

She studied her dinner plate, exhaled, and built up the courage to look into his eyes. "Probably that's some of it. Also, I've lived alone for a long time . . . well, except for Sappho . . . and I've developed . . . habits."

"Yeah. Me, too," Joe said. "I didn't say it would be easy."

"Can you give me some time? Enough to get through this HelioCorp project and lose this damn ankle bracelet, so I can truly be free to grab hold of my raging hormones, which are currently treating me like I'm a piñata and they're the stick?"

"Sure. Of course."

Joe gave her a crooked smile. "Like you said before, world's sticking its ugly snout in our love life again. We really ought to fix that."

CHAPTER EIGHT

MONGREL'S DRIVER STOPPED the Mercedes in front of what once was a fine statement of the people's socialist movement. Now it was another graffitied apartment building on Moscow's outskirts. His security detail exited their car, one man disappearing into the lobby. The second scanned the area, a practiced twenty-second action that would seem casual to a passerby. It took in rooftops, windows, and sidewalks. The third man watched anything moving. When he nodded, Mongrel got out and walked quickly into the building. He wore a cheap windbreaker, slacks, and athletic shoes. He had brushed his hair to show his incipient bald spot, which was never exposed in his TV interviews, and wore heavy, black-framed glasses he didn't need. He hoped to be unmemorable, an office worker approaching middle age, perhaps. As he entered, another Mercedes pulled up, then an Escalade. Within forty-five seconds, all the vehicles pulled away, and three men with their bodyguards crowded into the small lobby.

Residents who passed through the lobby or down the stairs did not make the mistake of noticing them.

Mongrel led the group up grimy stairs to the third floor and an apartment facing the inner courtyard. The bodyguards waited in the hall, neither talking nor showing discomfort at standing silent for as long as their employers required.

The three entered the apartment. Chairman rested hands knotted with arthritis on the windowsill, appearing to take an interest in the courtyard below while regaining his breath from the climb. His flat, Slavic features and threadbare jacket made him appear to be a pensioner, perhaps retired from the factory a few blocks over. Certainly not among the wealthiest of the thirty or so oligarchs who owned most of Russia.

"Dologov has disappeared," he said to no one in particular.

"Another." Mongrel sighed. "The new Premier is not comfortable yet."

"Perhaps the Premier will not survive so long," Borzoi said.

Chairman turned from the window to face the young man. His face, stiff from plastic surgery and beatings long ago, showed no emotion, but his eyes carried his disgust.

"We hope," the younger man added with a nervous smile. His blazer, surely tailored on Savile Row, and a silk shirt complemented a handsome profile he was apparently unwilling to disguise.

"If you hope in one hand and shit in the other, which fills up first?" Chairman asked. His smile came off as a leer.

The younger man's face gave away revulsion—a person of superior station observing a peasant's gaffe.

A table and three straight-backed chairs occupied the single room that had originally been allotted to a family of four. On the table were bottles of water, but no pads of paper or pens to record the meeting.

None of the men used real names; the FSB's ears were everywhere. When the original group of three agreed to act together after Putin died, Mongrel suggested calling the eldest "Chairman" out of respect. The man thought for a moment, pursed his lips, and said, "As you wish. And we will call you Mongrel, also out of respect." He paused, taking in Mongrel's expression, then continued, "A mongrel retains the best characteristics of the many crosses that bred him." Mongrel relaxed, hearing admiration in the name. He knew it spoke to his rise from the streets of Moscow to the corridors of power at the FSB. Perhaps to his Romanian origin, as well, and his great-grandparents who survived the Warsaw ghetto. A proud lineage, not conferred by a long family tree, but by grit, striving, careful planning, and not a little blood. Twenty-eight substantial businesses—oil, metal fabrication, software, rare earth metals, apartment buildings—all owned by the kid they called numb nuts back in Bucharest. But all of it depended on the web of association with the premier and his hierarchy, and Mongrel knew that could disappear—he could disappear—in a flash; thus, he was constantly observant, constantly on guard.

The last member of the original group, Volkov, had been called Laika. He had disappeared some months ago. A hacker released information that suggested he questioned the new premier's legitimacy. Rumor had it that the nephew leaked the incriminating information to the hacker. His nephew had inherited his uncle's interests, including membership in Sobaki. The informal web of the oligarchy that Putin had built had strict rules of succession.

Chairman gave the younger Volkov the name Borzoi, after the Russian greyhound. Sleek, handsome, stupid. The young man was charmed.

Borzoi worried Mongrel. He had a perfect pedigree—a family lineage that reached back before the revolution, connections within the government and Europe, a fine education. A man defined by privilege, which made him dangerous. He would be used to having the rules favor him, which would make him think he was clever. He would be the first of them to break in a FSB interrogation room, the first to sell Mongrel and Chairman out if there was profit in it.

The three sat. Chairman spoke first to Mongrel.

"You have called us together for a report?"

"Yes," Mongrel said. "Phase one is completed. The penetration went as planned. The Americans have not identified the source. But an analyst from their IAC has been assigned to the project, so they consider this important."

"They suspect a breach in their firewall," Borzoi explained, apparently for the benefit of Chairman.

The young always seemed to think they possessed

knowledge the old couldn't understand, Mongrel thought, and said, "That is correct."

"This man Raskov you have in charge in the States—is he any good?" Borzoi asked.

"Yes," Mongrel answered, noting Borzoi's raised eyebrows. "I have known him for a long time. He is reliable."

Mongrel paused, waiting for a challenge. When none came, he continued, "We were able to use McTavish's company's physical link to the IAC without raising suspicion, and the Estonian's software worked perfectly. McTavish will have HelioCorp for his toy. Raskov will make him understand his role in phase two."

"As we had hoped," Chairman said.

"So we're finished with that Estonian prick," Borzoi said, his voice curdling with anger.

Of course, Mongrel thought. He's pissed at me for using the Estonian. Well, screw him. The Estonian's the best man for the job. Borzoi's just afraid he'll let out the truth that the loyal nephew sold out the doting uncle.

"Not yet," Chairman said. "Raskov needs him for phase two, which may last longer than we expect. The Americans will resist our demands, of course. We will need to demonstrate our power to control their electrical grid."

"And the ransom," Borzoi said. "One billion is not enough. It should be much larger, given the damage we can inflict." He squared his shoulders, nodding at his own logic.

Mongrel gave a single sidewise shake of his head, almost a tic. "phase two's value is our ability to break through their firewall at will, not the money. But if we simply shut off power to show we can do it, the Americans will understand the intrusion as cyberwar and will respond with their full force. Instead, we will demand a moderate ransom, one they can pay without informing their Congress. It will perhaps look like an ordinary hacker demanding a fortune for himself. It will be a pittance considering the size of the problem we will create. They will pay it, then turn their considerable energies toward finding that hacker, whose trail we have created to lead to one of their own."

Borzoi shook his head. "I still think it should be more."

"Besides," Mongrel continued, "The premier will understand the value of our project and pursue our friendship." He paused and grinned. "Or he will not, and we will have a new premier, perhaps one we select."

Chairman looked from Borzoi to Mongrel. "Agreed?"

Both nodded, and Chairman said to Mongrel, "Contact Raskov. Give him coordinates for phase two."

MAKSYM RASKOV DID not like being a jailer, but the Sobaki hadn't asked his preference. He was uncomfortable in Miami, where his looks branded him foreign and his English cemented the impression. He was tall and broad-shouldered enough to get more than a passing look, though a bit overweight. Everyone around him was tan; he was pallid. Other men his age wore shorts and T-shirts. His shirts and slacks were nice enough but out of place. Too many reasons for people to remember him.

The office complex was more comfortable than his flat in Moscow, that wasn't it, and the bars and bistros along Ocean Drive in South Beach made his few free hours tolerable. Despite his reservations about getting close to those who would soon be dead, he liked the Estonian captive, Puusepp. Besides, there was the afternoon chess match while they waited for the software Puusepp had written in the morning to be tested. Raskov was a decent and enthusiastic player; Puusepp was brilliant, a European champion before becoming a hacker. Raskov had purchased a travel chess set with a metal board, magnetic pieces, and a brown plastic case. The game was a pleasure the Sobaki wouldn't have approved.

Yes, Raskov had little to complain about. Except Pyotr.

Puusepp had to be watched twenty-four seven. Even when

sleeping. He had to be near the site of the project. In fact, he *was* the project, the hacker able to pierce the firewall of America's IAC and complete the necessary adjustments. But he was a prisoner, not a willing participant. He could not be allowed near a computer, or phone, or e-pad—anything with a chip—without supervision. The Sobaki understood that Raskov alone could not provide reliable coverage for the four or five weeks the project would require. Pyotr, cousin of one of the Sobaki members, lived near Miami, and was "very reliable," they said.

They were wrong. Pyotr was a twenty-something guy studying to be an American surfer. When they met, he had given Raskov a crooked smile and said, "They call me Pete."

Raskov called him Pyotr. At least he spoke Russian.

This morning, Raskov passed out of the warm humidity of the Florida morning into the interior of the office building that housed Neva Imports. Why did these Americans keep it so cold? He sipped an espresso, nodded to the guard, and passed down the hall to Neva's offices. He knocked three times. A light went on in the reception area, then Pyotr's face appeared at the window. The lock clicked and Raskov entered.

"Last night?" Raskov asked.

"All cool," Pyotr said in English. "He slept most of the night. One trip to the crapper. Chess, as always. Not much else."

"The key." Raskov held out his hand. Pyotr dug in a reception desk drawer and produced a tagged key marked "storage."

Raskov took the key, nodded and went to a door tucked away on the right side of the reception area. He knocked twice, unlocked the door and entered. The room had served as storage for office supplies; they had pushed cabinets and multi-slotted bins to the walls to make room for a table, two chairs and a cot.

Puusepp sat at the table in the center of the room with his back to Raskov. The desktop was bare except for the magnetic travel chess set.

"Cicciolini-Brankovic, 1974," Puusepp said, still concentrating on the chessboard. From the back, Puusepp's head reminded Raskov of his grandmother's soup tureen: round and shiny but for bristles of hair scattered randomly; ears sticking out like the tureen's handles. He was a small man with a middle-age paunch. His short neck made it seem as if his head rested on top of his collar.

"Cicciolini should have conceded five moves before this." Puusepp nodded to the board, then turned toward Raskov. Intelligent gray eyes and a mouth a size too large for his face completed the picture. "But he did not." Puusepp gestured at the board. "Now, the endgame approaches."

Puusepp smiled as he raised his eyes to Raskov. "Ours, too, no?"

Of course. Puusepp knew.

The little man continued, his Russian softened by Estonian vowels, "Very few surprises in an endgame."

"But we are not at the endgame, Puusepp. We have only completed the first round. Another game awaits."

Raskov saw shock, understanding and finally hope, quickly muted, pass across Puusepp's face.

Don't hope, Puusepp. Raskov cursed himself. He had allowed the weed of friendship to grow. It would make duty more difficult when the time came.

Puusepp gave a small shake of the head and the hint of a smile as he did when Raskov made an unexpected move. "I should have known."

AFTER RASKOV OUTLINED phase two, he gave Puusepp the e-pad used to write the software to penetrate the IAC firewall and left him alone. Puusepp activated the e-pad, found where he left off the day before. Like he did every morning, he did a calculation of how long he could drag out the writing. The endgame was approaching, but the additional work Raskov had demanded guaranteed him a little more time.

To clear his mind, he pictured the quiet of the forest near Nikerjärve, then the water-scent coming up from Tallinn harbor to his window, the swallows' raspy calls from their nest under his eaves.

When they scooped him up on his way back from morning coffee down the street from his apartment, he thought it might be the police again. Maybe only the MuPo, who could not cause him much trouble. But they were hooded, and they pushed him into a black Mercedes. The last thing he felt was a prick in the arm, then tunnel vision and a long dream—car, airport?, fruity odor, humidity. He woke to a woman squinting at him. She wore a white uniform, and when he tried to sit up, she frowned. "Nyet," she said, with a single shake of her head. She turned away and spoke into a cell phone. A few minutes later, a mastiff of a man appeared. Broad shoulders supported a thick neck and jowls, above which perched a nearly flat nose and watery light-blue eyes that seemed intelligent and not unfriendly. He wore a gray buzz cut and a suit clearly tailored in the Eastern bloc.

"You may sit up," he said in Russian, but with some sort of accent. Ukrainian? Polish?

Puusepp sat up, then braced himself, feeling lightheaded.

"I am Raskov," the man said. "I will be your guide for the next several weeks."

Puusepp, not quite fluent in Russian, was puzzled. "Guide?"

Raskov smiled, revealing badly corrected dental damage. "Da. I am going to guide you through the steps that are required of you so that you can return happily to Tallinn and enjoy the admiration of your sister Tiina and her children."

Why would Raskov mention his sister? A threat, of course. So this Raskov knew of the relationship but didn't know how she had shunned him after the publicity of surrounding the Volkov hack. She told him bitterly that she didn't want her children growing up with a common criminal for an uncle. They hadn't been in touch for three years. Puusepp hurt for the missed trips to the park with the kids, the ice creams together, their exuberance. Their love.

"Where are we?"

"Very near where you are going to do your business for us," Raskov said with a half smile. "A chance to make you famous with all your hacker friends. A real opportunity, HoHumJr."

Hacker friends? Did Raskov know about Olegarten? He knew Puusepp's handle, but a lot of people had seen that. Only his friends at Olegarten knew where it came from, and only he knew that the HoHumJr was more valuable to him than the silver medal from the chess championship.

When Puusepp understood the task and refused to do it, Raskov shrugged one shoulder and slid a picture of his sister in the park where she took her children every day. It must have been spring, trees leafing out, flowerbeds full of color. His sister was laughing, and five-year old Kaia was setting up to do a somersault. Puusepp, nearsighted, leaned close to make out the lines on the edge of the picture and saw they were the reticle of a sniper's scope.

He asked for the specifications. What did they say in America? Jump, and you ask how high.

Over the next several days, Puusepp's head cleared. They gave him some clothes: a short sleeve shirt with no pocket, short pants, and some synthetic shoes with straps instead of ties. The hustled him into a messy Honda driven by a young man with long hair and an earring. They drove him several blocks to a modern building on a street lined with sickly-looking trees and shops with signs he couldn't read. Spanish? They marched him past glass-fronted offices around an indoor fountain, past a security desk, and down a hall to a door whose sign announced Neva Imports LLC.

In the process, Puusepp learned he was in Miami. Raskov explained the nature of the hacking task he was expected to complete in no more than three weeks. The project seemed to involve one greedy American trying to destroy another's company, and Raskov had inside help. They gave him software written by an unskilled person. Making it work was difficult but not impossible. Puusepp might have enjoyed the challenge of the work, except for one intruding thought . . . once he finished his work, it was only logical that Raskov would kill him. They were, after all, Russians.

Now, there was phase two, which gave him reason to hope. He was doubly happy to have kept silent about the inefficient design of the penetration software they had made him use for phase one. He almost told Raskov they didn't need help from inside the company whose power feed they interrupted. But he played dumb, which gave him that most valuable commodity: time. Since only he fully understood the software he was writing, he might stretch time a little, maybe enough. As in chess, his survival was a matter of acquiring small advantages. Time was his first advantage.

Then there was Pyotr.

The long hair brushed back, earring and tattoos seemed very American to Puusepp. Where Raskov wore long- or short-sleeved dress shirts in dull colors, khaki trousers and nondescript leather shoes, Pyotr affected bright shirts with surfboards, palm trees and near-naked women. His trousers were finer than Raskov's, and instead of shoes, he wore gray boots made of some sort of animal skin. He had sharp features and dark eyes that Puusepp supposed would be attractive to women. The only odd element was a high-pitched voice and a whinny of a laugh. Where Raskov was careful and observant, Pyotr was laid back, affecting boredom most of the time.

After escorting Puusepp on several evening trips to the men's room, Pyotr now waited outside; no need for pretense with nobody around. Pyotr's relaxed attitude offered Puusepp his second advantage. A small thing, like someone advancing the wrong pawn, but something a good player could exploit.

Pyotr usually spoke English and wanted Puusepp to call

him Pete. He pronounced Puusepp's given name "Cal-Jew," hardening the consonants. Puusepp corrected him. Pyotr began calling him "Ka-choo," said with a chuckle. Some sort of joke. It took Puusepp several days to realize that "Dude" was a way of addressing him. Pyotr seemed to enjoy Puusepp's confusion with his English, which suggested a third advantage.

Pyotr often let Puusepp come out of his cell, perhaps in rebellion against Raskov's lectures that this odd little fellow was dangerous. He had apparently decided Puusepp was not fluent in American English and loved to torment him with slang. One evening, he snapped his phone shut as Puusepp entered the reception area. Pyotr lounged is his usual position behind the desk.

"Man, that was Rosalyn, a real bimbo. But she has a set of knockers on her."

"She is a door?" Puusepp shot him a puzzled look.

Pyotr returned a pained grin. "I mean world-class tits."

"She is a cow, then?" Puusepp replied in Russian.

Pyotr bent double, choking on his laughter. "Not teats, dumb shit," he answered, gasping and giggling. "Seeshka."

Pyotr and Puusepp always had their conversation in the reception area late at night.

It took Puusepp several days of walking through reception, looking bored, stretching non-existent kinks out of his shoulders to get Pyotr to ignore him. Finally, seeing Pyotr absorbed with a magazine featuring a gorgeous, nearly naked girl holding a surfboard, he bent to inspect the business magazines on the table next to the glass panel. This gave him a limited view of the end of the corridor and the security camera on the far wall. Set in an L-shaped corner, it could not cover the whole hall.

Another advantage.

The last advantage came as a shock. Several days after discovering the camera, Puusepp had come out of his cell and was moving toward reception. Pyotr was at the desk, boots propped on an open drawer, talking on his phone.

"Yeah, boring, but important."

The person on the other end presumably needed to be impressed.

"See, I'm tight with the big dawg, junkyard dawg, know what I mean? European. Big time. My family trusts me. They've got me watching an important, uhh, asset. That's why no clubbing. But soon, baby, soon."

Puusepp froze at "dawg."

Dog. Big dog, Pyotr said. Sobaki.

Puusepp spun and retreated into his cell. He collapsed into the chair, elbows on the table, hands cradling his head. Sobaki. Of course. The Volkov hack. That was how they found him.

He stared at his chess board, retreating into the sixty-four-square world of logic. Hoping to see some reason that he might survive, some move that would stun the opponent, win the game. His vision blurred. Tears of fear, but also relief.

Now, the endgame was clear. He had to act no matter the risk.

CHAPTER NINE

IT HAD TAKEN Mac Renfro a week to assemble the board of United Energy, which consisted of his three uncles, the fourth generation of the Renfro family. As his uncles aged, they had become more interested in indulging themselves than in running the company. That was fine with Mac, but frustrating when he wanted to get business done. United Energy was still closely held, a situation Mac intended to remedy in the future, maybe the near future if HelioCorp came out the way he thought it would. Now, he swirled ice cubes in his nearly empty glass of eighteen-year-old scotch whiskey and worked to contain his impatience.

The uncles and Mac sat in the oak paneled meeting room at the United Energy headquarters. The room was patterned after one in the Duquesne Club in Pittsburgh, where his great-great-grandfather, Simon McTavish Renfro, Old Mac, had been accepted into the business elite more than a century ago.

Conversation had veered into yet another story about Old Mac and some mine in Yorkshire. The older Renfros enjoyed the stories, the scotch whiskey, and reminding Mac he was "Young Mac." The name was an honor, an accusation, and a burden. Young Mac, Donel McTavish Renfro, was the only male offspring of the fifth generation of the Renfro family to stay in the family business, thus the honor. He was the product of Choate, Yale and Harvard Business School. His uncles were proud mining engineers; thus, the accusation—that fine education didn't count for squat in the mines. Putting up with his uncles' attitudes and strategies, most of which were frozen in the early twentieth century, was the burden.

Mac's uncle James banged his glass on the table to conclude the story, and the three elders shared a hearty laugh. Mac and the two others in the room, the company's CFO and its legal counsel, smiled politely. Mac cleared his throat.

"On to bullet five, funding HelioCorp through the United Energy Venture Fund." Mac heard a sniff that camouflaged a laugh. He continued, "As you know, Brianna Kapoor turned down our proposed investment several months ago. She retained outside financial counsel and decided to do a public offering. Everybody expected it to be one of the biggest tech IPOs this year."

He paused, making sure he had their attention.

"You know from the news that their tie-in to the grid failed. The substation they were using to connect was wiped out, and one person died. The public offering is off, at least for now. This is the time to get in."

"Is that the Hahvahd B-School speaking?" James asked.

"No, common sense. This is a slam dunk. Kapoor stumbled, had one bad day. She's got a great technology but no money in the bank. That's what I call opportunity." He glanced at James, then the CFO, looking for concurrence. "The B-school would agree."

James gave a dismissive shrug. Mac said more firmly, "After my call to HelioCorp, I know that at least four other firms got interested. Let's get in before they do. Let's be leaders rather than followers." Mac suppressed "for once," but his listeners heard it anyway. He scanned the room, saw jaws tighten, knowing "followers" hurt and angered his uncles. "You know as well as I that we have only a few years left before coal is history."

"Government regulations," another uncle sniffed.

"More than that," Mac said. "Energy is going green."

He picked up his glass and took a sip of the water left by the melting ice cubes, then continued, "Simon was famous for his common sense. He would have cut the deal, no questions asked."

The conviviality had drained out of the room. Mac waited for an explosion, a temper tantrum denigrating his inexperience and insufficient respect for tradition, but there was none.

It took another hour to work terms and conditions. When the vote came, Mac did a mental fist pump. The HelioCorp deal would be great. United would go from being the bad, dirty coal guys to a visionary energy company. A Harvard case study would follow, for sure. A Forbes feature. He would be proud of United Energy for the first time in a long time.

As he left the meeting, he opened his e-pad. His calendar showed the rest of the day free but for a few calls. A secure message had come in from his source inside HelioCorp. He whispered the password as he walked down the hall toward his office. He stopped, stock still, when a text appeared:

they discovered the insert program was modified.

James nearly ran over him. "Damn, Mac," he said, taking in Mac's expression. "Looks like you just learned your wife's humpin' the pool boy."

★ ★ ★

MAC TEXTED HIS wife from his office. She said she was going to the gym. The kids were at a friend's. He decided to go home early. He would have liked to relax a bit after the success with the board, but the message about HelioCorp meant he had to move fast before they fixed the problem. By the time he pulled into his drive, he had mentally sketched HelioCorp's new business plan and management structure. His uncles would be impressed.

He grabbed his briefcase from the back seat. After the deal closed, he thought, maybe turn the BMW in for a Mercedes 500-series hybrid. Or an AMG. A present to himself.

He unlocked the back door. No warning beep from the security system? She forgot to activate, again. Must talk to her about that. He dropped the briefcase on his way through the kitchen to the refrigerator, where he found a bottle of beer. He angled through the living room toward his office, twisting off the cap.

The corner of his eye caught a shape out of place. He turned toward the overstuffed leather armchair beside the fireplace.

The gray butch cut, prizefighter's nose. Raskov?

"You did good work, Mac. Your uncles will now understand your brilliance, and United Energy will become, what do you say, a household name."

Mac gasped. "Why are you here? How did you—God, Raskov, this is too risky. My wife will be home any minute— How will I explain—"

"Your wife . . ." Raskov opened and consulted an e-pad, "is at the YMCA."

How did he know that?

"Your children are at a friend's house two kilometers from here and expect to be picked up in an hour. We have time."

Mac slumped into a love seat across from Raskov. Tangled thoughts—Why is Raskov here? He's following my family?— drained his rising euphoria.

Gathering himself, Mac said, "The successful financing will finish our work. I assume our technical specialist is on his way back to . . . Estonia, isn't it? You, too, should be on your way soon, unless—" he forced a smile, "your management will give you time off to spend on the beach."

An image passed through Mac's mind of Raskov, chest a mat of gray hair, wearing a speedo, lounging at the beach.

"Yes, that's the reason I need to meet with you." Raskov shifted in the chair. "Because the project is not finished."

"Of course it is," Mac said. "HelioCorp will have no more problems They don't know what happened. Even their IAC expert thinks it was a one-time problem."

"Actually, she does not, but we will take care of that issue later. Today we will speak of a further extension of the project."

As Raskov outlined the plan for what he called phase two, Mac's stomach began to churn. His breathing came short, and his vision blurred. Raskov's voice became tinny, like old phonograph recordings he loved. He saw himself in the bar at the Intercont in Vienna, back when he cut the deal. His friend, trusted after several years of conferences and conversations, said his organization needed United Energy's help. They wanted to lay a "a few kilometers of pipe"—admittedly impinging on Roman ruins. Regrettably, bureaucrats made it difficult to accomplish this. So it had to be on the "bottom side of the table." Simple. Mac had only to carry a message to his contact at the Secretariat for Environment and Energy Efficiency. In exchange, his friend offered to put Mac "back in the driver's seat" with HelioCorp. Mac was skeptical; after all, the Wall Street boys had scooped what he had hoped would be United's leap into solar energy. His friend had smiled, ordered another round, and said, "Favors for friends are good, no?" Mac had wondered too briefly why he deserved so large a favor in exchange for passing a message along. Not seeing the *quid* in the *pro quo*. He said 'yes, of course.'

"Mac?"

Raskov was staring at him.

"What?"

"Are you understanding? We are not finished with the project. You will need only to tell us when load-leveling instructions are inserted each day. You should not worry. This will be easy for you."

"It won't be easy or safe," Mac said, hearing the fear in his voice. "The Southeast Control Division is a secure facility. I have no reason to go there, much less ask about their schedule or entry protocol for the grid."

Raskov's raised eyebrows said this should not be a problem. "You should take a drink from your beer and listen carefully." He explained the consequences of failure as a teacher might to a recalcitrant student. When he had finished and Mac agreed, Raskov took his leave.

Mac stayed in his chair, staring at the label on the bottle of beer.

Rolling, rolling, rolling Rock. Rolling over me, over me.

Nothing came into focus. Only looping thoughts. Family, gone. Prison. Worse, Raskov, who would shrug, give that apologetic, world-weary smile and kill him. And his wife. And his kids.

Mac heard the back door open, his wife's voice coming from some other dimension. A kiss brushed his cheek. Happy chatter. Her cheeks rosy. The faint scent of exercise that he had always found arousing.

"I don't feel so well," he said when she asked him why he was so pale.

He escaped up the stairs, to a hot shower, where he could cry.

CHAPTER TEN

WHEN PUUSEPP FIRST saw the design of the phase one software, it had seemed stupidly inefficient, but he was not about to help them refine it. They wanted to ruin one small company for no apparent reason. They must have had some way to pass directly through the IAC firewall via a legitimate portal. Puusepp admired that part of the plan. They hadn't made the mistake of trying to get through using the internet. The Americans watched that avenue like hawks . . . thousands had tried; as far as he knew, nobody had succeeded.

Now he saw that HelioCorp was not a one-off, but a test. For this second phase, they again had a direct entry through the IAC firewall, but his software had to get them in without alerting any of the dozens of countermeasures the IAC had in place. Difficult, but he could do it. He could have made it easy for Raskov to drop in the required location numbers, but that would make Puusepp unnecessary, and he knew how that would turn out. Of course, in the end these Russians would take the software and use it without him anyway, so the hardest design task was to make sure only he could run it.

They accessed the portal from an unused warehouse in a row of drab industrial shops lined up along a potholed road on the seedy north side of Miami. Pyotr would take Raskov and Puusepp there each time they needed to make a connection. The unit was on the end of a series of similar units. The windows on the exposed side of the building were crusted with years of mold and admitted only faint light to the interior. Heat and humidity encouraged a variety of biological experiments. Many had failed, according to the stink that filled the place.

The space itself was eighty by forty feet. The end facing the loading area featured an entrance door next to an oversized pull-down garage door. Inside, a half-open interior door revealed a grimy toilet and two doorless offices lined up along the back wall.

They connected to the IAC through a cable that fed through a hole in a windowpane at the far end of the warehouse. There was a password that changed often. Puusepp had been directed to figure out what algorithm generated the password and defeat the biometrics that protected it. It was too big a task for the small computer Raskov allowed him to use, and he dragged out the process of finding that out. Raskov was unhappy, but what could he do? There had been another delay. Raskov announced he had "made arrangements." Afterwards, the biometrics were no longer a problem.

The "arrangement" meant sitting on overturned plastic buckets next to the workbench where they attached an e-pad to the cable. Then they sipped cans of Dr Pepper while they waited for Raskov to get a call. When it came, Raskov entered a password. He would then start up the connection, his eyes flitting to the window to watch for workers passing by the supposedly unoccupied warehouse. As a result, Puusepp saw and memorized part of the internet address they used to tap into the IAC.

The connection made, Raskov would direct Puusepp to begin pulling down data. The targets were strings of numbers, always in the same format. After a half-dozen passes through the warehouse and a search routine he designed to find specific characteristics Raskov dictated, the mass of data yielded four such strings.

The numbers meant something. But what? For several days, Puusepp nearly pulled out what remained of his hair. The more he concentrated, the more the meaning evaded him. He tried to relax, free associate. That only led him to think of a town in Ukraine near the Russian border where the servers that belonged to Volkov had been. What did that have to do with phase two? Then a flash of insight: *location.*

The numbers Raskov had him copy were map coordinates.

Puusepp memorized as much as he could. With no e-pad, no paper, and nothing to write with, he could only keep a limited amount in mind. Then he remembered one of the business magazines Pyotr let him look at had postcard-sized advertisements between pages. A day later he had palmed one. No ink, but he could incise the paper with a paper clip he found peeking out under a file cabinet.

A blemish in the drywall at the back of his cell looked suspicious. If they were monitoring him—they must be—he hoped that blemish was the camera. He put his travel chess set on the table, white pieces toward the door and black toward the back wall.

He would make a move with white, shift around the table to the black position, pretend to concentrate while marking a few numbers on the card. He couldn't take too long; Raskov and he played daily, and Raskov knew Puusepp's style of play—he would notice.

The second day after Puusepp began marking the card, Raskov ruminated too long on what seemed an obvious pawn exchange. His eyes flicked up to Puusepp. "To understand this, would I do better to move to the other side of the board?"

Puusepp tried to keep his face calm. Was there humor in Raskov's glance? Was he toying with him? Letting him know that he and Pyotr were watching? Perhaps only asking the advice of a master player?

"In a difficult situation, it helps to see the board from the other player's side."

Raskov grunted, took the pawn.

TO GET TO the warehouse from Neva Imports, Raskov and

Puusepp had to pass the guard desk and go through the front entrance of the building to Pyotr's car. If Puusepp walked slowly, but not enough to worry Raskov, he could see the guard's monitor screen for fifteen seconds as they approached the security desk from the corridor that led from the Neva office. The first time had been a bust. The guard had been dozing, and the screen had timed out. The second time, Puusepp saw the flag that said the network was protected by a commercial software he had defeated many times. The third time, Puusepp saw opportunity, tripped over his shoe, and dropped his travel chess set. The set bounced on ceramic tiles and the top flew off, scattering pieces. The sound startled the guard, who was again dozing at the information desk.

Puusepp bent over to pick up the pieces and inspect the cracked case. In his peripheral vision, he saw the guard reflexively tap a key combination on his monitor, bringing the computer alive to check the security cameras.

Success.

PUUSEPP HAD HOPED for more time to build his plan, make it foolproof. But the last entry into the IAC had been the first execution of phase two, he was sure. Time to go; now or never.

A week ago, after Pyotr had been reamed out by Raskov for laziness and dereliction of duty, he had made a half-hearted effort to escort Puusepp to the men's room but refused to follow him in. Over the next several days, Puusepp had stretched the time before Pyotr got cranky. Six minutes.

Puusepp asked for a large, greasy burrito for dinner. The result was predictable and satisfactory. He passed through the outer office a couple of times, causing Pyotr to grimace and say, "Jesus! What died in you?" and waved his hand in front of his face.

Puusepp returned to his cell and waited until he heard

Pyotr in a conversation on his phone. He'd hobbled to the front office, a pained look on his face, and signaled he needed to go to the toilet. Pyotr let him go alone, half-heartedly watching him go down the hall, still on the phone. As Puusepp turned into the men's, he saw Pyotr close the Neva door, presumably to continue his self-promotion to a woman he'd told Puusepp was a "prospect." Whatever that meant.

Puusepp let the men's room door swing shut and dropped to the hallway floor. He inched his way snake-like from the men's to the lobby, hoping he was right about a blind spot between the hall and lobby cameras. Also hoping nobody was working late in the offices up front. He had no story for why a slight, paunchy guy with a heavy accent would be trying to extrude himself down the hall at this time of night.

When he hit the guard station, two minutes gone, his task got harder. He crouched behind the desk, reached one hand up to rotate the monitor down so he could see it, and grabbed the keyboard. He was unsure of the last digit of the password, so it took another minute to get into the system. Accessing the internet took thirty seconds; he was home in the Olegarten site in another thirty. Sweat ran into his eyes. Two minutes left. He opened a message to both Hotcakes and Jake. The card with the scratched GPS numbers was hard to read in the shadow behind the desk. He spit, ground his finger on the floor of the foot well and rubbed. The numbers, one complete, one partial, and two vague code words, came clear. He entered them, using *x* for missing digits. He wrote *GPS* at the end. One more minute. He found a small file—no time to attach the terabytes of the full library—and renamed it Hell-Kit. He attached it to a move in the game called DMS that he had often played with his friends, followed by .AND. Finished, he crawled back to the men's door, pushed it open, crawled through, stood up, and opened the door. He walked back toward Neva, fastening his belt. Pyotr opened the door, angry.

"Where the fuck have you—"

Pyotr's eyes swept Puusepp.

"You been praying in there?" His eyes were on Puusepp's knees.

Puusepp felt his face flushing. He looked down—dust on his knees, light against the dark fabric. Caught. His mind raced.

"I . . . I . . . the paper. It would not go. I had to . . ."

"Jesus." Pyotr's expression let Puusepp know that he was terminally uncool.

Back in his cell, Puusepp dropped into his chair. He brushed off his knees. Had he left tracks outside? Would anyone notice? The excitement of executing the plan was wearing off, leaving him drained.

The die was cast. Finality sank in.

Now, he would be smiling when Raskov pulled the trigger.

CHAPTER ELEVEN

IN THE DAYS since Joe's dinner with Weezy, he had called her each evening, but suspecting some NSA creep was listening ruined intimacy. Stilted conversations were better than none, and he craved her voice, as she obviously did his. The marriage proposal was always front and center but never mentioned. On this evening, they talked about HelioCorp and the impending second connection, weather, news, anything to put off hanging up.

"I was thinking of calling Jake," Weezy said. "It was her birthday last week."

How would Weezy know Jake's birthday?

"Uhh, good idea." Then it hit him: she couldn't go to Olegarten without violating the prohibition against any "non-work" internet use. And she was asking him to—

"Yeah, I'll give her a call too," Joe said, reading Weezy's ghost of a smile that let him know he was right.

Joe hadn't been to the chat room in a year or more. The conversations were laden with obscure programming termi-nology, which made them both irritating and intimidating. The members tolerated Joe because of Weezy, but he felt like either an annoyance or a mascot when he did go on.

Olegarten was at least a decade old, predating the CyberWar. Its members were White Hats, dedicated to illuminating the dark side of the internet. Or maybe they were Black Hats, using advanced cyber skills for all sorts of nefari-ous activities. Weezy had explained that Olegarten didn't fit into a neat category. It had strict rules it called The Protocol that would make it more or less a White Hat organization, except when its members penetrated government data bases (no doubt with good intentions), violated intellectual property of selfish corporations and the like. And there was the "midnight gardening" of currencies and bitcoins that helped keep body and soul together. Frowned on by most governmental authorities.

Then came the CyberWar. The U.S. response was the super-secure firewall called the InterAgency Channel. All data the government considered crucial was herded behind it. Several years after the IAC went live—"impregnable," the press releases said—Joe, Weezy and Olegarten had exposed the major hack now famous as Phoenix. Back then, Weezy had set Joe up in Olegarten with the handle "Luckymonkey" so they could communicate safely. The exposure of Phoenix saved lives and brought the people behind it to justice, but it put Olegarten in the spotlight. As a result, its members had become even more security conscious than they had been in the early days. Which was what drove Joe to Starbucks.

Starbucks? He could see Adeeb, the current Olegarten security chief, text it, sarcasm dripping from the italics.

Yes, Starbucks. Joe couldn't go through HelioCorp's systems—too many skilled programmers who might see the connection. The website he had developed during Phoenix, razorblue.net, was too public. So, Starbucks. He hoped anybody listening would be one of those unsophisticated script kiddies the Olegarten members joked about.

Joe drove down to Deerfield Beach. Midmorning would be slow, he hoped. The place looked normal. A couple of guys doing a business deal. A man in a suit concentrating on his e-pad. Several women talking. Joe bought a coffee, took a place in a back corner, found the shop's Wi-Fi signal, and raised the Olegarten site.

The site appeared to be one of those old two-dimension sites that existed by the millions. Abandoned, forlorn, copyrighted a dozen or more years ago. Joe punched on a spiky white flower in the lower right corner. A string of HTML code appeared. He found the comment tag he wanted, selected it, expecting the Olegarten portal to appear. Instead, a blank screen, shortly replaced by: Move around the table to face the back of the building.

Joe jumped. How could they? He checked around him as well as he could without being obvious. Nobody watching him.

A picture appeared on his e-pad. It took him a moment to recognize the coffee shop and, sure enough, the men, the chatting women, and his own back.

Of course. They hacked the shop's security camera.

Joe got up and positioned himself on the window side of the table.

That's better, Luckymonkey. You've got two crackers camping on your machine. Next time don't call from a dirty location, or at least do the decompression protocol.

Crackers? Decompression protocol?

Two IP addresses appeared on the screen.

Number one's close by, probably in a car in the parking lot. He's malicious, but we have no record of him. So Rule Four applies. We'll shut him down.

Joe remembered Weezy explaining that Rule Four of the Olegarten Protocol was "No Overreaction."

Number two is in your shop. He's a bad boy. He's trying to install a logic bomb, presumably so he can freeze your data and demand a ransom. We know him, so Rule Three overrides Rule Four.

Rule Three was going to make Number Two's life miserable, as far as Joe remembered the Protocol. Sure enough, shortly thereafter, there was a muffled "fuuuuuuuuck" from the business-suited guy. He shot out of his chair, bumped his table. His cup sloshed coffee. His face froze in a rictus of fear and anger. He stomped to the door, went outside, where Joe watched through the window as he scanned the parking lot. After a minute or so, his shoulders sagged, and he re-entered the coffee shop looking ready to cry. On the way back to his table, he grabbed a handful of napkins. He slumped into his chair and wiped the table absently while he stared at his e-pad's screen.

Joe's screen announced: Cleared to enter.

He typed out: Luckymonkey to Jake. You home?

The reply came almost immediately: Jake is not home. Paging now.

After several minutes, Jake appeared on video, sitting at the same kitchen table where she had spoken by hologram to the Senate committee and brought down Phoenix.

"Do you know where Hotcakes is?"

"Weezy is in Bethesda," Joe answered, surprised at the lack of preliminaries.

"Do you know why she's gone silent?"

"I do," Joe said. "She's been prohibited from using the internet. In fact, the reason I called is to make sure you know—"

"It is urgent that I get in touch with her."

"Anything I can do?"

"Tell her there's a message from HoHumJr. She knows he went silent over a month ago. Yesterday a message appeared, apparently from him. Looks important. There's a reference to a logic game we play and a string of numbers, as well as an attached file only she has permission to open."

"I'll call her right now. I'm sure she'll figure out a way to get in touch."

After he signed off, Joe sat for a moment. What was Weezy getting herself into this time? First, she asked him to help her violate house arrest, and now she needed his help to get to Olegarten.

What was she getting *them* into?

CHAPTER TWELVE

RASKOV WAS IN line for an early morning espresso when his e-pad buzzed. He paid for the coffee, left the shop and took a chair at one of the tables in front of the cafe. The note was from a Sobaki technical operative. It said an encrypted message had been sent from the building's system last night. Maybe one of the law offices working late, Raskov hoped; besides, Puusepp had no device that could send a message of any kind. On the other hand, if anyone could figure a way, it would be Puusepp.

Raskov sighed. A decade ago, the challenge of outwitting an adversary sharpened his enjoyment of the game. Now, it seemed like every risk reminded him of the possibility of failure.

He arrived at the building, nodded to the guard, and passed down the hall to the Neva office. He knocked three times. A light went on in the reception area, then Pyotr's face appeared at the vertical window next to the door. The lock clicked and Raskov entered.

"Last night?" Raskov asked in Russian.

"All cool," Pyotr said in English.

Raskov extended his hand. "The log?" He had instituted the log after the first time Pyotr reported "all cool."

Pyotr crossed to the reception desk, picked up a sheet, and thrust it to Raskov in a way that made it clear that it was a personal affront. He had drawn a line from 11 to 4, as if watching Puusepp was like giving a 7-Eleven restroom a glance and a swipe and calling it clean.

"Nothing happened from eleven p.m. to four a.m.?"

Pyotr rolled his eyes as if this line of questioning was too much to bear. "He slept four hours, then TV, then chess. Playing with himself." He repeated "playing with himself" in English and smirked. Some kind of joke.

"And you had him in sight all of these hours?"

"Yes, except when he took a crap."

"I don't see that on the log. Did you not understand the instructions I gave you?"

"I didn't log it. He just had to go to the toilet."

"You went into the toilet with him, and you were certain he carried nothing into the stall?" In Russia, there would have been no stall, and things would have been much easier. This was one of several problems that gave Raskov heartburn. Failure to execute Sobaki instructions precisely typically led to termination. The kind with no pink slip.

"Jesus, Raskov." Pyotr switched into English. "I never follow him into the crapper, okay? That'd be weird."

"You let him go into the latrine alone?"

"Men's room, Raskov, men's room. Latrines are for soldiers."

"You were certain he carried nothing—"

"It was 11:45. He needed to use the men's room. Nobody in the building. Front door locked. I watched him go down the hall and into the—"

"You didn't follow him?"

"It's not an internet cafe in there, you know. What could he do?"

"You didn't watch him, though?"

"He took a dump and was back in five minutes, maybe seven."

Raskov turned away from Pyotr, unwilling to show his anger, to give away the young man's future. He needed Pyotr for at least another week or two.

He cracked the outer door. No one around. He walked the hall from Neva Imports to the men's room, then to the opposite end. No access for any device. His e-pad showed plenty of Wi-Fi, but he had made sure Puusepp had nothing that could transmit. He continued to the security desk. Monitors mounted behind the wooden facade showed alternating views of the interior of the building. That would be the only option. With Puusepp's skills, getting a message through those monitors would be like taking a favorite toy from a toddler, except there would be no crying. That is, if the system was active in the evening.

Raskov spent the rest of the day reading and thinking while he kept an eye on Puusepp. Video monitoring showed nothing unusual, except that Puusepp had started changing positions from the white to the black side of the chess board when he played alone. Pyotr appeared at six o'clock, half an hour late, as usual. Raskov left the building as the guard was preparing to lock the front door for the evening.

Raskov returned after a dinner in a Cuban place several blocks away. He swiped his entry fob and the door clicked open. The fob would leave a record, a necessary risk.

The monitors were on. Raskov's hope sank, but he had steeled himself for disappointment. He stood next to the desk, occasionally checking his watch. He would appear on the security tapes, but he might be waiting for a business associate. Hardly plausible, but possible, given the odd hours the guards knew Neva kept. Raskov focused his peripheral vision on the scans. A small slice of the hall and the area behind the security desk was not covered by the cameras. He thought through his options. Was he too suspicious?

At last, he got his satellite phone, left the building, called the emergency number, and explained his concern.

There was a short pause while the one they called Mongrel considered. "We must know what the Estonian did," he concluded. "We will look into this from our end."

THE TWO MERCEDES and the Escalade deposited their owners

in front of an apartment building, this time several kilometers southeast of Red Square. The men's security details made sure the entrance hall was clear. Their presence ensured that residents who might have been curious became deaf and dumb.

This time, the elevator worked. The three Sobaki gathered in a fifth-floor apartment, bare except for a table with a cracked linoleum surface and three chairs. The men of the Sobaki stood silent while one of the security detail passed a black box over the wall and ceiling, peered out the window and pulled down a decrepit shade. Finally, he gave the group a nod and left the apartment.

"Why are we together so soon after the last meeting?" Chairman asked. The question had a querulous edge. Mongrel waited to speak until Chairman sat down. Borzoi, showing his nerves, tapped a cigarette out of a fresh pack. Mongrel stared him down. The man tried to put the cigarette back in the pack. His hand shook. He slipped the cigarette into his pocket and shrugged.

"Several days ago," Mongrel said, "Raskov warned that the Estonian may have sent a message."

"Yes?" Chairman leaned forward.

"What?" Borzoi half rose from his seat. "This is the same Raskov you said you trusted?" His sneer suggested his opinion.

Mongrel paused, tamping down a surge of rage. He took a deep breath and raised his eyes to Borzoi. "Yes. This is the same Raskov."

He cleared his throat and continued, "Raskov needed a second person, a reliable person, to help watch the Estonian. We had no assets in Florida, and you suggested your cousin. Very reliable, you said, and living in Miami."

Borzoi sat down, perhaps seeing what was coming. He reached for the pack of cigarettes again, glanced at Mongrel, and dropped his hand.

"The message was sent during the evening, when this Pyotr of yours was supposed to be guarding the Estonian."

"That is what Raskov told you, but—"

"That is what the computer log told me." Mongrel's stare froze Borzoi. "In any case, this raises two issues. First, we do not know how much the Estonian was able to send. The message was short, possibly a call for help. The signal disappeared behind a firewall our people could not penetrate. It is a famous hacker site called Olegarten. We know Puusepp belongs to Olegarten, and we have identified the member he sent the message to. It included the location of a file called Hell-Kit. We don't know what is in the file. Closer inspection showed that the message included two of our phase two locations and some indecipherable characters, as well. Maybe he hoped his friends would be able to trace it to his location. Second, the IAC analyst I mentioned at our last meeting is also a member of Olegarten. The Americans may confirm that HelioCorp was not a random event, so we should move forward quickly"—he paused, looked from Borzoi to Chairman—"or pull out now."

Borzoi shook his head. "This message probably means nothing. An attempt by the Estonian to save himself. A smoke screen. We don't even know what is in the file or what will happen if it is exposed."

Mongrel let out a slow breath. "Our activities have not been invisible. There are people who know things and material that, carefully assembled, would put all of us in jeopardy."

Borzoi looked away from Mongrel and gave a dismissive wave. "This file of his is probably false propaganda."

"What about the hack that led to your uncle's disappearance? That was not false propaganda." Mongrel cocked his head and waited for the answer he already knew.

Borzoi shot out of his chair. "I want them both dead. The woman, now. The Estonian as soon as the last instruction is sent." He leaned forward, fists on the table, fixing Mongrel in an angry stare. "Why are we waiting?"

"We need him to complete phase two. I expect we will be

able to convince him to tell us what he sent," Mongrel said. There was no malice in his smile. "He will respond to pain."

"What about the woman?" Borzoi asked.

Mongrel stood, signaling the end of the meeting. "The assassin has been dispatched."

RASKOV SAT IN the back office of Neva Imports, working an Expert Sudoku. His e-pad chimed with an advertisement for a popular American truck. Raskov sighed—he was on track for a record time—and took a satellite phone out of his satchel. He hustled to the loading dock behind the building where the phone would have a clear line to the satellite system and called Mongrel.

"We have reviewed all outgoing traffic from your building's server." Mongrel's voice carried the modulated tone of encryption. "The Estonian sent a message. It included the location of a file called Hell-Kit."

The secure line hissed softly. Did Mongrel expect an answer?

"It is up to you," Mongrel continued, "to convince Puusepp to tell us what is in Hell-Kit. We will eliminate the woman he sent it to. Puusepp is your responsibility."

"Your responsibility" carried the weight of a death sentence.

"Also, the government or Olegarten hackers may trace your location. You must move. And Raskov?"

"Yes?"

"You may eliminate the Estonian when we know what is in Hell-Kit."

"I cannot do that until we finish phase two," Raskov said. "Puusepp is necessary to enter the instructions into the IAC."

A pause.

"Then keep him and use him, but he should not die in a humane manner."

"Understood." Raskov's heart sank. Even a simple, clean bullet in the back of the head would be difficult, but to look into the little Estonian's eyes while . . .

Raskov broke the connection. His finger left a smear on the number pad where a drop of sweat had landed. He sighed deeply, returned to Neva, and entered Puusepp's cell.

Puusepp was, as usual, working a chess problem, his back to the door. Raskov negotiated the narrow passage between the table's edge and the wall.

Puusepp kept his eyes on the board for a little too long, then lifted them, his smile fading as he took in Raskov's expression. But he asked, "You would like to play now?"

"Not yet today, Kalju. Perhaps later. We will go to the warehouse and wait for instructions."

PYOTR DROVE RASKOV and Puusepp to the warehouse late in the afternoon. They unloaded a beat-up card table, three mismatched folding chairs, and two cots that screamed 'uncomfortable.'

"You set 'em up," Pyotr said, not quite addressing Raskov directly. "I'm off until tomorrow." He turned without waiting for permission and made for the door.

Raskov inhaled, preparing to shout at Pyotr, but held off. They would be finished in a few days, maybe a week. Why waste energy on Pyotr. Let him have his little act of insubordination. Instead, he said to Puusepp, "Set up the game. We will be here for a while."

He extracted the computer they used for phase two instructions from the grip he carried. At the far end of the building, he pulled a thin cable out of a crevice next to a hole cut in one corner of a window. He attached it, turned on the computer, and verified the connection.

Raskov returned to the card table and laid his e-pad on it. "We should get a call soon."

Puusepp had arranged the chess pieces, giving white to Raskov. Raskov sat and advanced the queen's pawn two spaces. Puusepp advanced a knight.

Raskov's phone interrupted. He listened, repeated a string of numbers, nodded and disconnected.

"Come," he said. The two men went to the computer. Raskov checked his watch, waited for several minutes, and entered his code. He turned the keyboard toward Puusepp.

Puusepp brought the software up, found the place in the code he wanted, and nodded to Raskov, who read off numbers: two digits, two digits, four digits.

Raskov let out a relieved sigh as a confirmation appeared on the screen.

"Okay," he said. "Back to the game."

As they took their seats, Raskov said, "You are playing a dangerous game" and moved a second pawn.

"It is too early to say that. You must first develop the center of the board—"

Raskov pushed his chair back, elbows on the tabletop, big fists clenched under his chin.

"Kalju, what is in the Hell-Kit?"

"Hell-Kit?" Puusepp's gray eyes said he understood.

"We know you sent a file called Hell-Kit to a woman at this place called Olegarten. Some information about phase two as well."

Puusepp nodded the way he did when Raskov made a particularly smart move.

"You will have to show me this file," Raskov continued. "I hope you will do it voluntarily. I think you know the Sobaki, and I think you understand the methods they employ—" he cleared his throat "—I will have to employ—to find and destroy the file."

The Estonian's shoulders sagged fractionally. "Yes, I know," he said. "My family has been familiar with these methods for several generations, Maksym." Puusepp had never spoken Raskov's given name before.

"Well, then—" Raskov wanted to move beyond the threat, but Puusepp interrupted. "My great-grandfather fought with the Finnish in the Winter War in 1939. Brave men held off the Russian advance. He was a colonel in the Estonian cavalry and a saber fencer. He'd won gold in the 1930 European games, so he was well known. He returned home to Tallinn after the Russians invaded Estonia. They had executed his first wife and two of their children. After they raped the wife and daughter, of course. That was his reward for bravery." Puusepp's voice quavered. "When the war was over, the Russians deported a quarter of the country and forbade the teaching of the language. My grandfather was born in Siberia. But you know about Soviet depredation, don't you?"

Raskov exhaled.

"Belarusian? Pole? Czech, perhaps? You are not Russian." Puusepp's eyes bored into Raskov. "Why are you doing these people's bidding?"

Raskov sat back. A low chuckle escaped his lips.

"The file, Puusepp. That is what I need. No stories, no philosophy. If I don't get it, well, you know the consequences. For me, as well."

"Am I a chess player?" Puusepp grinned for the first time.

Raskov cocked his head.

"And you answer, 'Of course you are, Kalju'," Puusepp said. "Would I make the first move of a game without knowing the second, the third and expecting the fourth?"

Raskov's irritation was growing. This was not the time for rhetorical questions. But he was interested, too. Puusepp was not dumb enough to send off a message believing no one would catch on. He would have analyzed all possible outcomes.

"Yes, Puusepp, you are a brilliant tactician in the world of chess, so you have thought this diversion of yours through in detail. But we are not playing chess this time, and I have you. Chess does not involve pain, Puusepp. There is no blood shed in the sacrifice of a pawn. I am capable of terrible things,

Kalju, particularly when my life depends on them."

"Maksym, my friend. I hope by now I may call you friend. The endgame of this is obvious. We are both dead. The Sobaki hates me. The only reason they haven't had you kill me already is they need me. Do you remember the Volkov hack?"

"Of course. Many millions of dollars and euros. Volkov and several others disappeared."

"That was my work. Volkov was part of Sobaki back then."

Raskov grimaced. "Ahh. So you are correct, Puusepp. Sobaki wants you dead. Now I understand the 'very slowly' part of my instructions."

"How do I survive, Maksym? You must see the gambit . . . I make my survival contingent on the secrecy of what is in Hell-Kit. Your experts will identify the person I sent Hell-Kit to, so I must make that secrecy contingent on her survival, as well."

Clever, Raskov thought. He put some sort of time lock on the file. It would open if he didn't keep it closed. He had hoped it would be clean and easy. Use the software to carry out phase two. Then an 'exit' for Puusepp. But Sobaki would never buy leaving Puusepp's files as a legacy for others to use. For now, Puusepp and the woman he sent Hell-Kit to would have to live.

Raskov sighed and scanned the board. Puusepp had made a move. A second knight. Develop the bishop, perhaps. Eliminate the threat from the queenside knight.

Eliminate. The word stuck in his mind. Mongrel said they were going to eliminate the woman.

Raskov bolted out of his chair, hitting the table and scattering the chess pieces.

Puusepp cringed.

Raskov extracted the satellite phone from his grip and rushed out the warehouse door, already dialing.

CHAPTER THIRTEEN

THE HELEN RAWLS chugged past the Owl's Head light. She was a stout forty-footer, returning from two days on the Thomaston Shoals. The faint red glow on the horizon was almost gone; night was settling in. It had been a long day hauling traps, banding and tossing lobsters into the well in the center of the boat. Some good hard shells, fewer shedders than last week. The boat passed out of the cut into the last five miles of open water, and the lights of Camden twinkled across Penobscot Bay. The captain and his crewman were finishing the small tasks of homecoming: stowing lines and floats, securing the winch, returning gaffs to the catch hold. Finished, stretching, the captain turned back toward the wheel house, stopped and stared.

Black.

Camden had disappeared. Where was he? He ran the few steps to the wheel house. Not knowing exactly where you were in the rocky coastal waters of Maine was a recipe for disaster. The autopilot was on course toward Camden harbor. Depth four fathoms. He turned back toward Owl's Head. The powerful fixed beam was right where it should be. Puzzled, but breathing more slowly now, he cut off the autopilot, slowed to a crawl. Like his dad would have done. Figure it out, Dad would have said. Take your time. Dad had survived hurricanes, Nor'easters, equipment failures, bad luck, and low prices.

Off to starboard, the reassuring red and white of Heron Neck Light appeared on the horizon. He blew out a long breath, knowing he was going the right direction, not out to sea. To be sure, he checked the compass.

The only thing that made sense was a blackout in Camden and up the coast as far he could see. It was going to be a long night unloading.

THE FIRST TAP came through the Bluetooth chip under the skin behind Granston Harmon's right ear. He didn't recognize the tone, three notes ascending like the boarding call in European airports. Not his boss, not the President herself. Probably from some lower-level bureaucrat with an inflated ego. He ignored it.

He was finishing an interminable dinner with three cyber-security experts. One had launched into a boring disquisition on the dangers posed by old-style demodulation techniques. After the third tap, Harmon excused himself, walked toward the men's room, and pulled a small e-pad from his pocket.

1 bn USD

See Camden, ME

Instructions follow

He stared at the text. Nonsense. A billion dollars for Camden, Maine? To Camden? He realized he was buzzed from the two—or was it three?—dirty martinis. No 'from' address in the message to respond to.

He slipped the e-pad back into his pocket, dawdled in the men's room, and returned to find the expert in his peroration about modems.

Harmon returned home after midnight. A sense of foreboding he couldn't put a finger on made him look again at the message. Was it a prank? A mistake? How had it gotten through a supposedly secure channel? He checked news feeds. No mention of Camden.

He shrugged, set his implant to Sleep to prevent messages

from intruding on his rest, brushed his teeth and went to bed. At three a.m., he awoke from a dream featuring his former wife, blinked, and realized his implant had tapped him with the same tone as before.

He reached for his glasses and his e-pad. The message popped up, harsh to his night vision:

MCB-bank

1 bn USD. Double tomorrow.

Below the text, a string of numbers.

Someone wanted him to transfer a billion dollars to, what, an offshore bank?

He sat up, ran his fingers through what hair he had left. Both messages were time-stamped. If this was some real issue, admitting he hadn't done anything was going to be a problem.

He turned on his bedside light, sent a short message to the Vice President, asking for some time in the morning. Then he lay back, mind spinning.

CHAPTER FOURTEEN

HARMON PASSED THROUGH his outer office at flank speed and turned toward his secretary as he shrugged out of his coat.

"Lydia . . . My office."

She glanced up from a stack of mail, letter opener poised.

"What subject?" His long-serving secretary would know which files, what e-pad to carry in, and whether coffee or a Diet Coke was called for.

"Uhh. Confidential. No need for files."

She stood and followed him in, closing the door behind her.

Harmon took a seat behind his desk, rested his elbows on the desk and his chin on his fists. Should he confide in her? She had clearance for most secret matters, and he couldn't very well work the problem without her knowing about it.

"Sit."

She sat, her hands folding then unfolding, looking as if they wanted something to do.

"My secure line has been hacked."

She inhaled, eyes wide.

"How?" She stuttered "H-how do you know?"

"I received a message last night from an unnamed source. A serious matter. I need to talk to the vice president at eleven o'clock." He paused, then continued, "This is a national security matter. I need it to stay absolutely confidential."

"I understand."

"I need to know everyone who can see that number. POTUS can, of course, and VPOTUS. Morgan at Homeland. Three people in this office." He raised his eyebrows. "Including, of course, you."

Lydia gave a stiff nod and began to stand. Harmon wondered briefly if she was anxious to leave. She usually waited for a sign from him.

"Are there others?" said Harmon. "Someone, some technician, set my secure line up when I was appointed. Probably someone at the CIA they never told me about. I'll work on the CIA. You find out who else has the code."

"Yessir." Lydia stood and turned to leave. Why was she in a hurry?

"Also . . ."

She stopped midway to the door.

"Find me a power grid technical specialist and get his ass . . . or her . . . over here. And that pain in the butt woman from IAC . . . Napa? Naples? . . . some Italian city."

"Napolitani, sir. Louise Napolitani."

WEEZY'S MORNING BIKE ride had started her day off right. She arrived at the IAC relaxed, loose, ready to tackle the challenge of work. Like starting a run in the front row, knowing your time is the best in the pack. That feeling lasted until she entered the bullpen.

Keith Sanders, tense as usual, waited at the door.

"Louise, there will be a car from Washington picking you up in five minutes. The AVP wants to see you again."

"AVP?"

"Granston Harmon. The Assistant to the Vice President for Internal Affairs and Cyber Security."

"Oh, okay. I had the A part figured out, but I didn't know how Asshole fit with VP."

"Louise, there's nothing to be gained—"

"What's he want?"

"He didn't say. Except that it's important."

"I'm not getting in a car without some assurance that I'm

not going to be driven out of my approved range, then arrested for violating my house arrest, taken off to some black ops site or—"

"Louise, I'm sure he just wants advice. You and I both know that the HelioCorp intrusion was never satisfactorily resolved. Maybe—"

"Okay, Keith. I'll go, but I want it on the record that I'm going against my will."

Keith's expression went sour.

"Formally recorded, I mean. Then I move." She turned away and stalked to her cubicle, aware that her co-workers were ostentatiously not looking at her ankle bracelet. Two minutes later, a log note appeared on her monitor recognizing L. Napolitani was responding to AVP request under protest. Shortly thereafter, Car's Here popped up.

The driver of the car waiting for her was the same kid who had picked her up last time.

"You know what the Assistant to the Vice President in charge of silly projects wants this time?" she asked as she settled in the back seat.

The kid glanced at her in the rear-view mirror. He didn't smile, but it looked to Weezy like that took effort.

"No idea. I have an order to pick you up."

As they rode through morning traffic into D.C., Weezy's e-pad sprang to life with a message from Joe: You need to call Jake.

She tapped back: Will as soon as I can. Going to meeting.

The car turned into the underground garage Weezy recognized from her last trip. It pulled up to the same entrance, which might have belonged to a shopping center except for the guys in suits standing in the military "at ease" position on either side of the double doors.

One of the guards led her down the same corridor she had passed through before. They went through the same security procedure, then to an elevator instead of the room where she'd been interrogated. After a short silent ride, they emerged into a different world from the unadorned concrete corridor below. Weezy's companion led her past an elegant but unoccupied mahogany desk to a door, where he knocked.

"Come."

The guard opened the door for Weezy and stepped aside. Sunlight washed the large office through windows overlooking the Potomac. Bookcases down one wall held the trophies of a political life well-lived: pictures of Harmon with dignitaries and rock stars from all walks of life. A miniature golden spade, a football jersey, several statuettes crowded on a shelf. All surely carrying proud stories. A huge desk occupied the space in front of the windows, stacks of paper and a monitor covering most of the surface. An extension jutting from the front of the desk formed a sort of conference table. A tall, thin man whose complexion hinted that he hadn't been outside in a long, long time sat on one side. Weezy's tracker group called the man Grid Dweeb. Behind the desk sat the assistant to the vice president, whose quivering jowls said he was close to apoplectic. Grid Dweeb stared at Weezy's ankle bracelet, which prodded her simmering anger and embarrassment.

"Sit." Harmon waved at a chair across the table from the Grid Dweeb. Weezy took a seat.

"Why am I—"

"Hold on."

Grid Dweeb was tapping on an overlarge e-pad. He was breathing hard, his garlic breath a malignant mantle of stink. Garlic for breakfast? More likely those 'odorless' garlic pills.

"Sir, the initial reports from—" He stopped, frowned at Weezy, then turned back to Harmon. "Uhh . . . this is class—"

"Classified. Right." Harmon said. "Give us the overview without the details."

"The reports from the subject location show no physical penetration of the substation. No signs of a break in. Security cameras see state patrol doing regular checks, but nobody moving in or out of the buildings."

"So it was a hack into the IAC?" Harmon asked.

"The Tracking division shows no penetration—"

Weezy interrupted. "What are we talking about?" Being dragged here against her will to bathe in Grid Dweeb's garlic breath made the question a challenge. Harmon turned to her, a vein next to his eye pulsing. But instead of the explosion she expected, he said, "There's been another power grid event."

Turning to Grid Dweeb, he barked, "Was it a hack? Yes or no?"

"So far, no. There is no sign of an event that caused this, uhh, abnormality last night. They're reviewing the sweepers and should have a report by late tomorrow."

"Sweepers? They're checking the janitors?"

Grid Dweeb gave Harmon a tolerant smile. "Not janitors, sir. Sweepers are autonomous code—artificial intelligence entities—that review the flotsam and jetsam on the IAC—we review the contents—" He glanced at Weezy, including her in the "we."

"Okay. I get it," Harmon said. "Follow-up, right?"

"Right, sir."

"So, if no one hacked the IAC, how did I get this message on my private system address? I thought the IAC was impenetrable."

Weezy's frustration bubbled to the surface. "There are three-point-four million legal users of the IAC as of the end of last week," she said. "Two thousand have access that would allow them to add a message or affect code, if that's what you're asking."

The Grid Dweeb added, "Most of the users are entering secure archives, and those entries get scanned to be sure they are passive—"

"Passive?" When Harmon squinted, he really did look like a bulldog.

"Documents that have no executable elements in them, which is to say no code that could execute to—"

"Speak English."

The man exhaled. Weezy held her breath, then took over.

"Most documents that go into the IAC are just that . . . documents. They get read in, like putting books on a library shelf. But they are all scanned to be sure they carry no computer code, same as our email. That way, there's nothing that can take action once inside the IAC."

"So they couldn't be the source, right?" Harmon asked Weezy.

"The source of what?" She spread her hands and let her eyes widen in question. "Oh, yeah, that's classified."

Harmon locked her in a stare that she assumed was meant to intimidate. His jowls quivered. She sniffed, preparing to tell him what cliff he could jump off of.

The Dweeb jumped in, "But military applications and certain actions relating to infrastructure need to have real time access—"

"Infrastructure?"

"Yessir. Infrastructure consists of dams, some interstate guidance systems, power management systems, nuclear—"

"I do understand what infrastructure is," Harmon said through clenched teeth. "Tell me about power management systems."

"Yessir," Grid Dweeb said, apparently realizing that his GS rating was in danger of evaporating. "About fifty utility companies have direct access to the power grid. Most balancing and switching software is now inside the IAC, and the utilities need access to balance out demand and supp—"

"Holy crap. So whatever came in to shut down Camden must have come from one of them."

"I can't see how that would happen. The relatively few people that are certified are carefully vetted. But, yes, that would be the first place I'd look."

"That will be all."

Weezy shrugged and started to rise. Grid Dweeb stayed seated.

"Not you." Harmon turned toward Grid Dweeb. "I said, that will be all."

The man flushed. He shut his e-pad and stood.

"I will stay on call in case you need—"

Harmon waved the man out. Grid Dweeb carefully slipped his old school e-pad into a padded case, zipped it halfway before the zipper jammed, fought with the zipper. Weezy watched Harmon's color rise.

Finally, the man said, "If I can be of further—," took in Harmon's expression, gave an apologetic smile, and left the room without finishing the offer.

Harmon watched the door close and sighed.

"What's your security clearance?" Harmon asked.

"It was TS/SCI. Top Secret with Sensitive Compartmented Information for data services and IAC protocols, until you took it away."

"Well, at least you didn't lie about that."

What did the smirk mean? She restrained her desire to take the bait.

"I don't lie."

"Asking Joe Mayfield to act as a proxy and check in at Olegarten when you've been told specifically to stay off the internet?"

Weezy went cold. They really were listening in, and better than she thought.

Harmon straightened in his chair. "Listen, Miss Napolitani. You're playing with fire here. From what we can tell, you're not the person who caused the HelioCorp breakdown, but you might have been. And you just keep jabbing the bull's butt with a sharp stick."

"My job."

"No, it's not your job to ignore orders and freelance whenever you feel like it."

Weezy leaned her elbows on the table, steepled her fingers and willed her face to drop into a neutral mien. She told herself to shut up. The next step after the ankle bracelet was not something she wanted to find out about.

Harmon looked at her for a long moment, then said,

"Good to get that out of the way. Now, on to business."

No threats? No bluster? Weezy stifled the urge to ask why she'd been dragged up to D.C. for a reprimand that never came. Then she realized Harmon was, indeed, the bull whose butt she had been jabbing.

"As you have no doubt figured, there has been another grid incident. Camden, Maine, went dark last night for about half an hour. Not a big problem, except for two things. One, the IAC power systems management showed no sign of the problem.

"Just like HelioCorp."

"Right." Harmon's tone challenged Weezy to make a snide remark. He continued, "Two, we got a ransom message through a supposedly secure communication channel last night." He exhaled and looked perplexed.

"In other words," Weezy couldn't help saying, "HelioCorp wasn't some random IAC hiccup."

Harmon's eyes narrowed. *Here it comes,* Weezy thought.

He exhaled, seeming to deflate.

"Right. We need to find these hackers, or it'll be cyberwar all over again."

Weezy felt a wave of relief. Bad news that someone was clever enough to get into the IAC, but at least a clearer definition of the problem.

Harmon stared at Weezy for a moment, then said, "You're the best tracker we have. I need you to find the source of penetration of the IAC."

"Why would I help you? You took away my tools and humiliated me."

His lips twisted into what might be a grimace or a smile.

"Perhaps we can relax the rules a bit, but you will not be allowed internet access except at work. Anything else?"

She pushed back her chair and extended her right leg toward Harmon. The light-blue monitor contrasted smartly with her lime-green socks.

Harmon sighed. "I will petition the Cybersurveillance

court to discontinue your house arrest."

THE SAME ESCORT who brought her to the meeting appeared, and Harmon nodded to Weezy with something that might be interpreted to be a smile, ending the meeting. She left the office feeling on edge. It seemed like Harmon caved too easily. The ankle monitor should be off in a week, and her net privileges were reinstated.

She and the escort made their way down the elevator, through the corridor, and to the garage. Maybe Harmon really was convinced that she could find out who penetrated the IAC firewall. But going from asshole to nearly human in a heartbeat? Was that just normal behavior in the big pond of politics? Or was it something else?

Her escort held the door to the garage. Same car. Same driver. As they approached the car, Weezy saw the man was wearing reality goggles, his hands moving to some invisible game. Weezy's escort stiffened and rapped on the window. The driver started, ripped off the goggles and laid them on the seat, looking embarrassed. Weezy walked around the front of the car and pulled open the passenger door.

"How do you like the X-9's? My Sevens are okay, but the sound's not great." Weezy grabbed the goggles.

"Just got 'em. So far so good. Uhh, it's protocol for you to ride in back."

"I'm okay up here," she said, slipping into the passenger side seat. "Mind if I try 'em?"

The guy hesitated. "Sure. You'll want to change programs, though."

"Much more interesting to see your program."

"Uhhh . . ."

Weezy put the goggles on and became the lead syn-guitar player in a rawk band. The words of a current hit played out across the top screens of a stadium filled with a dancing, screaming crowd. To her left, a bassist, female, bright green hair to her waist, wearing the tiniest bikini imaginable. Her body moved in time to the music in a way that would make any guy stand at attention. On the right side of the stage, several keyboards surrounding another long-haired woman, blue hair this time. Also a tiny bikini. Also moving to the music. A custom program carefully designed to be a dream come true. For a guy.

Weezy pulled off the goggles.

"I like your band. Better sound on the X-9's, too. You write the code?"

"Yeah." Now he was blushing, the red rising up his neck to his cheeks. "You should ride in back."

Weezy glanced across the driver. Her escort had stepped back from the car. He wore an expression that said breaking protocol was not quite a felony, but close.

Weezy got out of the front seat, gave a shrug to the escort, and climbed into the back seat.

The driver buckled up and activated the autopilot. The car wheeled out of the garage. When they were clear of the city center, Weezy pulled out her e-pad and punched up Joe.

Now she'd find out how serious Harmon was about lifting the internet prohibition.

Joe appeared, looking concerned.

"Can you talk?"

"So they say. Assume everything's being recorded."

"Oh, great."

"I just got out of a meeting with Granston Harmon, or 'the AVP' as he likes to style himself. I suppose he hasn't figured out how to pronounce his full acronym."

The driver let out a chuckle, quickly stifled.

"And?"

"I'm now free to use the internet, but only at work," Weezy said.

"Ahh. Well, I talked with Jake. She had a good birthday and said she's looking forward to a call from you."

"I saw that. Will do. I'll talk to you after work."

She disconnected. The driver concentrated on the autopilot's display. In profile, Weezy saw a faint scar that puckered his right eye. That must explain the perpetual squint.

The man caught her look. "My scar, right? Nothing exciting. Bike accident when I was nine."

Embarrassed, Weezy asked, "Why do they make you pick me up when a self-drive or autocar would work?"

"Protocol."

"Yeah, but the car drives itself, and—"

"Sometimes people are, uhh, reluctant . . ."

"You mean, they thought I might not come voluntarily?"

"Well, uhh, you had made some pretty harsh comments . . ."

"Whoa. At what point were you going to overpower me and—"

"Look. You're an important person, and the AVP wanted to be sure you arrived in his office. That's all. I didn't expect to have to manhandle you."

They drove in silence for several minutes. Then the driver said, "I know about Olegarten. I watched that video of you and your friend Mayfield when they almost burned you up in Florida." He shrugged. "I guess I was kinda looking forward to seeing a famous person in the flesh."

"Ah . . . got it."

"And that was Mayfield you just talked to, right?"

Why was he so nosy? None of his business. But it probably didn't matter—she had no privacy with the monitor on.

"Yeah."

They were silent for the rest of the ride. As the car pulled up to the front entrance of the IAC, the driver said, "I was wondering if you would put in a word for me. You know, at Olegarten. Maybe . . ."

"If you want to keep your government job, you really don't want to mess around with Olegarten."

The guy nodded, crestfallen.

Weezy got out of the car. After a few steps, she realized she could have been nicer. She turned back and rapped on the window before she realized he was talking on his e-pad. He turned to her, a furtive look changing to shock. He palmed the e-pad. Strange way to end a conversation. But the look passed quickly, and the window came down.

"If you want, go to the website and punch on the 'Join the Olegarten Family' tab. You get what looks like an employment application. List 'programmer' as your skill. Show your names, games, I.D.s and URLs. All of them. Olegarten security will let you know."

"Ahh, thanks much. I'll do that."

He raised the window, gave a curt nod, and left Weezy standing there.

CHAPTER FIFTEEN

WEEZY WAVED HER butt at the security card reader. The reader didn't mind the layer of cloth between the card in her back pocket and the pad at the building entrance. She got what her team called "the DaveScan" at the guard station—a smile and a wave. Weezy entered the bullpen, checked out Keith Sanders's office. Empty. So much for "report right away."

Maddie Hollingsworth was at her workstation. Weezy homed in on Maddie's e-pad, which was on the shelf next to her monitor stack. She took a quick glance around the bullpen, "Can I borrow—" Maddie shot her hand to cover the e-pad, warning in her eyes.

"Sure," she said, standing and stretching. "You can borrow me. In fact, how about a coffee?"

The two strolled toward the break room. Maddie pantomimed holding an e-pad to her ear and gave Weezy a questioning look.

"Yeah," Weezy said. "The freaks and geeks are listening in to me. I'm supposed to work on this power grid thing, but I don't want to go to Olegarten on an e-pad they're monitoring."

They turned into the break room, which was quiet, only one table occupied at the far end.

"You can't use mine," Maddie said as she poured a cup of coffee. "As far as we can tell, they're listening to all our e-pads."

Weezy had that same spike of fear she'd had at Harmon's parking lot.

"For some reason, they thought we wouldn't figure it out. I've got about two days of patience left before I redirect their tap to a porn site." Maddie giggled. "Can't you imagine them, six levels underground in their nuclear-resistant listening post, trying to figure out how to interpret the heavy breathing?"

"Phew. Well, then I'll have to find another way—"

"Got you covered. I need to pick up an e-pad that's registered to my cousin Freddy, and—"

"Cousin Freddy?" Weezy said. "I didn't know you had—"

"When I was a young girl, I had an imaginary friend named Freddy. Now, with the help of electronic sleight of hand, Freddy lives." A trace of a smile crossed Maddie's lips. "He can be very helpful." She stood. "Pretty sure they have no visuals. I'll put a . . .report . . . on your desk in a few."

THE "REPORT" MADDIE put on Weezy's desk concealed a slim e-pad.

"I think you'll find this interesting," Maddie said, turned and went back toward her workstation.

Weezy waited about half a minute and then, trying to look casual, picked up the report and leafed through it. She felt silly. NSA would never get permission for video surveillance inside the IAC.

Nonetheless, she picked up the report, stood, smiled to no one in particular, and left the bullpen.

The curtain of heat hit as she left the building, reminding her of Panacea. Hot this year, but that was to be expected, according to climate scientists. Few people in the courtyard between the IAC and the NIH building. Weezy found shade under a beech tree and sat cross-legged on the grass, already sweating. She slid the e-pad out of the report, found the Wi-Fi of the coffee shop across from the NIH building. The Olegarten website came up. Weezy entered and did the decompression protocol required of an unrecognized device.

No one tagging along.

Jake, you around?—Hotcakes

She watched, tapping her fingers on the surface of the pad, as the system page went out.

Soon a window opened on the small screen, and Jake was there, her normal grandmotherly smile absent.

"Are you okay, Hotcakes?"

"Uhh, yes. Why do you ask?"

"Well, I hadn't heard from you, and your friend May—uhh, Luckymonkey—said you were prevented from using the internet."

Jake looked older than Weezy remembered, worry lines and wrinkles deeper and bags under her eyes. And there was something—uncertainty?—in her eyes.

"Jake, what's wrong?"

"I got a strange message from HoHumJr. He hasn't checked in for over a month. We all figured he was doing things that might not fit the Olegarten Protocol so was staying away."

Jake paused, removed her glasses. "The message came in three days ago. Looks like a DMS move, but with a string of numbers and a file reference added."

"He's initiating a game of Dead Man Switch as his first contact after a month? Odd. What's the move?"

"2DMS-Bx36.228,Bo.AND. Then a long string of numbers that seem to have nothing to do with the game, at least not the way I understand it.

"Whew! Complex for the first move in DMS Let's see . . . a two-person game, then Bx is a closed box, right? With thirty-six-point-something until it opens?

"Yes, a clock. It's counting down," Jake said. "In hours."

"So in a normal game, Bx would open when the clock hits zero, right?" Weezy asked.

"Right."

"Okay, then a second box that's open. That would usually be a starting move. Did you see anything in the box?"

"Yeah. A string of numbers and a file location. Here . . ." A window opened showing a series of numbers and a pointer to a file called Hell-Kit secured in the first box.

Weezy stared at the window, trying to make sense of the numbers.

"It looks like either HoHumJr or I can keep that first box closed," Weezy said, but that didn't explain the fear on Jake's face. "Oh, I got it. The .AND. We both have to sign in to keep it closed. Why would we want to keep it closed if this initiates a game?"

Jake rubbed her forehead, as if to pinch off thoughts she didn't dare acknowledge.

"You haven't had three days to think about this like I have. Why would HoHumJr disappear for a month then send only you and me a complex move in a game that usually starts out with ten players? Why would he show me the move but make you the only other player?"

Weezy thought for a moment. "You're right. Strange. Of course, HoHumJr always was a little—"

"Not strange, Hotcakes. This isn't a game. The only thing I can think is he's trying to pack a lot of information into a small message and hope it would look like gibberish to anyone but you and me. The numbers he added and that file he called Hell-Kit, those must be significant. I think the switch he set on Bx is real. If he doesn't get back to Olegarten to turn it off in thirty-six hours, the counter hits zero and that file called Hell-Kit opens. Apparently that's bad for someone."

Weezy began to see the picture fill in.

"Okay, so he'd only do that if he's trusting us with something valuable and if he's afraid he might not be able to . . ."

"Right. The only thing that makes sense to me is he's in danger, and the switch must protect him. Maybe someone is threatening him but doesn't want whatever's in Hell-Kit to be exposed. They must keep him alive to reset the timer."

"Any idea what's in the file—this 'Hell-Kit'?"

Jake shook her head. "None."

"And the .AND. means"—Weezy nodded, comprehension dawning—"I have to check in, too, to keep the file closed. He needed someone to control the file if he couldn't. Anyone he tapped would become a target of whoever is holding him. He included me to protect me, didn't he?"

Jake nodded.

"But from what?"

WEEZY'S CALL HAD set Joe on edge. What did that jerk Harmon want this time? Why couldn't she talk? Was it connected to the logic game Jake had mentioned? And why was the game so important? And—

"You alright, Finance Boy?" Brianna Kapoor said, cocking her head with a twitch of a grin. "Got an update on United Energy?"

"Yeah, Brianna. I've been over this stuff so many times—"

"C'mon, Mayfield. Gotta be on top of your game tomorrow or Mac Renfro will slip in some last-minute condition, and—"

"We'll be fine, Brianna. The deal's done, except for the signing. Mac's as excited as we are. He'll probably stay for a few days to witness the restart. Speaking of which, we have to let him share some of the press attention. This is a real turning point for green energy, and it looks impressive that United Energy is part of it. When you start scaling up—"

"We. We start scaling up."

Then she was gone, leaving the statement hanging. Was this her way of opening a new front in the employment issue? Had she forgotten he told her he was leaving? Part of him was intrigued by the change in Kapoor over the last couple of weeks. She had actually started asking questions, rather than barking orders. Had she noticed how Weezy's give and take with the programmers invigorated them? Or was it that HelioCorp now had a plan and the promise of enough cash to restart?

The hint at a HelioCorp offer was interesting, but the urgency in Jake's voice crowded out speculation about the job. "Hotcakes needs to call me, right away," she had said. Maybe he hadn't communicated that urgency when they talked earlier. The United Energy deal required no more work. Joe packed up and left the building a little early.

The parking lot was furnace-hot, the asphalt soft. He'd arrived at work too late to claim a shady spot. Heat waves rose from the Subaru. He said "window down, fan on" to his e-pad and walked to the meager shade of a palm to wait for the car to cool to just hot.

Leaning against the tree trunk, he called Weezy at IAC. A pleasant computer voice asked if Mr. Mayfield would like to page Ms. Napolitani. He left a message. "Weezy, give me a call when you can. I'm leaving work, and I'm anxious to hear about your meeting."

As Joe drove the several miles from HelioCorp to the low-rise apartment complex where he had lived for the last six months, Kapoor's 'we' floated back into his mind. What an opportunity an offer would be, with HelioCorp set to become a dominant player in solar energy. What about Weezy, though? She wouldn't just chuck it, quit IAC and move to Florida. Certainly not Boca. Maybe Panacea, though. Maybe that's why she didn't accept the marriage proposal. Maybe she saw this coming. He had no good answer really, except he didn't want to accept a long, sad withdrawal.

The car turned into his apartment complex. Thank the lord for autopilot. For the first two months, he'd had a hard time figuring which building his apartment was in amidst the sprawl of nearly identical boxes. Miles of pink stucco, undifferentiated by an architect's imagination. The main drag was a boulevard featuring evenly spaced palm trees, like most of the other main roads in Boca. Couldn't somebody have come up with an original design, an original color?

In his apartment, he changed to shorts and a T-shirt. He considered a run along the Intracoastal Waterway, but Weezy hadn't called. He sat down in the small living room and picked up the guitar he'd been struggling to learn. He turned on the internet tutor app he'd been using and put his e-pad on the floor to watch the instruction while he played. The program had helped him with chord shapes, but transition from one to the other was shaky. Picking out the notes like John Hurt or Rev. Gary Davis was in the indefinite future. He had been at it for half an hour when an incoming call tapped his implant. No Sappho meow, so it wasn't Weezy. He glanced at his e-pad. No number he recognized.

He went back to struggling with the B7 chord. A few minutes passed. A chirp from his implant announced a message, which popped up on his e-pad.

Curious, he set the guitar on its stand picked up the e-pad. The message said:

Chester Burnell, please call back.

His avatar? He hadn't used any of his avatars since Weezy caught him hacking the IAC several years ago. That earlier call must have been Weezy.

She answered on the first ring. The video showed her sitting on a park bench, with an on-the-edge-of-irritated look on her face.

"Why the secrecy?" Joe asked. "I thought you were now free of those restrictions the guy you called Bullshit Bulldog—"

"Harmon."

"Yeah, him."

"Oh, I'm free to help on the project he cares about—you know, the project that really doesn't exist because HelioCorp was some sort of computer glitch—but the boneheads at NSA are tracking my every move and listening to all my conversations."

"Or so they think, right?"

"Yup." Weezy smirked. "So they think."

"So, what's up?" Joe peered at the e-pad video. "Where are you?"

"I'm in the park about a mile from home. We came here last time you visited."

Joe remembered the park. They had walked there several months ago, back when their only problem was being separated by several states.

"Did you call Jake? She was upset about something, a message."

"There was a power grid hack last night," Weezy said. "Not the same as HelioCorp in detail, but maybe related. Both have no obvious cause. Both on the eastern seaboard, so the same infrastructure. But this one came with a ransom demand, so nobody can argue it was a computer malfunction. Now this whole deal is top secret. I'm sure the political machinery is churning, trying to decide whether to pay the money or not. Harmon would rather fight back, which apparently brought him back to the IAC and me."

"Holy crap." Joe slumped forward. His mind spun through the ramifications. No telling what Kapoor would do if she found out. What about Mac and United Energy? What if this is the government's attempt to spin this because they found the real problem? "This is huge. So HelioCorp was a hack job all along."

"Looks like it.

"Okay, but what about the message Jake was talking about? She said it was urgent."

"Slow down. I was coming to that."

"Jake said it was from HoHumJr. Some sort of code."

"Not so much a code as a move in a game Olegarten members play called 'Dead Man Switch.' "

"Dead man switch?" Joe had a vague recollection.

"Like the pedal the engineer on a train keeps his foot on," Weezy said. "If he, say, has a heart attack and his foot slips off, the train stops. We used one in Panacea when Snake and Curly were after us."

". . . And you've turned that into a game?"

"Yup. A simple idea that can get complex very quickly. But HoHumJr wasn't playing the game, he was passing information. He sent us what the military calls a fail-deadly . . . the opposite of a fail-safe."

"The opposite would be something happens if you *didn't*—"

Weezy grinned. "Like a hand grenade. Pull the pin, and it blows up unless you keep squeezing the lever."

"So, HoHumJr sent a fail-deadly?"

"Yes. And a lot more."

"Meaning what?"

"Meaning that he sent a string of numbers I just now figured out. They're map coordinates. The first series exactly identified the location of last night's grid hack. The second is missing some digits, so I can't be sure exactly where it is. Somewhere in southwest Georgia. There apparently are two more locations that he may not know, at least that's my interpretation. Anyway, then he gives a string of game instructions that establish both of us as fail-deadlies. If he doesn't check in and I don't check in, a file called Hell-Kit opens. I don't know what's in it."

"If *you* don't check in? Why did HoHumJr set up a fail-deadly?" The thought was taking shape. "And why did he include you?"

"He must be in danger." Weezy's taut face let Joe know she knew his next question.

"But why would he drag you in?" Joe felt as if he was a step behind understanding something really, really awful.

Weezy continued, "HoHumJr must have realized his message might be intercepted. The bad guys might be able to decrypt it and see it was sent to me. Giving me control along with him is the only way he could think of to protect me. They would have to leave me alone, or the file would open, and—"

"Weezy, goddammit. Stop. Go somewhere safe. Now. Get

on your bike and ride to, I don't know. IAC? Police? Better yet, call Harmon. The government owes you protection. They have no right to keep you in the dark, put you at risk, and—"

"It's probably nothing." She shot him a shrug.

"Damn it, Weezy. How can you be so brilliant and so dense at the same time? He could have done only one fail-deadly to protect himself. But he didn't. He thinks his fail-deadly might blow up. He's the one guy who knows what's going on, and he thinks you're in danger along with him."

Her jaw set.

"Weezy, c'mon. This is serious. Think about the times we've been in danger since you've known me. Three times? Four? And what's your standard answer?"

Her eyes were in full squint.

"You always think you can outsmart 'em. They don't care about smart. They might want you dead."

"Joe, I . . ."

"Weezy, you're sitting alone outside in a cute little park in Bethesda, and I'm in Florida worried as hell. But you're oblivious. I should be there with you."

"Huh? There's nothing for you to do here. Besides, Helio-Corp needs you, more now than ever. I promise to be careful . . ." She gave him the doe eyes.

Of course she was right. Logical.

Joe dropped his eyes and sighed his frustration.

"I love you. I don't want you to get hurt."

He raised his eyes to the small screen. Weezy's expression softened. "Okay. I have to think this through. I'll go home . . . carefully . . ." she gave him a hint of a smile, "and I'll figure the smart part out. Then we can both worry about the other part."

Joe stared at the screen after Weezy signed off. His next few days were fully programmed. Mac McTavish was due to arrive mid-morning day after tomorrow, then the run-up to the financing announcement. Kapoor would go ballistic if he left, but Mac would love to take over the publicity. He tapped his pad, already working up what he would say to Kapoor. Maybe send a text, leave, deal with Kapoor long distance.

The airline reservation app showed space available on the flight to BWI at nine o'clock the next morning. He tapped to select a seat, realizing he was panting. He forced himself to stop. He told himself to be reasonable, get a grip. There were a lot of ifs in the scary chain of logic he'd built. Not fair to HelioCorp to just send a message and disappear. Mac would be excited to step in for him, but he needed to be prepped. Get the meeting with Mac done, the financing announced, then go. Cool down, he told himself. What difference would a day make?

AFTER THE CALL, Weezy sat still for a few moments, taking in the park, quiet at this hour. A red-bellied woodpecker landed on a tree nearby and began her Morse code search for grubs. Nothing scary, nothing dangerous. Maybe she should call Harmon and explain the situation. Joe might be right even if his advice was tainted by concern for her. Harmon would understand that something bad might happen to HoHumJr if she didn't check in, so he would agree to let Weezy keep the file closed. She'd run the grid bandits down with the help of HoHumJr's message. A fantasy, but she wrapped herself in it the way she sometimes pulled the covers up to her nose on a cold morning. And in that warmth, she felt Joe's love for her, even through his hurt when she hadn't taken his offer.

Finally, she shook off her reverie, stood, nodded to the woodpecker, walked her bike to the road.

Harmon wasn't going to worry about her welfare, much less some faceless foreign hacker.

She mounted the bike, began pedaling the last mile toward home.

He would want to stop the grid invasion, sure, but also cover his butt for having blown off the HelioCorp failure. No one knew what was in the Hell-Kit file but HoHumJr, but it must hurt whoever pulled off the attack. So Harmon would want to open Hell-Kit ASAP to find out who was behind the ransom demand. He would put Weezy in a safe house "for her own good" and prevent her from sending the signal. The file would open. Harmon would get his information. But the bad guys would see the file open, too. The protection for Ho-HumJr would be gone.

She rode up the drive to home, put her bike away, and scanned the lawn and bushes, listening for a moment before mounting the steps to her apartment. She dropped her daypack next to the door. Sappho appeared from her bedroom, stretching and staring pointedly at her empty food bowl. Weezy opened a can of Feline Delight for Sappho and got a glass of water. She folded herself cross-legged into her overstuffed chair. So domestic, so normal. So not scary. Sappho jumped onto the chair's arm, then into Weezy's lap, purring.

Joe was right, she thought. There's something here they didn't understand. It made no sense that HoHumJr would make Weezy part of the fail-deadly. But if she told Harmon . . .

On the other hand, Harmon would remind her that withholding this information would be considered treason.

She shifted. Sappho uncoiled herself, gave a Halloween cat stretch and jumped down.

Weezy thought through several variations on the truth and how she would explain herself to a prosecutor. Finally, she opened her e-pad and began composing a message to Harmon.

CHAPTER SIXTEEN

WEEZY WOKE TO Sappho's nuzzle-purr. Her clock said 6:38. Sappho didn't care about the clock, but sun streaming into the bedroom meant breakfast. Weezy sat up and stretched. She worked a crick out of her neck while she reviewed the plan she'd put together the night before. No doubt Harmon would be on her case this morning, wanting to know more about where she got the location information she had sent. She thought about staying home and waiting for the call from his office, but she needed to talk with Maddie.

Sappho focused a laser-like stare at Weezy that said "Feline Delight." Weezy got up, shuffled to the kitchen, scratching. She said, "Morning blend, three cups" to the coffee machine and fed Sappho.

Back in her bedroom, she began dressing. The usual cargo shorts, her *Harvard Sucks* T-shirt, socks and running shoes. Then she caught a glimpse of herself in the mirror. It hit her that Maddie was right when she said clothes matter in some situations. If Weezy was going to be whisked away to the AVP's office again, maybe she should dress for it. She went to the closet, picked out slacks that covered her ankle bracelet and a cream-colored blouse with mother-of-pearl buttons. The low-heeled shoes she'd bought for Joe's graduation party in New York a couple of years ago completed the outfit. She glanced at herself in the mirror. Nice, but why should she be covering the monitor, particularly if she was going to see Harmon? He needed to be reminded. She took off the slacks and put on a deep blue skirt.

In the kitchen, she drank some coffee and fidgeted. Finally, she packed some cheese sticks and an insulated mug of coffee in her day pack along with her own e-pad and the one Maddie had lent her. Then, down the stairs to her bike.

Her skirt was fine for pedaling and she suspected more in keeping with the classic design of her Bianchi.

A few early risers were trickling in when Weezy got to her workstation. She began fleshing out a plan to locate where the intrusion that brought the Camden grid down originated. Maddie came into the bullpen a few minutes later, nodded and turned toward the ladies room.

Weezy joined her, carrying the borrowed e-pad in a stack of papers and feeling foolish. The cloak and dagger stuff was probably unnecessary. She pushed the ladies' room door open and said "Good morning" to Maddie, sounding entirely artificial to herself, then stooped to inspect the stalls. They were alone.

"Okay to talk?"

"I think so," Maddie said, running water, then pulling down a towel. "It would take ten pounds of balls to bug the Ladies."

She looked Weezy up and down. "Nice skirt. Showing off the monitor?" She grinned. "Where's your T-shirt?"

Weezy shrugged. "Like you said, sometimes clothes make the woman. And . . . thanks." Weezy handed the stack of papers concealing the e-pad to Maddie.

"Hope it helped," Maddie said. "I stopped at Operations on my way in this morning to ask about physical intrusion into the system. You said an engineer at HelioCorp brought the issue up. She was right. It's almost impossible to tap into the IAC physically."

"Yeah," Weezy said. "She talked about the electrical shield on cables that feed into the IAC. If you pierce the shield, it alters the conductance of the cable, right?"

Maddie nodded. "Exactly. Even if it was just long enough to attach another cable, the IAC software would notice. Also, any insert would have to be from a registered entry point."

"Because?"

"It's that same conductance deal," Maddie said. "The IAC knows exactly how long all cables connecting to it are. If you were somehow able to tap in, you'd add length to that particular connecting link. The IAC would notice the change."

"So there's no way to get in except through an existing connection, right?"

Maddie furrowed her brow. After a pause she shook her head. "I don't see how anyone could—"

"But—" The idea forming in Weezy's mind was interrupted by a sharp rap on the outer door. "Napolitani? Weezy? Are you in there?" Keith Sanders's voice.

"Keith?" Weezy said. "Yeah, I'm in here."

"Uhh. You need to meet with AVP Harmon."

"Can I pull my pants up, or do I have to hop out there like a—"

"So sorry. Uhh . . . take your time." Weezy almost felt him blushing. Maddie stifled a giggle, then held her finger to her lips and quietly moved into a stall.

Weezy opened the door to a red-faced Keith.

"The AVP sent a car. He wants to see you immediately. What's up?"

Weezy kicked herself mentally. He was her boss, after all. Not fair to keep him out of the loop, and not a good idea, either. She didn't need him pouting and prying.

"I did get some data from the net last night."

Keith's jaw set.

Weezy plowed on. "The AVP had warned me to keep my work confidential, but I should never have left you out of . . . sorry, Keith. I'm sure he didn't mean to exclude you. I'll send you the note I sent him as soon as I get in the car."

She saw him relax.

"Thanks," he said and patted her on the arm.

Weezy went to her workstation, picked up her own e-pad, and left the bullpen for Reception. There, the guard pointed her toward a government-gray autocar.

She was disappointed. She liked the guy who had driven her a couple of times and wondered if he had followed up on Olegarten. But the autocar must mean they trusted her to play ball. She got in the back seat. The car's voice informed her they were going to Assistant Vice President Harmon's office. The trip would take twenty-eight minutes on the privileged lane.

Weezy opened her e-pad, relieved that she'd drafted the note to Harmon on her own machine. She added the bit about the issue of physical intrusion and the engineer's conductance description. But there was something else about entering the IAC. A tic in the back of her mind. What was it? She put the thought aside, sent the message to Keith, and began rehearsing the story she was going to tell Harmon.

The anodyne voice of the autocar said, "We cannot move until your seat belt is fastened." Weezy swore under her breath and clicked the harness in place. The autocar pulled into traffic and commented that estimated arrival time was 9:13.

THE ASSASSIN EXITED the ramp from the Toronto-to-Dulles Air Canada flight.

At close range, he appeared fit, perhaps a runner or cyclist. He wore a tan suit, a European slender cut. His blond hair was brushed back, and a long nose and high cheekbones made him seem aristocratic. The predatory look in his ice-blue eyes could have been that of an up-and-coming junior executive intent on becoming senior. His passport's chip said he was a youngish specialist in health care management software representing a Canadian company. The customs agent at the entry kiosk glanced at his monitor and gave him a nod.

He carried no luggage other than a backpack. He strode purposefully to a men's room next to the arrivals hall, entered, and went to a sink to wash his hands. An older gentleman exited the second stall from the back wall. Anyone watching would have mistaken the small nod he gave as the sort of impersonal recognition men commonly give one another. After the man left, the specialist dried his hands and entered the stall. A couple of minutes later, he flushed and left the stall armed with a .25 caliber handgun fitted with a silencer. A toy in the hands of an inexperienced shooter. Deadly in his.

He was pleased with the setup. Assassination was an art form, one which demanded precision and careful thought. He took no projects involving crowds to derail carefully-made plans. No attention-getting explosions with collateral damage.

His client must want to send a message. One shot. Very little blood. Right under the nose of the message recipient, he assumed. The woman would not even notice him until the last second of her life.

He passed through the baggage area to the outside, scanned the arriving vehicles for the autocar he'd ordered, found it and directed it to a low-rise office building near the airport. He exited the car and walked through the building to the rear service area where an older step-van waited. On its side, a cartoon plumber rushed to provide twenty-four hour service. The driver, dressed in coveralls with the same cartoon plumber stitched on the pocket, was a local hire. The specialist took in the man's paunchy body and tattoos running down his neck as he got in the front seat. Not a good first impression. The man might or might not be reliable. But he was disposable.

The specialist had expected to take a day or more to find the right set of circumstances but had received a message as he boarded the plane promising a more immediate opportunity. So much the better. He'd be back in France tomorrow.

The driver explained that the target was attending a meeting near the Navy Yard. She would be driven to IAC headquarters when it finished. If they were lucky, they would be in time to pick up the signal from the tracking device hiding inside the bumper of the car taking her back to Bethesda. Even better, the specialist thought. Follow the car, do the job, and get out before anyone was the wiser.

THE AUTOCAR PULLED into the same featureless parking garage Weezy had been taken to twice before. Same guys guarding the door, same hallway, same security checkpoint, same man to escort her. The elevator took her and her escort on a short, silent ride up. The door opened to reveal the foyer in front of Harmon's office. The desk that had been empty last time now held stacks of files. A woman with her back to them was digging in a walnut-faced file drawer that was part of a battery of similar drawers that covered the wall to their left. The place looked like a mid-level legal firm, not an important political center.

The escort led Weezy to the AVP's door. The extension from the center of Harmon's desk had space for seven chairs, three per side and one on the end. This time, six were filled. Grid Dweeb was there, brows drawn together, serious. Next to him, a man in uniform with a lot of ribbons and a colonel's silver eagle on each shoulder. Then a woman looking too young for the business suit she was wearing. She had blonde hair, sharp features and a Homeland Security credential on a lanyard around her neck. Across the table, a man and two women who looked like staffers of some sort.

Harmon glanced up from a notebook, looked as if he was trying to remember her. He nodded toward the empty chair at the end of the table. "Sit." He turned his attention back to the notebook. "So you found some information on Camden and an approximate location in South Georgia, correct?"

The people at the table turned to Weezy. Grid Dweeb nodded. The monitor suddenly seemed heavy on her ankle. Most glanced quickly at it; the colonel stared. Maybe she should have worn long pants.

"Yes. An internet message gave the coordinates of the Camden power station," she said. "The same message gave partial coordinates that describe a sixty by seventy mile rectangle mostly in southwest Georgia. I included that information in my note to you."

"Where'd you get it?" The colonel fixed her in a stare. Did he expect a salute?

"From friends on the net."

"Don't be evasive. Who?"

Weezy felt an almost physical pressure from Harmon and the others at the table. "A hacker I know only as an internet presence. I think he lives in Estonia."

"One of these Olegarten people?" the Homeland agent asked.

"Yes."

"Or perhaps an artful story." The agent cocked her head, then looked around the table for concurrence. "Convenient, isn't it, that you have the first location, the one that's already happened, but only an approximate idea of the second. When do your hacker friends send the next ransom demand?"

The colonel nodded at the agent's supposition and turned to Weezy. "We need to get into that site, find out where this person is and why he knows these locations," He paused. "You will take us there."

"Bad idea," Weezy said before she had time to think through her response.

The colonel's face turned a shade darker, and his eyes narrowed.

Harmon interrupted. "Miss Napolitani, this is a matter of national security. If Homeland Security"—he nodded toward the agent—"wants to get into this site of yours, you will provide a way."

The immediate answer was No. Screw you. Weezy told herself to slow down. They didn't know about the fail-deadly, and she couldn't tell them, for fear they would sequester her and force it to open. If she got arrested, same result. HoHumJr would be dead. Maybe she could lead these people to reason.

She took a cleansing breath and turned to Harmon.

"It is quite clear that the hacker who sent the message is trying to help us. We hadn't heard from him in over a month, then this message appeared. Right now, Olegarten is on our side. If we violate their trust, the site will shut down and we'll get nothing more."

"Other way around, Ms. Napolitani," Homeland said. "If they don't cooperate, we'll shut *them* down."

Weezy shook her head. "These are the best in the world at what they do, and they're very testy about their freedom. In this case, they're white hats—"

"White hats?" The colonel's tone said it was Weezy's fault he didn't know the term.

The Homeland agent turned to him. "Good hackers," she said. "Black hats are the bad guys, trying to steal your secrets or get your kids in trouble."

"The group has strict rules about what it can and cannot do, but it doesn't trust governments," Weezy said. The colonel stiffened, and the Homeland woman sniffed. Weezy continued, "The people who hacked the grid most likely kidnapped our hacker friend. He's brilliant, one of only two or three people I can think of that might have pierced the IAC and pulled off this attack. I doubt he would have done it voluntarily. You can try to force your way into Olegarten. If you do so, the bad guys will most likely see your activity and kill our friendly hacker. We'll stop getting information, and the bad guys will know we're on to them." Probably the truth or close to it, she thought.

Close. Close to it. The idea that had begun to form back in the IAC ladies' room coalesced. Close. Parallel wires. That would be the way to get into the IAC unobserved. She wanted to call a halt to the conversation, ask them to hold on, she had to send a message.

Harmon drew himself up. "All right. Here's what we'll do. Ms. Napolitani will be our liaison to the Olegarten people." The colonel's jaw set. Harmon continued, turning to Weezy, "You will stay in the IAC facility under guard until this issue is resolved. You will tap Homeland . . . he nodded toward the agent . . . into all your Olegarten activity. She will report to me daily." His expression relaxed a fraction. "We appreciate your help on this problem, Ms. Napolitani. I hope you understand how serious this is. We may be at the brink of cyber war—" a small but audible gasp from several people punctuated his statement. "I will view any freelancing on your part as a violation of national security and treat it according-ly."

Harmon stood, ending the meeting. The others rose, as did Weezy. The colonel shot Weezy an acid glance as they filed out of the office. The young Homeland agent stopped Weezy at the elevator.

"I have sent my secure contact information to your super-visor. Don't even think about keeping me in the dark." But she smiled, surprising Weezy, and held out her hand. "Let's fix this problem together."

"S-sure," Weezy hesitated, then shook the agent's hand.

The group outside Harmon's office had dispersed, and Weezy rode the elevator to the garage alone.

CHAPTER SEVENTEEN

As the plumber's van cleared the airport, the specialist slipped between the seats into the cargo space. He took off his suit jacket and tie and put on coveralls like the driver's. Then back to the front seat to find a signal from the tracking device on the target's car. Nothing. They drove another five miles. Still nothing. It was close to decision time—turn toward Bethesda or backtrack to DC—when the signal appeared. "Probably was underground or in a parking garage," the driver said. "What do you want to do? We following her? Nobody told me."

The specialist nodded. "Yes, following her." He laid on the accent to make his English seem weak. His contact said the driver knew English, some Russian, but little French. It was natural to assume a language barrier. That way, he could skip conversation and camaraderie. A relief for the specialist. No telltales the driver might pick up.

Weezy expected the gray autocar to be waiting in the garage, but instead it was a blue sedan like the one she'd ridden on the last trip. As she approached, she recognized the driver as the one who had asked about Olegarten.

Weezy got in the rear seat.

"Written any more on that game you were developing?"

The driver grinned. "A little."

But he didn't mention having applied to Olegarten. Most likely, he was turned down. Best not ask and embarrass the guy.

He set the nav system, then turned to Weezy as the car began to move. "Big doings today, huh?"

"Yeah. Harmon is—" Weezy stopped short. The driver should know not to ask about the meeting. "—Harmon is in kick butt mode. And I am enjoined from any discussion on pain of Leavenworth."

"Sure. Everybody's ripped about this grid hack thing, Camden, then that message . . ."

Weezy said nothing, hoping he would get the hint.

She opened her e-pad to call Maddie, then hesitated. How would the driver, a guy at the bottom of the org chart, know about the message?

Maybe she was overly sensitive because of Joe's worry or the fail-deadly. Still, she switched over to text mode.

> Maddie, find out whether a parallel line into the IAC would be possible. Same exact length, terminating at an IAC entry point. Switchable. Would IAC software detect that? On my way to office. Will talk when I arrive. Lunch?

Midday traffic was light, and the rest of the ride passed quickly. The driver engaged in a monologue about the advantages and disadvantages of game coding software. Weezy smiled and nodded, her mind occupied with the IAC connection issue. The car turned off the beltway, and the driver took back control to navigate the side streets but continued talking. Weezy realized he had passed the main entrance to the IAC building. The driver blinked. "Shit. Oh, sorry. I missed it, didn't I? Damn. One-way, too."

"Yeah, no problem. Hang a right at the next street." Weezy pointed. "Let me off up near those trees."

The guy gave her a sheepish grin. "I really enjoyed our conversation."

★ ★ ★

"SHE'S TURNING," THE van's driver said, pointing to a dark blue sedan a block and a half ahead of them. They had fallen in behind the car five miles south of Bethesda, occasionally catching sight of it a quarter mile ahead but mainly following the signal from the tracker. As they neared the sprawling NIH campus, the driver began to close the distance. The parkway approaching the complex curved toward a cluster of buildings. The sedan turned on a service road that ran behind several of them. "She's going for the back entrance of the IAC," the driver said. The specialist prepared his weapon. The van was maneuvering around a stopped autocar when the specialist's implant tapped him with his client's tone. Irritated, he laid the pistol in his lap and whipped out his e-pad to answer the tap.

"What?" He realized he had shouted, startling the driver. He listened, punched the e-pad off. "*Merde!*"

The van slowed. The blue car had stopped a half-block ahead of them. A door opened and a slender woman emerged, then leaned back into the car. His target, definitely.

"We have to capture her," the specialist said through clenched teeth. He slipped the gun under the seat. The driver stared at him, dumbfounded.

"I can't—How do we—?"

The woman closed the car door and moved toward the walkway. The specialist scanned the walk and the buildings.

"Stop here. Get out and walk up to that door," he said, pointing. "Turn back toward the woman as if you have a question." He crawled through the space between the seats. "I'll do the rest."

WEEZY CLOSED THE car door and stretched as the car pulled away. On the walkway, she sauntered, enjoying the mottled shade of the maples arching overhead. Maybe she and Maddie should go off campus for lunch, have a chance to discuss some regular, women-men-relationship stuff. Joe's offer and her hesitation? Maybe.

A cream-colored van with a perky cartoon plumber logo on its side had stopped in the road. The driver got out, then the side door slid open and another guy in coveralls exited and strode to the back of the vehicle. The driver trudged toward the north entrance of IAC, passing in front of Weezy. He looked at the address, turned to her, a question in his eyes.

She heard an intake of breath before arms circled her, jerked her off her feet. She screamed, only it came out as a pitiful squeak as her breath rushed out. She kicked, tried to stomp her assailant's foot. He wrestled her off the walkway toward the van.

She flailed, almost got enough leverage to turn, connected an elbow with something soft. He grunted, swiveling her toward the truck.

Her shin struck something hard, and pain shot up her leg. She landed on the gritty bed of the van and felt the skin of her knees shred. She felt the rush of the side door slamming shut. She got her breath back and screamed as the van began to move.

"Shut your mouth!" A slap stunned her. She caught a glimpse of blond hair, a sharp profile. He reached to the floor, jerking at something. A clatter of metal, an oily-smelling burlap bag jammed over her head. A thunderclap in her left ear, then black.

THE SPECIALIST STARED out the window of the plumber's van, planning his next steps through a veil of rage. He had survived for so long because he controlled the details and contingencies of every contract. The "capture her" forced him to run blind, no plan, out of control.

The woman had fought. He had to hit her. Dumb luck that there was a bag of pipe fittings on the floor. He'd emptied it and used the bag to cover her head. Afterwards, he pawed through the compartments inside the truck looking for something to bind her. Cursing under his breath, he found a roll of duct tape. Luck again. He hated luck. Too many things could go wrong when one's only protection was luck.

He had seen the shackle when he threw her into the van. It was smaller than ones he'd seen before, but it was clearly some sort of monitor. Another damn problem. Fortunately, the truck had a heavy-duty cutter, probably for small pipes. The monitor looked flimsy, but it fought his effort to cut it off. Finally, it snapped, and he pulled it off the woman's ankle. A quarter mile later, he had the driver pull over. He jumped out of the van, trotted to a clump of trees, and chucked it as far as he could.

When the specialist returned to the van, the woman gasped a couple of times, coming to. Her breathing was labored, and blood seeped through the bag. Nosebleed. He tore off a piece of tape to cover her mouth but balled it up as he listened to her breathing. Delivering a corpse would not be a good idea.

The woman took a quick breath and seemed about to scream. He slid the barrel of his gun under the bag, up her jaw line to the soft tissue under her ear. He growled, "Keep quiet."

"Your phone's ringin'," the driver said, above the noise of the truck.

The specialist reached into the front seat, where he had left the satellite phone, and keyed it.

His contact said, "I need you to deliver the package to a location I will send you when you are close. For now, turn west on the next road, follow it until . . ."

The specialist memorized the directions. The satellite phone disconnected, and the assassin gave the first instruction to the driver. Another ring. He stared at the satellite phone's small display. Dark. Nothing. Another ring. He glanced around the interior. It was coming from the woman.

Prokljat'e! Stupide! He ran his hands down her sides, found a lump at her hip, an e-pad. Felt behind her ear. No implant.

Good. He opened the e-pad. A call from Luckymonkey an hour ago, then one from a Maddie half an hour ago. Luckymonkey again just now. The e-pad had standard security. He fished his own e-pad out of a pocket, ran the find-and-unlock app. Luckymonkey was a man named Joe who sounded impatient. He might be trouble if the woman didn't answer.

He considered a moment. The woman he'd captured was an employee of the IAC, probably some sort of analyst. He dictated a text message:

> Lucky: Busy with a project. Will have to go silent for several days. Will call when I can.

He sent a similar note to the person called Maddie, turned off the e-pad, folded and pocketed it.

THE TRACKING SYSTEM at Homeland noticed the biometrics on Weezy's monitor had stopped. Shortly thereafter, a signal that the thing had been cut off. The officer monitoring it and a half dozen other bracelets had dozed off. After five minutes, the flashing icon on his monitor became a loud buzz.

"Shit. We got a runner," he said, knowing he was going to get chewed out for missing the signal.

"Where?" His boss called out over the cubicle wall.

"Uhh, south of Germantown."

"Traffic cameras?"

"None out there, boss."

"When?"

"Umm, about five minutes ago."

There was short silence.

"Okay, send the locals the location." His boss's tone told him he was in trouble. He had been on the job for three weeks and had already been written up once for being 'lackadaisical.' He had to look up the word.

"Let's take a look at it." His boss had navigated around the other stations to his cubicle almost at a jog. The woman was not lackadaisical.

The officer opened the prior activity file. His boss stooped to read over his shoulder. Perfume or shampoo that smelled like a cross between drain cleaner and flowers.

"Napolitani. Hmm. From IAC and by order of the Cyber-surveillance Court. That's why the reason's blacked out, but she had clearance to go to the Navy Yard this morning, then looks like she went back to IAC. Managing contact is Harmon, an assistant to the vice president. Phew! Heavy hitter. Biometrics look—scroll back to her arrival—yeah, there. Some odd heart rate, maybe adrenaline. Then normal until the monitor goes dead."

She stared at the screen, chewed a thumbnail. Finally she said, "Yes. Definitely a runner. I'll contact Harmon."

CHAPTER EIGHTEEN

Lucky: Busy with a project. Will have to go silent for several days. Will call when I can.

JOE STARED AT the message, furious with himself for deciding to stay at HelioCorp until Mac McTavish arrived. He should have followed his intuition.

He ran his hand over his hair.

Damnit. She knows I'm worried. So she ignores my calls and sends a freaking text message?

He tried to convince himself it was Weezy being Weezy. One hundred percent focused on whatever she was working on. But the message didn't sound right—too formal—and she always used Luckymonkey to text him. The message filled his mind with something he couldn't name. The upside: it gave him license to go to Bethesda.

He called Maddie.

"Yeah, Joe, I'm wondering, too," Maddie said as video came up. "She called nearly two hours ago and said she was leaving Washington. Should have been here in thirty or forty minutes. But she didn't show. Then I got this text that she's working on a project and has to go silent."

"I got the same message. Something's wrong."

"Maybe this hush-hush thing about HelioCorp?"

"I don't know. I'm coming up, though. I have a three o'clock flight tomorrow."

"Let me know when you leave," she said. "I can pick you up. Maybe we'll know more by then."

He disconnected from Maddie, mind in turmoil. Not unlike Weezy to get engrossed in a project, but she would have let him know if she was planning to go off the grid, wouldn't she? So damn hard to be separated by a thousand miles. He couldn't do much more in Bethesda than in Florida, but he had to go, had to find out. In the meantime . . .

He stood, grabbed his e-pad and marched down the hall, needing to move, to burn off his frustration. In the break room, he poured a cup of coffee. Not a good idea to get jazzed on caffeine. He dumped it out, got a glass of water, and took a seat at one of the lunch tables. What to do?

He dialed Weezy's work number, punched the option to talk with the operator. After fifteen minutes of forwards and dead ends courtesy of the IAC's answering system, he got to a human and punched video.

"It's urgent that I connect to Louise Napolitani's supervisor."

"Sir, this is a secure facility. Unless you have a name, ID number, and contact number, I can't forward this call." The operator gave him the kind of smile he would expect from a clerk at the DMV.

So much for participatory government.

Frustrated, he called Maddie again. The call went to the IAC message center. Maddie was out of the office and would return tomorrow.

Puzzled, Joe looked up the private number she had given Weezy and Joe "just in case."

"Yeah?" Video showed Maddie, eyes wide in surprise. She must not have recognized Joe's private number. "Oh, hello, Joe." Her voice was brittle, not her usual friendly, deep-south drawl. She was outside, her daypack on her shoulder, walking briskly. The video was not clear, but she seemed stiff, breathless, maybe scared.

"Maddie, you okay? Anything on Weezy?"

She stopped, scanned the area around her.

"Joe, I . . . uhh . . . shouldn't say anything." She glanced again, then whispered, looking ready to cry, "They say Weezy is a fugitive."

KAPOOR'S OFFICE DOOR was open. Joe knocked lightly on the frame. Kapoor glanced at him, nodded, and went back to what she was reading. Joe entered and found the one chair that wasn't occupied by stacks of journals, white papers, and file folders. Kapoor continued to read, marked a line and smirked, flipped a page, finally looked up at Joe.

"Yeah?"

"Brianna, I have an urgent personal matter. I need to leave, I hope for only a couple of days—" Maybe it really would only be a couple of days. The mystery of Weezy's sudden disappearance would be explained, and—

"When?"

"Tomorrow."

Kapoor exhaled, quivering like a volcano about to blow. Joe resisted the urge to fill the silence.

"You can't do that, Joe. Mac Renfro is coming. Restart is less than a week away." She was calm, surprising him.

"I . . . uhh . . . it's urgent."

The eruption was almost a relief. "Urgent?" She half rose out of her chair, mouth a thin line. "Urgent is getting Helio-Corp financed. Urgent is getting to high ground in a hurricane. This is outrageous. You need to be here, not off on some . . . wait a minute . . . where are you going?

"Uhh, I have to go to Bethesda. There is a problem—"

"Bethesda? Is this about Napolitani?"

"She may be in trouble. I'm worried—"

"You're worried? About Superwoman?"

Joe felt his breath rasping, his anger knitting useless insults. Finally, he blew out a long breath.

"Yes, I am worried. I have to go."

Kapoor sneered and gave a tight-lipped shrug. "Blowing us off, huh, short-timer?" She turned back to the document she had been reading, anger radiating like heat off a tin roof.

There, he'd done it. He turned and left her office. He felt a strange mixture of relief and sadness as he walked back to his cubicle. The company had become a home of sorts. He had become part of its history. So many good people. Makayla passed him in the hall and smiled.

He would miss them.

CHAPTER NINETEEN

WAVES OF NAUSEA washed over Weezy, and something behind her left eye seemed to be drilling a hole in her skull. Her right shin throbbed in time with her heartbeat. Enough light penetrated the bag over her head to make her eyes try to focus, which made her dizzy.

They had been driving for an hour, maybe more.

"Next right turn, half a kilometer, up a hill," a French-accented voice said.

"Turn in here, go to the back."

The truck bounced as the driver turned into the gravel drive too fast.

"Can't even drive," Weezy said, muffled, from under the bag. "Dumbasses."

The van came to a stop. Doors slammed, then the side panel opened with a rush. Cooler air. Hands rolled her onto her back. Conversation in a Slavic language. Russian?

Footsteps crunching on gravel, what sounded like the rattle of a doorknob being tried. More conversation. The crack of wood breaking and the squeal of an unoiled hinge.

Hands pulled at her ankles. Pain shot through her shin. She was dragged across the floor of the van. Her skirt bunched around her waist. A hand on her arm pulled her upright. "Sit." Her feet found ground. "Stand." A rush of vertigo. "Move" and a push that made her trip and fall forward. Another shot of pain from the shin and the knees. Someone grabbed one arm and lifted her, then held on as they stumbled across uneven gravel. Oily-sweet smell. Sound of the door closing. They must be inside.

"Sit." The hand directed her downward, and she landed on the edge of what must be a chair. Two hands shoved her back hard.

The sack came off. Weezy's eyes took a moment to adjust. A man stood in front of the chair holding the sack. A single dangling light bulb highlighted his thinning light brown hair. He was ordinary-looking. He had hazel eyes and a carefully trimmed van dyke beard. His grin might have been friendly if it weren't for the predatory look in his eyes. Maybe the driver who had popped out of the van back in Bethesda? He turned, revealing Chinese logograph tattoos running up his neck. As he stepped aside, Weezy caught a fleeting glimpse of the other man—blond hair brushed back, trim and entirely out of place in baggy white coveralls with the van's cartoon plumber on its pocket. The man slipped into shadow and out of her field of view.

"Would you like some water?" The younger man asked in slightly accented English.

Weezy said nothing.

"We do not intend to hurt you, Ms. Napolitani."

"You already hurt me, dumbshit."

"So far, this is nothing."

She told herself he was just trying to scare her. They needed her for something. They wouldn't really . . . but the certainty in his voice bore into her, and she began to sweat.

The workshop they were in had four bays intended to service cars, if the oil stains on the concrete were an indicator. Two of the large windows on the front wall were broken, and plywood covered all four of them, making the interior gloomy, except for the single light over Weezy's head and a stripe of sunlight at the far end where the plywood had warped. A workbench stretched along most of the front wall of the building. A chain hoist ran above them on a track that went from sagging double doors at the back of the building across to the workbench.

Tattoo turned to her, his eyes traveling over her body with

an avidity that made her shudder.

The younger man, holding a phone of some sort, strode toward the door. He peered outside, then stepped onto the concrete apron and began a conversation. Russian. From her experience listening to hacker traffic, she picked out "woman," "the IAC," and "internet." His voice rose and fell in what sounded like an argument. Finally, he said "Da, da." He signaled Tattoo, who went to the door and took the phone. Weezy realized they had to stand outside because the clunky thing was a satellite phone.

The blond man came back into the building and moved toward her but stayed in shadow. He passed her, then came up behind. "How many hours?"

Weezy sniffed.

"Madame Napolitani, how many hours are left before you have to renew the lock on the file our man has put on this hacker website of yours?"

She struggled to piece together what was happening. HelioCorp, then the incident in Camden. They would need someone extraordinary to pull that off. HoHumJr could do it. Did 'our man' mean he was working with them? She mentally sorted through the analysis at HelioCorp and the conversation with Jake. They—whoever they were—must know quite a lot if they had figured out there was a locked file and that the lock was time sensitive. They may have gotten that from HoHumJr, with or without persuasion. But he wouldn't have set up the fail-deadly if he were working for them voluntarily, would he?

"You would be wise to answer me. I am far easier to work with than my associate," the blond man said. As if to prove him right, Tattoo came back inside the building, and strolled toward them with a leer on his face.

Tattoo spat out a string of Russian and jerked his head toward Weezy.

"No." The other man spoke from behind her.

Tattoo squatted, hands on thighs, face inches from Weezy's. "You will tell us now how Hell-Kit works." His accent amplified the harshness in his voice.

Weezy took a deep breath. She saw in Tattoo's eyes that he hoped she would refuse.

Tattoo slipped a folding knife out of the back pocket of his coveralls and opened it slowly. It was a delicate instrument with a pearled handle and a slender blade. Out of place in his hand. He reached out, caressed her shoulder, then rubbed a thumb over the thin fabric of her blouse. She forced herself not to pull away. She stared at the wall at the other end of the room with its hanging belts and gaskets, mold creeping down the wall.

Tattoo drew the point of the knife lightly down her cheek. His hand quivered a little . . . with excitement, from the look in his eyes. The blade continued down her neck and along the V of the blouse to the top button. Tattoo gave a flick, almost dainty, and the top mother-of-pearl button skittered across the floor. The blade pulled the material aside, as if opening a curtain. The point traced across her right breast to the strap. Another flick, and she felt the strap break. Tattoo licked his lips.

"No." It was the man behind her, again.

Tattoo answered in Russian. Then, to Weezy, "I am in charge now. Mr. Frenchie here was going to show up, put a cap in your ass, and disappear. Now he's got his balls in a twist because he doesn't want anyone to be able to identify him." Tattoo glanced over Weezy's head and smirked. "Right, Frenchie?"

The man behind her said nothing. Weezy felt the tension rise between the two.

"Thought so," Tattoo said and refocused on Weezy. "You will explain how to access this place called Olegarten and keep the file our hacker has put there from opening. You think I can't afford to kill you."

He grinned and drew the point of the knife lightly across her right breast.

"You're right about that, but I can make you beg me to do it."

THE FIRST HOUR had been the hardest. Weezy's shin throbbed. The zip ties securing her to the chair ground into her wrists. The man Tattoo called Frenchie paced behind her. Tattoo pulled a ratty chair from the bench, set it in front of Weezy, reversed, sat down, and began worrying the plastic back of the chair with his knife.

Finally the phone buzzed. Frenchie passed from behind her to the back door and had a short conversation. She caught a glimpse of high cheek bones, a finely sculpted aristocratic nose, but he was trying not to look directly at her. He stepped out of the white coveralls, revealing a well-tailored business suit. A few minutes later, gravel crunched under tires. Tattoo rose and sauntered over to Frenchie. The man handed Tattoo Weezy's e-pad, nodded toward her, said unfriendly words she couldn't make out, and left.

Tattoo sat down again and leaned his crossed arms on the chair's back. For the first few minutes, he just stared at her. Weezy forced herself to stare back.

"You will need to contact this place called Olegarten and stop the file from opening."

Pretty obvious he's not a techie, she thought, if he thinks Olegarten is a place. Maybe if he gave her the e-pad, she could contact Olegarten and reveal her location.

"Give me the e-pad, and I'll see what I can do."

He was not that dumb.

Jaw set, he stood, kicked the chair aside. In two quick steps, he was at her side. He did the knife routine again, tracing from her ear down her cheek, across the breast, cutting the other strap. He stepped in front of her, pushed her bra down, and smiled as he caressed her breasts. Then he squeezed her nipples, making her scream in anger as much as pain. His lubricious stare told her how much he was enjoying himself. She forced her fear and disgust behind a stone face.

Her fortitude spurred the man to greater creativity. He

speculated in accented English about what sorts of tracking devices she might have secretly stowed in which body cavity. He brought his face close to hers; fetid breath assailed her nostrils. "Where d'ya keep it, huh, smart lady? Right up . . ." She felt his hand creeping up her inner thigh and tensed, straining not to scream. "Here?" Maybe let him see her fear. Maybe he would stop.

But no.

"Why don't you ooze over to the corner and jerk off?"

He hit her then. Open hand to the side of her head. The chair rocked, and she almost fell sideways. The room went topsy-turvy.

He might have done more, but the phone buzzed.

Tattoo went out of focus. Gravel crunched again, a vehicle arriving. Doors slammed, muffled conversation.

A woman entered, led by Tattoo. She was dressed as if she had stepped out of an upscale law office. Her short hair was expensively coiffed, and she wore a fine gray suit, crisp white blouse, and low-heeled pumps.

Had she seen her before? Weezy was fogged, but there was something about the hair, the suit . . .

The woman came directly to Weezy, jerked up the remnant of the bra, closed her blouse, and inspected her face. She had a friendly, plain face that contorted with . . . sympathy? She produced a tissue and dabbed at Weezy's nose. She turned to Tattoo and fired off some Russian, her expression and tone needing no translation. He curled his lip but grabbed the satellite phone off the bench and retreated to just outside the door.

The woman turned the chair in front of Weezy, brushed off the seat, and sat. She leaned toward Weezy and offered a tentative smile.

"You may call me Marka, Ms. Napolitani. I am so sorry you have been treated badly."

Weezy said nothing. Was this their idea of good cop? Still, Weezy almost gave in to tears of relief.

"Ms. Napolitani, you know why you are here, do you not?"

Weezy focused on a point over Marka's shoulder and said nothing.

"Let me put this another way, Ms. Napolitani," Marka said. "Our position, our need, is simple. We must enter the Olegarten chat room and refresh the lock on the Hell-Kit file our rogue colleague has deposited there. We must do this without setting off any alarms."

Rogue colleague? Weezy heaved a sigh of relief. HoHumJr wasn't one of them.

"You find this amusing?" Marka leaned forward in her chair. "Your situation is simple," she continued, her expression softening. Now she was counsel for the accused, on Weezy's side. "You can instruct us as to how to go into Olegarten and renew the lock. Or you can refuse to cooperate with us, which will open Hell-Kit. You will then be responsible for our colleague's death—I believe you call him Ho-HumJr?—as well as your own."

What would they do if she cooperated? Throw her a party? She was dead regardless . . . unless. If she could warn Olegarten, buy some time, keep Hell-Kit from opening, Olegarten might trace an incoming signal.

Marka gave Weezy a long minute of silence to make up her mind. Getting no answer, she shrugged, looking a bit less sympathetic now. She stood and went to the workbench and rummaged in a backpack. She took out a small kit, unzipped it, and busied herself with something she withdrew from it. She called out in Russian, and Tattoo came back into the building.

Marka gave Tattoo what sounded like orders.

He passed by Weezy, gave her a smirk. A minute later, there came the screech of metal on concrete. Tattoo appeared, dragging a small table that must have been heavy. He positioned the table just inside the back door. More Russian, and Tattoo turned to Weezy and produced the knife again.

Weezy drew in her breath, preparing.

But Tattoo only cut the zip ties and pulled Weezy to her feet. The world spun, but she steadied herself.

"Over there." Tattoo pushed her forward with his right hand and grabbed the chair with his left.

They sat her in the chair in front of the small table. More zip ties. The sun had come out, bathing the trees in soft afternoon light. Incongruously beautiful. Marka put Weezy's e-pad in front of her, set the satellite phone on the far side of the table just outside the door, and connected the two with a cable.

Weezy came as close to crying as she had all day.

Of course. They needed to run the e-pad through the satellite phone. The signal Olegarten saw would appear to originate in some remote server. No big surprise. But a server they didn't recognize would get extra attention. She could at least warn them by failing the protocol, then they would be waiting when she was forced to try again. Maybe they would figure out her locat—

She felt a sting in her shoulder. Then Marka spoke.

"I'm sorry you're unwilling to help us. I have given you a shot to loosen your tongue. You are going to help us access the Olegar—" the words began to slow and echo. Weezy wondered if this was the word of God the ancients heard in their rituals "—ten. Web. Site. You will tell—" *Hotcake. Hotcake. Take off the "s."*

The sound of Marka's voice became muddy, but Weezy wanted so much to answer her questions. No "s," though. She had to remember: No "s."

WEEZY FLOATED IN a gauzy, half-conscious state. Happy, warm. Children playing, grass, swings. Beautiful children, a girl and a boy. Or two girls? Her children. Joe at the door of the single-wide trailer, calling them, calling her. "S," he said, smiling.

"Ms. Napolitani."

Not Joe. Sweet, oily industrial smell. Face close to hers.

"Ms. Napolitani, wake up."

Marka.

Weezy's eyes fluttered open. The sunlight was gone from the shop floor. How long had it been?

She was still at the table next to the back door.

"We were not successful in getting into Olegarten. You told us the protocol, the fingerprint ID, the several levels of security. But the site would not recognize 'Hotcake.' "

Relief burst through the fog in Weezy's brain. She had held the S. She was fully awake now, trying very hard not to let Marka see her triumph. They'd tried and failed. That would raise an acre-size red flag. Now, all she had to do was wait. How long would the security team need to set up a trap?

Weezy closed her eyes and tried to look dazed again.

"Ms. Napolitani, wake up."

" 'S okay?"

"Ms. Napolitani, it is essential that you wake up. You revealed that there is less than a day before the file opens. You must wake up."

"Uh-huh." Weezy made it look as if it was an effort to keep her eyes open. She hoped they didn't know how long it took for the drug to wear off.

The slap came hard, shocking her eyes open. Marka's face was twisted in fury.

"You have been playing with us. You will get us into Olegarten. Now."

"No." They couldn't go in so soon. Olegarten wouldn't be set up.

Marka's jaw twitched. She turned to Tattoo, said something in Russian. A grin spread across his face. She turned back to Weezy, a look that might be pity on her face.

Then she left.

CHAPTER TWENTY

MAKSYM RASKOV WOKE in a foul mood. His back hurt from the thin, lumpy mattress. Puusepp's snoring most of the night hadn't helped. The warehouse that was now their home stank. But mainly, he had been unable to keep from cycling through the disaster the project had become. And more, the fear of knowing what would happen to him if he didn't fix it.

Mongrel had called last night and reminded him that he was responsible for the project. Now they had added a West Virginia operation, and Raskov was in charge of that, too—from Florida. A dozen years of working with Mongrel first at the FSB then the Sobaki taught Raskov tidiness. To the Sobaki, tidiness meant ending a project with only one person alive—the man who would report success, be rewarded, and win a new assignment. At the start, Raskov assumed he would be that person. Now, he was not so sure.

Puusepp had made the grid hack more than untidy. Now, Raskov had to deal with Puusepp's fail-deadly and the complication of the Napolitani woman. The change in plans opened too many opportunities for things to go wrong. The nice, tidy assassination had turned messy when the assassin pulled out after learning that Napolitani had to be kept alive. That left hired muscle and an operative Raskov had never met in charge up in Virginia.

Raskov turned on his side. Gray light filtered into his room. A new day, one with no obvious solution. The woman in charge in Virginia, Marka, had seemed capable when he first talked with her. But she was using physical and chemical persuasion. It hadn't worked, at least not yet. Raskov wasn't surprised. He knew from experience that torture wasn't often effective on people who believed they were protecting something larger than themselves. Friendship and moral suasion might work but took time. A threat to a child or lover worked best, but took time, too. They had less than a day before Puusepp's fail-deadly blew open.

Raskov sat up, working the kinks out of his back, thinking his line of work was better suited to young men.

He had arranged to get United Energy's grid update schedules directly from Mac Renfro, who was going up the coast to get together with HelioCorp later in the day.

Raskov stood, dressed, and moved quietly to the grimy toilet at the far end of the building. After a piss, he turned on the single faucet in the sink, rubbed his teeth, rinsed and spat into the iron-tinged basin. The mirror was cracked diagonally, breaking Raskov's reflection. He shivered. The evil eye. His grandmother would have been sure of it.

THE BREAKFAST CROWD was thinning at the North Miami IHOP when Mac entered. He found Raskov seated at a table on the far side of the building by the window.

Mac had arrived the evening before and visited the United Energy's Southeast Control Division. It had been late, no managers around to get in his way. A technician at the grid control desk had been friendly, a bit awed, and more than willing to talk with one of the owners of the company. Mac left the building with the specific time he needed for the next action. More important, the tech had explained how the schedule was set. Mac would drop that intelligence on Raskov and be done with it.

He had rehearsed a story about being in a hurry, needing to get up to Boca. Then it had come true. Joe Mayfield left a message on his phone last night about having a late afternoon flight to catch. Strange that he would leave, given the importance of HelioCorp's upcoming announcement. Mayfield said he was sure Mac and Kapoor could handle the press release. Why would Mayfield give up the opportunity to be interviewed on Bloomberg, by the *Journal* and the finance talking heads? An emergency, apparently.

Mac crossed the open dining area and sat down facing Raskov, who was addressing a stack of pancakes topped with bright red strawberries. "I'm afraid I'll have to keep this short," Mac said. Raskov's right eyebrow, the one split by a scar, rose. "I'm meeting with HelioCorp's finance guy, and he has to catch a plane this afternoon."

Raskov gave Mac a look somewhere between irritation and pity. "You can leave when we have completed our business."

Mac swallowed, throat dry. A waitress appeared and offered a menu. Mac waved it off. "Just some water, please." The waitress retreated, scowling.

"The schedule for daily updates and password sequences?" Raskov said.

Mac nodded. "I have something better."

Raskov finished a bite, swallowed, and said, "Better?"

"Here is the formula they use for scheduling." He produced a single, handwritten sheet. "This is good until the end of the month."

Raskov took the paper, studied it, gave a small nod.

"That should finish our business," Mac said. "I hope the project will—"

Raskov's single shake stopped him. "The first interruption has not yet produced results. We must increase the pressure on your government."

The waitress appeared with a carafe of water. "Is there anything else I can get you?" she said, took in Raskov's glare, and left without waiting for an answer.

"Our agreement is clear," Mac said, projecting confidence he didn't feel. "I have given you access to the IAC. That is really all I can do without—"

Raskov interrupted with another shake of his head and scanned the area. They were now alone but for one family, parents concentrating on their children. A busboy cleared dishes two booths away.

After the busboy hoisted the tray of dishes and made for the kitchen, Raskov said, "You will use your contacts to release details about the first event today by four o'clock so they will be reported this evening. You will hint at events to come."

Mac swallowed again. His voice cracked. "That was never part of the plan. It exposes me to . . ."

Something in Raskov's eyes silenced him. Mac took a slug of water, building his courage.

"If I leak to a blogger," Mac said, "it might lead back to me, then expose HelioCorp, then phase two, then . . . you. Our agreement was for me to get you to the IAC feed line. I have done that. Now, I have given you more than you asked—a full month of schedules."

"We are not finished." Raskov didn't appear angry. It was as if Mac had simply misunderstood something obvious. "Perhaps, after the leak, we can talk about this finishing. You have what you wanted. Now you must finish what we want."

"The HelioCorp project is at risk. You should hold off further action for now." Mac hadn't wanted to play the card, but it was his last.

Raskov tilted his head in question.

"What is the problem?"

"There's a woman who works for the IAC. She may have helped HelioCorp figure out the problem. She's famous, and so is Mayfield. They were involved in the Phoenix issue a couple of years ago. She and Mayfield—"

"Phoenix?"

"Yeah. It was a big deal in this country. It's all over YouTube. Mayfield and this woman Napolitani—"

Raskov's fork paused halfway to his mouth.

"Napolitani?"

A gob of strawberry sauce dropped off the bite onto

Raskov's pants. He took no notice. Mac wondered if he should mention it, but Raskov's look of puzzlement stopped him.

"Yes. She's a big deal at the IAC, and—"

A look Mac couldn't read passed quickly across Raskov's face.

"Where will he go? What airport?"

"Mayfield? He didn't say."

"You will find out, and you will drive him to the airport."

"But he may not want—"

Raskov's jaw tightened. "You will text me the airport, and I will give you further instructions."

CHAPTER TWENTY-ONE

JOE'S CONVICTION TWO days ago that it was okay to stay in Boca and brief Mac had been ripped away by his call to Maddie. Weezy a fugitive? Was she on the run? Hurt? Why hadn't she called? His mind spun through the possibilities, getting no traction. Earlier, he'd called Maddie again and got no response. He'd called Weezy's work, home, private numbers. Nothing. He didn't have time to do the Starbucks trick with Olegarten, even if they would let him in. Best to get to Bethesda and try to figure out what had happened. But first, Mac Renfro.

Joe entered the HelioCorp lobby. Mac was chatting with the receptionist. He spied Joe, raised a hand in greeting, and picked up his briefcase.

"You got my message about leaving Boca for a few days?" Joe asked as they walked toward his office.

"I did," Mac said. "Tough time to have to leave. I bet Kapoor went nonlinear when you told her."

"Yes, she did," Joe said. "And I'd be really worried if you weren't here."

"I'll do my best, Joe, and . . . thanks for your confidence in me." His excitement crept through the serious words and expression. "We'll miss your command of the numbers and the deal, though."

"I'm sure you'll do fine," Joe said, "but I want you to see and understand the new hardware before you talk with the press. Engineering is expecting us." They walked toward the back of the building, greeted by smiles as they went. The company grapevine had let everyone know about Mac's life-saving investment, and the staff was energized and happy. A young engineer proudly showed Mac and Joe the improvements she and the team had made to the control panel. They were a week from what everyone was calling Restart, three days from the announcement of it, and optimism reigned. Brianna Kapoor joined them for a few minutes, greeting Mac formally and ignoring Joe.

Joe and Mac finished the tour and took over the conference room where they'd talked an eon ago—two-and-a-half weeks—when HelioCorp was facing failure and Mac offered a life-saving infusion of cash.

They spent an hour preparing Mac for the announcement. The financial press would demand numbers, so Joe concentrated on covering projections of how fast the business could scale up and how much capital would be needed. Joe knew the numbers backward and forward, could discuss them without much thought, which freed him to worry again about Weezy. Where was she?

"Joe?"

Joe realized Mac had asked him a question.

"Pardon?"

"When do you leave for the airport?" Mac asked.

Joe checked his watch. "I need to leave in about an hour."

"If you're going to Lauderdale or Miami International, I can drop you off. It would give us more time to talk, and—"

Joe's mind raced, trying to come up with a plausible excuse to go by himself. He should let Mac do the favor for him, but he felt too keyed up to carry on polite conversation.

"I'm going out of Miami, but I'll grab an autocar, Mac. Traffic'll be ugly. Besides, you've got homework to do." He tried a disarming smile.

Mac glanced at the open door of the conference room, then leaned across the table to Joe. "I need to talk with you in private. I'll be bringing in several other investors for the scale-up, and I need to have a plan about Kapoor." He dropped his voice. "I'd rather discuss it off site."

Mac checked his watch. "Let's do a late lunch on the way to the airport. I know a great little Cuban place over near Coral Springs. Neighborhood's sketchy, but they serve a great *arroz con pollo.*"

Before Joe could argue, Mac said, "Don't worry, it'll be quick. Plenty of time to get you to your plane."

When they had finished their work, Joe took his suitcase from his car and stashed it in the back seat of Mac's. They pulled out of the HelioCorp lot, and Joe braced himself for the conversation about Kapoor. Mac pulled onto the interstate, set the autopilot. He launched into a monologue about United Energy, his uncles, and how the world was changing its ideas about energy. It sounded like a speech he might give at an investment conference. Certainly not the discussion about Kapoor Joe expected. Maybe he was waiting to have it at the restaurant.

Mac directed the car off the interstate and took over control from the auto pilot. They were now on a side street, passing through classic Florida commercial clutter—small strip centers, cheek-by-jowl spas, tanning parlors, second-hand shops. Mac turned to Joe. "You have to stay with HelioCorp. I heard about the blowup with Kapoor. Everyone is scared."

"Yes, we argued," Joe said. "But Kapoor is changing, Mac. Whatever the cost of the failed connection to the grid, these last weeks have matured her. We're going to be all right. I should be back in time for the announcement, but you really don't need me."

Mac squinted. "Hiding your light under the basket again, Mayfield?" They both chuckled.

Mac checked his e-pad and turned a hard right and slowed. He checked the e-pad again. Joe glanced at the businesses they were passing, then back at Mac. Didn't he know where the 'great little Cuban place' was? But then Mac nodded and said, "Aha. Here we are," as he made another right at the end of a clutch of shops.

Mac hung a left into the area behind the buildings. "I

always park in back. Only a few spaces up front." He drove slowly toward the end of the strip, steering around dumpsters and a couple of nondescript older cars. Finally he stopped, turned off the engine. He sat for a moment, glanced at the rearview, then opened his door.

Joe cracked his door, smelled the rich mix of cooking fat and spices. He relaxed and swung a leg out of the car. Suddenly, a man rushed toward him. Hawaiian shirt, earring, and a deep tan. A chrome-plated revolver flashed.

"Back in the car! In the car!" He screamed, nearly soprano, and waved the gun.

Mac thrust his hands up, "I can give you money. I have money. No problem. No *problema.*"

Joe fell back into his seat and turned to Mac, still in the driver's seat. There was a second man on Mac's side—a thick torso, a hand, a gun.

Earring guy produced a black sack. "I said, in the car, asshole!" Joe pulled his leg back. The guy dropped the bag over Joe's head. Sounds dulled. Mac said something he couldn't make out, his voice rising. There was a loud pop like a firecracker, and something wet splattered Joe's hand. Then a rush of breath from Mac sounding like an exasperated sigh.

Joe pulled at the bag enough to see blood and bits of something else on his hand. A strong hand pulled the bag down. A voice, accented and deeper than the one that just yelled at him said, "Leave it alone."

Then hands felt both sides of his head and the deeper voice said, "Implant."

The voice moved away and said a few words. A hint of breeze let Joe know the door was still open. More words, closer now. Joe leaned toward the door, swung his feet out at the same time he pulled the bag off. His feet hit the ground, and he curled into a crouch, then drove toward the two men. He dropped his shoulder and hit the earring guy, rucking him up, pushing him toward the bigger guy and the dumpster. Muscle memory from those August two-a-day practices kicked in. Zone blocking 101.

"Goddamsonofafuckingbitch!" The earring guy took a step, trying to get off the bigger guy, tripped and fell. The big guy sidestepped with surprising grace. Joe cut toward him, but too late. A hollow metallic sound detonated inside his head, then a light show as his vision blurred and the pain hit. He lost balance, stumbled and fell onto concrete, the skin of his palms tearing. He lay stunned for a moment, then strong hands lifted him by his shoulders. They bound his wrists, jammed the bag back over his head, and manhandled him into the car. Something metal, rough surface was put in his hand, his fingers wrapped around . . . what?

Grips of a gun?

It was taken away, and the passenger door closed.

A hushed conversation ensued, maybe not in English.

Then the sound of movement of something heavy on the driver's side.

"Christ, there's blood all over my—"

The deeper voice, in another language, angry.

The driver's door slammed, and the car started. It jerked into reverse. The driver mumbled to himself.

Joe shook his head, a mistake that brought a stab of pain. He tried to formulate a question, heard himself say. "What's—"

"Shut up or I'll shoot you right here," the high voice said.

Joe's mind careened. This was no robbery. Why the bag over his head? Mac driving to the back of the building had to be a setup. Why would Mac do that? Something about HelioCorp? Then the thought that froze him. What happened to Mac? The blood.

After a short while, the car slowed, then swayed. Must be pulling off the road.

"Out."

Joe felt for the handle, numb. He opened the door and was wrapped in humidity and the thick, woody swamp smell. A car door slammed nearby.

He felt a presence, and the bag was yanked off. They were

in a crushed-rock parking area somewhere in the outback. Sawgrass, a row of live oaks and palmetto. The big man was approaching from a car parked on the grassy margin between them and one-lane track overlooking a wetland extending to the horizon.

The ear ring guy shoved Joe toward the rear of the car.

Catbirds argued in the distance. Was this the place Joe was going to die? Joe flinched as the big man pushed Joe's shoulders and chest onto the rear deck of the car firmly but not brutally. As he went down, Joe glimpsed clothes in the back seat, then open, staring eyes and blood. Mac.

"We are going to take your implant. It will be easy and quick if you don't move."

The big man's hand held him down. Metal hot from the Florida sun burned his cheek. He didn't care. After what he had expected . . .

There was a moment of silence, then another person, probably Earring, said, "You gotta be kidding—"

"Go quickly, right here." A finger touched the bump behind Joe's ear where his Bluetooth implant was attached to his mastoid bone.

A stab of pain, searing hot. Wetness on his neck. Then something pulling, reminding him of when his wisdom teeth had to come out. This time there was no anesthetic, and it felt like they were pulling his brain out the side of his head.

"Good. Put it over there. In the grass at the edge of the clearing. His e-pad is inside. Throw it far, but not in the water. Now—"

The black sack dropped over Joe's head. A hand between his shoulder blades directed him across grass, then gravel or rock, to what must be the other car. A door creaked open, and the hand guided Joe in, then the two were in the car with him.

The car jerked as it backed up. Joe's head spun and the spot where they'd ripped out the implant burned.

Why had they shot Mac? Why not Joe? Drugs? Gambling? White-collar crime would be more Mac's style, but wouldn't get him killed . . . would it? How did Joe fit in? Was this about HelioCorp?

Then, like a punch to the chest, Weezy.

JOE WENT INTO stasis, concentrating on timing how long they rode and what direction to stave off thoughts over what would happen next. Twenty minutes, maybe twenty-five? Finally a sharp right turn, the car proceeding slowly, then stopping.

They took the black bag off, then pulled Joe out of the car. He blinked in the sunlight. The right side of his white shirt was brilliant with blood and his left forearm was spotted with clumps of something else.

Joe had a moment of vertigo and stumbled. Big Guy's hands steadied him.

They faced a row of concrete-block buildings, each with oversize garage bay doors. The long asphalt apron held dumpsters, rusty machinery, and sun-bleached pickup trucks.

Big Guy prodded, and they moved across the apron toward the end unit. They passed through an entrance next to the roll-up door. Dirty windows along the building's outside wall filtered sunlight to gray-green. The shafts of light illuminated a workbench near the entry door. There were three doors at the near end, one opening into what looked like an office, the other two closed. Most of the space sat empty, a warehouse of some sort. A card table and three folding chairs stood in front of the office. The place stank of mold with subtle overtones of something long dead.

Big Guy pushed Joe into one of the chairs at the card table. He took an odd-looking phone from his grip and put it on the table along with an older e-pad. A travel chess set occupied the middle of the table, pieces at the ready for a game. Its cover lay next to it, a crack running from corner to center.

He spoke to Earring in another language, calling him something like Peter. Slavic, maybe? Peter answered. Big

Guy's name sounded like "Razcoff."

Earring was younger . . . brown hair slicked back, slacks and lizard-skin boots. He would be at home in one of the upscale South Beach bars. He crossed the space in front of them, undid a padlock on the middle door, opened it and yelled, "Get your ass out here."

A small man appeared. He was a middle-aged, rumpled version of the retirees who played at lawn bowling in Boca: Polo shirt, baggy shorts, and walking shoes with Velcro straps. He spoke to Peter and turned toward a third door. Peter said, "Nyet." The man spoke again, his expression pained.

"Okay, but make it quick."

The man opened the door. Joe glimpsed ratty linoleum and a toilet. The man entered. After a few moments, he reappeared, zipping his fly. Big Guy asked him a question, pointing to the phone. The man picked it up, turned it over, then inspected the e-pad.

Big Guy seemed to be in charge. He was tall and broad-shouldered with a bit of a belly. His gray hair was sparse and cut short, his face flat with high cheekbones and a nose that might have been broken, perhaps often. His eyes were watery blue and seemed capable of humor. After he'd hit Joe, he'd handled him almost the way an EMT might. Firmly, but taking no pleasure in causing pain.

Joe didn't understand what they were saying, but he recognized problem-solving. The big man listened to the little man almost respectfully, finally giving a small shrug. He motioned for the man to take a seat across from Joe, grabbed the phone and walked to the far end of the open area. He held the phone up to a window partly cleared of the crusted crud that had taken over the others.

Peter emerged from the open office and strolled toward them, a large bottle of Mountain Dew in hand. He looked away to take a generous swig. The man across from Joe gave him a hint of a smile of recognition and said, "HoHum" softly. Peter rushed to the table and kicked the leg of the folding chair.

"Shut up, douchebag."

Joe realized he was staring open-mouthed. Was the man the Olegarten member Weezy called HoHumJr? Pieces of the puzzle fell together. Olegarten. The Dead Man Switch game. So HelioCorp wasn't a computer glitch. Joe's hopes soared. Weezy would figure this out. Then he caught sight of the blood on his shirt, remembered the sharp crack that sounded too small to take Mac's life.

"This is Pyotr . . . Peter in English. He is unhappy when I speak," HoHumJr said in accented English, "but Raskov is less concerned."

Pyotr grabbed a handful of HoHumJr's shirt, nostrils flaring. "Listen, asshole, you—"

HoHumJr, if he was HoHumJr, went slack, but seemed more bored than scared.

Raskov was coming back toward them, holding an e-pad and looking perplexed. "Stop," he said, in a voice that betrayed irritation, as if he were used to Pyotr's behavior.

Raskov switched to the other language, addressing Ho-HumJr as "cal-hoo" and pointing to the e-pad. HoHumJr listened, nodding as Raskov continued.

Joe stared at the small man across from him. Was he Ho-HumJr? He had sent the fail-deadly message, so he must be a prisoner. But now, he was behaving like a colleague to Raskov, sucking his teeth, contemplating some apparently abstruse problem, shaking his head.

Raskov checked his watch, then addressed Pyotr.

Pyotr put the bottle of Dew on the table, picked up the e-pad, and grabbed Joe roughly by the arm.

"Up, asshole. Over there." He shoved Joe toward the workbench. Joe's anger surged, and he half-turned. Pyotr pulled back, but then put on a sneer, daring Joe. Raskov barked Russian, Pyotr flinched and pushed Joe toward the end of the bench.

Raskov set a folding chair in place and seated Joe at the

bench next to the cleared windowpane. Joe got a glimpse of palmetto fronds obscuring another building.

Pyotr set the e-pad down in front of Joe. Raskov leaned close to the clear spot, keyed the phone, and spoke briefly. Pyotr tapped on the e-pad, raising a video link.

Pyotr smirked. "You're gonna love this, asshole."

AN ARRAY OF Florida State Patrol cars crowded the parking lot of the Sawgrass Trailhead on the edge of the 'glades. Raisa Jarvinen parked and walked across to the levee, then down a lime-rock track toward the site of the murder.

The Miami FBI field office had been notified of the murder of a man connected to a case some DC mucky-muck was interested in, and Jarvinen drew the short straw. She'd been about to leave the office when her e-pad chimed, showing an incoming call from AD Henry Barber. It wasn't every day that a newly minted special agent got a call from one of the dozen highest-ranking members of the Firm, so she put on her best officious tone, knew it would sound phony coming from a twenty-eight-year-old just graduated from the Academy, and answered. Barber turned out to be down to earth, happy to review the HelioCorp case and the murdered guy's possible connection to it. He answered her questions, his tone indicating collegiality. When he was finished, she felt as if she was on a team of two.

So, by the end of her several hundred-yard walk to the scene, her collar and armpits were wet with sweat, but she was walking tall. There wasn't much to see. A couple of patrol cars and the medical examiner's meat wagon were pulled into an open area that held piles of sand and gravel probably used to maintain the bike trail she'd just walked down. The rear of a sedan poked out of bushes at the edge of the clearing. An ME team was moving a gurney into position near it. One cop was taking pictures of the area around the car, another of the inside. Two cops were inspecting the perimeter. All the cops were male and at least a decade older than Jarvinen. She braced herself, preparing for either the avuncular, don't bother-your-pretty-head treatment, or the fellows-in-uniform sleazy hit. A gray-haired sergeant saw her first. He stood, stretched his back and grunted in relief.

Most likely avuncular.

She held up her wallet. "Jarvinen, FBI."

"Joe Mraczek." He cracked a grin. "Don't try to say it. Just Joe."

"What have we got?"

Joe turned out to be neither avuncular nor creepy.

"Passing bicyclist saw the back end of the car this morning, called it in. Dead guy in the car had an implant that ID'd him as a Donel McTavish from Wheeling, West Virginia. He was down here visiting a company in Boca. One shot to the head."

The officer still working the perimeter stooped and passed his scanning device near the ground. He put the scanner down, pulled on rubber gloves, and picked a small item out of the grass.

"Bluetooth implant," he said, holding it up. "Bloody."

"They left the implant in the guy they killed, took it out of somebody else?" Jarvinen said.

"Probably the guy who did the deed knew we could track him if he kept it," Mraczek said.

"Given the fact that he had to do a painful operation out here, he probably didn't expect to suddenly become untraceable," Jarvinen said. "And he must have had help."

"Good thought," Mraczek said. Then he grinned. "Or he could just have had an 'Oh, shit' moment. Twenty years on the job says never underestimate perps being stupid."

The other officer pulled an e-pad from his duty belt, held it close to the device, swiped, and tapped. "Registered to a Joseph Mayfield, permanent address up on the panhandle, but most activity in Boca. Device went stationary just before noon yesterday."

Mraczek and Jarvinen crossed over the open area to Renfro's car. The officer photographing the inside of the car popped up on the passenger side. "Looks like a bullet lodged in the floor."

"Where?"

"Front seat, passenger side kick panel. There's blood on the driver's side and blood and some bone material on the passenger seat, mainly down the side."

Jarvinen looked in the driver's side window to where the tech pointed. Odd. Renfro must have been driving. They stopped, Mayfield must have gotten out, went around the car, shot Renfro. The way Renfro's clothes were wrapped around him said the body had been moved. Mayfield must have dragged his body out of the driver's seat, jammed it into the back seat. But no drag marks here. So Renfro was shot somewhere else. Then Mayfield drove here . . . but how did he leave?

Mraczek must have been following the chain of logic, too. "Mayfield wouldn't have been dumb enough to call an autocar, but"—he turned to the officer that discovered the implant—"will you check any autocars coming to this area today?"

Jarvinen walked the fifty feet back to the road. The grass between the open area and the road was tramped over now . . . *locals, gotta love 'em* . . . but tire tracks still showed. Just the one car in the maintenance area. The road was lime-rock, hard-packed and made for bikes. She squatted and studied the verge of the road where the rock tended to collect.

"Hey, uhh," . . . *what was the guy's name?* "Joe . . . You should cast this track."

"Sure. On it."

The upside was locals tended to be excited about this stuff, Jarvinen thought.

She unrolled her e-pad and left a short report for Henry Barber. She concluded, "Looks like Mr. Squeaky Clean isn't so clean after all."

CHAPTER TWENTY-TWO

WEEZY STIRRED AND tried to raise a hand to rub an itchy eye. The pain hit, and she cried out before she came fully awake. Both hands were strapped to the arms of the chair. The little finger of her left hand was swollen and purple at the knuckle where they'd broken it.

The acrid scent of her own body brought back the horror of yesterday's torment. Marka learned HoHumJr had reset the clock from his end. Weezy had to do so or the fail-deadly would open the file that frightened the Russians. She refused, buying Olegarten time to trace the signal. But she had refused once too often. Marka said something in Russian to Tattoo. He came to Weezy, put his hands on her wrists and leaned forward so that his lips brushed her ear and whispered softly, almost lovingly, "It is time to contact Olegarten . . . NOW!"

His scream deafened her and made the room spin. She heard a snap like a wet twig breaking. Then the pain hit, and his face, leering, went out of focus.

She had struggled against the restraints, bending forward, rocking, wanting to cradle the pain radiating from her finger, make it go away. They were talking at her, but words didn't matter.

Behind the red veil of pain, the need to hold on just a little longer, give her friends time.

"This hurts you?" Tattoo said, touching her finger. "Here?" Almost sympathetic, like a lover might be. "Or perhaps,"—a smile—"here?"

She began crying. It didn't take much effort and it bought her a couple of minutes.

Marka stood behind Tattoo and said almost apologetically, "We have so little time, Louise, so little time. And you have seven more fingers, two thumbs, ten toes . . ."

Weezy nodded, trying to look resigned. Finally, she reset the clock, hesitating as if recalling the security protocol was a challenge, taking as long as she could to do the reset. Hoping.

They had given her water afterwards, probably drugged but she didn't care, and she had slept.

Weezy shifted in the chair. The pain in her finger shrank to a throb. The itch in her eye receded. Afternoon sun shone on the floor, leaving most of the building interior in shadow.

Her eyes swept the room. No Marka. Panic. She searched again, more slowly. Marka was huddled in a chair in the shadows, apparently asleep. Weezy let out a long sigh. Relief. As long as Marka was there, he couldn't . . . wouldn't . . . do it again.

"I have to go to the bathroom."

Tattoo roused himself and clipped off her restraints. Marka gave Weezy a half smile and said something to Tattoo. He grinned and took Weezy's arm, pushing her to the primitive toilet stall on the far wall. When she tried to close the door, he shook his head.

Weezy stared into the rust-stained bowl, wanting to plunge her hand into cool water. When she turned, Tattoo was leaning on the door frame, arms crossed, a smile playing across his face.

"Really?" Weezy said. "You want to watch me pee?"

His grin broadened.

She shrugged and hiked her skirt with her good hand. She struggled to push her underpants down, trying to look nonchalant when she saw the dried blood, and sat. Peeing was painful, but she tried to make it last, hoping Tattoo's attention would shift.

A tone out in the main room announced an incoming call on the satellite phone. Tattoo turned away from Weezy, releasing her from his prurient stare. She took the opportunity to pull her pants up and push her skirt down as best she could with one hand. Tattoo turned back to her after a few words with Marka and motioned Weezy toward the center of the room and her chair.

They must not have expected the call, because they had to set up an e-pad and attach it to the satellite phone. Why hadn't they figured out satellite phones were not easy to secure? Was the sat phone a necessity, not a choice? Where the hell were they? No traffic noise, no lights outside at night as far as she could remember. Must be in the country.

Tattoo carried the e-pad over to her, shoved it in her face.

A blurry picture. She tried to focus.

Joe.

A dark stain ran down his shirt. The e-pad's camera adjusted, and the stain turned red. Blood. They had hurt him. A lot of blood. Her breath caught in her throat. What would they do with him? He was angry, mouthing words she couldn't hear.

Relief and fear flooded her. Why had they . . . of course . . . to make her throw the switch. Her tears were for Joe. They had succeeded. No way to hold back now, no way to give Olegarten more time to find her. But underneath the fear for Joe was relief. No more broken fingers. No more Tattoo. No more reason to endure pain. Keep Hell-Kit closed. They'll think her resistance died because they had Joe, not her fear of another broken finger or another session with Tattoo.

They were right, she realized, as a second wave of fear hit, the undertow as the first receded.

She tried to speak through her tears. Nothing came out but a moan.

Now there were three people they would eliminate as soon as they got what they wanted.

THE WATER. SOMETHING in the water.

The thought surfaced long enough to register before Weezy fell back into the lazy comfort of pain-dulled, no-worry half sleep. Had she done one reset after seeing Joe? Two?

Dreaming, she saw Joe's face after he asked her to marry him. She, wanting to justify, the words forming, floating toward Joe, stopping midair, dissipating like smoke. Hands caressing her shoulder, then her left breast. Joe? But this was rough, almost painful.

She shook awake. Tattoo, leering. She repressed the enraged scream she knew he craved.

"Wake up, little bird."

He held the bottle of water to her mouth. She was thirsty, but something in her dream told her to refuse. He shrugged. "You don't drink, you die. Don't be stupid." He held the bottle to her lips and forced it against her teeth. She took some, then shook her head.

"Your funeral."

Weezy fell back toward the void as if she had pounded the snooze button after the alarm woke her. But now there was a set of synapses that drove her to wake up.

A bare lightbulb on the far wall cast weak light. Tattoo sprawled on a sleeping bag on the floor. No one else around. How long had it been? She tried to concentrate. No Marka. That should worry her, but she forgot why. How many times had she reset the switch since the awful vision of Joe? It was dark then, too. Had it been a day? Two days? Three? She recalled at least one reset.

The drug dragged at her powers of reason and tangled the threads of logic before they had a chance to work themselves out. She fought to concentrate. How many times into Olegarten to reset the fail-deadly's timer would it take for her friends to trace the signal? They wouldn't be expecting a satellite uplink, but Adeeb was better at this stuff than anyone at IAC. Maybe only two. What would they do if they did locate her? Would they break Olegarten's rule against governmental involvement and contact someone who might help?

Weezy stared into the gloom of the workshop, straining to figure some way to tilt the odds in her favor. Maybe more, in Joe's favor.

For now, the system was in balance. She was throwing her switch, HoHumJr must be throwing his. These Russians must be accomplishing their hacking of the grid. They'd started with HelioCorp, gone to Camden, then Georgia. Probably more. Closing the jaws of the vice. They had to keep Joe alive to threaten her. But would the government give in to their demands? Was their goal money, or did they want to set off CyberWar Two?

She felt the urge to sleep, to dream, to hope. She, Joe, HoHumJr, the Russians . . . all in balance. On a high wire.

CHAPTER TWENTY-THREE

JAKE PUSHED BACK from her keyboard and let her head fall forward, trying to relax her neck muscles. It had been two days . . . pushing three now . . . since Jake talked with Louise about HoHumJr's message with the fail-deadly. Louise hadn't checked in as promised, and Jake kept circling back to worry that HoHumJr had made Louise a player to protect her. Why?

To add to Jake's rising unease, Olegarten's security chief had reported that Louise had tried to get into the site; at least, the biometrics were Louise's. But she signed "Hotcake" twice. If it were a simple keying error, why not try again? But she hadn't. Then, without explanation, she had signed in and performed a reset to prevent the Hell-Kit from opening. Now, the clock was ticking closer and closer to the deadline to reset yet again. What bothered Jake most was that the source of the Hotcake signal was shrouded, bounced through many servers. Louise would know that violation of protocol might get her ejected from the group.

Jake stood and stretched. Maybe another coffee. In the kitchen, she poured herself a cup. The light of a warm Wisconsin afternoon flooded through the windows, tinting everything gold. The familiar mugs on the shelf above the coffee maker, the plates, the curtains and the smells always calmed her. A rainbow trout, frozen in motion on a wooden plaque on the wall, regarded her through one bright glass eye. She thought of her husband Kermit, gone these five years. She smiled at the fish, and the tension in her neck and shoulders eased.

Back at the computer, Jake checked on HoHumJr's file.

Still locked. She and Adeeb hoped whoever this Hotcake was would try to sign in again. When they tried, Adeeb would be ready, waiting to trace the signal's origin.

What would they do after that? Olegarten had the best tracking and hacking capability in the world. No problem to steal a list, plant false information, move money. But Olegarten couldn't put boots on the ground.

In the silence of the Wisconsin afternoon, Jake felt the weight of the decision she feared she would have to make.

To save Louise, if it was Louise, somebody—the FBI, the police or Homeland Security—would have to act. Jake would have to direct them where to strike. And that would violate the Protocol. Rule One, No Exposure, allowed no cooperation with government authorities. To make matters worse, chatter on the internet indicated that Louise was a fugitive, possibly responsible for a penetration of the power grid. Olegarten members would have to vote to violate Rule One for the benefit of a single member.

The group had named Jake Grand Poobah. She would have to decide.

Jake poured cream into the coffee and watched the white spiral into brown. A muted bing interrupted her reverie. She hurried to the computer. Adeeb, again. His feed came up on video. He looked haggard but alert, as if only adrenaline stood between him and badly needed sleep.

"Jakee, another signal!" In his excitement, the usually formal Pakistani gentleman forgot the "-e" was silent in English.

"From Hotcakes?"

"Yes, yes . . . and I found it."

"Uhh, you know where it came from?"

"Yes. Almost. You see, they are using a satellite phone. Fewer in use these days, so a bit easier to find. They were popular years ago when the world was less connected, but now using a slice detector for a specific region—"

"Adeeb, did she reset the lock?"

"—I was able to detect a signal coming from your state of Maryland, perhaps West Virginia. Of course, I had to go high, so I can't—"

"Adeeb, that's wonderful, but did she reset?"

"Yes, this time she . . . they . . . got in and performed a reset."

"Brilliant of you to find them," Jake said, and Adeeb sat straighter. "Where are they exactly?"

"I had to sample a slice ten kilometers above ground to eliminate electronic noise, so the circle is twenty kilometers." A map popped up on Jake's monitor, quickly followed by a topographic overlay.

Jake nodded. "Pretty hilly." She expanded the map. "Sure, rising toward the Blue Ridge. I bet it's sparsely—"

Another overlay, this time with population density.

"Yes, yes. Not many people there. That should help find them," Adeeb said, nodding several times. "But who will be sent?"

Jake heard the real question. Rule One. Was it worth losing Olegarten to save Louise?

IT HAD BEEN an hour since Adeeb signed off. He had been relieved when Jake suggested a good night's sleep. "Sleep late," Jake added, realizing it was already the wee hours of the morning in Pakistan.

She had posted a bulletin explaining the Hotcakes situation. She had been candid about the rumor that Louise was the person responsible for the US power grid hacking. She made a case that it was in the best interest of Olegarten to inform authorities confidentially rather than ignore the issue and possibly bring unwanted scrutiny.

She watched the discussion ricochet between members. Assuming Louise hadn't lost her mind, there were only two possibilities.

Bawboy2, always skeptical, outlined the first: "If Hotcakes and HoHumJr were involved in some doubtful enterprise, they might have created the fail-deadly as a red herring."

Adeeb weighed in. "That doesn't make any sense—why would they create the fail-deadly if they wanted secrecy? They would know Ockham's Razor was right: keep it simple."

No, it had to be the second possibility: something was terribly wrong. HoHumJr set up the game and the fail-deadly to protect himself and Louise. The fact that Louise had gone silent must mean she was in trouble. HoHumJr, too.

Jake's coffee cup shook when she picked it up to take the last sip. She realized she hadn't eaten in eighteen hours. She raised herself from the chair in front of her monitor and made her way to the kitchen.

The refrigerator held leftover stew she didn't want, as well as milk, cheese, eggs, and some aging vegetables. There was lettuce in her garden, growing so fast the rabbits couldn't keep up. But she'd have to pick it, wash it, make it into a salad. That felt too complicated. She settled on eggs.

She set a pan on the stove, added a pat of butter, and watched it melt. She cracked two eggs into the pan and rotated it to keep them from sticking, remembering how Kermit flipped them with a twist of the wrist she had never mastered.

What would happen when she made the call to the government? Weezy was probably being held against her will. But was she with HoHumJr, or were they in two different places? If Weezy was rescued and HoHumJr wasn't with her, she might not give the signal to keep the file closed. What would happen to HoHumJr then?

The eggs were crackling and spitting, the edges browning the way she liked. Kermit never let them get brown enough, but she ate them just the same. She didn't need brown edges. Her eyes misted over. She tried Kermit's flip and broke both yolks.

She carried the eggs to the kitchen table. She salted and

peppered them and added a squirt of ketchup. Kermit would have made fun of the ketchup.

As she ate, she replayed her options. Her plan sounded sensible, but who would she talk to? She could try to talk to Joe Mayfield first. But he didn't monitor Olegarten like full members did. She could probably find a way to get to Homeland's Office of Cybersecurity or the FBI. But that might expose her. She sighed. So many uncertainties.

As she pushed the last bit of egg through the ketchup, she remembered a person Louise worked closely with at IAC. A woman, southern accent. Jake took the plate to the sink, trying to remember the name. Melanie? Madeline?

At the computer, she scanned her contact log for two years ago, when she had worked with Louise on the Phoenix project. Hollingsworth, that was it. Madeline. Louise called her Maddie. Jake hoped she was still at the IAC and tapped the contact info card to make a call.

WEEZY'S PRIVATE TONE chirped on Maddie Hollingsworth's monitor.

Maddie gasped, dropped the signal she'd been tracing, and answered.

"Weezy?"

A voice, probably female, tone shifted, asked, "Madeline Hollingsworth?"

"How did you get this recognition code?"

"I am an associate of Louise Napolitani. I am concerned that she missed a dinner date."

One dinner date missed wouldn't lead to a call to IAC through a privileged channel. Maddie set a trace routine to work on the signal.

"She's not available."

Maddie hesitated, then punched in audio recording. The NSA was listening. When Keith told her Weezy was part of a plot to disrupt America's power grid, she'd known that was bullshit. He had warned her that she would be named a co-conspirator if she conspired with Weezy. That was not bullshit. They probably wouldn't put her in prison, but the effort to defend herself would bankrupt her and ruin her career. On the other hand, if this was a message from Weezy . . .

"We haven't heard from her in a couple of days."

The tracer was getting nowhere after several thousand iterations.

"Hmmm," the voice said. "Your reticence tells me I should disconnect immediately. You may already have enough data to find me. So let me say two things before I leave you. First, I believe Ms. Napolitani is being held against her will by people who mean the United States no good. Second, she is located somewhere northwest of Harpers Ferry, West Virginia."

"Somewhere?" Despite her better judgement, Maddie was drawn in.

"Probably in wilderness. We have traced a satellite phone to a six-mile radius centered on map coordinates 39.448217, -78.076803."

"How do you know this?"

"We are friends. But we have no ability to save her."

"And so you need us," Maddie said, but the connection had been broken.

JAKE TOOK OFF her glasses and pinched her nose, tired but knowing she had more work to do.

Louise's friend had understood right away why she was calling. No "what's this all about?" Concern in Hollingsworth's voice. The signal must be monitored. If they were any good, they would find her. Better shut down and pack up.

Jake sent a short message to Adeeb, explaining that she had passed along location information. She told him she had to go silent for a few days. He would understand that she was quarantining herself. She hoped he would plead her case with the rest of Olegarten and she would not be impeached.

She went to the basement. In the interior corner, across from Kermit's work bench, was a twin bed frame supporting a stack of moldering cardboard boxes. Each was marked with its contents. An old carpet lay across the top of the boxes. Jake lifted the carpet carefully, so as not to disturb the layer of dust. She took three sewing machine cases from the hollow behind the wall of boxes—two Necchi and one old round-top wooden Singer. She carried them one by one up the wooden ladder-stairs to her kitchen. Then to her sewing room, which housed perhaps the most sophisticated network monitoring operation in the state. If her friends noticed Jake never produced any clothing, embroidery, or tchotchkes, they were too polite to comment. She hadn't been the same since Kermit died, they whispered to each other.

She packed the advanced gear, the high-speed modem, the monitors, and the computers she had designed herself and built from parts purchased on trips to Milwaukee and the Twin Cities. She moved a sewing machine from a cabinet to the tabletop next to her desk where the main processing unit normally rested.

As she moved the cases down the stairs, she rehearsed how she would sound confused and afraid if the government did come. She hoped it would be the local sheriff—what was his name?—because he would assume she was no more than the widowed school teacher everyone in Solon Springs knew. But she needed to be prepared for FBI or Homeland agents, who would be harder to fool.

When the cases were safely back in the basement, she set up the big-box computer that would make her friends on Olegarten dissolve in giggles. "Gonna swat a gnat with that thing, Jake?" they'd say. Then she plugged the puny modem provided years ago by the cable company into the wall outlet.

It was near midnight when she returned to the kitchen, scraped the dried egg yolk from the plate she'd left in the sink.

She nodded to the rainbow trout on the wall, went up the stairs, changed into her nightgown, and went to bed.

THEY CAME MORE quickly than Jake expected. She had slept a few hours, but her internal clock woke her before five, as usual. She had rinsed the coffee pot and was spooning coffee from the ceramic canister into the coffee maker's basket when the back door burst open, glass shattering.

Jake screamed and dropped the canister. It also shattered, scattering ground coffee and bits of crockery over the kitchen floor. Five agents crowded into the kitchen, huge and alien. They were black-clad and body-armored, faces covered with tactical shields. The leader trained a short-barreled automatic weapon on her.

"Take her down."

One of the black-clad figures approached her, seized her arm.

"No weapons, Sarge." A woman's voice from behind the face shield.

"On the floor," the sergeant shouted, gesturing with his automatic.

"Okay."

The agent took Jake down to the floor, first to kneeling, then with a hand between her shoulder blades, to prone. Forceful but careful, trying to avoid the shards of pottery.

Jake watched, head to one side, cheek on the floor, as the sergeant directed the team, mostly with gestures. Two of the agents moved out of the kitchen into the living room. Heavy boots pounded on the stairs to the second floor.

"Where's your computer?" the sergeant demanded.

"In the sewing room," Jake answered. She discovered that sounding confused and afraid was not hard at all.

The sergeant raised his face shield, which exposed the lined forehead and gray stubble of a middle-aged man.

"Where might the sewing room be?" he asked, his words telegraphing irritation.

"Behind you." The sergeant gestured again with his gun.

"On it," said an agent next to him. He glanced at Jake, presumably saw no imminent threat of violence, and raised his face shield to reveal a dark-haired kid who looked about the age of Jake's eldest grandson. He turned toward the open door of the sewing room, took a couple of steps and froze. The damaged back door, one hinge broken off when the troop entered, leaned against the wall that separated the sewing room from the kitchen. He gave a low whistle. "Got a weapon, Sarge."

He pulled a shotgun from behind the door. "Damn, a Winchester Model 12. A beauty, too."

"Status?" the leader said, still more irritated.

The young man lifted the gun, pointed toward the floor, pulled the slide to open the chamber. "None in the chamber," he said as he pumped again several times and green twelve-gauge cartridges clattered to the floor. "Three in the mag."

The leader turned back to Jake. "What's the shotgun for, Ma'am?"

"You wonder what a widow living in the forest half an hour away from the nearest police station is doing with her husband's shotgun next to the door?" she said. The sergeant's expression changed from irritated to uncomfortable.

"Get her up and into a chair," he said, pointing with his gun toward the breakfast table next to the broken door.

The woman who had stayed crouched next to Jake held her elbow to help her up. Jake leaned heavily and groaned as she rose. Maybe they'd think she was a helpless old lady.

Jake collapsed into a chair. Her knee really did hurt, and a spot of blood clashed with the pink roses on her nightgown.

"What are you doing? Who are you?" Jake asked, adding a querulous note to her voice.

"Homeland Security." The sergeant produced an identity card, held it toward Jake.

"And what are you doing stomping around my house?" Jake's voice came back strong, taking on a commanding tone honed by years as a high school history teacher.

"There is terrorist-related computer traffic coming from your home."

"Sarge?" the young agent who had found the shotgun called from the sewing room. "Found the computer."

The sergeant gestured toward the room, and the woman who had helped Jake joined the young agent. There was a hushed conversation, then she appeared again.

"Is this your only computer?"

"Now, why would I need more than one computer?"

"What is its primary use?"

"My grandchildren talk to me on it."

"Any banking, bill paying?"

"My husband did all of that before he passed on. I do some bills online now, the automatic ones. But mostly I pay by mail."

"Right."

The woman returned to the sewing room. One, then two of the team members came into the kitchen from the dining room.

"Report," the sergeant said. Each, a man and a woman, raised face shields and gave the sergeant a slight shake of the head. Apparently the upstairs, living room, and dining room held nothing of interest.

"Basement?" the sergeant said.

"I'll check it," the woman said.

She peered down the stairs and took the first step tentatively. The Homeland agents in the kitchen looked everywhere but at Jake, who dropped her gaze to her lap and concentrated on looking weak and scared. The agent returned from the basement after only a minute or two, pausing on the top stair to sneeze. The sergeant raised his eyebrows in question.

"Lotta dust. Furniture, a tool bench that doesn't look recently used. Fishing gear. She's got a world-class set of classic

Rapala lures and a St. Croix Legend and—" she belatedly took in the sergeant's glare. "And, um, an old bed. Boxes that look like they've been there a while."

Jake kept her eyes on her lap, hoping to conceal her relief.

The woman in the sewing room called out, "The modem's not password protected, and I found a virus."

"So this is a backdoor?" the sergeant said.

"Probably," the agent said as she came into the kitchen.

Jake peered at the broken door, then at the sergeant.

The agent took in Jake's look and sat down at the table across from her. "A back door is something a person put on your computer," she said. "It's not a physical thing."

"I don't understand what you mean."

"Someone has taken over your computer and used it to send signals on the web," the woman said, pleasant but condescending. She asked Jake to join her at the computer and gave Jake the expected lecture on computer security. Jake showed her pictures of the family reunion a few years ago, she and Kermit posed behind a sheet cake, many identical pictures of grand babies, and . . .

They unplugged the computer and took it and the modem for "further evaluation."

"I talk with my grandson in Illinois every Monday. How—"

"Use your e-pad," the sergeant said. He cleared his throat and studied the kitchen floor. Jake saw that he was covering embarrassment.

"But the picture's so small." She succeeded in looking disappointed.

The sergeant gave Jake a card with several numbers in the Milwaukee office. "They'll be contacting you to fix your door," he said, eyeing the agent who looked like Jake's grandson. The young man had been brushing pieces of crockery into a pile with his foot. "We're done here," he said toward the kid.

The kid finished the pile and said, "Sorry about the coffee," before leaving. The sergeant left last, nodded, and hoped

Jake would have a nice day.

Jake listened as several vehicles started and drove off. She sat for a moment in the quiet of the morning, then stood, chuckled, and retrieved a new bag of coffee from the pantry. She knew they would eventually conclude that the call she made to the IAC had come from room 103 at the Super 8 Motel in Tempe, Arizona. She hoped they would break that door down, too.

CHAPTER TWENTY-FOUR

GRANSTON HARMON SHUTTLED between his situation room, the president's office and that of the vice-president. Everyone's tension notched up a click with each visit. They had decided to pay $500 million and hope the hackers were interested in money rather than politics. The NSA had created a tracing process to follow the money, retrieve it, and lead them to the perpetrators. The size of the ransom made sign-off by the president mandatory, and finding a pot of money large enough and secret enough had been difficult. As tension rose, small issues got tangled between Harmon, the vice president, and the vice-president's volcanic temper. Add to the mix that the president was a cultured Boston Wellesley grad, and the vice president was a 'Bama good ol' boy, and the result was agony for everyone. Piled on top of it all, the original messages had come to Harmon's supposedly secure e-pad. Which raised the issue of Lydia, who seemed to have disappeared. Her family knew nothing about the gall bladder surgery she'd mentioned, and calls went to voice mail.

Harmon sat at his desk running through, for the nth time, how he was going to explain the breach to the FBI. An intern leaned in his office door.

"Valdosta, Georgia," the kid said.

"When?"

"Now. This one's pretty serious. Georgia Power sees nothing. Someone switched the city off."

"How long?"

"It began about an hour ago. At dusk, like Camden. We just learned about it."

"No message yet?"

As if in answer, Harmon's implant bleeped the same tone he'd heard when the first message came. His e-pad, which he had centered on his desk, came alive:

12x this time. 6 bn now. Same instructions

He stared at the message. *12x.* What did they mean by that? Twelve times? The intern still stood at his door, no doubt curious.

"Find me the population of Camden, Maine, and Valdosta."

"Uhh—" The kid apparently realized asking why was not a good idea and turned to leave.

A second bleep was followed by a second message: Next time, 28x

"Hey . . ." What was that kid's name? Jason, wasn't it? "Hey, Jason?"

The kid kept going a few paces, then stopped and turned, looking miffed. "Ethan. It's Ethan."

"Yeah, sure, Ethan. Listen, I need to know all the cities with a population twenty-eight times the size of Valdosta."

Ethan raised an eyebrow. "The city or the MSA?"

Harmon puffed his cheeks out. Was the little prick trying to impress him or just being a jerk? How would he know whether it was the city or Standard Metropolitan Statistical Area?

"Both. Get me both."

BRAD THE NANOWIZ sat at his desk in his garden apartment in the old building, listening to the water pipes rattle in the ceiling above him and his neighbors arguing through the thin wall.

He read over the post he'd drafted, poked uncomfortably

by the horns of a dilemma. He knew that the piece would draw a reaction. Maybe good; maybe bad—in the blogosphere, any reaction brought him a few cents.

Late last night, his anonymous source had called. A 'routine' power failure in Valdosta, Georgia was really a hack. Brad nosed around. A couple of lower-level Georgia Power and Light employees admitted that they had no idea why the city went dark. NanoWiz's leaker hinted that something much bigger was coming. If he got out in front of it . . .

Since his first announcement about Napolitani . . . *the* Napolitani . . . the click rate into his blog had gone up thirty-five percent. He'd supplemented it with several more posts. Napolitani had dropped out of sight, and he sensed that she wouldn't talk to him anyway. It made the posts easier to write, the hints and speculation more . . . piquant. Another click rate bump.

This news would drive his click rate into the stratosphere. His reputation in the materials science industry meant invitations to speak on various related subjects from time to time. The honorarium usually paid for transportation and a chain hotel. He loved the science and the writing. A bump like this might mean he could move out of this dump and wouldn't have to supplement his income by working as a barista on the weekends.

On the other hand, it was off-the-record information, and he had no way to validate it. But it was so logical. First HelioCorp, then Camden, then Valdosta . . . which he had verified, sort of. Now the most recent call. He'd tried again to get background on the leaker. A good reporter would demand it, and to report something this inflammatory in the press without a true source would be an invitation to jail or at least financial ruin. In the blogosphere, maybe nothing. He knew he was cruising near the guard rails. He had already irritated the government. On the other hand, there was no real penalty for dubious reporting except loss of reputation, and maybe not even that. The person had given him some concrete details about stuff he already knew, which established she was pretty high up in the government. Energy, maybe Cybersecurity. Brad pressed, but the person behind the voice cloaking device did a verbal shrug and mentioned she'd call Brad's competition.

The headline almost wrote itself: **Power Out in Valdosta: More Evidence Grid Hacked.**

CHAPTER TWENTY-FIVE

GRANSTON HARMON HAD gotten Homeland to shake loose eleven drones to search the three-hundred-square-mile area IAC identified. Easily done, because Napolitani's disappearance had allowed him to convince them she was part of the problem. Now Harmon stood in his hastily constructed situation room, tempted to call for an update but realizing probably not much had changed in the last half-hour. NSA had estimated a day, a day and a half at most, to complete the survey.

He punched the intercom button.

"Lydia."

"Yes, sir. This is Renaldo Stone, sir."

Ah, yes. Lydia, gall bladder surgery, except . . .

"Get me Volcom."

"Uhh. Yessir. They are . . ."

"She, goddammit. She's at NSA surveillance."

"Ahh, yes. Of course."

Harmon's monitor blinked awake, showing a middle-aged woman wearing a headset, her military bearing apparent in her squared shoulders.

"Status?" Harmon said.

"We have spoken to the IAC person who received the coordinates. We have traced the source of the communication to Tempe, Arizona.

"And this 'dead-man switch'? Have you identified it?"

"It appears to refer to information the oppositional actors do not want public."

Harmon drew a long breath. Now they were oppositional

actors. "Yes, but what is the information?"

"We do not know."

"What *do* you know?"

Volcom seemed unperturbed by Harmon's tone. "The communication with IAC appears to have come from a hacker group called Olegarten." She tapped a keyboard and a backgrounder on Olegarten appeared as a new window on Harmon's monitor. "Napolitani is known to have worked with Olegarten. The message stated that Napolitani is under compulsion to sign into Olegarten and prevent this file from opening. Our analysis indicates it is equally likely this explanation is a red herring."

Harmon signed off and leaned back in his chair, fingers interlaced behind his head, staring at nothing particular. *Napolitani.* He thought back to his meetings with the slender young woman who had turned to whipcord and steel when he raised the issue of this Olegarten group of hers. She had not been what she seemed then. What was she now?

THE WOMAN WHO called herself Marka turned into a Sheetz Quick Stop outside of Harpers Ferry. She felt bad about leaving Napolitani with the troglodyte they'd had to hire when the job turned from assassination to abduction, but it couldn't be helped. She needed to report on time, and she had been warned not to call from the warehouse unless absolutely necessary. She pulled past the gas pumps to the far end of the parking lot, out of range of the surveillance camera, and made her call.

No payment from the government so far. She didn't have perfect knowledge of the conversations that had gone on in Harmon's office in the days before she had to take over management of Napolitani. But the volume and vocabulary that leaked out to the reception desk told her that the AVP's soft nether parts were in a vise. Also that the government suspected Napolitani was responsible for the grid interruption.

How long would they have to hold the Napolitani woman, she wondered. And what would happen when they no longer needed her? If the government thought Napolitani was part of the plot, they must be searching for her. She knew the massive reach of the FBI and Homeland was only restrained by the AVP's fervid desire to keep the whole thing under wraps.

Marka had pulled into the Sheetz because out here in almost-country, stopping at the side of the road might get the attention of the cops or some helpful citizen. On the other hand, the local Sheetz had gas, beer, and food, making it the social center of the small town after everything else was closed by nine. A safe place to make a call.

There were several other cars in the parking lot, none suspicious. She was thirsty and decided to take the small risk of entering the Sheetz. A guy in a paint-spattered coverall stood at the register buying beer. A couple of people faced the wall-long cooler. They moved off toward the register as she selected a Mountain Dew. She approached the counter, only then taking in the two people. A man and a woman, both professionally dressed, looking fit. Did the man say he had to check in? A chill went down Marka's spine.

She watched the two leave. The man pushed the door open, did a quick scan of the parking lot, and turned left out the door. The woman went right. Marka paid for her soda, realizing that her nervous desire to put it back and leave would only make her more memorable . . . the place still had a human clerk. Outside, she watched two cars leave the parking lot, one turning north, one south.

Back in her car, she dug the satellite phone out and called her contact a second time. Her Washington handler had once called him Mongrel, then winced and told her to forget the name. After the time delay, he answered in the same clipped tone she had come to expect.

"I believe the FBI is closing in on us. We may have only a few hours," she said.

"We will move you to a new location. You must be sure Napolitani keeps the file closed for at least another two days. Then you may dispose of her."

Marka stowed the phone in the glove box, hands shaking. She had not signed up for "dispose of her."

When they recruited her, they said they only wanted insight as to what Harmon was doing. It was such a lot of money for her, as well as a fine job for her sister in Volgograd. A conversation, some gossip over coffee once a month. Then, last week, the order to leak details of the power grid hack to a blogger, followed by the order to babysit a female being held "to assure her assistance." They had not mentioned breaking her finger or the awful man she had to work with. The gall bladder surgery excuse would fool no one, and she would be discovered.

She sat in the car, window cracked. Pine scent and new-cut grass. A chorus of tree frogs. Her vision blurred.

Her happy life was over.

She blinked away tears and started the car.

"Up! Get up!"

Weezy startled awake, recoiling from Tattoo, whose nose was almost touching hers.

"Can't."

Tattoo's lips curled into a snarl. "Don't give me your shit, bitch."

"I can't get up," she said, inclining her head toward the ties that restrained her hands.

Tattoo snorted, brought out his knife and severed the ties. "Up."

Weezy stood, stumbled forward.

Tattoo grabbed her arm.

"Don't screw with me," he said.

"Leg's asleep," she mumbled.

Gray light silhouetted Marka at the door.

She caught an odd smell, the piercing clean odor she associated with public restrooms and the biology lab in college. Bleach.

Now fully awake, she shook out her leg and shuffled toward the door. Outside, ground fog surrounded them, deadening sound. The plumber's van was gone. Tattoo pushed Weezy toward a dark green sedan.

"Back seat," he said.

Weezy sat. Tattoo waited to get in until Marka got in the driver's seat, then got in the back seat next to Weezy. He extracted a black fabric bag from his pocket and pulled it over Weezy's head.

"Get down. Lie on your side," Tattoo said.

"Can't. Not enough room."

"Put your head in my lap, darlin'. Plenty of room that way." His hand pulled Weezy toward him and down. "And while you're down south, baby—"

Weezy heard an explosion of Russian from Marka.

"Aw, for chrissake. That rod up your ass getting uncomfortable yet?"

More Russian from Marka.

Tattoo was silent, and Weezy felt his sullenness soaking through the fabric of the bag.

THEY DROVE FOR what seemed like a short time, but Weezy knew the stuff in the water altered her perception.

"It's up the hill." Marka's voice.

She felt the car laboring, then coming to a stop. Tattoo's hand on her arm. How did the simple act of pulling her out of the car seem both suggestive and creepy? A breeze, brief scents of wild magnolia tempered with pine. Too lovely for the current situation.

"Step up."

Her foot on a step that gave under her weight. Finally, the bag came off. A trailer. Like Joe's single-wide in Panacea but older, shabbier. A sofa on one wall sagged under an untidy pile of magazines. It looked as if it had weathered many nights of snoring, drunken stupor. Next to the door, several plastic crates stacked as if someone were on the verge of moving out. A table abutted the pass-through from the kitchen . . . same design as Joe's. A couple of kitchen chairs were askew, as if someone had finished dinner, pushed back, and left. Dirty padding peeked through ripped green Naugahyde seats. Rust freckled once-shiny chromium legs.

Marka's lips curled in disgust. Tattoo didn't seem to mind.

They sat Weezy on one of the chairs. It had no arms, so Tattoo bent her arms behind her and secured her wrists with a plastic tie. The broken finger screamed at her. Tattoo must have heard her intake of breath, because he tweaked the finger. "Seven hours to decide how many more you want broken, little lady."

He ran his knuckles down the side of Weezy's face, to her neck. Marka spat out some Russian. Tattoo let the hand rest where it was, and fear and hatred almost overwhelmed Weezy. Finally, he shrugged and leaned over to rummage through one of the duffel bags sitting next to the door. He pulled out a water bottle and twisted off the cap. He drew a vial with amber liquid from his pocket, smirked at Weezy, poured a small amount into the bottle, and replaced the cap. Then, grinning as if a good thought had crossed his mind, he reopened the bottle and poured another dose of the amber liquid, nodded as if satisfied. Marka, clearly irritated, spat out something in Russian.

"Don't worry, she's getting to like this," Tattoo said as he turned to Weezy, "aren't you, darlin'?"

As disgusting as Tattoo was, he was right. Weezy was getting to look forward to the water. They needed to keep Hell-Kit closed. At some point, they either were or weren't going to kill her. They either were or weren't going to kill Joe. When she was awake, she exhausted herself worrying. Better to doze.

Weezy drank the offered water. Marka said something to Tattoo, then turned away and took packages of crackers, cheese, and lunch meat out of one of the duffels.

Marka crossed to Weezy. "I must sleep. You are going to sleep, as well. If he"—she jerked her head toward Tattoo—"if he touches you, I want you to scream as loud as you can." Marka's face was falling out of focus as the drug hit. Weezy concentrated on nodding. Words caromed off the inside of her skull. "How am I going to scream if . . ."

THE DRONES HAD overflown the area Olegarten identified, sucking in images. The eleventh most likely location of the "target" was halfway to the crest of a hill. A weathered sign advertising *Casto Bros. Transmission* hung lopsided over the front door. Bilious green paint peeled away from concrete blocks. Windows along the front were covered in graying plywood.

The Entry and Analysis team blew through the door and declared all clear. The technician following them in sniffed and said, "Bleached. Bet we're in the right place."

The team leader raised her face shield and looked at the technician quizzically.

He shrugged. "You ever hear of anyone using bleach in a transmission shop? They wiped this place down. If they did a good job, no DNA."

It took the team two hours to find the single spot of dried blood on the floor. The tech lifted it, dissolved it and processed it in his portable sequencer, which transmitted its results to the IAC gene bank. Napolitani.

At the NSA computation center, the analysts and algorithms zeroed in on the video the drones had taken of the building hours before and saw Marka's car. They sewed together stills that formed a connect-the-dots map of the car going west, deeper into the hills. The last shot was from the edge of the circle the drones had inspected. It was taken about two hours before the E and A team hit Casto Bros. But the wilder country allowed few options. It took the redirected drones several hours to spot Marka's car partly hidden under a pignut hickory tree next to a dilapidated trailer near the Virginia border.

Somebody up in the hierarchy wanted the people captured, detained, and held with no access to electronic devices. Their coordinator, sitting safely underground in D.C., warned that the subjects might be heavily armed. The same E and A team that had cleared the warehouse climbed the hill leading to the trailer, scoped out the approach lines. A drone no larger than a sparrow circumnavigated the building, producing hi-res pictures. Pretty straightforward insertion. No way to get to the one entrance entirely under cover, so the leader decided to wait until dusk. Then the team could cross twenty yards from the edge of the forest to the northwest corner of the trailer mostly in shadow. Unless, of course, they'd put up video surveillance.

The leader took a last look through her binoculars and sighed. Can't ever reduce risk to zero, she thought as she gave the signal to move.

WEEZY WAS AGAIN swimming toward the surface of consciousness. The interior of the trailer was quite lovely in the deep orange light from the west-facing windows. She blinked. Marka was nowhere to be seen. Sleeping, she reminded herself. Tattoo slouched on the couch, something playing on his e-pad.

Weezy drifted toward the comfortable oblivion of sleep.

The door swung open, crashing against the crates. A black cylinder rolled across the floor. Tattoo kicked at the thing.

Then came a blinding flash and a deafening blast.

CHAPTER TWENTY-SIX

SWISH-SWISH-SWISH. CEILING TILES swimming by. Pain when she tried to move. Someone talking, far away. There was something she needed to do. Right now. She struggled to remember what it was.

Weezy came awake with a start. Ceiling tiles again. This time not moving. She craned her neck. Instruments, monitors next to her bed. A shot of pain from her cheek made her recoil, and she realized her face and neck were bandaged. She coughed, and a face appeared, mumbling something. The face belonged to a man with close-cropped hair. He was wearing a shapeless blue shirt, a blurry name tag, and something around his neck . . . stethoscope. The voice came again, far away, behind an ocean sound, as if someone was standing in the surf, calling, and she was on the beach. The man looked across her at the instruments. His voice came in stronger.

"Ms. Napolitani? Louise? Can you hear me?"

"Uh-huh." Then, "Where am I?"

"You're in the hospital. You were injured when the entry team used a stun grenade, but—"

"What time"—Weezy struggled to sit up—"is it?"

"Take it easy. Lie back. No need to—"

"What. Thefuck. Time. Is it?" She had risen almost to sitting position. Her cheek, her left leg, and her left arm were screaming. The instrument cluster at her bedside bleeped. At the top margin, above the heart rate trace (110 and rising) was the time: 9:14.

"My e-pad. I need my e-pad." She felt herself breathing hard, getting dizzy.

Too late, too late pounded behind her eyes. *Too late, too late.*

"I can't do that, Louise. I . . . ahh." He glanced toward the door, where another man stood.

"I need an e-pad. Please."

Her breath came in short gulps. *Too late, too late.*

The man at the door came toward the bed. "You are under arrest, Ms. Napolitani. You are not allowed access to electronic dev—"

"Two men are going to die if . . ." Sobs came in great gasps. *9:14. They are already dead. My precious love is already . . .*

Then, panicked, "Get an e-pad. You can run it yourself. I'll tell you what to do. I'll—"

The man gave away no emotion. "Not gonna happen."

Weezy rolled to her side, away from the man. She folded into a fetal curl, arm clasping arm, and cried, gasping, almost retching.

They've killed him.

THE NEXT HOURS were a blur. Weezy was vaguely aware of the nurse giving her pills and offering water. She didn't care. She supposed they were giving her something for pain, but whatever it was only made her numb.

At length, she woke. Gray light of dawn, rain against the window. A woman in light blue scrubs was straightening her pillow. Her name tag said Keesha, RN.

"Let me take a look at those dressings." Her voice was a rich contralto, comforting. Tiny braids swayed, colorful beads clicked as she leaned toward Weezy. She smelled of soap and something floral. She pulled gently at the bandage on Weezy's face, then checked Weezy's arm. She pulled back the sheet covering Weezy's legs, stopped, grasped the privacy curtain.

"Leave the curtain open." A gruff male voice.

Weezy raised her head. The same man she'd seen before sat across the room on a straight-back chair.

Keesha's eyes narrowed. "I'm fixing to do a pelvic. You really think I'm gonna let you look on?"

The agent stood and squared his shoulders.

"This woman is subject to Homeland Security Restriction. She must be in my sight at all times and can't use electronic devices. I see that you have an e-pad in your pocket, so you cannot—"

Keesha crossed to the agent, extracting her e-pad. Her body mass index possibly said obese, but her grace said solid, and her attitude said watch out. The agent had eight inches and maybe sixty pounds on her, but he stepped back. She slapped the e-pad on his chest.

"Hold on to this while I complete my examination."

Back behind the curtain, Keesha pushed Weezy's gown up. Her fingers were gentle, probing. "Men," she said under her breath. Then, "You got a small tear, but gonna be fine, girl, just fine."

Weezy lay back, staring at the ceiling, tears running down the side of her face, collecting in her ears.

I'm never going to be just fine.

CHAPTER TWENTY-SEVEN

HELLO KITTY? HELLO fucking Kitty?

Granston Harmon stared into the monitor, watching a white cartoon cat with a pink bow dancing across the screen.

Hell-Kit was Hello Kitty? Not the crushing blow to the hackers who had made his life miserable?

He'd been duped. They'd all been duped.

First, the money. Then Lydia, the secretary he'd trusted with important secrets turned out to be a Russian operative. Shock enough. She was as close a friend as a person five grades below him could be. Now this.

Lydia could be explained, spun. Anybody might be taken advantage of by a skillful operative . . . after all, she made it through a full background check. Not his fault. And she had to be the source of the leak to that pipsqueak blogger, Nano-something or other. But Hello Kitty? Hello Kitty would come out, and it would be worse by far. He imagined the talk show hosts cutting him, the laughter. It would turn to brutal broadsides when the press discovered the half-billion dollars he had paid for a bunch of kids' videos. The chain of command that signed off on the payment would be silent. After that the beltway knives would come out.

Tactical options swirled in his mind, none of them good. His career was over.

HELLO KITTY? WHAT is this Hello Kitty? Little cats dancing?!

Mongrel slammed the satellite phone shut, dropped his

head, and leaned back into the soft cushions of the Mercedes. His hand came up to rub his temples, and a moan, half laugh, escaped his lips. He caught his driver's quizzical expression in the rearview mirror and gave a quick shake of his head. The driver's eyes shifted away from the mirror.

Mongrel thought for a moment. Then he punched a number, put the phone back to his ear. There was a brief delay, then an answer. "Execute the Philadelphia interruption," Mongrel said. "We must go now, not day after tomorrow. Then leak the news. The Americans will pay one more time." He signaled his driver to go, then cut off the call.

He waited as the big car nosed into the boulevard, then dialed again. "The Philadelphia interruption will happen tonight. Verify that the instructions are in place. Then kill them," Mongrel said, a tremor in his voice, "Kill them all."

CHAPTER TWENTY-EIGHT

GRANSTON HARMON PUSHED himself up from his desk.

"Let's get this over with," he grumbled to himself.

There was no way around the meeting. He would have liked to have it in his office where the appurtenances of his position were arrayed. His new secretary had seen the headcount and set it for the conference room instead. Now, as people arrived, they would be confronted by Renaldo. That would remind them of Lydia. Lydia, whom everyone knew and loved, who was so helpful, so friendly. Lydia, who had been leaking secrets to Russia for years. Lydia, who had dropped his life in the crapper and flushed.

The conference room held an omnium gatherum of heavy hitters, most trailing support staff. His own chief of staff, the ambitious prick, was sucking up to the Homeland deputy director. Her trailing case officer had taken a seat along the wall behind the director. The head of the IAC was there, also a step above normal, with two support staff. The president's national security advisor herself had replaced the colonel who would have been the normal choice. The FBI representative, Assistant Director Henry Barber, was also a grade above the usual attendee for such a meeting. He was alone, apparently not needing support.

Harmon saw the schadenfreude in guarded smiles as he entered. A screwup this massive required sacrifice, and he felt like Leviticus's original scapegoat. No doubt he would be cast out of DC and into the desert like that goat.

Coffee had been poured and minimal pleasantries exchanged. When people had taken seats, Harmon turned to

Barber. "Bring us up to speed."

"The cell in West Virginia has been deactivated. Homeland breached a trailer there. I believe most of you have seen the video." Several heads nodded. "Napolitani was rescued with some injuries. The team captured a man with a long criminal history and a woman who was a deep cover agent acting as the AVP's secretary."

Several eyes swung to Harmon.

"What about Napolitani?" Harmon asked, anxious to move on. "Why was she there?"

"She was apparently being forced to keep closed several data files that the power grid hackers feared would expose them," Barber continued. "The protection mechanism operated through a group called Olegarten Manufacturing."

The national security advisor's brow furrowed. Barber turned to her. "It's an internet chat room comprised of high-level technical experts. Your staff is familiar with them."

"Hackers," Harmon added.

Barber shrugged. "Sometimes, I'm sure. The department has had two interactions with them. Both times, they helped us. And they're as good or better technically than our people. Your folks"—he nodded at the IAC director—"got intel from Olegarten that led to the capture of Napolitani and the two Russian operatives."

"I don't like the government working with a bunch of hackers," Harmon said. He turned to the Homeland deputy director. "Did you find the source of that supposedly friendly hacker who sent the location information?"

"We traced the signal through many servers to a house near Solon Springs, Wisconsin," she said. "Way out in the sticks. Nice lady there had a rudimentary setup. She seemed clueless about technology. Our bad guys probably put a back door on her machine. We're working to trace the signal beyond her."

"Who's behind this?" Harmon addressed his question to Barber, but his glance swept the room.

"We don't know for certain," Barber said. "It appears to be a Russian group, possibly connected to an oligarch named Volkov. He was one of the new premier's confidantes until he disappeared about a year ago."

"What's the motive?" Harmon asked.

"On the face of it, money. A variation on ransomware, where a hacker would put a virus on a computer, encrypt all its data, then demand money to decrypt. But I think it's more than that." Barber paused, as if considering whether to continue.

"I think this power grid hack is designed to showcase software that would offer the new premier a powerful tool to increase his status by disrupting our economy. I'm speculating of course, but there's some evidence—"

"CyberWar Two." Someone said it softly.

Barber glanced downward, lips pressed together. "Yes."

"Where are we on finding them?" Harmon asked.

"The woman who was posing as the AVP's secretary tried to commit suicide and was nearly successful. It's not clear when, if ever, we will be able to question her." Barber paused for what seemed to Harmon like a small eternity. "The man we picked up with her appears to be hired muscle. He's anxious to cooperate, terrified of going to prison, but he doesn't seem to know much. There's a dead man in Florida named Renfro, possibly connected to the HelioCorp hack," Barber said. "Meanwhile, Mayfield has disappeared. Homeland's working hypothesis is he was involved with the Russians, Renfro found out, and Mayfield killed him. Evidence at the scene—Mayfield's fingerprints on the murder weapon—supports that hypothesis. Most of the rest of the evidence doesn't."

He paused again. "In the first place, the motivation is unclear. Renfro was the key to HelioCorp's survival and by extension, to Mayfield's success. He saved HelioCorp from bankruptcy by a last-minute investment, and he'd put together a consortium of follow-on investors which will probably collapse now. Hard to imagine what reason Mayfield would have to kill him."

"Those fingerprints, though." The Homeland deputy director looked to Harmon. "Pretty clear. Maybe that first interruption at the solar power company was pulled off by Mayfield, Napolitani, and this Renfro. Mayfield planned to off Renfro, then join Napolitani."

Barber steepled his fingers and nodded, but continued, "Another possibility is that it was Renfro helping the bad guys. If Renfro knew the original failure was the first Russian grid hack, that would be an opportunity to invest at a bargain-basement price. Maybe he was eliminated because he was no longer useful. In that scenario, Mayfield may be a hostage. If Napolitani believed he would be killed if that file opened, she would keep it closed."

Harmon squared his shoulders and put on his no-nonsense face. "So, speculation, but no hard answers, right?" He scanned the room, found none, and continued, "Last item. The blackmailers . . . hackers . . . sent a threat about the next strike." He turned to his own chief of staff. "Where will that be?"

The man consulted his papers, savoring his time in the spotlight. Harmon exhaled noisily. The man said, "The message said '28x,' probably meaning twenty-eight times the population of Valdosta. A half-dozen cities fit that profile, but only two are served by the Eastern Interconnection: Philadelphia for sure and San Antonio, assuming they can get into the Texas subsection. Our analysis says Philadelphia."

Harmon leaned back in his chair, laced his fingers behind his head. After a moment, he squared his shoulders. "Bottom line . . . How close are we? Homeland?"

"We have only speculation." The woman, a well-known retired marine commander, clipped her words, as if lack of certainty offended her.

"Barber?"

"Clues, no conclusions."

"IAC?"

"Nothing, but knowing Philadelphia is the target, we may be able to protect the big plants on the Delaware."

Harmon sniffed. "So, we got nothing, right?"

Silence.

He cleared his throat. "Put another way, we're playing defense with no plan for offense. We think they might attack Philly, we may be able to protect power there, but then they'll still be out there . . . or do you assembled geniuses think these mystery bad guys will drop the whole project when they haven't tried Washington, New York, or LA?"

"Couldn't be LA," Harmon's chief said, "because the attacks have all been to the Eastern—" Harmon's stare silenced him.

"They may want to eliminate Napolitani," the Homeland director said. "She may know enough to damage them."

Barber spoke up. "We plan to put her in a safe house in a day or two. You,"—he nodded to the Homeland director—"are guarding her in the hospital, correct?"

"Yes, of course."

Harmon stood, signaling an end to the meeting. As people filed out, Harmon gestured to his chief of staff to remain, then caught the Homeland deputy director as she prepared to leave.

He lowered his voice and said, "We need to know if there are other operatives in our system. If they want to eliminate Napolitani and know where she is . . ."

". . . they'll show themselves," the chief said. Harmon glared at the man, whose desire to impress Homeland apparently overrode caution. Which gave Harmon the idea he needed.

"Perhaps you could take over management of Napolitani from the FBI," he said to the Deputy Director. "I'm sure you will be able to arrange that, given the international implications of this hack. Put her in a safe place, of course, but one which may flush out our hackers."

The deputy director gave him a quizzical look, then the meaning hit. "We can do that," she said with a curt nod.

Harmon strolled back toward his office, some of the weight off his shoulders. Both the Homeland deputy director and Harmon's chief of staff knew exactly what he was suggesting. He would turn this around yet. Maybe he would be the hero of The Great Grid Hack. A book deal? A six-, maybe seven-figure advance.

Too bad about Napolitani, though.

CHAPTER TWENTY-NINE

Raskov moved a knight. It was early in their second game of the morning. The first had ended in a draw. Raskov was sure Puusepp let that happen. Easier to keep playing than sit silently or contemplate the real endgame. Raskov shifted on the metal folding chair, easing the tightness in his lower back. A high-pitched motor started in the shop next door.

Regret tugged at Raskov. He cursed himself for having made the mistake of caring about Puusepp, when he knew . . . and Puusepp knew, too . . . what the endgame would be.

Raskov had worried too much about the instruction to pull forward the attack on Philadelphia. United Energy was nothing if not schedule driven. Puusepp was able to breach the IAC at exactly the same time United Energy was load leveling. They had "dropped the bomb" as Pyotr liked to say. Philadelphia would go dark that evening. Perhaps this would force the Americans to pay the ransom, and this project would be finished.

Raskov was ahead a knight and a pawn, hoping for a win and irritated with Mayfield. The guy talked and talked. Napolitani was well-known, he said, an important person. Homeland Security would be on the case with all their resources. The IAC trackers would figure out what was going on. Any electronic signal could be traced. The FBI would find Napolitani and then this warehouse.

His yammering had the ring of truth, which ruined Raskov's concentration. Speaking Russian, he described which animals had done what to Mayfield's mother, what she had done back to them, and how much she had enjoyed the interactions. He used all the artistry of the *mat* he had perfected growing up in the streets of Minsk. He noted Mayfield's blank stare during the soliloquy. He turned to Puusepp and said, "He does not speak Russian."

He then turned to Mayfield and told him to be quiet or he would let Pyotr break the boredom by removing some of his body parts. Slowly. He said it in a matter-of-fact voice. Mayfield shut up.

Raskov had sent Pyotr out to buy food for a midday meal. He and Puusepp returned to their chess match and a discussion that had been building over several days.

"Maksym, the Sobaki are playing a game Pyotr would call 'old school.' "

"Old school?"

"Yes. Their response to a challenge to their power is to kill the source of the problem. Their plan has always been to execute phase two, or three, or whatever is necessary to achieve their goals, then eliminate the participants. Except, maybe, you." Puusepp moved a knight out of danger. "They think they are in the endgame, and they think they know all the moves. Old school," Puusepp said.

Raskov, seeing an opening, advanced a bishop, but held his finger atop the piece as he scanned the board. Then, embarrassed, took the piece back when he realized he would lose it in two moves.

"What the Sobaki don't understand is that you can kill me, but I will continue to exist. There are two Puusepps, Maksym. The one sitting here, about to capture your rook—" Raskov's eyes jumped to his remaining rook, seemingly safe on the first rank—"and there is HoHumJr, a person who exists only on the internet. Like you said earlier, the man in front of you has blood, feels pain. That man is weak and can be made to do almost anything, but the Sobaki can't torture, can't eliminate, can't intimidate HoHumJr."

"The real Puusepp must destroy Hell-Kit." Raskov said. "All the copies. And you must convince me that it will never surface."

"You must look to your own survival, Maksym."

Raskov covered his rook, which drew a nod of approval from Puusepp.

"You are an intelligent man, Maksym. You must understand that Sobaki's operating tactic blunts any threats to destroy Hell-Kit. If I'm dead anyway . . ."

"You must destroy Hell-Kit, Kalju. The real Puusepp is still alive, still feels pain."

"The real Puusepp and HoHumJr know Hell-Kit is infinitely replicable, how many copies of it exist, and where they are stored."

Puusepp paused to inspect the board and move a pawn. "You must know this project, this phase two, is in jeopardy," he continued. "How do the Sobaki respond to failure, Maksym? A pat on the back and 'better next time'?"

Raskov felt a spike of anger. This little man understood the project so well. He saw its motivation and its outcome. Sobaki projects usually involved people who were hopeful or greedy. They were shocked in the instant before Raskov pulled the trigger.

Puusepp gave an elfin grin.

"You know Zugzwang, Maksym? In chess?"

"When you have to make a move, and there isn't a good one?" Raskov said, thinking back to the chess club and the mentor who taught him to value himself when no one else did.

Puusepp beamed. "Exactly. The German translates to 'tight spot,' though. You are in a tight spot, Maksym. Maybe no *good* move, but that is not the same as having *no* move."

In spite of himself, Raskov wanted to hear Puusepp's always-brilliant analysis. He'd been in plenty of tight spots before and survived. Maybe . . .

"Let us lay out the endgame, Maksym. One possibility is that this project will come to whatever conclusion the Sobaki envision. But it's not going according to plan, is it?" Getting no confirmation, he continued, "Do you want to return to

Moscow to report a partial success?"

Puusepp gazed owlishly at Raskov the way a professor might, waiting for him to draw the correct conclusion. Raskov shrugged.

"But there are other, more likely options," Puusepp continued. "The Napolitani woman may have been rescued. She will want to keep the file closed to save Mr. Mayfield, here." Mayfield raised his head at the mention of Napolitani. "But I suspect her government will want to expose the Project. They will want to open Hell-Kit. What will you do then, Maksym?"

Without waiting for an answer, Puusepp continued, "Simple, you say. Execute Puusepp and Mayfield. Pyotr, as well. Then disappear. But no, you will think, I cannot use the papers the Sobaki gave me. And what will I do for money? The Sobaki will watch my cash accounts. I will be looking over my shoulder for the rest of my life."

Drawn in, Raskov said, "But if Hell-Kit opens . . ."

"Ahh, yes." Puusepp grinned, the happy teacher of a bright student. "Of course. The Sobaki will be destroyed, and you, Maksym, will be free. Of course, it will be prudent to perform the executions to make a clean break. But where will you go? Back to Russia and explain to the FSB that, while you used to work for the Sobaki, you are now anxious to serve Mother Russia? No, you will need to disappear."

Puusepp frowned, a theatrical gesture, Raskov thought. "But you will need papers. Money, a place to live, a believable occupation. A new life, Maksym."

Raskov had been through these calculations many times, tossing sleepless on the cot's lumpy mattress.

"It may be that I can help you, Maksym. I have many resources, many contacts. Of course, I will have to be alive to do these things."

Raskov turned his attention back to the board, rolling the possibilities over in his mind. Hell-Kit is the king, he thought. Like the king, essential, the focus of the game, but almost powerless. Also more valuable to him closed than open. Odd to think it, but maybe . . .

"Puusepp, give me the file. All copies. I may let you live."

JOE HAD ALMOST dozed off. The heat of the Florida morning baked through the corrugated roof of the warehouse. Raskov and the little guy they called Puusepp had been playing chess for hours, as if waiting for something to happen. Pyotr had gone out a while ago. Joe had done his best sell job on why they should give themselves up. Raskov had let him talk for a while, then told him to shut up.

Joe's chair was rickety, a condition he was careful to hide. At first, they had secured each foot to a chair leg with plastic straps. There were no arms on the chair, so they'd bent his arms around the back of the chair, which cut circulation. They didn't care about the pain it caused him, but the irritation of having to cut the straps every time they took him to the toilet did get to them. Finally, they'd given up and strapped his wrists together in front of him. After all, he wasn't much of a flight risk. If he ran, Napolitani would die. And he'd have to make it thirty feet to a door he couldn't easily open to get away. They had positioned him between the two decrepit offices and the table, which was near the center of the room. Raskov sat on Joe's right, in position to keep an eye on both Joe and the entrance, which was over Joe's left shoulder. Puusepp was across the table from Raskov, back to the door.

Still, Joe had some hope. He knew the "your woman will die" threat was bogus . . . they needed her to keep the fail-deadly file closed. They had run short of straps, so they bound only his right ankle to the chair. The chair had metal legs that allowed the ankle strap some slippage. He had considered trying to work his foot free but held off. Despite the chess game, Raskov was observant. Nighttime might give Joe cover.

Raskov and Puusepp were having an intense conversation, or maybe Russian always sounded that way. But Joe picked out Napolitani and Mayfield often enough to think they were talking about the current situation. Was Puusepp trying to convince Raskov of something? Was Raskov looking interested?

PUUSEPP WAS PLEASED that Raskov had discovered the logic of his plan. He had come to think of Raskov as a promising student. If he gave Raskov Hell-Kit, he would have to do it in such a manner that he wouldn't open it right away. Raskov would not be impressed to see countless Hello Kitty pictures and videos.

The game ended in a draw. Raskov went to the far end of the work bench, presumably to check on the software they had injected into the IAC. Or maybe it was to give Puusepp time to reflect on his options.

Raskov returned and set the board up for another game. "So, we wait," he said, advancing his queen's pawn. Puusepp moved a knight.

The warehouse door opened. Pyotr entered, carrying a bucket of chicken and a twelve-pack of the watery stuff they called light beer in America.

Pyotr crossed to the table where Puusepp and Raskov sat. Raskov glanced up, then back to the board. No thank-you, no recognition. Puusepp caught the anger in Pyotr's clenched jaws.

Pyotr slammed the bucket of chicken on the table. Two of the chess pieces fell over and something dropped from the underside of the table. Raskov's surprise quickly became anger tinged with contempt; his jaw set as he prepared to dress Pyotr down.

Pyotr ignored the coming tirade, stooped to put down the beer and pick up the bottlecap-sized thing from the floor.

"Well, smack my ass and call me Judy. What's this?" Pyotr held up the device as if to inspect it. "Seems like your conversation has been broadcast." He flipped the device onto the chess board. "Including that part about screwing Sobaki to save your worthless—"

Raskov's thighs hit the table as he shot up, scattering chess pieces and launching the bucket of chicken in an arc toward Pyotr. It fell between them and burst, ejecting wings and drumsticks. Pyotr's hand went to the small of his back as Raskov rose. Puusepp watched the choreography play out in slow motion. Pyotr's hand rising with a snub-nose, chrome-plated pistol; the blast, echoing; Raskov sitting back down, his expression one of puzzlement, a red third eye in the middle of his forehead.

Pyotr grinned at the dead man. "You thought Sobaki would put you out here without a watcher, did you, Maksym?"

Then he swung the short barrel toward Puusepp.

"Well, little man, you managed to screw things up pretty bad, didn't you? Bet you thought you were real clever to create a file with junk in it. See, Napolitani has failed to set the switch. And, like they say here in the USA, you're toast."

Puusepp thought of the real fail-deadly. Only a month until it opened. It would be too bad not to see the look on this cretin's face when the tide of data flowed across the internet and drowned him and the rest of the people who killed his family.

Puusepp stared into the dark eye of the gun. A movement in his peripheral vision, a sound. The hammer came back.

BLAM!

Joe's shoulder smashed into Pyotr's rib cage as the gun went off. Dragging the chair attached to his leg, stumbling into the table, disoriented and half-deafened by the blast, he drove Pyotr. The two hit the floor, tangled in the chair and broken table, Pyotr screaming in Russian. Joe's arms, still bound in front, were trapped against Pyotr. Pyotr was trying to raise the gun, which was wedged between his side and the ground. Joe used his weight and leverage to stop the motion. His bound hands found Pyotr's waistband and jerked, trying to turn him face down. Hot breath rasped in Joe's ear.

Blam!

The blast, muffled this time, seared Joe's left leg. In reflex, Joe rolled away from the hurt, dragging Pyotr with him, freeing the gun. Six hands fought for control.

Puusepp was standing over them, trying to pry the gun out of—

Blam!

Pyotr uttered a surprised "Huh?" Joe rolled off him, feeling his leg go numb. Pyotr sat up, holding the gun loosely. He made brushing motions over the patch spreading rapidly on his Hawaiian shirt, red clashing with the yellow and green of the pineapples and palm trees.

Puusepp grabbed the gun, grimaced as if he found it disgusting, and tossed it toward the office door behind him. He turned back to Joe. "It is, I hope, not so bad. I will get help." Then he was gone.

Joe propped himself on his elbows, then sat up. There was a long, charred tear in his pants, blood obscuring a wound in his thigh. Blood pooled on the floor, engulfing a chicken wing, its tip reaching aloft as if sailing in a red sea. Joe's vision blurred.

Don't bleed out.

His hands shook as he pulled at his belt. Black crept from the outer edges of his vision as he used his last energy to cinch it around his thigh, seeing Weezy's face as she turned to him from the bow of their canoe, her lips forming a word he could not understand.

Don't bleed . . .

CHAPTER THIRTY

PUUSEPP PUSHED THE warehouse door open to a blinding sun. His breath came in staccato spasms So much blood. He'd never seen so much blood. They must have emergency responders here. How would he call them? What would they do to Puusepp himself?

As his eyes adjusted, he saw that he was on an asphalt loading area, probably the back of the building. A chain-link fence separated him from a road. Too high and too exposed to go over. He stood at one end of several similar units. An open field lay at the far end. Go that way? He took a few steps. No, too risky to cross the open space. To his right, fan-like bushes separated him from the next set of buildings. Maybe that way? He hesitated, still breathing hard. When he turned to look down the row again, four men were staring at him. One was talking on a phone.

They had come out of a machine shop next door to the warehouse. Both overhead doors were raised, and work had stopped.

"What the fuck's going on over there?"

"Doctor," Puusepp said. "We need a doctor."

"We heard gunshots. Called 911 already. What happened?"

In the distance, Puusepp heard sirens.

"There is a man with a gun inside."

He jerked his head toward the door he'd just come through. "Perhaps go inside your building and close . . ." The men were already scrambling toward the nearest unit, one reaching to pull the chain that brought the overhead door down.

Puusepp scuttled onto the gravel path that separated the warehouse from scraggly palm bushes. The sirens grew louder. He caught a glimpse of two white cars, lights flashing, turning onto the service road a block away. Shortly, tires screeched and doors slammed, very near and farther off. Shouts came from the front and back of the warehouse.

Puusepp moved up the path, cursing under his breath at the crunch of gravel. A high, dense hedge blocked the path at the front of the building. More sirens sounded. Two boxy, yellow ambulances followed the same route as the white cars. The sirens cut off when they reached the entrance to the loading area. He heard shouted questions, an overhead door grinding open.

Puusepp stopped, calculating, tempted to stay quiet in the shade of the tree and hedge. Hide in plain sight. They might not look carefully. A radio squawked, startling him. "All clear in front" from the other side of the hedge.

The palm bushes were low but dense. Water runoff from the roof had created one bare spot. Puusepp glanced toward the back of the building. Nothing . . . yet. He paused, uncertain. Help had arrived for Joe. Perhaps he should walk back down the path, give himself up. But he was a foreign national with no identification. With one, maybe two, dead in the warehouse, he was the obvious suspect.

He pushed through the spindly bushes.

He brushed himself off. The benign-looking fronds had scratched his arms and shins in a dozen places. Gravel crunched. He dropped to his knees, crawled behind a particularly dense stand of the nasty palm bushes and lay flat. Footsteps passed a few feet away. They moved toward the hedge at the front edge of the building, paused, then returned and stopped. Puusepp stared through the bushes at black brogans, box-toed, no more than five feet from him. Cop shoes. Ants navigated his face and legs. One found his left nostril inviting. Puusepp clenched his teeth. *Don't sneeze . . . don't sneeze.* A radio squawked a garbled question. "All clear on the north edge," the owner of the shoes said, and the shoes disappeared toward the back of the building.

Puusepp blew out his nose as quietly as possible, rose to hands and knees and took his bearings. Then he rose and stood stock-still, listening. All the voices now seemed to be coming from the loading area. The neighbor to the warehouses was a small strip mall. He walked as quickly as he could without jogging across the open area between the bushes and the back of it. He made it to the partial cover of the buildings and dropped behind a dumpster overflowing with stinking plastic bags. Must be behind a restaurant, one which served a lot of fish. He peeked around the edge of the dumpster. Sweat ran into his eyes, stinging. More sirens. They would come searching. Puusepp brushed the sweat away, stood, and pulled one of the bags from the dumpster.

He held the bag carefully away from his side and walked toward the far end of the strip of buildings, hoping the police wouldn't be too curious about an employee taking out garbage. A few more steps to the end of the building and a trash bin. He began to relax, to hope. He tossed the bag into the bin, turned toward the street, and . . .

A police car was parked directly in front of him.

Puusepp froze, trying to control a rising sense of panic. He dared a closer look. Nobody in the car.

He trudged slowly toward the car. As he passed to the front of the building, two uniformed officers emerged from one of the businesses. One shrugged. They turned away from Puusepp, then into the next business down the strip.

Puusepp crossed the street and walked a couple of blocks, forcing himself to keep a casual pace. The scratches from the palm bushes were now showing scarlet. On his legs, too, below his cargo shorts. His face stung, and his left ear was still ringing from the gunshot as Mayfield tackled Pyotr. He again saw the gun, cylinder rotating as Pyotr prepared to send him home. The acrid smell hanging in the air. Him shocked, in stasis while Mayfield fought Pyotr. So close, so near death.

He stopped, hands on his knees like an exhausted runner, and sobbed a couple of breaths. Raskov, Mayfield bleeding. Napolitani probably dead. He had to stay among the living and stay free. He owed them.

Puusepp straightened and continued at a controlled pace. After a couple of blocks, he came upon a park. In Tallin, they would have called it a pocket park. Here, it was three or four lots of stunted grass losing its battle against sand and sun, a rusted swing set, and a trash can. Two benches angled from each other were set beneath the spreading branches of a massive tree. One of them was occupied by an old man, hands and chin resting on a cane, staring into space, perhaps dozing. Puusepp, suddenly exhausted, dropped onto the other bench, his back obliquely to the old man.

"Y'all been fightin' somethin'." The old gentleman wasn't asleep after all. Puusepp turned toward him.

"Yes, I have tried to pass through some small palm trees, and—"

The old gentleman laughed, "Y'all been bit by the saw palmetto." He turned to contemplate Puusepp. "Where you from?"

Puusepp had seen very few black people except on video. This man had deep mahogany skin, lined and polished like old leather. A smile let Puusepp know he sympathized with the pasty-white, bald guy with the bruised face and scratches on his arms and legs.

"Y'all ought to take care a' them marks, son. They can blow up somethin' fierce." He looked Puusepp up and down, another smile spreading over his face. "You better stay out of the sun, too. Otherwise, you gonna get fried, sure enough."

Puusepp felt himself relaxing, building a story. "I have only been here a few days. Two men asked me for money. They had a gun. They pushed me into the little palm trees. I missed my bus. All my informations are in my hotel." He laid on the accent. "They stole my e-pad. I need to replace it so I can call my sister. Is there a place near here—"

The old gentleman was working an e-pad out of his pocket. "Where you callin'?"

Puusepp thought quickly. Some place few would know. "Montenegro."

"I don't expect this here pad gonna want ta call Monte—what you say?"

"Montenegro. But I need to buy a new pad anyway."

The gentleman slipped the e-pad out, said to it, "E-pad store near here." He handed it to Puusepp. The map showed a couple of stores within walking distance. Puusepp bowed his head to the old man. "Thank you for your help."

"You take care a' them cuts and scratches. And you be careful in this part a' town, too."

THE *E!!* STORE was on a main street of wherever Puusepp was. The displays included every imaginable electronic gadget, from basic e-pads to personal security, replacement modules for appliances to single-task robots. It was free of customers when Puusepp entered. The young woman at the counter did a double take, eyes wide, gave him a thin smile and trotted to the door marked employees only. Puusepp waited, inspecting e-pads under glass and advertisements for communication plans. In due course, a young man appeared. He also did the double take Puusepp was coming to expect.

"Can I help you find—"

"Yes. I need an e-pad. You see"—the heavy accent again—"mine, it is stolen."

"Ahh. So sorry. Do you have an account with a telecom service provider?"

"Yes, it is Eesti Telia."

The young man's brow knit. "I don't think that's a regular telecom—"

"It is in Estonia."

"Oh, well, I'm sorry. We can't set up an account with that firm."

Perfect. Better than he had hoped.

For the next several minutes, Puusepp let the young man grind through all the possibilities. It was difficult to sound clueless yet direct the young man to the right answer. But he finally got there.

"I'm sorry sir. The best I can do is sell you a temporary data service subscription. You will have to get in touch with your service provider when you get home to transfer this new e-pad to your existing account."

Puusepp tried to look disappointed.

"You can purchase temporary service blocks in one-half, one, two or five terabytes."

"Ten."

The young man, helpful now, said, "You probably won't need that much capacity, and these one-off subscriptions are quite expensive."

Damn.

"I . . . umm . . . I don't mind paying. I want to take many pictures. To send home."

The kid shrugged. "That's an awful lot of pictures." But Puusepp's apparent lack of sophistication and the opportunity to sell high-margin data services apparently got the kid over the speed bump of wondering why this strange-looking man might want to take five million snapshots.

The kid read off the list of purchases and announced the total, $976.47.

"And in bitcoin?" Puusepp raised his eyebrows, knowing the likely answer.

The kid's face fell. "I'm sorry sir, we're not allowed to transact in bitcoin."

"No?" Puusepp put on a shocked look. "In Europe . . ."

"Sorry. Company policy. But if you could convert . . ."

"I would have to do it through a secure connection, and that is only on my stolen e-pad."

"If you like, I can run you through our secure store connection, and you can perhaps trade some bits into dollars?"

Fifteen minutes later, Puusepp left the store. He carried a new e-pad, the access code to the store's secure connection, and enough data capacity to move his files—the ones he protected with the real fail-deadly—to Olegarten.

PUUSEPP SAT IN a bar a couple of miles from the warehouse. Late afternoon sun slipped through bay windows, and idle conversation surrounded him. He took another sip of the first good beer he'd had since his capture.

He'd written every number and web address he remembered on the new e-pad. He did not have a photographic memory, but years of chess had sharpened his recall. He'd been able to record most of the entry codes to the IAC. He'd memorized part of the bank routing instructions Raskov transmitted when the government paid some of the ransom Sobaki demanded. He would need time and quiet to flesh out the connections and run down the money.

He hoisted the beer and gave a small tip of the glass in celebration of capitalism. He'd been able to acquire an e-pad, open an online bank account, convert enough bitcoin for his reasonable needs, purchase some clothes he thought quite stylish, get rid of the ridiculous running shoes, hail an autocar, and buy a beer. All in an afternoon. Of course, he still had the problem of identity.

The Wi-Fi signal was strong from the restaurant next door. The secure connection he'd memorized at the e-pad store had allowed him to download his security software so he didn't have to go naked into Olegarten. The familiar website came up, and memory flooded him. He was a child, sitting on his grandfather's lap. The scent of home, the warmth of the fireplace, the rumble of the old man's voice as the poetry of the *Kalevipoeg* rolled off his tongue. Puusepp tapped the last few keys, oblivious to conversation around him. He touched the spiky white flower in the lower right corner of the Olegarten home page and began the sign-in protocol. He was HoHumJr again. He was home.

JAKE WAITED A couple of days to unpack her gear after the Homeland agents left. She had dragged the sewing machine cases up from the basement and set up the computer, monitors, modems. The cases had gone back to their cave under the rug downstairs. She was back up to speed.

She had gone to the kitchen for a glass of water after a conversation with Adeeb. Still no word on Louise, and they hadn't heard from Mayfield again, either. A ping issued from her monitor. Someone wanting to chat, no doubt. She let the water run a little longer, then filled her glass and returned to the sewing room.

::HoHumJr to Jake blinked on her monitor.

Her heart leapt. Hands shaking, she keyed Are you OK?

::OK but need help.

Are you with Hotcakes?

::No.

Is she OK?

A pause. Jake's pulse beat in her throat.

::Don't know. Files open, not by me. Could be bad news.

Are you safe?

::Yes. Safe for now. Escaped. In Miami. Got money; no papers. Russians captured me and Hotcakes and another man. Mayfield. I must destroy them before they kill me. Need safe place to go. Can you help?

Let me think. Check back in an hour.

JAKE STARED AT her blank monitor. Her fingers hovered over the keyboard. Someone in Olegarten would know a safe place for him. How to phrase it? She imagined the honest request, and chuckled: Olegarten member needs a place to stay in USA, preferably east coast or south, for an unknown amount of time. Volunteer needs to be willing to risk scrutiny or arrest by U S government or possibly assassination by a terrorist group. Please contact Jake as soon as possible.

She stood, stretched, went to the kitchen, took a pitcher of iced tea out of the refrigerator. As she reached for a glass from the cupboard, a flash of light stopped her. The glass eye of the trout on the wall above the sewing room door reflected a ray of the afternoon sun.

What would Kermit say?

"Don't be foolish." His brows would scrunch the way they did when he thought the answer was obvious. "Think it through. Makes no sense to get involved."

And of course, he'd be right, she thought. The government was on this project like sweet on honey, no question about that. And the people who captured Louise . . . who knew what they would do to keep their project secret?

"But you're not here to say that," she said, wiping a tear from the corner of her eye. "You wouldn't want me to become a sad, lonely old woman, talking out loud to her dead husband because she has no one else, would you?"

She sipped the iced tea.

"And missing out on doing something valuable."

She glanced at the door, still off-kilter even though she had screwed the hinge back on.

She saw the Homeland agent forcing her to the floor, remembered the sleepless night spent with Adeeb searching for Louise's location.

She smiled at the trout, returned to the sewing room, signed into Olegarten, and began looking at bus schedules.

★　　★　　★

JAKE'S TEXT HAD said Check back in an hour.

Puusepp finished his beer. His waitress smiled at him as he stood to leave, reminding him that in the States, he should leave something for the service. Not just the European "round up to the next euro." He left a forty percent tip (she did have a lovely smile) and exited to the heat of the street. He walked several blocks, reconnoitering. His e-pad map showed a pond or small lake nearby, and there he found a bench partly shielded from the street. Several Wi-Fi signals appeared on his e-pad. He worked for a few minutes until one of them yielded to his list of common passwords. Unlikely anyone but the most observant tracker would see his signal. Then he waited, pretending to play a game on his e-pad, until the hour had passed.

Jake's video came up.

"You are in Miami. Is that right?" Businesslike. An older woman, brilliant white hair, looking fit. No-nonsense.

"Yes, I am."

"What identification do you have?" she asked.

"None. Nothing." Did she look disgusted? Puusepp's optimism deflated like a party balloon. Why had he thought a person he had never met would risk arrest or worse to help him?

"How did they get you into the country?" she asked.

"I don't know. They may have counterfeited a passport," Puusepp said. "Do you know how to get that done here?"

"Passports are very difficult since the International Security Treaty," Jake said.

Puusepp exhaled. He was not surprised, but he had hoped Jake knew something he didn't.

"Could they have stolen your valid one and used that?"

"I doubt it," Puusepp said. "It is very well hidden."

"Is there a way for you to get it?"

A reasonable question, but frustrating.

"If I had time, certainly. A friend I trust could go to my apartment with a story about my need to travel out of the European Union. But I do not have time."

Puusepp heard desperation in his voice.

"I have already given away my location," he continued. "I had to convert bitcoin to get US money for this e-pad. To the people who kidnapped me, there is only one solution: they need to kill me. I am the only one who understands what they did and how to protect against it in the future."

"Perhaps you should turn yourself in to the FBI. I can make a contact—"

"No. I have no passport. I have violated what your government calls the most secure data vault in history. And these people—the Sobaki—have enormous resources. Even inside your FBI." The problem grew larger in Puusepp's mind—insurmountable—as he explained it.

"The only way I will ever be able to use my passport, ever use my name again, is to destroy the people that made me do this horrible thing. To do this, I need more computer power than I have, more time than I have, and Olegarten. But first, I need to get away from where I am. Where should I go, and how? To a big city?"

Jake went silent for a moment, then sighed. "Come here until it's safe to retrieve your passport."

"Thank you, but no," he said. "Too much risk to you. We cannot have the passport mailed until Sobaki is dead. That may take some time."

"We can take as much time as necessary," she said, but her expression seemed stern, not pleased.

She had no reason to risk her life for him. He wanted to say something articulate, give her a sign of the rush of gratitude he felt. Instead, he just nodded.

"If you pay cash," she continued, "you can still travel by bus without identification."

"I can do that," Puusepp said, almost choking with relief.

"You will need to buy a ticket to Superior, Wisconsin. It

will be a long ride."

"I have a great deal to think about," Puusepp said. Then, glancing around the park, "We should keep this short." His hand paused above the e-pad's keyboard, about to shut down. "Thank you," he said softly.

"You are a brave man," Jake said. Then the screen went blank.

"And you, too," Puusepp said.

He rose from the bench. As he walked toward the street, he realized he was humming a tune his grandfather taught him.

CHAPTER THIRTY-ONE

GRANSTON HARMON SWIVELED his chair to face the floor-to-ceiling windows on the west wall of his office. The sun had dropped behind the buildings surrounding the Navy Yard, painting them red. What was the saying? Red sky in the morning, sailors take warning; red sky at night, sailor's delight? He hoped the saying was right.

Those windows, the office whose square footage spoke to his importance, the massive desk, all had mattered to him when he was tapped to support VPOTUS. But the opportunity to be at the leading edge of the United States' effort to protect its massive database seemed a cruel irony. Now it was a bleeding edge, and he was doing the bleeding. The IAC, the most significant government project since the moon landing two generations ago, had been brought to its knees. Worse, with the help of people he trusted.

He had briefed the vice president for the fourth time. The IAC had at least partially protected Philadelphia, whatever that meant.

Henry Barber had conferred with him by secure uplink a couple of hours ago. It was clear by now that a Russian cabal was responsible for the grid interruptions. It was also clear that NSA's oh-so-sophisticated algorithm that was supposed to follow the money had been left in the dust. Why had everyone thought a group that had breached the IAC would be incapable of disabling a financial tracking algorithm?

Napolitani was, as usual, an enigma as well as a pain in the ass. Barber was inclined to take her into protective custody. He argued that the Russian group might want to eliminate her for any number of reasons. The IAC was bitching about needing her back to work on the grid intrusion problem. The shrinks said she was apparently suffering some form of PTSD.

Harmon had figured the VP would throw him under the bus. Either problem . . . the hack or the money they'd spent . . . would have been justification. Of course, VPOTUS had signed off on the money and spent political capital to get the president to squeeze the $500 million out of a budget hidey-hole. Harmon had been working out how best to use that leverage, fully expecting a confrontation. But the VP had been friendly and human. "Shit, Harm, everybody makes mistakes. Don't worry so much."

Which made Harmon know he was done for.

He poured a glass of water, went to the discreet bar concealed in the bookshelves, selected a bottle of twelve-year old bourbon, hesitated, put it back. Bourbon wasn't going to help tonight.

He returned to his desk and sat facing the windows. Red faded to ochre as night fell, and Harmon contemplated the disaster his career had become.

THE LEAD SUPERVISOR of the PJM interconnection facility outside Philadelphia pushed back from her desk. After eight o'clock. It would be sunset outside. The monitor bank that occupied the wall above the desks in the main control room showed no unusual activity. She half hoped there was something to the mysterious warning about a grid attack that might happen tonight. Probably management covering its ass. She'd never heard of a breach in the IAC firewall. But she'd had to hold everyone in position, making her people miss soccer games, high school musicals, dates, and dinners.

She tilted her head side to side, stretching muscles, and sighed. It would be a long night. Maybe she should order out for some food to show she cared about upsetting plans. Coffee and treats? Pizza?

She was weighing the options when Merion Township dropped off-line, then in short order Radnor and Tredyffrin. Shit . . . the Main Line. They were outside the extra protection the IAC had thrown around the big plants. She chuckled, picturing the sylvan gracefulness of the fine old homes engulfed in the noise of personal generators coming online. Small potatoes to the system, but they'd bitch louder than anyone tomorrow. She punched her keyboard to bring up the Delaware plants, then Limerick, then Three-Mile Island. The dotted yellow line around each of them showed entry attempts, but none had succeeded. It brought back memories of being in this room, helpless, during CyberWar I.

She had twenty-three years in. Maybe time to hang it up.

CHAPTER THIRTY-TWO

MONGREL ARRIVED AT the dacha outside of Moscow before the others. Their agreement, never broken before, was that all three of the Sobaki should arrive together. Chairman had trusted him with the operation, and Mongrel concluded that the breach of protocol was necessary to ensure security.

The Philadelphia failure suggested caution. It might well have been reported to the FSB through their American resources. Perhaps it had been a mistake to hint to the Americans that a larger city would be attacked. It was necessary to focus them on the ransom money, convince them the attack was a hacker at work. In any case, the software had been proven to work.

The dacha conformed to the communist regime size restrictions. A covered porch that would have been a minor size violation had been added. The dacha probably had been the prize of an upper-level apparatchik. It was set off from the others in the cooperative by a wall of trees, left untrimmed by the owner to simulate deep forest.

Mongrel's security team covered the Mercedes with netting that would suggest vegetation to all but the most inquisitive of drones. Mongrel knew from his FSB days that a Mercedes at a dacha of this size would not be unusual, but three might bring extra scrutiny.

One of the members of the team went around to the back of the building to inspect wiring and disable the security system. The team leader opened a briefcase, selected a scanner into which he plugged an antenna that expanded like an umbrella. The man stared at the small screen for a few seconds, brows knit. Mongrel caught his look of concern.

"Problem?"

The man continued to concentrate on the display for a few moments, then turned to Mongrel. "Drone at five kilometers but moving away. I have latched onto the control signal and will monitor it."

Mongrel watched the device's screen with the leader and saw the all clear text from the man in back. The third member of the team entered the dacha with a handheld scanner. Several minutes later, she reappeared and approached Mongrel and the leader.

"I have disabled the security system. There is no video, and I can see no other signals."

Mongrel moved toward the porch as the security team melted into the trees. Chairman and Borzoi arrived a few minutes later. Mongrel stood on the porch, watching their security teams fan out to duplicate what his had done.

"I see you arrived early," Chairman said. Only a slight flaring of his nostrils gave away his displeasure. The old man mounted the steps, leaning on a cane. Mongrel resisted the temptation to lend a supporting hand.

"Yes. This building required a more complicated security sweep than our usual meeting places, and we had to be concerned about drones."

Borzoi joined them. He was flamboyantly dressed in a green linen jacket, silk shirt, and the newly fashionable flare leg trousers atop elegant boots never intended for the country-side. Mongrel showed his disgust and turned to lead them into the house. Borzoi stepped in front of him, close enough that the medicinal odor of vodka overrode his cologne. "Security check," he said. Mongrel contained his anger. He would have done the same in the circumstance, but Borzoi's vodka breath showed lack of control and might make the meeting conten-tious.

Borzoi's security team repeated the check of the inside of the building, gave their clearance, and the three Sobaki entered. The main room was a careful reconstruction of a hunting lodge from the time of the empire. Paintings of wolves and the borzois who would have run them down hung on the walls. The tusked head of a wild boar commanded the wall above a stone fireplace, which held an iron grate on which his body might have sizzled to celebrate the end of the hunt. A massive pine table occupied the center of the room.

"Why have you brought us to the country?" Chairman asked.

"My report will take longer than usual," Mongrel said. "Here, we can safely take the time we need to make some decisions. Let us sit."

Bad news first, Mongrel thought, then butter the broken bread.

"The Philadelphia intrusion was only partly successful."

"Partly?" Borzoi's jaw muscle twitched.

"Yes, the Americans were able to protect most of the city." Mongrel paused. "Perhaps they guessed the location from hints in the ransom message."

"Stupid," Borzoi sniffed.

Mongrel restrained himself, instead nodding ever so slightly to Borzoi. "Granted." Better to concede than to explain his logic and point out that the main purpose of the plan had succeeded—the software worked. "They threw up a firewall around critical power plants. It is unlikely that they have a general solution that can protect places they do not have advance knowledge of."

"How much have they paid?" Borzoi demanded.

Mongrel did not contain his look of irritation, but said levelly, "The single payment of five hundred million dollars after Valdosta."

"Then we must attack New York or Washington," Borzoi said, slurring slightly.

Mongrel drew in a long, deliberate breath. The frustration of having to deal with this blockhead almost made him lash out.

"Right now, that is impossible," he said as patiently as he could manage. "Which is why I asked to meet here, where we can spend the time to adjust our plan."

"What does Raskov say?" Chairman asked.

"We have lost contact with both Raskov in Florida and the group in West Virginia."

Mongrel paused, letting the message sink in. He continued, "Two days ago, our operative in West Virginia signaled that federal agents were close to the original hostage location. We moved the Napolitani woman, and we know they arrived at the backup location. We lost contact with them a few hours later. It seems likely that our people were compromised. The Napolitani woman did not send the required signal, and the file opened."

"And it had . . ." Fear thickened Borzoi's voice.

"Nothing." Mongrel let the word hang. "Nothing" was better than "Hello Kitty."

"We have been tricked," Chairman said with a single nod.

"Yes."

Borzoi slammed his hands on the tabletop, rose, and leaned toward Mongrel.

"This is what I suspected. Where is the fucking Estonian?"

"As I said, the Florida location was also compromised."

"I told you we should have taken the code the Estonian wrote and killed the little bastard," Borzoi said, his vodka breath enveloping Mongrel. "Now he has made fools of us all. He knows what we did. He wrote the program, and he can destroy it. He must be found and eliminated . . . now."

"Raskov was able to set up the Philadelphia action," Mongrel continued, staring down the younger man. "But he failed to report later that day, and we learned that there had been a disturbance at the warehouse."

"Pyotr?" Borzoi pulled back.

"We know from local reporting that one person is dead, two people are wounded but alive, and one person may be missing."

"Who is dead?" asked Chairman.

"We do not know yet."

"In other words, you have failed." Borzoi smiled in triumph.

"Enough." Chairman interrupted, steel in his voice. "How do we move forward?"

"Phase two is finished," Mongrel said. "We have valuable software and the money. We can claim moderate success and the promise of future—"

"No!" Borzoi said, still standing. "This is not acceptable. They have not paid the full amount of the ransom. We must teach them to obey us. We will insert the software into the IAC and shut down Washington. Then they will pay."

Mongrel felt his own fear rising. Bad luck, poor execution, bad timing could sink a project. But stupidity could get them all killed.

"The money we have extracted from the Americans is a reasonable return for our efforts," Mongrel continued in a level voice. "We've moved it through several bank accounts and a transaction involving copper ore. I believe it will be safe to distribute in several weeks. We will use the normal process. Chairman will give us routing instructions."

"It should be safe to distribute now," Borzoi said, too loud, as he retook his seat.

Chairman shook his head once. "No," he said. "Too soon. We will continue to move it until we're sure no one has traced the transfers."

"We have the Estonian's software," Mongrel continued. "It can penetrate the American IAC. The premier no doubt will see its enormous value." He shrugged. "Perhaps the power grid again. Perhaps the next American election."

The corner of Chairman's mouth twitched in what might have been a grin. "What is our next step?"

"I believe we should contact the premier," Mongrel said "with a gift of two hundred million of the ransom, then proffer the software."

"Agreed?" Chairman looked from Borzoi to Mongrel.

Borzoi's look was sour, but he nodded acceptance. He stood, knocking the heavy chair backward, almost tipping it, and leaned toward Mongrel. He opened his mouth to speak, but snapped it shut, turned, and made for the door.

He shoved the door open, took the steps, his security detail trailing.

Mongrel glanced at Chairman, who gave an almost imperceptible shrug. Soon there would be two Sobaki.

CHAPTER THIRTY-THREE

AFTER THE ALL-HANDS meeting with AVP Harmon, Henry Barber had returned to his comfortable office, top-notch support staff, and the perquisites of an FBI assistant director. He had plenty to do, but the issue of the grid hacking wouldn't leave him alone. There was that young agent at the Miami office who'd done an excellent job investigating the Renfro murder, what was her name? Jarvinen, he remembered. Unusual first name.

She answered on video, brushing a hand over her hair. "Yessir."

"Great job on Renfro. Nice, clear report."

"Thank you."

"Anything new? Leads on Mayfield's whereabouts?"

"Matter of fact, yes. We got a call from the North Miami PD about a possibly related incident. A shooting at a warehouse. One dead, two wounded. Mayfield is one of the wounded."

"Mayfield, huh?" Barber said.

Barber had tried to erase what he knew about Mayfield from prior experience: smart, honest, no-nonsense. Jarvinen's precise, carefully-constructed report made no sense at all. The idea of Mayfield killing a guy who'd just saved his company, jamming his body in the back seat of the guy's own car, and driving away with an accomplice struck Barber as ridiculous. Something obvious was evading everyone on the case. The secrecy of the investigation had the DC establishment constructing sandcastles of logic based on partial knowledge. The cops in Florida saw a murder case with one suspect.

Someone needed to put it all together.

Barber used the pretext of national security to book an evening plane to Miami, politely nixing the suggestion to follow protocol and take at least one other agent with him.

He had called Jarvinen when he arrived. She had learned both men were in surgery. Probably a good idea to get some rest, check them out in the morning, she said. Was she looking at his face and seeing exhaustion or just assuming he was an old, tired guy? Barber got an autocar and went to the hospital.

In the waiting room, he picked up a months-old *Sports Illustrated* to fight off his body's inclination to doze. He thumbed through the articles absently, his mind occupied with confusing evidence. The local police thought Mayfield killed Mac Renfro. But what was his motive? After all, he'd scored ten million for his company from the guy he shot. Then, a couple of days later and a few miles away, this shootout. One man dead and Mayfield and a young guy named Wilcox wounded. A fourth man disappeared after asking workers in the adjacent building to call for help. He had an accent, they said, but not Spanish.

The double doors at the end of the hall whooshed open and a woman in green scrubs emerged. She consulted a clipboard. "Barber?"

Barber stood as she approached and produced his badge. She glanced at it and said, "Mayfield is under heavy sedation. You can't talk to him yet." At close range, he saw fatigue lining her face. "We fixed his femoral artery, but the surgery was complicated by bone fragments from his femur. We'll have to keep him sedated for at least eight hours—"

"Doc, this is a federal investigation."

The doctor exhaled. "You want a witness or a corpse?"

"What about Wilcox?"

"He's sedated, too, but he should be good to talk when he wakes up. Hell of a lucky guy. Shot in the abdomen at point-blank range. The bullet missed major arteries and the small intestine, clipped his left lung, and broke a rib. We got the bullet, repaired tissue damage, and he'll be almost as good as new in a couple of weeks. One lucky fellow. An inch up, down or sideways, and . . ." She shrugged. "Give it an hour, then you can ask a few questions. A nurse will be with you—"

"I can't do an interview with a non-vetted person in the room."

"—and you will limit your questions or we will cut you off." The doctor's voice said exhaustion was wearing through her patience. "Hospital policy. Take it up with our legal staff tomorrow if you like."

The doctor turned and stalked back toward the double doors. Barber took a seat again and opened the magazine, remembering the part of field work he had hated: the waiting. After a few minutes, bored and nodding off, he shook himself, stood, and checked on the Miami cops guarding Mayfield and Wilcox.

A little shoptalk, then back to the waiting room. Someone had taken his magazine, and he realized he hadn't eaten since lunch.

He took the elevator to the ground floor and followed signs to the cafeteria, which was long closed. A bank of vending machines offered sandwiches, sodas, and coffee. Barber bought a ham and cheese. Another machine vended a light brown liquid that was called coffee, apparently without irony. Barber opened the sandwich and added a squirt of bright yellow mustard to the graying slice of ham, which lay exhausted over processed cheese food on wheat bread. He chuckled. He was the one who wanted to get into the field.

He left half the sandwich in the triangular plastic holder, slid his e-pad out of his jacket pocket, and called Jarvinen. Video opened, showing her elbow on her desk, head leaning on her fist, looking tired.

"Good evening, Agent Jarvinen."

She straightened up.

"Any news on the shooting at the North Miami warehouse? Have you ID'd the fourth man?"

She cleared her throat and answered, "No. That guy disappeared. There are two men in the hospital. One we ID'd as Joseph Mayfield. He's a businessman up in"—she reached off camera and came back with an e-pad, which she swiped—"Boca, at a business called—"

"HelioCorp. Yes, I know Mayfield. Who's the other person?"

"His ID has him as Pete Wilcox, but his real name is Pyotr Volkov. Came here from Russia as a kid about eleven years ago." Her brow furrowed. "He has a short sheet, nothing serious." She tapped her keyboard, and a forensics lab sheet popped up on Barber's screen. "All the bullets they retrieved look like they're from the one gun." She swiped a trackpad. "Uhh . . . that'll be confirmed tomorrow, and they'll have run the prints and DNA."

She flipped through papers on her desk, swiped again, and a new window opened on Barber's e-pad.

"I'm looking at this slip of paper from the dead guy's pocket," she said. "Linguistics says it might be chess moves, plus some notes in Cyrillic. Looks like Russian to me."

"Thanks," Barber said, preparing to sign off, but the woman held a finger up. "Hold on."

She swiped again, "Got the warehouse video from the local cops." After a moment, the video appeared in a window on Barber's e-pad. The camera swept across the inside of the warehouse. A man, seated as if at ease, arms hanging down, head tilted to one side. Might be napping, but for the hole in his forehead. The camera panned to a guy on the floor, lying in a pool of blood. A medic cutting pants away, then she moved, revealing a face. Mayfield. Another pan, then a young guy sitting up, legs splayed out, moaning.

"Is he saying something? Maybe another language?"

The agent nodded. "Yes. The linguistics guys can't figure it out. Mix of Russian and English, something about dogs and a proper name. I can't quite get the name, but it sounds Finnish, maybe Estonian."

"You speak Russian?"

"Russian, some other Slavic languages . . . they're pretty close to each other . . . Finnish, some Hungarian and Estonian . . . they're related, too. Limited Mandarin. Language was my first FBI gig."

"Whew! I thought my college Spanish was pretty impressive."

She grinned. "You probably get along a lot better than I in Miami."

BACK ON THE third floor, the uniform cops guarding Mayfield and Wilcox stood as Barber got off the elevator. Neither had anything to report. Barber found the nurse in charge and did a practiced job of being a serious, not-quite-intimidating federal officer. The nurse seemed suitably impressed that this was an Important Matter and assigned herself to accompany him to the interview.

The guy who called himself Wilcox was dozing as Barber and the nurse entered. His eyes opened at the sound of the door. Guarded. Barber saw it right away.

"Good evening, Mr. Wilcox. How are you doing?"

Wilcox cracked a slanting grin. "Not so bad, I guess, considering."

"Can you tell me what happened?"

"I was bringin' in lunch. That guy they were workin' with . . . Mayfield . . . had a gun. They were arguing. He shot Raskov. I knew he was gonna shoot me next, so I charged him. He shot me right before I hit him. There was another shot when I was wrestling, then I kinda faded."

"Why did you change your name?"

The half-drowsy smile again. "Ever try to get a job with a name like Volkov?"

Volkov. A name Barber had heard before. Where?

"How did you get employed by Neva Imports?"

Volkov reached for a plastic cup of water on the table beside his bed. A telltale stall—rehearsing his story. Barber had seen it a hundred times before.

"A couple of months ago, I get a call from my uncle in Russia. He says he wants to start an importing business here. He wants me to work with a guy named Raskov. I'll be the English-speaking associate, set up the business, work with Customs to get permits, and like that."

Volkov took another sip, constructing the next scene.

"Anyway, about a month ago, Raskov arrives. I show him all the work I've done to set up importing and ask when shipments will start arriving. I ask if I should be calling on potential customers."

"What were you going to be selling?"

Volkov's eyes did the sidewise shift that gave him away. Only talented liars were able to construct fantasy worlds while keeping eye contact. Volkov wasn't talented.

"Umm. Software."

"What sort of software?"

"Custom stuff. For doctors' records, inventory, stuff like that. We were going to contract the work out in Russia."

Another sip of water.

"Raskov blows me off. 'Later, later.' After a few days, he brings in this Estonian guy. Says he's supposed to do some programming. 'For what?' I ask. Raskov blows me off again."

Volkov's eyes narrowed, and he shifted a bit toward Barber.

"Raskov has these meetings, 'with clients,' he says. They're about some 'investment' "—Volkov's eyelids drooped—"of my uncle's."

The nurse tapped her watch. End of interview. Volkov was lying anyway, so Barber didn't argue.

On the way down in the elevator, he texted Jarvinen, asking her to run down "Volkov" and Neva Importing.

★　★　★

BARBER WOKE UP feeling gritty. The hotel's famous name mattress hadn't helped his back, still sore from yesterday's flight. A shower, hot at first then cold. A small bottle of body wash helped . . . floral was better than day-old sweat. He remembered a diner across from the hospital and skipped the motel's complimentary breakfast.

The diner was dominated by a large table of men arguing politics over coffee refills. But the smell of bacon cooking, honest-to-god coffee, and something sweet and cinnamon justified Barber's expectation. He took the booth farthest from the noise.

A waitress followed him and took his order for over-easy eggs, sausage, and . . . he really shouldn't, but what the hell . . . a cinnamon roll. He settled into the booth, sipped coffee, and tapped his e-pad to call the Miami office.

Jarvinen was back at her desk.

"The gun in the warehouse has DNA from Wilcox . . . uhh, Volkov . . . and 'unidentified' in the US database. They're running them through International. But definitely not Mayfield's, so it looks like he's clean on this dead guy. And they confirmed all the bullets in the warehouse are from that one gun."

"Did you see my message about the name Volkov and Neva Imports?"

She nodded. "There was a Russian oligarch by that name. He was involved in the rise of the current premier and was enormously wealthy. Banking, electric power, mainly. About a year ago, a hacker—no one's ever figured who—released a mass of documents . . . emails, texts, financial statements, videos. Short story: they implicated this Volkov dude in shady dealing related to one of the premier's personal projects." She paused and grinned. "And maybe one of his, uhh, lady friends. Then . . . poof. No Volkov."

Back to serious. "Apparently it's okay with the premier if his friends steal from Mother Russia, but not so much if they steal from him, money or love. Seems like the premier eliminated his good friend."

"Great job," Barber said. "Did you sleep at all?"

"Uhh, a little." Her half smile told Barber that she hadn't.

"I checked that business, Neva Importing," she continued. "It has a website . . . here." A window opened on Barber's e-pad showing pictures of nesting dolls, Russian alphabet blocks, and stuffed animals.

Barber chuckled. To the agent's raised eyebrow, he said, "Volkov told me they were selling software."

"Obviously a different product catalog. Maybe two companies?"—she glanced offscreen—"nope." She tapped keys. "One Neva Importing in the Florida business registry, classified as toys, other consumer goods. It has an office near Miami Beach," she continued. "Building management says it was rented a couple of months ago. The guard at the information desk says there were people in there until about a week ago, but no one since then. He recognized a picture of the dead man."

"So, Volkov's story is right in some regard."

"Yes, but there are no payroll tax records filed, and it doesn't seem as if they're doing much business, if any."

"Thanks for your help," Barber said, reminding himself to write a note for her personnel jacket.

A tone in Barber's ear had let him know the hospital was paging him. The doc had cleared Mayfield for an interview. He paid at the counter, left the men still arguing about whether the Rs or the Ds were responsible for the dismal state of the stock market, and crossed the street toward the hospital. Maybe Mayfield could tell him who the mysterious fourth man was.

JOE FLOATED SOMEWHERE in featureless space, trying to grab hold of a fleeting thought. Under water, reaching for the surface, lungs almost bursting, grasping. But the urgency evaporated, and he drifted until he awoke, sun in his eyes, pain down his left side.

Weezy.

The fight, Pyotr, Puusepp.

Weezy.

If Puusepp didn't send the message to keep the file closed, then . . .

He coughed, tried to move. Some part of his lower body screamed at him.

He took in soft gray-green walls. Rails on his bed. Wires and tubes snaking between the rails. Wall-mounted monitor seeming to float and wobble. Drugs.

The door to his room opened. A scrub-clad middle-aged man entered.

"Welcome back, Mr. Mayfield."

The man came to the bedside, inspected a hanging bag of fluid beside the bed, and made a note on a chart.

"How are you feeling?"

"Where am I?"

"You are in Holy Cross Hospital."

Joe tried to focus through the haze in his mind.

"I need an e-pad."

The door swung open and a man entered. Barber? Henry Barber? The rumpled suit, the open collar. Was he hallucinating?

"E-pad. It's important. Weezy is—"

"Safe. Weezy is safe," Barber said. "She was rescued two days ago."

Safe. Beautiful word. Joe felt himself lift off the bed, float on a cloud of happiness. She was safe. He began to drift. Barber was speaking, but what really mattered was . . . safe.

He realized Barber had asked him a question and was repeating it.

"Joe, what were you doing in the warehouse, anyway?"

"Keeping the file closed. Raskov was unhappy with Pyotr. Shot him. Puusepp said he was going."

Barber leaned toward him. "Joe, focus. Who is Raskov? Who is Puusepp? I need to know exactly what went on in the building and your story . . . all of it."

"Raskov and Puusepp were sending instructions somewhere, I think to the electrical grid. HelioCorp wasn't—"

Joe's eyelids were heavy. Like trying to lift ten pounds more than his limit.

"Who are the people who captured you?"

"Raskov . . . I think he's dead. A young guy, Pyotr, shot Raskov, then shot me and got shot himself. They killed Mac—"

"Got shot? Who shot him?"

"We struggled. Gun went off. Don't know. Puusepp threw the gun away."

"Puusepp? Who is he?"

"Hacker. Their prisoner." So tired.

"Mayfield, stay with me."

The eyelids tried to stay open and failed. Red spots floated on a background of black. Far away a voice, Joe's own, said, "HelioCorp wasn't a glitch."

CHAPTER THIRTY-FOUR

WEEZY HAD FALLEN into a doze. Better to zone out. Not sleep, not dream. The day nurse who replaced Keesha woke her. She was a middle-aged woman who seemed to have gotten the impression that Weezy was fine except for the burns. "You should get up, move around," she said.

Weezy's burns were painful but not disfiguring. The stun grenade had ruptured her left eardrum, but it would heal. The red spot that occupied her vision when she closed her eyes was shrinking. The finger Tattoo had broken was painful but splinted. She should be mending rapidly. She should not stare at the wall for minutes on end, chewing the fingernails on her good hand. She should not curse the nurses, then break into tears.

But they hadn't been through what she had. She knew they were whispering about her. The forensic exam should have been private, but she knew the test results had made their way back to the nursing station. She saw it in the mingled pity and curiosity in their eyes.

The nurse gave up, made unnecessary noise moving Weezy's untouched lunch tray. "You'll be fine, dear," she harrumphed, and left Weezy alone to replay Tattoo's knife, the sound of the chain hoist clanking, the fear, and the pain.

Weezy rolled over and stared out the window. She was not "fine." How would she ever be "fine" again?

Sometime later, the door opened. She lay still. Maybe they'd go away.

"You have a call." The day nurse's voice had lost its judgmental note. "It's important."

Weezy took the phone.

"Ms. Napolitani? Louise?" A voice she knew, but who? Curiosity got to her, and she punched video.

That homely, honest face. Henry Barber? Why would Henry call? Where was he?

"Louise, good to see you're mending."

"Why are you—"

"I'm looking at this grid hack for the FBI."

Weezy fought back tears of relief. Finally, someone who knew her, someone smart enough to understand. Someone who cared.

"Joe. Do you know about Joe? They say he was rescued, but he's in a hospital. No one will tell me—"

"Joe is here with me."

"Is he . . ."

"He was shot, but they say he will make a full recovery. Let me put him on."

Barber spoke with someone off camera, nodding several times, negotiating. Weezy tried to follow the conversation, increasingly frustrated. Finally, he turned back to Weezy. "Joe is under arrest at this moment, although it's looking more and more like charges will be dropped."

"Charges?"

"Let's get you through to him. We can talk about the other stuff later."

Weezy clutched the e-pad in both hands, realizing she was shaking. Barber's face disappeared. Then a man's face. Not Joe.

"It's not . . . it's not . . ."

The picture blurred, then refocused.

Joe.

They stared at each other for a long moment, speechless.

"You're hurt," he said.

She touched the bandage on her face.

"Not bad. You're hurt, too."

"But better now." He gulped in several breaths, smiling.

"Much better now."

"You got shot," she said.

"Yes, but our buddy HoHumJr saved me."

"So he was their hacker. I should have known."

"It wasn't voluntary. And Mac Renfro—" Joe looked up, away from the camera. "I'm told I have to stop. I guess this is my one phone call. I love you."

The image of Joe blurred.

"Love you, too," Weezy said.

The video showed movement, a door being opened and closed, passage through a hall, a sitting area, Barber.

"There, now we can talk."

"Your Florida rat-bastard took away the e-pad before I said goodbye."

Barber let out a long, relieved sigh. "That's the Napolitani I know." Then, "Are you able to talk about what happened?"

"Wait a minute, Joe's under arrest?" She sat up too fast, making the burns on her side scream at her. "For what?"

Barber was tapping on his e-pad, looking sheepish. "Murder."

"*What?*"

"Mac Renfro was shot and killed. The circumstantial evidence points to Joe."

Weezy shook her head in irritation. "That's stupid. He raised ten million dollars for the HelioCorp restart from Mac. Why would he shoot him?"

"Exactly. So if circumstantial evidence leads to a strange conclusion, either you don't understand the evidence or—"

"—Or somebody managed the evidence." Weezy saw Barber smiling.

"Right."

"So, while you folks are stomping around hoovering up false evidence and bothering my lover man, you're not getting much done on solving the grid problem. I bet you don't know who did it and how it got done, do you?"

"Do you?"

"I don't know who . . . HoHumJr does, I bet. Maybe Joe does. But I'm pretty sure I know how."

"I was afraid of that."

Weezy raised the bed to a sitting position. "You were afraid . . . why?"

"Seems to me," Barber said, "there are two people who can figure out what happened. One is your hacker friend, who has disappeared."

The mental picture formed, lines connecting HoHumJr, herself, Joe, the government. Roles sketched out. "And I'm the other."

Barber nodded.

"So the government still thinks I've gone over to the other side."

Barber nodded again.

"And, oh yes, these Russians need to kill both of us."

Barber nodded yet again.

"And you're going to tell me I need to go to a safe house. Or witness protection. Something like that."

Barber shrugged.

"And now I'm going to explain to you, very slowly so you can see my lips move, why that's not a good idea."

Barber grinned. "I'm watching your lips."

"There are two ways to solve this: the government way and the good way."

"I'm guessing you've figured out both ways."

"Sure. The government way is to stash me in a safe house or prison. Then you'll try to find HoHumJr. If you do find him, you'll try to convince a terrified, suspicious foreign national to help you out." Weezy gave one irritated shake of her head. "And that's if the Russians don't get to him before you do."

She paused, tempted to scratch the itch under the bandage on her cheek. Then she continued, "That's not even the main problem. Whoever did this probably has the software my friend HoHumJr wrote. To have the ability to hack into the

IAC . . . that's too much power to remain unused for long. And without HoHumJr's help, you have to wait for the next hack and play defense."

She leaned forward. "You need me free to operate."

She reached for the plastic cup on her bedside table and tilted toward Barber in a mock toast before taking a sip. "If HoHumJr is alive, he will contact Olegarten. He won't talk to you, but he'll talk to me. Between the two of us, we will figure out how the power grid was hacked. Then we'll go on offense."

She forced herself to shut up. Let him draw the right conclusion.

Barber rubbed his chin absently.

Good, she thought. At least he's considering it. Maybe she would be free to operate, but more important . . .

"First, I have to take care of Joe. I'm good to travel in a day or so, and—"

"You can't travel. Particularly not to Miami . . . it's the one place these Russians know to look for you, Joe, and the Estonian."

"You're not very good at reading lips, Barber."

"Louise, you're not going to risk your life to see Joe. He's recuperating now, and he's in danger, too, you know. Besides, you're under protection, which is about the same as being under arrest."

She was working up righteous indignation, about to argue. Barber held up his hands in mock surrender and said, "Let's change subject. Can you tell me exactly what happened when you were held hostage? There were two people with you when you were rescued, a man and a woman. Can you tell me about them? And were there others involved?"

Weezy knew Barber was on her side. She had to give him something if he was going to figure a way to thread the bureaucratic needle for her. "Yes," she said, and told him everything . . . almost everything . . . she could remember.

Barber had been scribbling in a small notebook as she

spoke. She remained silent while he wrote the last few words.

"What happened to the tattooed guy," Weezy asked softly.

Barber's head snapped up, eyes inquisitive. "The tattooed guy? He was captured. He's a small-time thug with a record as long as your forearm. Connections to the Russian mafia here, but not high-test. What did he do to you?"

Weezy looked away from Henry's penetrating stare.

He sees. He can tell.

"He beat me and, uhh . . ." Suddenly, Weezy had a lump in her throat. "He . . . He threatened . . . He made me . . ." She stopped, trying to swallow, trying to erase his stink, the knife, the rage, the helplessness.

Henry was staring off-camera, veins standing out on his forehead, jaws working. He cleared his throat. "They have the tattooed guy in custody. If you want to talk—"

"I don't."

She hadn't expected to start bawling. The pain, the fear, what she'd been through . . . suddenly she was gasping, blubbering, hiccupping, hopeless.

Barber bowed his head. He said nothing, but his expression of pain was better than all the shrinks strung together.

Finally, she wiped her eyes, reached for a tissue, blew her nose, and said, "Sorry."

"Don't be sorry," he said. "Get better. We have work to do, and I think I know how to do it your way."

CHAPTER THIRTY-FIVE

AFTER INTERVIEWING MAYFIELD and talking with Napolitani, Henry Barber called an autocar. As the queue of vehicles oozed down I-95 toward the center of Miami and the FBI office, Barber tried to make sense of the evidence.

Mayfield's story squared with most of what the Bureau had learned in Washington. Not much more to mine there. Volkov, who called himself Wilcox, was more interesting. His prints on the weapon found in the warehouse gave Barber pretext to hold him, at least for a while.

There was the lingering issue of Mayfield's guilt, though. Not clear-cut. Barber, who generally put himself in his own Good Investigator column, knew more data was almost always a good thing. He called the office and learned that a tech crew was at the warehouse where the shootings had taken place. He decided to join them. The autocar extracted itself from the I-95 scrum and turned north.

Barber stopped and bought coffee and scones for the crew. When he arrived, they were unpacking gear in the back of the building. The crew appreciated Barber's gesture. The lead tech was cranky. "Some IAC broad"—he gave Barber a guilty look, maybe hoping for a chuckle—"some IAC *person* has a theory that these warehouse guys hacked into the IAC physically. Something about an exact length of cable we're supposed to find." He sniffed. "Went over this place with a fine-tooth comb yesterday," he said as he unrolled a 150-foot power cord that served tripod-mounted work lights. "We would have noticed a cable."

"If you didn't know to look for it . . ."

The team leader snorted.

Half an hour later, they had been through the offices. "Alright, let's start with the perimeter, then move inward," the team leader said. The temperature in the building reached warming-oven level, and one of the two other guys on the team had shucked his shirt. Barber would have liked to do so, too, but neither his status as agent-in-charge or his sensitivity about his thickening waist would allow it.

Progress around the perimeter was slow because a work bench ran the length of the wall on the window side. Junk, old boxes, discarded bits of pipe and wire made false *aha* events frequent. Barber, wanting to escape the stifling heat in the building, excused himself to make a call.

Outside, he took off his suit coat and dropped it in his car. He rolled up his sleeves and walked the length of the loading zone. The unit he had left was at the north end of a series of eight attached bays. The missing person had come out of the building, urged the men in the next bay to call for help, convinced them there was danger. Then he disappeared.

Barber walked the length of the connected units. Emergency rescue personnel and the police had responded quickly... there was a fire station two blocks away. If the missing guy had run along the back of the building he would have arrived at a parking lot separated from an open field by a sagging chain-link fence. Based on the description ... middle-aged, short, paunchy ... the guy wouldn't be vaulting the fence and sprinting to freedom. A more substantial chain-link fence separated the loading area from the street that ran behind the building. A portion was broken down, probably from an accident long ago based on the rusted links. He might have slipped through there, but that would have put him where the cops would have seen him.

Barber turned and walked slowly back toward the north end of the building. Palmetto bushes separated the property from the next set of buildings. Hard to pass through, but not impossible. There was a path down the north side of the building, unpaved, uneven stones washed by a broken downspout. This would be the more likely escape route.

He squatted and inspected the stones. No marks or displacement. But it had rained overnight. He stood and walked gingerly down the path, evading the palmetto fronds that threatened to tear his shirt. At the front of the building, dense ornamental bushes made passage almost impossible. Besides, the missing guy would have ended up in the front parking lot . . . right where the emergency vehicles would have entered.

Barber retraced his steps toward the back of the building, looking for any indication of where Puusepp might have slipped away. Several feet from the front of the building, there was an uneven patch in the stones. Barber stopped, scanned toward the palmetto. An almost imperceptible lump between two stems, probably nothing. He was at the point in the wall where the brick facade gave way to windows, spotted with moss and mold. His eyes swept the wall. Everything normal, except . . . a thin vertical line from the ground to the sill of the first window? Barber leaned toward the wall. In the bottommost corner of the first window, a cable painted the color of the brickwork passed through a hole in the glass and down the wall to the ground.

As Barber stood, a muffled call from inside the building. "Got something."

LATER THAT DAY, and in considerably better mood, the tech team leader announced to Barber that the team had been able to trace the cable. It ran 543 feet to a junction box. The box was buried at the edge of the parking lot of a modern, nondescript building.

The front door of that building bore no marking other than its address.

Barber pulled open the outer door, entered a small foyer.

A uniformed guard eyed Barber from behind a desk on the other side of a glass security door. A sign next to the doorjamb instructed visitors to push a button on the intercom above it.

"May I help you?" The voice was tinny.

"Federal Bureau of Investigation business. Open the door."

"Please state your business, sir."

"Special Agent Henry Barber," he said, holding his credential to the glass. The door buzzed, and Barber entered.

The guard handed over a sign-in log. Barber signed it, then glanced at the guard. "What business do you do here?"

The guard looked uncomfortable, checked the log as if to be certain Barber had signed it, and said, "This is a division of United Energy."

Barber's mind ticked through the HelioCorp hack, Mayfield, the dead investor. Renfro's venture fund was part of United Energy. The cable, the warehouse, the murder. Possibilities crowded into Barber's mind. He put on his interrogation face and asked, "What does United Energy do in this particular building?"

The guard picked up a phone. "I need to have you speak to building management. Can you have a seat?" He nodded to the chairs hugging the wall next to the entrance door.

Barber sat, more perplexed than irritated. The FBI credential usually got instant cooperation.

The guard had a short conversation. Two minutes later a middle-aged man came down the hall from the inner building. The collar of his sport coat was turned up on one side, as if he'd put it on in a hurry, and he was smoothing his combover.

"Mister, ahh . . ." His smile suggested constipation.

"Special Agent Barber, FBI, Miami office. And you are?"

"Forbes . . . Randall. I'm assistant director here. What can I do you for?"

Forbes started to extend his hand to shake but apparently thought better of it and let the hand fall to his side.

"Okay, Mr. Forbes, I'm investigating a recent incident at

the warehouse down the—"

"Oh, yes. The shooting. Terrible. The neighborhood used to be so quiet. Now, with the change in . . . uhh . . . demographics."

"What does United Energy do in this building?"

"This is our Southeast Control Division."

"Which does what?"

"We conduct analysis and load leveling studies and certain control functions."

"Mr. Forbes, is there a place we can talk privately?"

"I'm afraid I'm not authorized to discuss—"

"All right." Barber gave a small shrug. He loved this part. "Give me a minute to order a car. We can continue our discussion in the field office. You can consult with your superiors and your lawyer from there."

A sheen of sweat appeared on Forbes's forehead. Maybe it was the effort of making a decision.

Forbes turned toward the corridor he'd emerged from. "Follow me."

The corridor led toward the back of the building past framed pictures . . . grainy black and whites of men with shovels standing beside an enormous pile of coal, a plant belching smoke, and a portrait of a serious-looking man in the formal wear of a century ago. At the end of the corridor, Forbes turned left, leading Barber past a twenty-foot-long window. Behind it, a dozen people at monitors. On the far wall, a display that looked like a multi-colored circuit diagram.

Barber paused, taking it in when he realized Forbes had turned off the corridor into a conference room. Barber followed to find a standard-issue, Formica-topped conference table with six chairs.

"May I see your credentials again?" Forbes asked.

Barber flipped open his wallet and pushed it across the table toward Forbes, who raised his glasses to inspect it. Barber took the wallet back, extracted a card, and slid it across the table toward Forbes.

"You're physically connected to the IAC, right?"

Forbes took a long moment to think over his answer.

"I really should communicate with upper management." He looked unhappy and cowed. "I could lose my job for discussing our operations here. This is an IAC level-two facility."

Barber almost felt sorry for him.

"Look, Mr. Forbes. Someone has used your facility to hack into the IAC, and—"

"That's not possible." Forbes sat taller, his mouth a thin line.

"Some very clever people did it. Our tech folks traced the cable they used. It joins your cable at a junction box."

"We'd see anyone tapping in." Forbes was back on familiar territory, the expert. "It would have to be someone on the inside. Anyway, why would anyone go to the effort? We've seen no interruption in our activities."

"I'll need a list of all people with clearance to enter the IAC. On second thought, better include all the people who work here. Think back, Mr. Forbes. Has anyone that's not normally involved in your operations been to this facility in the past couple of months?"

"The normal visits from headquarters, but those folks don't enter the . . ." Forbes's face lost color, and the sheen of sweat returned.

His eyes grew huge.

"They killed Mac Renfro, didn't they? Police said it was a robbery, but they . . ." He was breathing hard.

"Why do you say that?" Barber asked.

"Mac was down here a lot recently. He was investing for United Energy in a startup company—"

"HelioCorp?"

"Right. He wanted to understand how our load leveling worked. He said it was because HelioCorp was having difficulty connecting with the grid. It seemed odd at the time, but he is—was—an important guy. One of the original family, and I . . . I . . ."

"You helped him understand how those instructions enter the grid, didn't you?"

Forbes's features sagged, giving Barber his answer.

CHAPTER THIRTY-SIX

"Ms. Napolitani? Louise?" The voice was soft, with a professional veneer. Another shrink. They'd been coming every few hours, led in by the nurses to perch on a chair beside Weezy's bed. Vultures, anxious to pick at the bones of her experience. As if she'd tell them.

Weezy sighed, kept looking out the window. A riding mower crawled across the grass plot fronting the building across the highway, creating comforting geometry in green. Weezy watched it for several seconds, then turned to the woman.

This one had brownish curly hair and looked about Weezy's age. She wore a vaguely meso-American pendant, a checked blouse and practical pants. A name tag pinned to her blouse said *C. Garcia.* A visitor badge told Weezy her case had been escalated. Earlier social workers had been hospital employees. The woman's eyes were too small for her face and her mouth too big. When she smiled, fine lines around her eyes suggested humor. No, sympathy. Anger rose hot in Weezy's chest. Sympathy?

She introduced herself as Camila. "I wanted to check in. The doctors say you are responding well to treatment, but you have been through a very difficult time. I wonder if you would like to talk about what happened and how you feel about it."

There it was, the concerned look. They always trotted that out. But they weren't sent to comfort her. They wanted details to hold against her. Get her to admit how she'd ignored the internet prohibition and talked to Jake, then tell the cops so they could use her admission when they interrogated her. Or, even better, glean some succulent tidbits about what Tattoo did to whisper about over coffee back at the office.

Weezy sighed, reached for the bed's controller, raised herself to sitting position and leaned toward the woman. "I was captured, beaten, forced to keep some data files closed. That was after the moron AVP"—Garcia's brow furrowed—"Harmon . . . the Assistant to the Vice President of the U S of A . . . decided I was a criminal because he couldn't stretch his tiny mind around what I do to protect the government's data from the kind of people who kidnapped me." Weezy took a breath.

"Louise, can you tell me about what happened while you were captive?"

"I had to send a signal every day to a website—"

"No, not what you did. How were you treated."

A fleeting thought—maybe this one was different. But the dumbass shield popped up to protect her. She held up her bandaged hand.

"That's how I was treated. And a creepy tattooed guy liked to watch me pee. It was a frickin' picnic."

"Louise, you have been through an incredibly difficult time. You were hurt, violated, and you feared for your life. I understand that you feared also for the life of an internet friend and a lover. Is that true?"

Weezy's angry resolve began to fail. To be comforted, to tell C. Garcia and her clunky necklace how nothing would ever be the same again, how her life couldn't . . .

But no.

"Yes. They say Joe is okay, but they won't let me talk to him. See, I'm under suspicion. The guy you're calling my hacker friend is out there somewhere. Safe, I hope. He's the only person who can stop the people doing this. If they let me find him and talk to him."

Garcia's professional smile faded. She cocked her head to one side.

"Being combative is a natural reaction to the stress you've

been under. But to get better, it will help if you tell your story. It must have been terrifying to be grabbed the way you were. They must have hurt you . . ." She paused. Weezy fought to control the fear, the blast of sweet-acrid smell from the warehouse, Tattoo's face too close, the clanging of the hoist as the hook came down. She was sure Garcia saw her fear. Did she hope Weezy would open up, spill her guts?

After a silence that seemed to last for minutes, Garcia said, "Weezy, if you get to the point where you want to talk, give me a call." She stood, reached into a pocket and produced a card. Weezy fixed her in a stare, raised her hand. Garcia held out her card. Weezy scratched next to her eye and dropped her hand. Garcia shrugged and put the card on the bedside table.

"Your anger is entirely normal," she said. "But you need to release it, Louise, or it will eat you alive. Please . . . if it's too early to talk, or if you don't want to talk to me, fine. But talk to someone. And soon." She waited for a response, a concerned look in her eyes. "From a practical point of view, someone like me will have to certify that you're capable of going back to your work at IAC."

She paused and gazed at Weezy. Not with sympathy, Weezy realized, but sadness.

"There are people who want to help, Louise. We admire your bravery. You don't need to suffer alone."

Weezy shrugged, pressed the button to lower the bed, turned away from the woman, and stared out the window at the green-on-green stripes of freshly mown grass.

PUUSEPP WAS SQUEEZED into a mummy-like position against the bus's window wall. The person next to him from Miami to Nashville was big, much larger than Puusepp. Her bulk lapped into his seat after she raised the arm that separated them. The woman spoke English with an accent harder to understand than Pyotr's. Apparently, Puusepp's name was Y'all.

In Miami, he had traded caution for speed, called an auto-car to take him to the International terminal of the Miami airport.

He walked the short distance to the main bus terminal and paid for a ticket to Superior, Wisconsin. The trip would take him through Orlando, Atlanta, Chicago, Milwaukee, and a couple of small towns in the Upper Peninsula of Michigan. The first leg to Orlando left that evening. He had forgotten how big America was. It would, indeed, be a long trip. The time it would take was like a punch to the gut. He needed to follow the money trail to sniff out the Sobaki, and it would be at least two days colder than he had hoped.

For the first day on the bus, Puusepp planned the steps he would take when he got to a computer system with the power he needed. He wanted desperately to record what was in his mind but realized dictating it in Estonian would draw the attention of his seatmate. She had finally given up on starting a conversation and taken out a book whose cover featured a blonde-haired woman hanging on the improbably muscled shoulder of a square-jawed, bare-chested, AK-47 toting man. But she was inquisitive; even trying to key it on his new e-pad was a risk.

In the Orlando station, he strolled into the gift shop, look-ing for a notebook or pad of paper. In the sundries display, a small diary with an attached pencil stood out from the others. Puusepp chuckled and reached for it. He paid, drawing an odd look from the gum-chewing cashier. Why would this funny little guy with an accent pick a Hello Kitty diary?

On the Orlando to Atlanta leg, he opened the diary only halfway to screen most of the page he was writing on. His seat mate took in the Hello Kitty title, eyed Puusepp suspiciously.

"What'cha writin'?"

Puusepp closed the diary. "Mathematical notes. Non-linear programming, a particular optimization problem with nine constraints. It is my specialty. You see, it cannot be a simple linear algorithm because—"

"Can'tchall ask your 'pad?"

"No, is too difficult for my e-pad. The parsing algorithm alone . . ." Puusepp shrugged as if conferring with a colleague and laid on his accent. "This is why I needed paper to write."

"Where y'all from, anyway?"

"I am from Montenegro."

She peered at him, a puzzled expression on her face. "Monty neegro, huh? But you ain't no . . ."

"I am not . . . ?"

"Never mind."

The Y'all lady resumed her heaving bosom book, and Puusepp wrote every number and web address he remembered into Hello Kitty. In the layover at the Atlanta station, he sent a request to Jake to monitor the web addresses. On the Atlanta-Nashville leg, he closed his eyes to stave off further conversation and began planning. The Y'all lady got off in Nashville. Puusepp pretended not to wake up. A different woman, black and mercifully much smaller, got on and read the Bible all the way to Chicago. When his plan was as complete as he could make it without access to the net, his mind drew him back to images from the warehouse—Raskov's surprised look, the blood spreading on the floor around Mayfield. The Sobaki. His grandfather. Revenge. Fear that he was too late. Two days to get to Wisconsin. He felt opportunity slipping away as the bus motored through the night.

In the Chicago bus terminal, he ate a piece of "Chicago Pizza" unlike anything he'd had in Europe. More like a crusty bread bowl filled with meat, sauce and cheese. Very like the United States, he thought . . . big, over-the-top, strident. Also delicious.

The last leg of the trip took him north to Wisconsin. As they crossed out of Illinois, his excitement built. At least he was finally in the right state.

The bus stopped at a terminal in Milwaukee, then rolled north, into birch and spruce forest that reminded Puusepp of his grandfather's house outside Nikerjärve. Evening came, and he slept fitfully, waking for the lights of small towns. Much later, after a long spell of darkness, he startled awake. The bus had come to a halt. Lights glared over the entrance to a small concrete-block building with a sign over the door. Escanaba? *Michigan?*

He checked his ticket. It said he needed to transfer, but there was no other bus. In fact, no sign of human activity beyond the cone of light around the station. He left his seat, puzzling over his ticket. Outside, the driver pulled a couple of bags from the under-bus compartment for another passenger, who dragged them toward the single car in the center of a small parking lot.

"I am going to Superior, Wisconsin."

"Yeah?" The driver was a big man, belly riding above a large belt buckle. "Lemme see your ticket." The man angled the ticket toward the light. "You gotta transfer. Fifty-three minutes. Best be standing out front, so the driver don't think there's nobody and just keeps going."

Puusepp nodded his thanks and entered the small waiting area.

The Milwaukee bus's doors slammed, its air brakes hissed as they released, and it was gone. In the silence that followed, Puusepp realized he was framed in light, a sitting target. Would the Sobaki figure out his dodge at the airport? He'd hoped they would imagine he had the resources to get a passport. Then they would spend a couple of days combing through passenger lists looking for Estonian nationals or someone who looked like him. If they did catch on to his ploy, could they trace his bus ticket? His mind ground through possibilities, each one seeming unlikely. But unlikely didn't mean impossible.

A small truck passed, slowing as it approached the building. Behind a cracked windshield, the driver turned, seemed to study him. Puusepp realized he was sweating in the cool of the night. The truck accelerated and soon was gone. As the time for the next bus approached, Puusepp left the waiting area and took a seat on the bench in front of it. Close to three a.m., nine minutes late, a bus rolled into the parking lot. Above the front window, "Superior," brightly lit. Puusepp let out a huge sigh of relief.

As the bus left Escanaba, Puusepp curled across two seats and fell asleep. When he awoke, the sun was up. He stretched and scrunched himself into a semi-sidewise position, gaining momentary relief from the pain in his back. The bus was on a larger road now. On the horizon, steel skeletons of some great industrial activity. A shipping port with cranes, docks, barges and cargo ships crept into view.

The bus skirted a harbor, drove through the outskirts of the city, and pulled into a car park next to a building called Perkins. The driver stood, announced, "Superior. End of the line, folks."

Puusepp stood, stretching cricks out of his back, and picked his way down the aisle.

She told him she would meet him in a green pickup truck.

He'd been confused. "Pickup truck?"

Jake had scratched her head. "A small, two-seat lorry," she said, her voice ending in a question mark. "You will see a lot of them when you get to Wisconsin."

When Puusepp got off the bus, sure enough, there were several two-seat trucks. None were small by Estonian standards. It took a minute to spot a green one and, emerging from it, a white-haired woman wearing a red and black checked shirt and blue jeans. Smaller than he'd imagined from the video, but Jake, he was sure.

Puusepp's throat constricted. Maybe it was relief from the fear that had been with him for a month. Maybe the worry over Napolitani, maybe losing his friend—yes, friend—Raskov. Or Mayfield on the floor in the warehouse, bleeding to death.

"Puusepp?"

He put his hands to his face to cover his tears.

"Don't worry, Kalju. Let's go home."

JAKE HAD SEEN Puusepp only as a brief video image, but there had been no doubt about which of the dozen people who got off the bus he was. Amidst the shorts, flip-flops, and distressed jeans, he stood out in a tattersall shirt, dress slacks, and Italian leather shoes. Such a homely man, bald, small, paunchy. Now, he had his hands to his face. Was he crying?

He wiped his eyes. "Thank you."

Jake, embarrassed, said, "You're welcome. Can I call you Kalju?"

"Of course."

The bus driver was pulling bags out of the luggage bay. Passengers grabbed them and scattered toward vehicles in the lot behind the bus. Jake considered Puusepp's clothes. "We have to do some shopping." She turned toward the truck, "and we have to build a story for you."

"Yes," he said, "Did you track the URL's I gave you?"

"I did, and there was some activity. I didn't try to analyze it. I kept it for you."

Happiness spread over Puusepp's face. Jake wondered if he would break into tears again.

"That is good. Very good."

"And you are Estonian, correct?"

"Yes."

"And, if I remember, Estonian and Finnish are similar languages."

"Yes." Puusepp's brow rose in puzzlement. "Mostly. I can understand some of what a suomalainen . . . uhh, a Finnish person . . . says.

"Good."

Puusepp's brow rose further.

"An Estonian person would be easy to trace," she said. "But the little town where I live has plenty of Finnlanders."

Puusepp nodded. "When I tell them you're my husband's distant relative, come over to visit from Finland, your accent will make sense. We can work out the details later."

They drove a few miles to a Target store in Duluth. Jake picked out khakis, blue jeans, T-shirts, underwear . . . Puusepp was definitely a boxer shorts guy . . . while Puusepp spent quite a bit of time selecting toiletries. "So many choices. What is best?" he asked.

Jake steered him away from cologne Target seemed to think would be popular with adolescent boys and helped him select from among several pairs of sunglasses.

Back in the truck, Jake said, "Tell me the whole story, Kalju. It's almost an hour to home."

And Puusepp told her. His capture in Tallinn, imprisonment in Florida, the phase one attack on some energy company.

"HelioCorp?" Jake said.

"Yes, that's right."

Puusepp continued, outlining phase two, the fail-deadly and realization that he couldn't use the real files—

"Real files?" Jake turned to stare at him. They drifted across the center line; the truck's lane departure warning bleated.

"Yes. Many files, much informations."

Jake brought the truck back to its side of the road.

"What's in the files? How did you get them?"

Puusepp explained how he had amassed the data and painstakingly assembled it into a weapon to destroy the Russian oligarchs—heirs to the people who killed his family. The techniques he used were fascinating, brilliant. In the beginning, he said, he made some mistakes. The shadowy Russians—he called them "the Russian hounds"—had come within one web address of finding him. He diverted them, but only by getting convicted of an unrelated hacking crime. That gave him a month in the Tallinn jail to plan more carefully. What they would have done to him if they caught him was terrifying, but the greater horror was giving up his immense research.

"I had to protect the informations. Even if the hounds took me, the informations had to stay alive." Over three frenetic, coffee-fueled days, he had buried his terabytes of data together with all his bank accounts but one behind many layers of security. "No passwords to memorize and give up under torture, no clever hints," Puusepp said. Only an individual steeped in Estonian poetry, adept at programming, and possessed of an encyclopedic knowledge of the great chess games back to Lasker, Morphy and Steinitz could pass through the outer wall protecting the data. And behind that, an iris scan. "I am the only one in the world who can answer the questions, which are different each time I enter. And each year, in the week before the day of my great-grandmother's rape, I must go into the data cave and renew the lock."

"Your first fail-deadly." Puusepp nodded confirmation.

Jake was silent, thinking of the immensity of the work Puusepp had done, the pain of loss of family, and the hatred he must feel.

"But then, why Hello Kitty? Why not use the real files?"

"Time," Puusepp said. "I had only six minutes to send the message I gave you. It would have taken much more time to transfer even a small part of my treasure."

"So, the real files are safe?"

"Yes, and now I must use them."

"To destroy these Russians? Can you do that with your files?"

"My informations can destroy them, and with your help, I will find them."

"Why do you need to find them?"

"I need to know they are destroyed, or I will never be sure any of us—you, me, Olegarten, my family—will be safe."

They were silent for a couple of miles. "It may not be as bad as you think for Weezy," Jake said. She glanced at Puusepp, whose brow wrinkled. "Sorry, Hotcakes. Her real name is Louise."

"Weezy?"

"Yes. A nickname. I don't know what you call it. A short, informal name."

"Ahh." Puusepp nodded. "Like Ho Hum."

"Yes, a little. Anyway, Adeeb found approximately where Weezy was being held. I passed that along to the government. Maybe . . . maybe they were in time," she said.

"Dogs. They call themselves 'dogs.' " Puusepp's expression was tight, nostrils flaring.

"Dogs?"

She slowed the truck, approaching the dirt road that led to her home.

"The Russians. Zlye Sobaki. It means more than 'dogs,' I think. A group of dogs, wild, angry."

She glanced at Puusepp as she made the turn, saw fear and hatred on his face, and wondered again if inviting him to her home had been a good idea.

CHAPTER THIRTY-SEVEN

MONGREL'S MERCEDES ROLLED through ground fog, the result of heavy evening rain, unusual for Moscow in June. Thoughts passed through his mind like the cars appearing out of the fog, then disappearing. The Estonian. The Napolitani woman. Volkov. The money.

The plan had soured like milk in summer heat. His nostrils filled with the memory of the stench of it. And his father's blast of stale vodka and cigarettes as he screamed at Mongrel and drew his belt out to carry out the whipping that was his answer to any transgression. But Mongrel was fifteen, strong enough to rip the belt out of the old drunk's hand. He had beaten his father across the back, then the neck and face, left him a blubbering mess, walked away from his home with his mother's screams in his ears. He'd recovered from that and a dozen other failures and had come out stronger. This was not the end of the world, he told himself.

His driver turned off the ring road. They made their way through a neighborhood of older apartment buildings. Cranes punctuated the skyline—gentrification, using concrete and steel from one of Mongrel's companies. He had arranged to purchase the dilapidated buildings from the state, but some apparatchik in MoskomArchitektura expected to suck at his teat. He applied leverage. The project now seemed promising, and the apparatchik was attending to housing issues some-where to the east . . . he forgot where. Where was his leverage on this power grid project? Much more complicated.

The Mercedes passed into a grittier neighborhood. As it pulled to the curb, Mongrel's security squad was finishing their scan of the street and disappeared into a building defaced by graffiti. Borzoi's Escalade, a new, garish blue one, followed Mongrel. Chairman's older Mercedes arrived from the opposite direction. Too much action for midday, Mongrel thought, particularly Borzoi's flashy car.

The three men, together with their security teams, took the stairs to an apartment on the second floor, vacant but for a table and three chairs. When they had seated themselves, Chairman spoke.

"What has happened to Raskov and the project?"

Mongrel nodded. "As we suspected, the trailer in West Virginia was compromised, and the Napolitani woman was freed. Marka attempted suicide and is in a coma. She cannot talk . . . yet." He cleared his throat. She had been, after all, a precious resource, developed over years. "She will not be allowed to recover."

"And the man who was with them?"

"We hired him only as a driver, then kept him when we determined we needed to keep the Napolitani woman alive. He is in jail in Virginia and will go to prison.

"Perhaps he should not survive?" Chairman turned to Mongrel.

"One needs to balance the risk of carrying out such an operation in an American prison with the risk of exposing us."

"Which I'm sure you have done, my friend," Chairman said. "And your conclusion?"

"He knows little, and nothing about what we might do in the future. Let him rot in prison. He is easy to observe there, and his sentence will be a few years at most. Perhaps an accident when he is released . . ."

"And Raskov?"

"He was eliminated by Pyotr. That has been confirmed."

"Unfortunate," Chairman said, "to lose such a man." He bowed his head briefly. "He will be difficult to replace."

Mongrel knew Raskov had been with Chairman since before the Sobaki. "Pyotr was not able to eliminate their

hostage, and the Estonian escaped, as well," Mongrel continued. "Pyotr was wounded and is recovering."

"What shall we do about Pyotr?" Chairman said.

Mongrel exhaled and massaged his chin with his thumb
and forefinger. "He was certainly aware of some aspects of the
project. If the police question him, he may talk. The question
is—"

"No, there is not a question." Borzoi looked from Chairman to Mongrel, jaw set. "He is family. Anyway, he doesn't
know enough to hurt us."

Chairman cast a long appraising look at Borzoi. "The
people who work in our organization always know they are at
risk. When a project goes wrong, no one who can expose us
can be left alive. Surely Pyotr understood that."

"He did not," Borzoi shot back. "We had to pull him in
because Raskov couldn't guard Puusepp one hundred percent.
He had no idea of the risk you speak of."

Chairman tilted his head and inspected Borzoi. "You suggested him," he said. "You did not explain the situation when
you promised to pay him far more than he could have
expected for a job without risks?"

"But—"

Mongrel interrupted, turning to Chairman. "It would not
be wise to risk eliminating him, at least not now. We must
assume that he's heavily guarded. Assassinating him would be
risky, and if it failed, he would surely talk to them."

Chairman shrugged acceptance. "The Estonian, however,
is dangerous," he said.

"I agree," Mongrel said. "Unfortunately, he has disappeared. He drew money from a bank near the warehouse. He
may have gone to the Miami airport. But it does not appear
that he took a flight."

"You have lost him?"

"Yes, for now." Mongrel continued, "But he has no papers
of any kind, limited money, none of the substantial resources
he would need to track us. To be a problem, he would have to

develop those resources, and that would expose him."

Mongrel felt none of the confidence he put in his voice. By assuming they could control the Estonian, he had botched the project. The little bastard was brilliant. He would find resources to strike back at them; it was only a matter of time. But he could not admit his error, so he chuckled and said, "Besides, this store of information we feared he had turned out to be nothing. We have the software he wrote, which will be in the premier's hands shortly and will establish our loyalty. If he surfaces with information that compromises us, we will convince the premier it is false news."

"No." Borzoi's face contorted in a sneer. "That is not acceptable. If you had listened when I said we needed to destroy him—"

Chairman cut Borzoi off with a sidewise slash of his hand.

"I am inclined to agree with Borzoi," he said. "The Estonian is too great an unknown. We must find and eliminate him. The Napolitani woman, as well. We have no idea how much she knows. Based on her reputation, it is almost certainly too much."

"If anyone knows where the Estonian is, Napolitani does," Mongrel said. "He will communicate with her before anyone else. The government has Napolitani, and our resource in Homeland will find out where she is. But as before, we must force her to help us before we kill her. The Estonian is easier. If we can get to him, we can use his family as leverage."

"What about the hacker group they both belong to? Do we have options there?" Chairman asked.

"A couple of members might help us, but it would take too much time to find and convince them," Mongrel said with a shake of his head. "We have only one resource left in America. He is a Homeland computer expert, untested in the work of convincing unwilling subjects. It would be a shame to waste our last—"

"Yes, a shame," Chairman said. "But we have no choice, don't you think?"

Mongrel thought through the options. Chairman was patient, a trace of a smile on his lips. Borzoi tapped his hand-tooled Italian loafer and sighed every few seconds. Finally, Mongrel said, "Yes, it is necessary."

"We are agreed, then," Chairman said to Mongrel, ignoring Borzoi. "We will activate the man in Washington to capture Napolitani and through her, the Estonian."

Mongrel considered speaking out against the idea, but the time for that had passed. They were throwing resources at a project that was finished. It was unlikely the Estonian's supposed information could hurt them. They should withdraw, take no more risks, and be satisfied with the software and the money.

"What is the status of the money? Is it safe to divide it?" Chairman asked.

"It would have been," Mongrel said. "If this man"—he nodded to Borzoi—"had not moved it."

Borzoi's face flashed surprise, which he tried to cover with anger. Before he could speak, Mongrel turned his attention fully to Borzoi and continued, "Presumably you think Chairman and I are old fools." He raised eyebrows, waiting for Borzoi's concurrence.

"You thought we wouldn't know you transferred the funds? Were you going to keep all the money yourself? How were you expecting to explain that to us? Or did you think you wouldn't have to?"

Borzoi pulled back from the table and sat straight in his chair. Mongrel leaned forward, now the prosecutor. "It took me two days to find your account, and I was able to do that because you let the money sit for *three days* in a Netherlands Antilles bank!" Mongrel shook his head in disgust.

"You do know that anyone trying to follow the money—the Napolitani woman, or the American government, or the little Estonian—may locate it because of your incompetence." Mongrel's lip curled in disgust. "We have only tolerated your stupidity because we owe allegiance to your uncle. But now—"

A loud, metallic-sounding *ping-ping-ping* came from the hall. Mongrel startled. A sound from his past. Or perhaps a water pipe rattling.

Borzoi gave a half smile, then a frown of concern, quickly gone.

The door swung open, and a man wearing a bulky windbreaker with a patch bearing the initials ФСБ stepped over legs blocking the entrance. He scanned the room, a silencer-mounted pistol following his eyes.

The smile that crossed Borzoi's lips morphed into a sneer. "As you said"—he nodded to Mongrel—"the premier will find the software valuable. He will appreciate my sacrifice in giving it to him, and he will understand that the plot against him"— Borzoi put on a look of false surprise "oh, yes, of course you didn't know—there are documents from our meetings. They will explain the plot, my effort to uncover it, and the subsequent confrontation which regrettably concluded in your deaths."

Mongrel took this in, his smile growing from thin to broad as he listened. He stroked his chin, looked to Chairman, gave a tiny shrug. Borzoi saw this, and his jaw clenched in fury. He turned to the FSB agent.

"Kill them."

The agent raised his pistol.

"Gennady Aleksándrovich," Mongrel said, stretching out the patronymic. "The years have been good to you since our time together."

Doubt crept into Borzoi's eyes.

Ping.

Borzoi slumped back in his chair, eyes wide, as if considering the reality of his own demise.

CHAPTER THIRTY-EIGHT

JAKE'S HOME WAS nestled in pine and aspen forest, the walls built of logs weathered to a rich brown. Green window frames with window boxes full of bright flowers.

"It is a very fine house," Puusepp said, beaming. "My grandfather had such a house. Practical. Good in the winter." The memory of wood smoke, the taste of his grandmother's cinnamon kringle, his grandfather's bellow of a laugh crowded into his mind.

"Not fancy, but it's home," Jake said, pride in her tone.

Jake stepped out of the truck and took the bag of purchases from behind her seat. Puusepp opened his door to follow, but paused, taking in the scent of the forest and the quiet. So welcoming, so safe.

The feeling lasted only a moment, replaced with urgency. Puusepp caught up with Jake as she turned the key, put a shoulder to the door, which opened with a rasping squawk. This must be the door she said the Homeland Security agents broke.

She showed him the kitchen, the coffee pot, the refrigerator, and finally the computer gear in the converted sewing room. As he was preparing to sit at the computer, Jake touched his arm and said, "Let me show you your room." Reluctantly, Puusepp followed her through the tidy living room, up the stairs to a small but comfortable-looking bedroom. Jake gave him towels, showed him the bathroom, then returned to the bedroom and opened a bureau drawer to put away the Target purchases. Puusepp, finally gave in to frustration. "Very nice. And thank you. I must get to the computer. Every minute wasted makes my job harder."

"Sure," Jake said, looking surprised and a bit miffed.

A rush of shame warmed Puusepp's cheeks. Jake had most likely saved his life; more importantly, she had given him the opportunity to strike the Sobaki.

"I . . . I apologize. Thank you for taking me into your nice house. But I must get started."

Jake gave a nod that accepted the apology.

In the computer room, she showed him how she had set up monitoring on the accounts he had sent her.

He stared for a long minute at the screen, scrolled down, then back up, and heaved a great sigh of relief. Jake had identified a group of candidate banks from the partial transfer instructions Puusepp had sent. She had written an algorithm to track and organize their transaction flow.

"Thank you, Jake. Now my job is only difficult, not impossible."

"What is your job? What do you need to do?"

"I need to find the money trail," he said. "The money will lead me to the Sobaki."

"Money trail?"

"Yes. Your government paid the Sobaki to stop attacking the power grid. I saw the transfer instruction when I was a prisoner. I memorized the first part of it . . . the country code, the check digits, and some of the bank identification code, too. From those numbers, I could tell you some likely places to— how do they say it in the movies?—'stake out. Places I thought the money would pass through, because these Sobaki are probably clever at cleaning up money—"

"Laundering?"

"Yes, that's it. They transfer bank to bank many times. Or they buy things in one name, then sell them immediately to another person or company, move to another bank, and so on."

Puusepp turned back to the monitor.

"Can I help you?" Jake asked.

"It is complicated to track the accounts, so it is faster for me—"

"How complicated?"

"I am sorry to be . . . umm . . . I don't know how to say it. You have been good to me, but now speed is the most important thing. If I don't act quick, these bad people will slip away like water through my fingers."

"If two people work the problem, even if one is not as adept as the other . . ."

Puusepp's answer sat at the tip of his tongue. Better to do it himself. He turned to Jake, prepared to deliver it as diplomatically as possible. Her simple logic caught up with him at the same time as his exhaustion. He bowed his head and exhaled.

"Perhaps you can help me find the banks. You see, the first characters of the transfer information are check digits, and that means—"

"—they reduce the number of places we have to look."

Puusepp smiled. "Yes. You have it. And I apologize. You have understood the problem better than I. I should have seen that in the brilliant way you organized the URLs I asked you to track. The check digits mean the number of ways to find one of Sobaki's transactions is millions, not billions—"

"Which makes the problem manageable," Jake said with a satisfied nod.

"And there are only twenty-five thousand banks in the world—"

"And I could set up a second computer—"

"You could." Puusepp beamed.

"But first, Kalju, you must eat something."

Lunch. It would be so nice to have lunch.

"No, I must not . . . coffee, perhaps?"

Jake nodded and left the room. Puusepp was vaguely aware of clattering in the kitchen, then the aroma of coffee.

The first bank was easy to find with the partial address he had. It was a smallish Bulgarian bank, which would require a delay to confirm that the huge transfer was real. It would make only a few hundred bank-to-bank transfers on a normal day. If the banks held the money for two days, maybe three, he might catch the Sobaki in three, even two transfers. They were seven days ahead of him, but he was reeling them in.

A mug of coffee appeared at his elbow, along with a sandwich. He slurped coffee, burned the roof of his mouth. He took a big bite of the sandwich and returned to tapping at the keyboard, chewing. The sandwich was delicious, some sort of ground meat, tomatiketšup like at home, wheat bread.

Puusepp became aware of activity behind him. The squeak of metal on metal. He glanced over his shoulder. Jake had set up a folding table. Twenty minutes later, a computer and monitor occupied the table and Jake was fussing with wiring.

"I have check digits and country codes from the first bank," Puusepp said over his shoulder. "Are you ready to analyze?"

Jake nodded. Shortly thereafter, a window popped open on Puusepp's monitor, and groups of bank names began appearing. He watched the list drop from a hundred to fifty to a dozen as Jake's algorithm chewed through the possibilities.

"Brilliant." Puusepp shook his head in amazement. "Your algorithm is better than I could have designed. Now, to the transfers."

Might she do anything to help? More coffee, of course.

Jake's second algorithm inspected outbound transfers to the likely target banks. Nothing three days post-deposit. Nothing two days. He checked even one day after deposit, which would violate international protocol and risk losing the bank's entire capital. Still, it was a Bulgarian bank, so maybe?

Nothing. Had they not transferred it? Or was there a problem with—

"Jake, can you check the logic of your algorithm?"

Puusepp wished his English was better, that he could ask more subtly.

"You think it didn't—"

"None of the transactions your algorithm identified are

from our Sobaki."

It took an hour for Puusepp and Jake to check the logic. Everything seemed in order.

"I am sorry to waste our time," Puusepp said by way of apology.

"Not a waste," Jake said. "We had to know."

She paused, exhaled, maybe irritated underneath it all. After a moment, she turned to Puusepp, a question knitting her brow.

"Where is the money, Kalju? . . . I mean, if none of the transactions you had me trace were Sobaki's, and the money's not in the bank, where did it go?"

Puusepp pushed back from the monitor, rotated his head to loosen cramped muscles. Dusk had become night. Had they really been working for eleven hours?

Of course, Jake was right. The five hundred million would be huge for this bank, should be easy to spot. Puusepp had hacked into the bank's internal records, searched every transaction, except . . .

He bowed his head, closed his eyes, cleared his mind, and saw the awful solution.

"Kalju, what is it?"

Hands shaking, he tapped the instruction to pull transfers the same day as the deposit.

And there it was. In at nine thirty, out at half past two. *No. Not possible.* The bank was crazy to allow it. They'd go naked for the cash, risk their own bankruptcy. It made no sense. There were no answers. Puusepp stared at the screen, his mind rebelling, not wanting to admit the truth. There were now eight days of exponentially expanding possibilities ahead of him. Five, even six, would be achievable. But eight days . . .

Exhaustion weighed on him. He leaned forward, put his elbows on the table and cradled his head in his hands.

"What's the matter, Kalju."

"We have lost."

CHAPTER THIRTY-NINE

WHEN KEESHA REPORTED for the night shift, Weezy was on a walk down the hall. She leaned on a cane and was escorted by a uniformed officer.

"Who's the uniform?" Keesha asked.

"FBI business," the charge nurse said. "Personnel wouldn't say much either, only that he's supposed to guard Napolitani."

"How's she doing?"

The charge nurse gave a quick shake of her head. "It's like, who turned on the lights? All of a sudden she wants to get out of bed, move around. Won't take a walker."

"Since that big-shot FBI guy visited her."

Keesha caught up with Weezy and the cop. The strain on Weezy's face showed her pain. "You need to take it easy, girl. Those wounds don't heal *that* quick."

They returned to Weezy's door and entered her room. Weezy slipped into bed, Keesha put a hand on her shoulder. "You need to get some rest."

Weezy reached to pat Keesha's hand. "I have work to do." But she accepted the pain pill and fell asleep.

The next morning as Keesha was finishing her shift, two men appeared. One looked like a model out of J. Crew, hair neatly trimmed, pressed khakis and a button-down oxford shirt. The other leaned toward unkempt, managing to look shifty even in the harsh light of the corridor. The night supervisor stopped them, checked their IDs. J. Crew was FBI. The other guy was Homeland Security. The supervisor checked hospital security and was bounced to the hospital's CEO, who vouched for them.

They had a brief conversation with the guard at Weezy's door. Shortly, Weezy appeared, fully dressed. Keesha met her in the hall, and the two hugged. "You take care of yourself, hear?" Keesha said, leveling a look at Weezy that held worry and command in one raised eyebrow.

"I promise," Weezy said, eyes filling. "Thank you."

When an orderly appeared with a wheelchair, Weezy's jaw stiffened. "I'll walk." The charge nurse said firmly, "Hospital policy." Weezy appealed to Keesha with a glance but got a "she's right" nod. Weezy shrugged and lowered herself into the wheelchair. Homeland went to the elevator, scanned the connecting corridors. She watched the trio disappear into the elevator, Weezy looking small and frail next to the big cops.

Keesha knew otherwise.

THE TWO AGENTS rolled Weezy past the front entrance of the hospital down a corridor to the parking garage. The FBI agent waited with her until a dusty orange Toyota that must have been ten years old pulled up to the door.

Panic crackled through Weezy's chest. Federal agents driving a junker? She willed herself to breathe deeply, to think. No autodrive meant no signals to track. The better to take her to her safe house.

The Homeland agent drove, steering the hybrid manually. They took her to a low-rise apartment building west of Bethesda. It was the kind of place that offered reasonable rent close to Metro lines to DC or the NIH headquarters. She still felt fogged by the pain meds she'd been given, but it didn't look like the safe house she'd expected.

"How did you pick this place?" she asked as they parked across from the entrance. Homeland answered, "The best hiding place is in plain sight. Most of these tenants are young, overworking in one of a dozen government agencies spread around here. No nosy neighbors with time on their hands.

Ideal, really."

The speech sounded rehearsed to Weezy. She caught a look of irritation, quickly suppressed, from the FBI agent.

Homeland scanned the parking lot and said, "I'll check in when I get inside," stepped out of the car, and entered the building. A couple of minutes later, the FBI agent tapped his implant and said, "All clear. Let's go." He took Weezy's backpack from the trunk, as well as a suitcase she had never seen. In the entry, he waved the electronic key at the keypad, then handed it to Weezy. "Hold on to this. You won't be going out of the building, but you might need it in an emergency." Weezy wondered what kind of emergency he was talking about.

The agent passed the elevator and led Weezy toward the stairs.

"Memorize exit routes," he said over his shoulder. Weezy lagged behind him, tired after only a few steps, leaning on the cane. He opened the door to the stairs and turned back.

"Oh, man," he said. "That was dumb of me. Let's take the elevator." He came back toward her and pushed the Up button. They waited, silent, for what seemed like a minute. The agent cleared his throat. "I . . . uhh . . . should have . . ." He nodded toward her cane.

"No problem. I'm almost better." Did he know? Had he read the file? Or was he just being polite?

The elevator door hissed open, and they entered. The agent pressed "3." The door closed, and they began a labored ascent. "Stairs are better if you need to get out fast," the agent said. "This elevator's too slow, and it boxes you in. Now you know where the stairs are, anyway. There's a building plan in the apartment."

The door opened on a nondescript beige hall. The apartment was a few steps away. Homeland stood in the doorway. The FBI agent led the way in, Weezy following. He stopped, thrust out an arm to hold Weezy back. "Stay away from windows."

The entry opened on a living room with a couch, a couple of chairs, and a small dining area. To the left, a picture window overlooked the parking lot. Beyond it, a berm shielded the building from a main road. A small kitchen with a pass-through to the dining area faced the entry door. To the right, two rooms separated by a bathroom. The drug haze was lifting, and Weezy thought again that the apartment was an odd choice for a safe house. The picture window, a hollow core door? And why was the FBI agent on edge?

The FBI agent passed through the living area and dropped Weezy's backpack and the suitcase in the room beyond the bathroom. She followed but stopped to check out the other room. It was furnished with a desk and a computer with dual monitors on the outside wall, like a mini version of her set up at the IAC. A window on the back wall showed a scraggly lawn, a small play area. The FBI agent brushed past her, went to the window, and twisted the louvers of the blind mostly closed.

Weezy fought the temptation to sit down and sign on, but there were more instructions to be relayed and warnings to be given. She was not to go out of the apartment for any reason. The kitchen was stocked. Homeland produced what he called a "crash band." It was incorporated into a sports bra and would deliver her vital statistics and location to Homeland. In the center of the bra was a yellow button. "If you're concerned about anything, anything at all, punch that button, and we'll respond."

"Nobody's staying with me? I thought you always did that."

"We'll be monitoring the building . . . the entrances, the hall, your apartment twenty-four seven. In the event of a problem, we'll know immediately."

"Ummm. If you're protecting me from assassination and it takes you five minutes to respond, I'll be dead, won't I?"

The FBI agent's single, small headshake and sour expression let her know his opinion of the arrangement. He was being forced to play nice with Homeland, she was sure. Why?

In the bedroom, she tried on the bra. Its elastic, body-conforming material fit well and was comfortable. The button was set in a contoured pod between her breasts. She pulled on a T-shirt and returned to the living room. The Homeland agent checked the signal and gave her a thumbs up.

The FBI agent said Henry Barber would call to check in shortly, drawing an exasperated look from the Homeland agent.

The agents left, and Weezy sank into the couch. The pain meds had worn off, leaving her tired but jumpy. Too many odd details. *Just sit for five minutes. If Barber doesn't call, I'm outta here.*

CHAPTER FORTY

"KALJU?"

Puusepp was playing a chess game in which his opponent reset pieces each time Puusepp made a move.

"Kalju?"

He startled awake, blinked, and coughed. Early morning light filled the room. All his muscles hurt, and his bladder was painfully full.

Jake was peering at him, looking worried.

"You fell asleep in your chair. You needed the rest, so I let you sleep."

The enormity of the situation returned, amplified. The Sobaki was too far ahead to ever catch them. Puusepp dropped his head, close to tears.

"The second bank held onto the money for almost two days."

"The second bank?" Puusepp shook his head to clear cobwebs. How would she find the second bank?

"When you learned about the quick transfer, that gave me data to run the algorithm, and it quickly identified the second bank. And like I said, they held the money for more than a day and a half. I thought you said that was too soon for them to do that."

"Yes, but they already did it once. There is something here we do not understand. But I must—"

He stood, gave Jake an apologetic smile, and hop-skipped to the bathroom.

He flipped up the seat and groaned in relief.

He asked himself again how they could transfer on the

same day. It was stupid. Their board would fire them all if—

"Ha HAH!"

He missed the bowl, peed on the upraised seat, zipped up, swiped the seat with toilet paper. Rinsed his hands—no time for soap. He rushed back toward the computer room, nodding to Jake, who had moved to the kitchen table. A slice of toast was poised halfway to her mouth.

"Breakfast?" she asked.

Puusepp waved a hand, not wanting to take the time to translate a polite "no, thanks" into English.

Of course. Someone had to clear such a dangerous transaction. He keyed the web, and there it was in plain sight on the first bank's *About Us* page. Volkov, the man Puusepp had destroyed, was the bank's founder. The board of directors included another Volkov, a younger one. He was quite handsome, with sharp features and dark hair worn fashionably long, but a look that made Puusepp sure of the relationship. He knew this younger Volkov from his research. He must be one of the Sobaki. He would have been able to intimidate the bank operations people into making the transfer.

Energized, Puusepp found the second bank's home page. The board included a shadowy Russian oligarch who owned many companies—steel, oil, manufacturing. Another of the Sobaki?

Still, they were six days behind.

Jake pinned the next transfer to Deutsche Bank. Why did they risk using a big, visible bank that would no doubt follow transfer protocol? Puusepp pushed aside the tendril of hope that wound through his calculations. Still too far behind.

Puusepp found his answer four hours later: the commodities trading desk. They had bought copper futures, held them for a day (a full day!), and sold. The resulting cash was converted to euros and transferred again. Clever of them, but costly in time. Also, the futures required a trading instruction, which the ever so well-organized Germans kept in a file Puusepp cracked. The sign-off from a functionary at a massive conglomerate owned by, yes, an oligarch close to the former premier. Another one of the Sobaki, he was sure.

Now they were three days behind.

Puusepp chuckled.

Jake, back to him at the other computer, asked, "Are you alright, Kalju."

"Yes, I am better, much better."

"You need to eat and sleep. You can't keep this up. You can't be thinking straight."

"Coffee, Jake. No, I am not thinking straight. I am thinking in circles, and they are getting smaller and smaller. They look like the sign on the store we went to."

"Target?"

"Yes. Target. These Sobaki are my target."

He turned back to the keyboard, feeling a surge of optimism. He was gaining on them.

On the evening of their second day, Jake found the next bank. Her algorithm was learning, slicing through possibilities more quickly. They gained another day. Two days behind, now. But Puusepp knew his concentration was failing him. Like an exhausted competitor in the last round of the World Chess Olympiad, he reached deep into himself to find the last bit of energy to make it over the finish line. Except the finish line kept moving.

That night, the money skipped through another eastern European bank. They gained a day, but only a day. And neither of them could make it through another night without sleep. They agreed to take three hours.

PUUSEPP WOKE, MOMENTARILY confused. Where was he?

Ah. Wisconsin. Sobaki.

He padded down the stairs, smelling coffee. Another day was breaking, filling the house with a soft orange glow.

Jake was at her computer.

"Did you sleep?"

Jake shrugged and continued tapping on her keyboard. "A little. My internal clock doesn't care when I go to bed; it always wakes me early." She rotated her shoulders and said, "They transferred while we were sleeping."

Puusepp exhaled. Not a surprise, but it probably eliminated yesterday's gain. "Could you follow?"

"Yes, it went to a Netherlands Antilles bank."

"Are you sure?" Puusepp perked up.

"Yes, quite sure," Jake said. "Why?"

Puusepp peered over Jake's shoulder. Sure enough. Antilles.

"It is a foolish choice," he said. "This bank's main business is helping the rich avoid taxes. It will be almost impossible to move out of that bank without a regulator from some country following it."

And the money did not move. Puusepp could not believe their good fortune. The bank's security was excellent, so it took him several hours to get in. He found the account and injected an algorithm that would transfer the money to a midsize American bank in Chicago instead of wherever the Sobaki directed it next time they tried to move it. It would take them at least a day to realize what had happened, and then Puusepp would be ahead of them.

When he finished, another day was breaking.

He punched Return with a flourish and sat back.

"Look, Jake. We have them!"

Jake came into the room from the kitchen and leaned close over his shoulder. His ears were ringing and his head throbbed. When Jake pulled back, he realized he needed a shower, too.

"I didn't think we'd catch them. I feared they would keep the money moving until the probabilities got too small for us ever to find them, even with your fine algorithms and your computer's power. But they must have decided no one was tracking them because they let their money stay in one place for three days."

He pushed himself out of his chair, grabbed Jake in a hug, and danced her in a circle, laughing. "Zlye sobaki, they call themselves. Bad dogs. Stupid dogs. And now we have them." He stopped, realizing the bear hug might be too personal, too smelly, or both. He pulled away but did not let her go. Instead, he grasped her shoulders.

"We have done it," he said, knowing he must look like a grinning maniac. Not caring.

"Now I will destroy them."

CHAPTER FORTY-ONE

WEEZY STARTLED AWAKE. Afternoon sun slanted through the picture window.

How long had she slept?

She stretched, pushed herself up, wiggled a foot that had gone to sleep, and limped to the study. The secure line went live, and the dual monitors delivered a replica of Weezy's workstation at the IAC.

Perfect.

"Call—"

The IAC electronic auditor interrupted her. "You have 733 unanswered messages. Seventeen are Eyes Only High Priority. Please attend to them." Weezy punched the X in the upper right corner of the message box. Instead of disappearing, it retreated to the corner of the screen. Sulking?

Weezy sniffed. "Call—"

A window popped open, revealing Henry Barber, eyebrows knit.

"Louise, I called earlier. You okay?"

"Yes, I fell asleep right when your guys left."

"We need to cover some procedures. First off, this line is protected. You can freely—"

"Do you know how Joe is doing? He looked terrible when we saw him. Nobody will tell me anything."

"He's recovering faster than the doc expected but still moving pretty slowly. I saw him earlier—"

"You saw him? Where is he? Where are you?"

Barber grinned. "Glad to see the impatient Napolitani is back. I'm at the FBI office in Miami. I saw Joe this morning.

He was up, on crutches. Right now he's on a plane."

"Where? How?"

"To Bethesda. Everybody down here tried to talk him out of it. They really want him to recuperate here and go back to HelioCorp. Apparently there's an announcement coming, and they think he's a crucial part of it. But he's determined to get to you." Henry shrugged. "I told him you have to stay in the safe house indefinitely, but he decided to go anyway."

"When?"

"He's landing later today."

"I need him here with me."

"You'll get him, but with conditions."

"But I get him." Weezy cracked a grin. "How'd you pull that off with Harmon?"

"Like I said . . . conditions, a raft of 'em. The main one is you both stay put—inside, absolutely no trips out—until Homeland and I conclude the threat to you and Joe is over. You must wear a crash band, report all conversations you have online, particularly Olegarten. And—"

"Your guys briefed me, chapter and verse. But thanks, I owe you."

"Are you wearing the crash band?"

"I am. It's not too bad, comfort-wise."

"I'd like to add a second level of security."

Weezy took in Barber's guarded expression.

"Because you wonder if that weasel Harmon is using safety as an excuse to"—she lowered her mouth close to the crash band—"listen in to what I do when I'm not on the internet?" Barber ducked, unsuccessful in his attempt to hide a wide grin.

"They're not listening. Just monitoring vitals."

"What's that second level?" Weezy asked.

An acorn icon appeared in the upper right corner of her screen.

"The acorn sends a signal to me and to the agent nearest you. It also turns on audio."

"You don't trust the crash band, huh? Why don't you send

an agent to babysit me?"

"This is a Homeland gig, and they're, uhh, sensitive about FBI involvement—a little more so than usual bureaucratic border wars."

Henry's straight face almost hid his irritation.

"Homeland has adopted the crash band approach, which they say is as good as having on-site personnel. They sent out a white paper about their AI algorithm. They say it cruises through the data the crash band transmits and picks out a problem faster than a human would. They have made it standard in low-risk situations. Of course, it's a hell of a lot cheaper, too. Me, I'm an old school guy. Let's call this belt and suspenders."

He leaned toward his monitor. Weezy saw concern in his eyes.

"Use your intuition. It has served you well before. Don't hang back. Call us. If something has to happen fast, my guys will get to you quicker than Homeland's."

"That makes me more . . . comfortable . . . to know you're involved."

"Me, too." Henry's face crinkled in a smile.

"When's Joe landing? When's he getting here? Who's bringing him?"

"He should be there in two or three hours. Homeland is picking him up at BWI. You'll get a message when they have him, and they'll come directly to the safe house."

"Okay." She exhaled. "Let me talk with Maddie."

"Stay in touch," Barber said. "I'll be back in DC tonight, and I want you to keep me in the loop."

Barber's image blinked out before Weezy had a chance to thank him.

She let out a long breath. Joe was coming. The thought filled her with hope and dread. How was she going to explain? She swallowed, blinked back almost-tears, and squared her shoulders.

"Call Maddie Hollingsworth."

Her friend appeared on the screen, her features wrapped in a smile.

"Weezy?" Maddie's voice quavered. Her sweet smile warmed Weezy. "So happy you're—"

"What's going on with the government? Harmon? Did they catch the grid hackers?"

"—Okay." Maddie chuckled. "No, not that anyone at Homeland will tell us. We know two people were captured with you, but—"

"My apartment? Is Sappho all right? Is Bo—"

"Weezy! Slow down." Maddie drew a long breath. "Damn, it's so good to see you. They wouldn't let any of us visit you. We knew you were rescued, but it was a big hush-hush deal about where you were." Her face came closer to the monitor. "You're hurt."

"Yeah. They used a stun grenade when they rescued me. I got some burns." The words, the real words, stuck in her throat. How could she tell her friend about the horror of what she'd been through? How could she not? Her pain wanted so badly to come out, to bleed away in her friend's understanding. "They're healing."

Maddie sat back. "Everything's okay here. Your buddy Harmon has put us back on the power grid hack, 'full time, twenty-four seven,' as he likes to say. What he lacks in technical chops, he makes up for in vacuous business-speak."

"I talked with Henry Barber," Weezy said. "He says Joe's coming to Bethesda."

"Yes," Maddie said. "We were planning to pick him up and take him to your apartment, but we got a call from Homeland a couple of hours ago. I hope that means they're transferring him to wherever you are. I'm sure they don't want us to know where that is."

"Yeah, I just heard about that."

"That's great news, right?"

"It is." Weezy paused, fear overcoming elation. "Yeah, great news." She knew it came out flat and hurried to change the subject.

"Any communication from my friends at Olegarten?"

"I think so. Haven't you read your Eyes Only inbox?"

"Uhh." Weezy glanced at the minimized auditor button, which was now blinking mauve. "Was about to."

"There's a cryptic message about calling a 'Jake.' If that person is related to Olegarten—"

"She is."

Maddie pulled back, one eyebrow raised. "She?"

"Olegarten best buddy," Weezy said. "Her handle is Jake."

Maddie nodded several times, eyes thoughtful.

"I think it was your Olegarten friends who located where you were being held," Maddie said. "Someone with scanning ability at least as good as NSA, anyway. We got the message from a woman. No name."

"Might be Jake," Weezy said.

"Oh, and speaking of mysterious women . . . to answer your question, Sappho is okay." Maddie chuckled.

"I was afraid . . . cooped up in my apartment, no food, no water . . ."

"When you didn't meet me for lunch, then didn't come back at all, I called Bo," Maddie said. "She went across to your place, opened up, fed Sappho."

Weezy sighed in relief.

"Bo says Sappho sits at the top of your stairs every day about the time you'd be home from work. She waits until dark, then goes across to Bo's for dinner." Maddie giggled. "Bo feeds her tuna . . . from the butcher, not the can . . . and braised chicken. You're going to have a hard time going back to Feline Delight."

Weezy chuckled, and her tension drained away. No threats, no violence. A normal conversation about mundane things. But . . . back to business.

"I have to call Jake," she said. "How do I get out of the IAC system?"

"The setup you're using there is almost identical to your

workstation at IAC. The signal comes to us, then you can go directly out to the web and Olegarten, except . . ." Maddie grimaced, "NSA is listening."

"Right. Henry told me. I'm wearing a gizmo like one of those buttons they give old folks in case they fall at home. They say it's not transmitting audio, but . . ."

"So, no bedroom talk with Joe, right?" Maddie said.

Weezy realized she had laughed for the first time since she'd been captured.

NEXT, TALK TO Jake. She blew out a short breath and opened a link to Olegarten. The security firewall popped up, a reminder that her signal was being monitored. Did she want the offending tagalong disabled? Such a temptation; she imagined Homeland going crazy if the feed went dead. But she answered no. And no to video. Homeland wasn't going to see anything that might identify Jake. They wouldn't hear Olegarten's side of the conversation, only hers. Which meant she had to consider her words carefully.

Jake, you there?

And Jake was there, as she'd always been for Weezy. A rush of affection, of relief, made Weezy forget the Homeland listeners. She heard Jake's joy when Weezy told her Joe was safe.

Could Jake connect Weezy to HoHumJr? In a few minutes, he was there. She had never heard his voice, his hesitating, sing-song English, effusive in his thanks for Weezy's bravery, hugely relieved Joe was okay. He explained the confusion over the Hell-Kit files. Weezy's burst of anger . . . she went through hell for freakin' Hello Kitty . . . flared out when HoHumJr explained how he had so little time. And damn, his solution was brilliant.

She explained that she had limited permission to work with Olegarten friends to solve the problem of the grid hack. HoHumJr described his software, and the flag he had added to prevent future users from getting into the IAC.

"A flag?" Weezy asked.

"Yes. It will warn your IAC when someone tries to get through your firewall," he said. He went on to tell Weezy the government had paid a ransom. He said he and Jake had tracked it. Could Weezy help him get the software and the money back to the government?

"Of course," she said. "What about the hackers? Do you know who they are?"

A Russian group, he said. When she asked if he could identify them, perhaps to Interpol or the FBI, there was a pause. Then the line came live again.

"They call themselves Sobaki. You and I and Jake will destroy them. Alone."

THE CALL ENDED. Weezy sat for a moment, considering HoHumJr's last statement, relishing the thought of payback. Another part of her brain began listing out reasons going it alone was a very bad idea. Finally, she shook herself and checked the time. Still at least two hours until Joe arrived. In the bedroom, she opened the suitcase they'd given her. Someone with taste had picked out several outfits. She took out a couple of tops, jeans, slacks, a cotton nightshirt, shorts, and a simple pleated skirt. They got the sizes right. The skirt almost brought her to tears, remembering the warehouse and Tattoo. No shoes other than the flats they'd given her in the hospital. She settled on slacks and one of the tops, a simple cotton scoop neck, medium blue, and laid them out on the bed.

She went to the bathroom, cranked the shower to almost too hot to bear and stripped. She considered taking the crash band off, but realized she'd probably have a squad of Homeland agents gaping at her shortly after she did that. She decided the band must be waterproof and took the shower, luxuriating in the needles of heat.

Finished, she toweled off, wrapped up and rummaged through the vanity's drawers. They, whoever they were, had set the place up pretty well: toothbrush, toothpaste, hairbrush, basic cosmetics she wouldn't use . . . well, maybe some lipstick. She twisted the tube. Scarlet, the hooker look. Skip that. She took a couple of swipes at her hair, stared at herself in the mirror. Scabs from the burns traced down the left side of her face. Her puffy eyes bore the yellowish bruises of Tattoo's beatings. Lines of fatigue framed her mouth. She felt the nervous, I-look-like-hell feeling she'd had before her first prom date. This time, though, she really did look like hell. What he sees is what he gets, she thought, which brought a shiver.

She returned to the bedroom and dressed. Staying in shadow, she returned to the living area and peeked out into the parking lot. It would be an hour at least, she told herself. No phone, no e-pad. She discarded the idea of signing into the IAC and checking arrivals at BWI from somewhere in Florida. Joe would arrive one way or another.

She realized she hadn't eaten since the hospital, dug in the freezer, and microwaved a couple of tamales. Her mind spun between the Christmas morning feeling when she was a kid and fear of what it would be like to see him. Much worse than a first date.

How would she tell him?

CHAPTER FORTY-TWO

IT WAS MIDAFTERNOON when Joe's plane touched down at BWI. His injured leg, trapped in tourist cabin spacing, throbbed. The "free to move about" announcement came, and Joe stood slowly. Managing the cane and his daypack created an impatient queue behind him. He kept to the left in the jetway, protecting the leg as people pushed past him.

"Mr. Mayfield?"

A young man in rumpled khakis and a polo shirt met Joe as he emerged. He was of medium build, carrying a few extra pounds, and looked about twenty. He had a round face with close-set eyes and the pucker of a scar that forced his right eye into an odd squint.

"Yes, Joe Mayfield."

"I'm here to pick you up."

Joe drew back. He knew he was hypersensitive after all that had happened, but how did this kid get to the gate?

The kid glanced at the stream of passengers exiting the ramp. "Let's step aside," he said and reached into his pocket.

He produced a credential, shielding it so only Joe saw it. Homeland Security.

"I was supposed to find an autocar when I arrived." Joe opened his e-pad to check messages. "I didn't expect a person to meet me." He found the note about the autocar from Maddie Hollingsworth, but nothing more. "A colleague of Ms. Napolitani is expecting me."

"An adjustment," the kid's expression shifted to formal. "We understood you were injured." He took in Joe's cane. "Should we get a shuttle cart? You have baggage?"

"No, I'm okay," Joe said. "And, yes, I have one bag."

The kid's expression softened. "Great, let's pick it up," he said and turned to leave the gate area.

"Who made the adjustment?" Joe said to his back.

The kid stopped, tense again, waited while a young couple with a baby carrier passed. He turned back to Joe and said, "I got a call to pick you up, that's all I know."

"Ms. Hollingsworth hasn't texted me about the change."

A look that might have been confusion passed across the kid's features.

"Uhh . . . They will have talked with Hollingsworth. You're going to Ms. Napolitani's temporary residence. I'm sure Homeland didn't want that information shared."

"They told me I wouldn't be able to see her," Joe said, stunned.

"I guess you have friends in high places. Anyway," he said in a lower voice, "it's a secure location, so you can't go in an autocar. I need to take you."

Could it be? Joe ignored the pain in his leg and hustled to keep up with the kid. The secrecy made sense. Someone would straighten it out with Maddie. The joy of seeing Weezy, home again . . . safe . . . together. Was it Barber? How did he work it? Joe laughed out loud.

The kid cocked his head. "What's so funny?"

"Nothing. Just happy to be home."

THE KID LED Joe to a dusty, late model Tata electric with a dented rear panel, popped the trunk, and deposited Joe's bag. Certainly not a government car . . . not after Congress passed the American-only rule. Suddenly, Joe was sweating. This wasn't right. Joe forced a few breaths. *Calm down. Think this through. The kid has a valid ID.*

The kid apparently saw Joe's concern. "Best way to stay under the radar, use a foreign car," he said. "Why don't you take the back seat?"

On the trip from BWI, Joe retreated into his excitement, rehearsing the meeting he imagined, preparing himself to not react to her wounds. What would it be like to see her? Would she be tough Weezy or soft Weezy?

The kid wasn't talkative, but often glanced in the rear-view mirror at Joe. Was he nervous? Maybe a rookie intent on doing his job perfectly.

The trip took an hour . . . through Bethesda, then west into the setting sun. The car passed a series of low-rise apartments, franchise food stores, older charging centers. The kid checked his e-pad and turned into the driveway of a several-story apartment building. They pulled into a space near a lighted entry. The place was not at all what Joe thought of as a safe house location. It was certainly unobtrusive, though, sandwiched between several other identical buildings.

"Want me to carry the bag?" the kid asked as he opened the trunk.

"I got it." Joe jerked the bag out. The kid walked to the lighted door and held it for Joe, motioning him to enter the small vestibule. "It's 314," he said. "You gotta call for access." He stayed outside. There was a black keypad next to the door frame. Joe touched "3," "1," "4."

It was a long few seconds, then a tinny "Yes?" Weezy's voice.

"Weezy, it's—"

The door buzzed.

"—Joe."

The kid followed Joe in and punched the elevator button. Joe pulled his shirt to straighten it, feeling the clinch in his gut like he used to get before running into the stadium with the team on Friday night. He glanced at the kid, whose brow had a sheen of sweat.

The elevator rose slowly to the third floor. Joe exited and turned right—wrong way—reversed himself, nearly running into the kid.

Three-ten.

Three-twelve.

Three-fourteen. He knocked.

"Joe?" from behind the door. A click of the lock.

She opened the door and stepped back, a tentative smile on her face. Behind the scabs and yellowing bruises, a look he'd be happy to spend years drowning in. He dropped his bag, let the cane fall, and took a couple of wobbly steps toward her.

She folded into his arms and he into hers. He felt her laughing . . . crying . . . both. Like him. "I'm so . . . so . . ."

He felt her stiffen, drop her arms to his hips. Had he embarrassed her in front of the kid?

"Keep your hands where I can see them, Ms. Napolitani."

What?

"Seriously. I know you're wearing a crash band. If your hand moves toward it, I'll have to shoot Mayfield." It sounded as if the prospect scared the kid.

Weezy dropped her arms to her side. A tear from the joyful reunion ran down her cheek, but her eyes flared hatred. Joe craned his neck, turning slowly.

The kid stood at the door, a pistol, elongated by a silencer, pointed at Joe's back.

"GodDAMNit! I should have known," Weezy said. "Pretending you were so fascinated by my notoriety and Olegarten that you missed the turn into the IAC so you had to let me off right where your buddies could grab me."

"Mayfield, step away from Napolitani."

A weight tugged at Joe. *Forever, hold her forever. Protect her. Love her.*

"Move!" The kid's voice went up half an octave. Not the calm assurance of a professional.

Weezy said softly, almost tenderly, "Do as he says, Joe."

Joe forced his arms to release her, straining almost as if lifting a too-heavy weight. He stepped aside and faced the kid.

The kid was trying to look tough, but the veneer didn't

hold. He looked . . . scared. Probably had never done this before. That explained the nervousness, the sheen of sweat, the pistol shaking.

The truth hit Joe like a sledge. The Sobaki had told him not to leave Joe and Weezy alive—and he was afraid he wouldn't have the nerve to execute them.

The kid paused, seeming to consult a mental checklist.

"Ms. Napolitani, you have to get on your computer and talk to the hacker." He rushed the words. "I know you can do that, because—"

"Because you've been listening in down in your bunker with all the other Homeland sleuths, right?"

Fear flooded Joe. Weezy had no common sense when she was angry. Joe stared at her, hoping to drive home his message to be cool.

No luck. She had passed beyond fear to contempt.

The kid motioned with the gun. "You spoke to this 'Jake' on Olegarten. We need some data files and some money from the hacker, and you are going to get them for us."

Watching Joe and Weezy, he moved to the office door. He quickly scoped out the room, then stepped back into the living area and jerked his head toward the door.

"Mayfield, you first."

Joe limped toward the office slowly, searching for any object, any leverage. Nothing.

"Move that chair over next to the desk." The kid pointed to one of the straight chairs against the opposite wall. Joe took it in both hands. Something in his eyes must have given away his plan. "Drag it," the kid said. "One hand. Then sit."

Joe sat, careful of his leg, deliberate. The kid moved to keep Joe in his line of fire, then gestured to Weezy. "Go to the computer, nice and slow."

The kid followed Weezy into the room.

Eight feet, maybe less. One lunge.

Now Joe saw warning in Weezy's eyes. *She's telling me not to act? Why? She must know he's going to kill us.*

"You will go to Olegarten and contact this 'HoHumJr' you mentioned when you were on before. Be certain not to do anything clever. If I suspect anything, I will shoot Mr. Mayfield's uninjured leg. If I need to, I will proceed northward." The gun swung from Joe to Weezy to Joe.

Fancy words, but the gun was shaking.

Weezy tapped the keyboard to wake the monitor. Then she tapped again.

"What's that? What did you do?" the kid was practically shouting.

Weezy gave him her best dumbass look. "Uhhh. Signing into Olegarten like you told me."

"What's that acorn? Why did you click it?"

Acorn? Joe knew his face gave away his surprise, but the kid was focused on Weezy.

Weezy sighed the way she did when someone missed something totally obvious to her.

"You didn't apply to Olegarten after our conversation, did you? You never got the acorn, right? But you do understand two-stage security, don't you? Start by qualifying the device you're using? Remember that from school, maybe?"

Now the guy looked embarrassed.

Weezy followed with, "So, you want me to connect or not? Olegarten now sees my computer."

The kid cleared his throat, a blush rising from his neck toward his cheeks. Joe almost chuckled. Only Weezy could embarrass a guy holding a gun on her. Only Weezy would. God, he loved her.

"Yeah. Go ahead."

Weezy tapped a staccato series then stopped.

"What's the dots circling?" the kid said.

"Decompression. You know, security?"

Joe hoped Weezy's eye roll of incredulity wouldn't register.

The kid was watching the screen, drawn into the process.

Joe shifted his feet to position himself to strike. The movement caught the kid's eye, and he swung the gun to Joe and gave a small shake of his head.

"Okay," Weezy said. "They're paging HoHumJr ... and here he is."

More staccato typing.

"Don't say that," the kid said.

"You really want me to tell my friend it's my idea that he should do whatever your weird organization wants? He wouldn't believe me. You want him to sign off right now?"

The kid looked perplexed, as if there was no item to cover this on his mental checklist. He squinted at the screen.

Weezy sighed, "See, he's suspicious." Her tone said she was explaining an easy lesson to a difficult student. "Look, the only way this conversation's going to continue is if we tell him the truth."

Joe almost felt pity for the kid, having himself been skewered by Weezy's didactic logic more than once.

The kid appeared to think over Weezy's proposal. "Uhh. Send him this exactly: 'You will deliver all the files containing any material detrimental to any European individuals to our representative within two days and agree never to publish it in any way. You will do this in person. You will return the money to the account you stole it from within one day. If you do not do this, your sister Tiina and her two children will be killed. We have them in custody. We will start with the youngest.' "

Weezy finished typing and rested her hands on the keyboard. Her nostrils flared. "Bastards," she whispered.

And they waited.

"What's taking so long?"

Weezy squeezed her face into a look of hopeless disdain. Joe hoped the kid hadn't seen it as clearly as he had. After a couple more minutes of uncomfortable silence, during which the kid took care to watch Joe more than Weezy, she said, "He's answered."

The kid let out a sigh. Relief, or the next step in the plan, the one he's afraid of, coming closer? Joe tensed, ready to strike, and move a bit to force the kid to keep the gun on him and off Weezy.

Two steps and an open-field tackle. The kid would probably get Joe, but maybe he could—

"He's asking how to make the transfer."

"Tell him to come here."

Weezy tapped at the computer.

She turned to the kid. "As you can see, he says five days to get here." She turned back to the monitor. "He can meet you in two days, but only if you make the exchange in Chicago."

Weezy's brow knotted in concentration. "He says he's in this country without papers." She opened her hands and shrugged in an unspoken accusation that the kid hadn't done his homework. "No planes or rental cars. He can get to Chicago in two days, apparently, but not here." She paused. "Then he says international banking transactions can't be done in one day. Two is minimum."

"We gotta have the files in two days," the kid said. Desperation broke through the facade of command he'd been struggling to project.

Weezy gave him another shrug, "Guess you're going to Chicago." She hunched forward, concentrating on the screen. "He says you should be at the main hall of Union Station between noon and two o'clock, two days from now. Look for a short man in"—she squinched her nose—"a bright yellow CAT hat. He must mean Caterpillar."

She half turned to the kid. "He asked if we understand."

"Say yes."

A cicada buzz started soft, then entered the room. Joe spun toward it. A big insect? bird? . . . coming straight at him. He flinched, but it veered to his left and smacked into the kid's head, spreading to cover his left ear. There was a flash of surprise in his eyes, then they rolled up, his knees gave way, and he hit the floor like a rag doll.

Joe dove across the inert body, trapping the gun.

"Freeze!"

A black shoe, a black pant leg, a gun trained on him, an

imposing figure in a bulky blue jacket with white letters. FBI.

JAKE STARED AT the cursor blinking at the end of the question "Have you understood?" After a long moment, the cursor clicked down to a blank line and a single "Y" appeared. Then the screen went blank.

"What happened?" Jake asked, apprehension building.

"I am not sure," Puusepp said, eyes closed, pain spreading across his features.

"But you think . . . ?"

"Hotcakes was the, what do you say, inter—"

"Intermediary?"

"Yes. They got what they wanted from me. She was no longer useful. So—"

Jake's hand flew to her mouth. "No. They wouldn't."

"The Sobaki have a single, simple solution to every problem."

They were silent. A wrenching at Jake's heart drew the memory of Weezy chatting in Olegarten, then seeing her earlier in the day, bandaged but unbeaten. Kermit left her; now another part of her was gone.

The monitor reflected Puusepp's face contorted in fury.

Jake put her hand on Puusepp's shoulder and found her voice. "Kalju, what are you thinking?"

"They know they can't be sure I will give all my files. I might leave copies. So they tell me if the files are ever released, they will kill my family." He gave a mirthless grin. "The simple solution." He was silent for a few moments, then raised his head to gaze out the window at the towering white pine at the edge of the forest.

"My sister Tiina thinks I am a criminal," he said. "She has forbidden me to talk with my niece and nephew. Her son Jakob is young and doesn't know me well. But Kaia," his voice caught, "Kaia does the turning over, the *saut perilleux*, the . . ."

"The somersault?"

"Yes, that's it. She is so beautiful when she does it." He covered his eyes. "She is five."

Jake squeezed his shoulder, feeling it quiver as he sobbed.

After a time, Puusepp took a deep breath, cleared his throat, and wiped his eyes on a sleeve. "But they don't know what is in the real fail-deadly," he said. "If I'm dead, maybe they will think they're safe and not watch so carefully."

Jake saw hope in his smile.

"Here," he said. "Sit by me."

Jake dragged a chair next to his.

"Good," he said. "We will make the plan together." A smile tugged one corner of his mouth. "You and I will go to war with Sobaki, and you will lead the charge.

"I . . . I don't know how I will do that, Kalju."

Puusepp's eyebrow rose. Jake imagined gears grinding as he calculated next moves and probabilities. "We will give them enough to make them believe they have—how do you say it?—the genuine article." He nodded in agreement with himself.

"After they kill me, they will relax. The real fail-deadly will open and there will be much work for you to do."

"No."

"No?" Puusepp gave Jake a sidewise glance. "You will not help?"

"They won't kill you. Damn it, Kalju, don't be so stubborn." Her voice rose. "This is crazy. Let's call Homeland Security, Hotcakes's people at the IAC, the FBI. This is a goddamn international incident. They'll help."

Puusepp gave a small shake of his head, then pushed on. "The files will come to Olegarten. We will write instructions, addresses and lists of what to send and where. We will make— you will make—a massive explosion of files. You will need help from Adeeb and perhaps another member you trust. Some files will go to the Russian government, some to your CIA and Homeland Security, Interpol, newspapers, blogs.

These Sobaki attempted to discredit the current premier in the uncertain days after Putin's heart attack. They almost succeeded, and the evidence of their attempt will destroy them."

Puusepp paused for a moment, sighed. "Maybe before they kill Kaia and Jacob and Tiina."

"Kalju—"

He read her tone. "Jake, I know you want me to trust your authorities. But I cannot. They will act in their own best interests. My material will fascinate them, and they will spend weeks—months, perhaps—analyzing it. By the time they decide how to use it, my family will be dead. We must move quickly."

"Kalju, there is a better way."

Puusepp cocked his head.

"You yourself said the government will take weeks to evaluate what you give them. So . . . give them the files before the fail-deadly explodes. Let them begin to analyze. Hotcakes has"—*was*, she thought, but couldn't say it—"has a connection to the FBI. If they know you're helping them, perhaps they will protect your family."

Jake saw Puusepp's acceptance of the idea in a minute shrug. He cleared this throat. "That might work," he said. "For me, it is all the same, but for my family . . . . Thank you, Jake. That is a good idea."

"Kalju, there is no need—"

"I must go to Chicago for our plan to work. I must give them something to give our plan a chance to work. We have told them two days. How long will it take to get to Chicago?"

"Four hours, I think, if we leave here very early the day after tomorrow. It's best to go on the train from Milwaukee, which is why I suggested Union Station. You'll arrive exactly where you need to be for your . . . meeting. It is a big place, crowded. It will not be so easy to . . ." her voice drifted off.

She unrolled an e-pad and began tapping. "Yes, about an hour and a half to Union Station from Milwaukee." She scrolled some more. "The intercity express needs only a ticket, which I can buy—"

"It will identify you. I cannot expose—"

"Don't be silly, Kalju. I go to Chicago several times a year. No one will connect you and me."

Puusepp tilted his head, contemplated Jake with a skeptical squint.

"Really," she said. "Almost no risk."

"I do not like this 'almost.' I have already lost too many friends."

"Kalju, damn it, I'll be careful."

Puusepp turned back to the monitor and rubbed his hands together, reminding Jake of a piano virtuoso preparing to attack a particularly challenging etude.

"You must stay with me so that you understand the instructions completely. You will be the maestro of this orchestra."

"No, Kalju, you will come back. You will direct us."

Puusepp's smile was at once sad and resigned. "I will be dead, my friend."

CHAPTER FORTY-THREE

FOUR HOURS AFTER the Homeland agent dropped to the floor, Weezy finally stopped shaking. She sat beside Joe on the couch in the safe house living area. Henry Barber had taken a chair across from them. He had arrived half an hour after his squad took the kid away, alive but incoherent.

Weezy squeezed out a wan smile for Barber. "Thanks for giving me suspenders."

"Yeah, first thing we heard was your brilliant explanation of why you had to use the acorn," Barber said.

"What's going to happen now?" she asked. "I see why Puusepp is so adamant about wiping out Sobaki. They don't quit, do they?" Then, to Joe, "We'll always be looking over our shoulders, won't we?"

"I don't think so," Barber said. "The person you call the kid is not a seasoned operative. I think these Russians have exhausted their resources. But I wish Puusepp or your friend Jake would answer you."

"Not a chance," Weezy said. "The way the signal cut out with no proper sign off would have consumed them. Our attempts to reconnect would look suspicious, like someone trying to find their location."

Barber sighed. "It would be easier if Puusepp was part of our plan," he said. "As it is, he's unpredictable, but I think we can pull it off anyway. As long as Puusepp shows up in Chicago."

"How is the plan going to work?" Weezy said, incredulous. "If these files of his start leaking out, they will kill his family, one by one."

"First off," Barber said, "whoever these Sobaki are, they believe both of you have been eliminated. They're expecting Puusepp to appear in Chicago"—he glanced at his watch and raised his eyebrows—"tomorrow."

"Wait a minute," Weezy said. "How did you manage that?"

"Our turncoat Homeland agent is a thinking man, at least he was after his brains unscrambled from our sonic drone," Barber chuckled. "Faced with the virtual certainty of lethal injection or the possibility of prison, he chose prison. He sent his contact a message about his success with you two and the Chicago meeting. Of course, we tagged along and are following the communication path back to its source . . . and I hope, to Chicago."

"Okay, that buys time," Joe said, "but they still have the lever of his family."

"Actually, no," Barber said. "That was an empty threat. I suspect they threw this plan together at the last minute when they learned you two had been rescued and Puusepp had escaped. We identified the man you call HoHumJr from Joe's debrief in the hospital. Kalju Puusepp, a famous guy, actually . . . chess champion . . . so we tracked down his sister and kids in Estonia. They're his only family. Tomorrow, they will begin a nice vacation at a very secure B&B in England courtesy of the US of A, MI5, and Interpol." He sucked his teeth.

"So there's hope," Weezy said and leaned on Joe as exhaustion and relief hit.

"Yes, there's hope," Barber said, "if Kalju Puusepp is willing to die."

JOE AND WEEZY went to bed at two thirty, after Henry left and the crime scene team finished their work. Joe brushed his teeth and stripped down to boxers. Weezy kept on her clothes.

"Don't you want to change?" Joe said. Weezy eyed him quietly. Angry? Fearful? But she said only, "Too tired" and fell into the queen-size bed. Joe climbed in beside her, exhausted, leg in pain, and troubled.

He stared at the ceiling, tired past the point of sleep. That first hug when he arrived had been all Weezy, welcoming, relieved, hopeful. But after Barber left, she had been almost wooden. What had he done? Was it the stress of the last few hours?

He must finally have fallen asleep because the alarm woke him at eight. There was barely time for coffee before an FBI agent picked them up for debriefing. He took them to the FBI office in Rockville, led them to separate glass-windowed conference rooms—the kind one might expect to find in a lawyer's office or a financial advisory firm. Over coffee and later, sandwiches, two agents took Joe through painstaking reconstruction of every action he could remember from his capture, Mac's murder, and his time in the warehouse. And over it again. And again. Then came the questions about minuscule differences between the first telling, the second and the third. Weezy described a similar process on the drive back to a new safe house, this time an unobtrusive home near Tyson's Corners.

They entered the home with their FBI escort, who checked the rooms, spoke with an outside team, checked the rooms again, and finally left.

"I should have known the apartment was a set-up," Weezy said. "This feels more like a safe house."

Joe flopped on to the couch and waited for Weezy to join him. But she disappeared into the bathroom. No further conversation, no contact. The shower started.

Joe sat for a couple of minutes, feeling let down. Maybe just tired, he told himself, but a shower would feel good. A shower with Weezy, well, that would be much better than good. But he hadn't been invited, and that hurt.

Finally, he sighed, pushed himself off the sofa. In the kitchenette, he dug in the freezer, prospecting for dinner. He went to the bathroom door, cracked it, pulled back from the cloud of steam. "How about chicken Kiev? Be ready in forty minutes."

An unenthusiastic "sure" issued from the shower.

"And there's a steamer bag of veggies that looks pretty good."

"Sure."

He shut the bathroom door, returned to the kitchen, slipped the Kievs into the oven. He found a bottle of Cabernet Sauvignon in one cupboard, wine glasses in another. The shower went off.

"Want some wine?"

A muffled "Sure."

After several minutes, Weezy emerged from the bathroom, steam wafting around her. She was fully dressed in jeans and a T-shirt. Joe wondered how much of a struggle that must have been in a steam-filled bathroom.

She offered a tentative smile. "That felt good."

Joe handed her a glass of wine.

"What would you like to do, other than collapse into bed and sleep for sixteen hours?"

A gambit. After they had been separated, it usually took a little time before they fell into the easy, comfortable conversation that led to the intimacy they both craved. It might be a story about HelioCorp or the boyfriend who was pursuing Maddie at IAC or some Olegarten gossip. Just something to drop the needle into the groove. The wine might help.

Weezy took the glass, sipped. "It was a long day." She sat down on the couch, expression still guarded. Well, Joe thought, this wasn't a normal two-or three-week separation. He took a seat, half turned toward her.

"Yeah," he said. "My main interrogator would have made a certified public accountant seem loosey-goosey."

Weezy gave a puff of a laugh. She looked into her wine glass for a long moment. "It's unbelievable to be sitting here with you. I didn't think that would ever happen," she said. "It seems so . . . normal." She smiled, but her expression remained tentative.

"Normal is good," Joe said. "More than good. Seems like a gift. Sitting in that ugly warehouse, all I thought about was those ordinary times. Panacea. Your apartment and Sappho. How I never valued them the way I should have. I thought we would never have those times again."

He slipped his arm around her shoulders and felt her stiffen.

"Weezy, what's wrong?"

"Nothing."

She took a sip of wine. "It's just hard to . . . act as if nothing happened to us. You got shot, Joe. I got stripped half-naked, and a pervert watched me pee."

Joe choked.

"Half-naked? He watched you pee? Why?" He tried to keep his voice level, but some part of his brain screamed *kill the fucker*.

Weezy twisted toward Joe, her mouth a tight, angry "o."

"He was a pervert, Joe. Perverts do that kind of stuff."

"Good God, Weezy. Did you tell the FBI about that? They have the guy in custody. He should have to pay for that." Joe realized he was nearly shouting.

"Joe, for Chrissake, can you keep your hormones in check?" Her mouth was tight, her eyes wide with anger . . . or disbelief. She looked away, then bowed her head. "Sorry. It's hard to get back to normal, if there is ever going to be such a thing."

"Maybe we won't get back to the old normal," Joe said. "Maybe there's a new one that's even better."

Weezy shrugged in a way that made Joe feel like a cheerful, clueless idiot. "To answer your question," she said, "of course I told them. It doesn't matter a damn. The guy was a lowlife piece of crap. He's not some big shot foreign agent, just muscle for the local Russian mafia. It's over. Forget it."

They finished their wine, almost in silence. Dinner was uncomfortable at first, but they soon retreated into bringing each other up to date. Easier to talk about facts. Weezy told Joe about the meetings with Harmon, the trip to IAC, but veered away from the pain of the capture and beyond. Instead, she settled on family—her mom and dad, Auntie Tonia's battle royal with her neighbor. Joe picked up the thread of family—his sister, her kids. Mundane stuff, talking just to savor each other's voices.

They cleared the table, cleaned the dishes. Safe action, no contact.

"Let's see if we really can sleep for sixteen hours," Joe said as they finished.

"Sure." Weezy disappeared into the bathroom again and soon reappeared wearing a nightshirt. Joe went to the bedroom for his Dopp kit and found Weezy in bed, lying on her side, turned away from him. He took off his clothes quietly and went into the bathroom. Slow, take it slow, he thought as he brushed his teeth.

He sighed, switched off the bathroom light, and went to the bedroom. A waxing moon shed a faint light through the window. He got into bed, careful not to disturb her. She shifted and turned her head toward him, what seemed to be a small, sad smile on her lips.

He lay a hand lightly on the curve of her hip, then slipped under the nightshirt and ran his hand over the smooth luxury of her belly.

"I'm really fine, you know. You don't have to cover your beautiful body for fear of getting me excited. My leg's almost healed. Besides, just thinking about you gets me excited . . ."

He kissed her shoulder and felt a rhythm like waves lapping the shore—quiet sobbing.

"What's wrong, my love?"

Finally, muffled, "He made me dance, Joe."

Joe kissed her shoulder again but had a watery feeling in his gut that something terrible perched between them.

"Who?"

"There was an old hoist in the building. They had my hands tied in front of me with a plastic strap. The pervert put the hook between my hands and pulled on the chain that raised the hook. I had to stand up. He kept going until I was on my tiptoes. The hoist was on a rail. He dragged it toward the bench, me with it, and jerked the hook up and down. He said, 'Dance for me.' "

The words arrived and piled up in some anteroom of Joe's mind, at a door with insanity on the other side.

"When we got to the workbench, he gave the chain a huge pull. The hook clattered down, and he bent me over the bench."

She made an animal sound. "I fought him, Joe. I tried so hard." The words were coming out in bursts. "But he pushed me down. 'Like a dog, bitch,' he said. 'I take you like a dog.' "

"My own sweet love," Joe choked on the words, hers as well as his. "I am so sorry." He slipped his arm from under her nightshirt and caressed her arm.

When Weezy began speaking again, her voice was thick.

"When he was finished, he said, 'Marka goes away to make her calls. I can take you then, any time I want.' He had this knife, a long slender blade. He touched me with it . . ." Her shoulder shook.

Rage almost burned through Joe's desolation.

"He took my jaw in his hand and turned my head so I had to look into his eyes. He said, 'Until next time,' and winked. The bastard winked."

Joe felt helpless to soothe the hurt, to put back together what had been broken in Weezy.

"May I hold you?"

For a painful moment, no answer.

"Yes."

He pulled her to him. They cried together and finally slept.

CHAPTER FORTY-FOUR

"I WILL WAIT for you here, and we will go home together," Jake said. She handed Puusepp the ticket to Chicago and a packet of sandwiches he didn't want. Puusepp supposed Jake meant to sound firm and confident, but her voice quavered. He started to tell her again to go home, but only nodded and turned toward the intercity train cars.

He managed to walk steadily, though his body resisted his brain's firm resolve to go to Chicago and play out his destiny. His senses seemed to open, as if to sample the fecundity of life in his last hours: the oil-metallic smell of the train, the swish of the doors opening, the bright colors of the flowing robe worn by the woman across from him, her deep nut-brown skin, the screech of an arriving train and the long glissando of the piped-in country music.

It is going to work. It has to work, he thought. He had packed five cubes with a terabyte each of documents, email, videos, articles. He carried them loose, rather than in a storage tray. Perhaps he would give them over one at a time. Anything to put off the inevitable.

The train jerked as it accelerated out of the Milwaukee station. He resisted the urge to turn and look to see if Jake was on the platform. It would be foolish for her to wait.

He kept the CAT hat inside his jacket. They said Union Station, but they might have people on several trains, hoping to catch him unawares. He took deep breaths to calm himself, and he was back in his grandfather's smoke sauna. A place to become quiet, to speak to one's ancestors.

"You okay?"

Puusepp woke. A young woman in overlarge glasses, stylishly baggy shorts and a T-shirt that said *Love Your Librarian* was peering at him. Sweat ran down his face, dripped off his nose—almost as if he had been in the sauna. He smiled at her. "Yes, I am okay. It is a . . . a disease."

The woman pulled back. "I am sorry," Puusepp said. "My English." He shrugged. "You say, 'a cold.' Very strange, because a cold makes one hot, no?"

She relaxed and grinned. "Hope you feel better soon." She moved down the aisle.

Puusepp gazed out the window. The pine forest of Jake's home was gone, replaced by deciduous trees and houses. He imagined Jake sending the first flight of his precious data and it arriving at a desk somewhere in Washington, DC. What would Jake's FBI contact do with it? Would they understand it? Would they act on it? Thinking through the wealth of information helped hold off the thought of what it would be like to die. Would there be pain? Would he be brave?

He checked his watch. *Almost time.* Jake had advised him to say between noon and two o'clock. He wished now that they had given a specific time. Noon, or quarter past one, or 1:18. Show up at 1:17, and it would be over by 1:19. Now, he had to wait. And Hotcakes had cut off before giving him any sign or password. A "Dobriy den' " or "Do you know the way to . . ." would have been nice. Something to give him time to prepare.

The train stopped. The woman in the colorful robe swished by him, leaving a whiff of flowers and soap. He stood and waited for others to pass toward the door. Perhaps they thought him polite. His legs shook, and he almost tripped as he stepped onto the platform. He squared his shoulders. *You must do this. The sacrifice of one to destroy the evil . . . .* He walked haltingly down an echoing corridor, following arrows to the Great Hall. At the entrance, he put on the hat.

Sunlight streamed from the vaulted ceiling, making the white marble floor glow. Why did he have to die in such a beautiful place?

Jake had said it would not be too crowded in midweek. Puusepp was surprised to see so many people. On closer inspection, there were plenty of spaces on the elegant back-to-back wooden benches that occupied much of the hall. He walked the length of the hall. No one showed interest in the hat. 12:10. He turned and retraced his steps. Much easier now.

He had always wondered at the calm in the eyes of the field mouse run to ground by grandfather's tomcat. Now he understood. The mouse had accepted its fate.

Still no one. He took a seat in the middle of an unoccupied bench toward the center of the hall, hoping the yellow-and-black CAT hat was a beacon.

And he waited.

A panhandler approached. Was this the contact? No, but he said he was hungry, though he reeked of alcohol. Puusepp offered up a dollar.

And he waited some more.

At a few minutes past one, a young woman—an executive, from her tailored pantsuit—sat a couple of feet down from him, nodded, and began tapping and swiping at an e-pad. She'd glanced at the hat, but it seemed to be a fashion judgement, not recognition.

At 1:20, he stood and again made the circuit of the hall. When he returned, the woman had left. Her seat was taken by a young man wearing coveralls with a bright blue logo featuring a fish. Puusepp retook his seat, thinking it better to stay in one place in case they were watching. A man in a blazer had taken a seat on the opposite side of the bench, his back to Puusepp. Might he be the contact?

Maybe it was the adrenaline wearing off, but Puusepp had a hard time keeping his eyes open. Maybe he should eat. He chuckled. Die on a full stomach. He had stuffed Jake's sandwiches in a jacket pocket. He took one out, bread and delicious cheese in a plastic bag, crushed but still good.

Someone slid into the place next to him.

"Looks good."

Puusepp startled. The panhandler again. A complication. Puusepp held out the partly unwrapped sandwich. "Here," he said. "Eat." Maybe he would take it and go.

The man snatched the sandwich and tossed it on the bench. "The files," he said, "Gimme the files." The alcohol smell was gone, and the panhandler's eyes were cold.

So this is how it ends.

Puusepp leaned back to reach into his pants pocket and came up with one data cube. He held it out, hand shaking. "There are four more of these." Puusepp eyed the entrance to the hall, people walking by. If there were enough of them, maybe he could slip—

"Don't get cute, asshole. All of 'em. Now." The panhandler pulled a device from the folds of his ratty coat. Not the gun Puusepp expected, not exactly a knife. It looked like a high-tech toy with a blade, which made it all the scarier.

Puusepp dug in his pocket. He brought out the four remaining cubes. The panhandler rose from the seat and grabbed the cubes with his left hand, his nails scraping Puusepp's palm. Puusepp saw the snarl, the muscles bunched to drive the weapon toward his neck . . .

. . .And a hand gripping the wrist, twisting it away. A scream and a snap as the panhandler's arm broke. The coveralls man pushed between Puusepp and the panhandler. A remarkably calm voice saying, "Take down the lookout."

"You okay?"

The blue coveralls man turned from the panhandler, now moaning and inert beneath the man with the blazer from the other side of the bench.

The next five minutes were a blur. The coveralls man showed FBI credentials. The panhandler was hustled off between two agents. The woman in the business suit appeared between another two agents, handcuffed. Coveralls man watched them being marched out, tapped his implant and confirmed a "handoff," and turned to Puusepp.

"Do you have ID? A passport?"

Puusepp's hopes sank. He dropped his head. "N-no. I have nothing."

Coveralls man seemed to find this unsurprising. "Technically, you're an illegal," he said as he pulled handcuffs out of a pocket. "We gotta take you out in cuffs." In a lower voice, "You'll be going to the Estonian Consulate. You can apply for emergency status there."

"No," Puusepp said, rubbing his temples. "They will know I am alive."

Coveralls looked at him strangely.

"The Sobaki cannot know I am alive."

Kaia.

CHAPTER FORTY-FIVE

GRANSTON HARMON WAS deep in the text of an appropria-tions bill when there was a knock on his door.

"Come."

The door opened to reveal a woman from the finance division, Penny or Penelope or some such. She crossed to his desk, examined her e-pad, brow furrowed.

He gave her a tight smile intended to remind her of the value of his time.

"We have received a very large transfer into the special activities fund."

Harmon snapped to full attention. "Yes?"

"It included a note directing us to notify you confidential-ly."

"Ahh, yes. Your security clearance is . . .?"

"Top secret for financial matters only, sir."

"Fine. This matter is to be classified top secret." He cleared his throat. "What is the source and the amount?"

"The source is a 'Skrillex Trust' transferring from an An-dorra bank. I can find no listing of such a trust. However a search produced an electronic dance music artist, which may be—" she glanced at Harmon, perhaps sensing an imminent explosion. "The amount"—she adjusted her glasses and referred to her e-pad—"the amount is four hundred seventy-two million and change. The transcript accompanying the note refers to a five hundred million initial payment"—she stroked the face of the e-pad—"transferred out of the special activities account over the vice president's signature on June third. It seems as if—"

"Where did the twenty-eight million go?"

"The transcript is quite detailed. Most are bank transfer fees. The money went out of our account to Deutsche Bank in New York to a smallish bank in Kazakhstan. Then there were nine transfers through banks using shell companies, as well as a commodity transaction." She sniffed. "Classic money laundering." She paused, perhaps waiting for a response from Harmon. Getting none, she continued, "The transaction fees were considerably higher than normal. The Kazakh bank got eight-tenths." Her voice radiated disapproval. "And a haircut for the commodities of nine-tenths.

"Haircut?"

"The fee they take off the top of a transaction. Between the bank transfers and the commodity futures discount, twenty-three million."

She paused, swiped again.

"Finally, a Lehman Formula entry with the notation 'HHjr'."

"What the hell is that?"

She brightened and pushed her glasses up her nose. "I was unsure myself, so I looked it up, and"—she glanced at Harmon, took in his expression, and hurried on—"the Lehman Formula was used thirty years ago to determine the amount charged for advising on financial transactions. Lehman Brothers failed in the financial crisis of '08, of course, and the Lehman Formula is rarely used anymore because it yields smaller fees than the big investment banks—"

Harmon shot out of his chair, causing the woman to step back. "A fee? Who?"

"It only says 'HHjr.' I thought you would know . . ."

"How much?" Harmon felt the heat radiating from him.

"Uhh, one percent, sir. The Lehman Formula prescribes one percent for amounts over—"

"That's five fucking million dollars!"

"A little less, sir. Four point seven million. It was calculated on the balance remaining after the bank transfer fees, so . . ."

"OUT!" Red spots danced in Harmon's vision. His fury crushed the tiny voice reminding him nothing good would come from screaming at a GS12 staffer who managed the department's expense account.

The woman blanched and withdrew.

Harmon yelled through the closing door, "Lydia!" *Shit, she's gone.* "Renaldo!" His new secretary appeared, looking offended as usual.

"Get me the Napolitani woman. Now."

"Right away, sir." Renaldo ducked out, but returned after several minutes, looking troubled. "She is available only through a special link from the IAC, sir. Any outside contact except for the FBI requires the IAC director's permission, and I am sorry to say the director is unavailable."

"Unavailable?" Harmon felt acid crawling up his esophagus, or maybe it was a heart attack. He fumbled in his desk for an antacid. "Goddamnit, I am the director's boss. I need to get in touch . . ." He chewed. The antacid began to work. "Ahh, screw it. Get me the Homeland deputy in charge of this program."

"Right away." Renaldo retreated.

"Right away" stretched into five minutes, then seven, before Renaldo appeared, eyebrows knotted.

"Homeland says it is locked down on this case."

Harmon's well of patience, never large, was nearly dry. He took a moment to inhale, then exhale.

"Okay, find me that FBI guy, the AD, Baker, Brewer, Butcher—"

"Barber, sir?"

"Yeah, right, get hold of him. He'll be able to get me through."

It took Renaldo fifteen minutes to get through to Henry Barber, who appeared on video. Did he look guarded?

"So, where is this hacker, this Junior guy?"

"Puusepp. He is under protection of the Estonian consulate in Chicago."

"What?" Harmon's well ran dry. "Look, Barber, this fucker stole five million dollars from us. He was supposed to have crucial information about these Russian mafia people and some sort of software to identify the program that broke into the IAC. So far, bupkis." Harmon snorted. "I want him arrested the minute he sticks his nose out of—"

"Mr. Harmon, we are on the record."

"I don't give a crap if we're filming a goddamn documentary, this little prick—" Harmon paused, the import of Barber's statement arriving late. "Wait a minute, are you investigating *me?*"

"The incident and circumstances surrounding this power grid hack are subject of an FBI investigation. A Russian operative in your cyber security unit is a significant breach, particularly considering Russia's history of cybercrime and your position."

"I had nothing to do with vetting her." Harmon drew a quick breath, remembering Lydia, always so helpful, so quiet, so . . . sympathetic.

Barber's gaze hardened. "Also, Homeland chose to downgrade Napolitani's safe house assignment to crash-band monitoring. They chose a building that made access easy for our would-be assassin. That strategy was your suggestion, against the full-time coverage recommended by both NSA and the FBI."

"It worked, though. We got the bad guys. Not the way we expected, but it worked, right?"

Anger flashed beneath Barber's professional demeanor. Harmon's mouth went dry. Barber had some hang up about the Napolitani broad. Harmon realized too late that he should have swallowed the five mil and buried the ransom payment.

Barber paused and cleared his throat. "My understanding is that the hacker has delivered software that will flag intrusions to the IAC. Also, the NSA is reporting receipt of a mass of data which on first look is significant. The analyst I spoke with called it a 'treasure trove.' "

Barber was enjoying this. The heartburn returned.

"We understood that there were funds involved," Barber continued, "but did not know the amount."

Of course. The slush fund was a well-kept secret.

Harmon realized he had grabbed the paint can and the brush, popped the lid, and painted himself into a corner. "There was a ransom demand after Camden and Valdosta," he said. "We, uhh, negotiated a substantially reduced payment and," the last words came out in a rush, "transferred funds to that organization."

Harmon paused, thinking about how this must sound to a rod-up-the-ass FBI agent. "This sort of negotiation is not uncommon for the government in difficult situations like these." He tried for a smile. "The sausage factory, you know."

Barber's expression did not change. "And how is the hacker involved in this?" he asked.

"He agreed to claw back the money, which he was able to do. But he kept almost five million dollars as some sort of fee for service. We had no agreement to pay him. That is theft, plain and simple." Harmon heard his voice rising.

"You have received money from him? How much?"

"Four hundred seventy-two million."

The surprised silence at Barber's end of the conversation gave weight to the amount.

"So you got back ninety-four percent of the money." Not a question.

"We did, but we didn't authorize this HHjr to take a fee for the return."

"But he did recapture four hundred seventy-two million. Would you have been able to do that without him?"

"I'm sure that, given time and the resources of Homeland, we could have—"

"Ahh . . ." Barber paused, as if searching for appropriate words. They apparently didn't come to him. Barber's tone shifted to formal. "You will be required to deliver all documents, communications and data related to this project to the

FBI investigators. I believe they sent the request this morning."

"Look, Baker . . . uhh, Barber, I'm as shocked as everyone else about the grid hack. Of course we will cooperate." Harmon put on his best collegial smile. Barber matched it with a colder one.

After Barber signed off, Harmon dropped his chin to his chest and exhaled. He needed another antacid. He needed a drink. He needed to move to a sunny tropical paradise far, far away. He stood and trudged to his bookcase bar and pulled down a crystal tumbler. The silver clock set in Connemara marble that commemorated his long-ago accession to city council president back in San Diego said 11:18, which seemed like an accusation. He sighed and poured himself a bourbon. Two fingers.

CHAPTER FORTY-SIX

MONGREL HAD BEGUN to believe that they had come to a satisfactory conclusion to a messy project. A news report from Chicago mentioned the murder of a foreign national in Union Station and the apprehension of a suspect. The Estonian had probably been eliminated. Not certain closure, but close. Unfortunate to lose Raskov, of course. But they had the most important bargaining chip, the software the Estonian had written. The female computer expert Puusepp had enlisted to keep files secret had been rescued, but it was not likely she had any damaging knowledge. US security would have whatever the Estonian was carrying at the time of his murder, but his remaining Washington asset had heard nothing. Borzoi, for all his faults, may have been right—the Estonian created a red herring to delay his inevitable execution. It turned out to be Hello Kitty. The simplest explanation was often best; most likely there was nothing more.

Then hints like the lambent, almost-granular moisture in the air before a blizzard: a tincture of fear in his secretary's usually serious expression, chatter in cyberspace about upcoming actions from the premier.

He called a contact from the old days at the FSB. The man had always been humorless. Now, he laughed a lot and evaded the openings Mongrel gave him.

Someone was asking questions.

Mongrel had put his withdrawal plan together long ago and updated it religiously since the Sobaki formed. He and Chairman knew that someday the premier might find them too powerful, perhaps too popular. Too bad to leave his companies and most of his wealth behind, but the plan required him not to be too greedy. All those assets, he hoped, would function like a bright red ball thrown sidewise in front of an angry dog.

He sent a message to Chairman.

No response.

Time to execute.

He told his secretary there was a problem at the metal-stamping business in St. Petersburg. Might she get him on that evening's train? With an empire that included twenty-eight businesses and his penchant for hands-on management, such a request was not unusual. He kept a suitcase at the office for such situations. A change of clothes, toiletries, an e-pad. While she made arrangements, he called his driver.

His office, a luxurious suite in an older building near the Bolshoi, was outfitted in the ornate style of the nineteenth century. When he occupied the suite, he had a modern safe installed in an anteroom. His staff assumed it held money and records the taxing authorities did not need to know about.

He opened the safe with a fingerprint and a combination. The safe clicked open, and he took out a nondescript daypack. He knew its contents: euros, dollars, three passports, two cell phones, bearer bonds. He opened the suitcase. The nicely folded slacks, shirts and a sport coat came out and went into the safe. The daypack fit inside the suitcase. Clothes that a working man or a farmer might wear came from the safe, together with work shoes that had seen better days. He jammed them in the suitcase with the daypack.

His secretary, always efficient, had the ticket confirmation ready. He gave her the standard handshake, perhaps a second longer than usual.

After the car passed out of the scrum of Moscow traffic, Mongrel had changed clothes. He folded the suit he had been wearing and put it into the suitcase.

Mongrel's Mercedes had made it west from Moscow to a Eurogas station in sight of the Latvian border in just over six hours. The driver, as directed, went into the cramped café in the station for a coffee. Mongrel slipped out of the car and shouldered his daypack. He kept under the metal canopy, invisible to drones watching the border. Keeping the car between him and the café window, he moved into the shadow of a stanchion supporting the canopy.

In the gathering dusk of a warm evening, the driver would see a maroon BMW sedan stop next to the Mercedes. He would have seen doors open and close quickly and the BMW pull away, turning back toward Moscow. He would have noted the single driver when the car came in, but two heads in silhouette as the car drove away. After considerable persuasion, he would admit all of this to the agents who scooped him up a day later. The BMW would be discovered at the train station in Pskov.

As the BMW pulled away from the station, Mongrel kept in the shadow of the canopy. In that position, he was invisible to anyone in the café. He watched his driver finish coffee, check his watch, and leave, just as Mongrel had directed.

Mongrel slouched across to the truck parking area and slipped into the back of an old delivery truck. He unfolded a tarp that had been placed at the rear of the bed, crawled forward to a space between bags of onions and sacks of fertilizer, and covered himself.

Outside, the trucker told a last bad joke to another driver and got a laugh. The door creaked. A moment later, the truck's ignition fired, hesitantly at first. Then the smell of diesel exhaust joined that of the onions and fertilizer, and the truck lurched out of the station. It turned south, paralleling the border on its way to deliver the cargo to Smolensk.

The driver would stop at the side of the road for a piss halfway through the four-hour trip. It would be dark, and he would ignore the shadow passing into the trees on the border with Belarus.

CHAPTER FORTY-SEVEN

TWO WEEKS AFTER the Homeland agent's failed attack, Weezy was cleared to move from the safe house back to her apartment. Joe half-heartedly offered to go back to Florida, hoping Weezy would ask him to stay a while, which she did. Both the NSA and Henry Barber were close-mouthed about what happened in Chicago, except Barber told them Puusepp was okay.

There were news reports that one of Russia's wealthiest oligarchs had been grabbed by the FSB, and rumors were circulating that both the nephew of Volkov and another oligarch had dropped out of sight, but nothing from Barber himself. His reticence puzzled them until news leaked of an FBI investigation of Russian penetration into the US cybersecurity arm. Closed door House and Senate committee hearings were scheduled, and the assistant to the vice president for cyber security was hounded by reporters as he hustled through hallways.

Weezy told Joe that Harmon still looked like a bulldog to her, but that he was thinner and more drawn than she remembered.

A few days after the move back to Bethesda, Joe caught Weezy sitting at the breakfast table glowering at a business card.

"Gotta be cleared by the fixit brigade to go back to work," she said.

"Probably not a bad idea to have someone to talk to, considering—"

Weezy turned on him. "No. Not a good idea to have some

oh-so-understanding certified professional feed me smarmy bullshit about how she understands that it must have been very difficult. I've already heard 'Your anger is natural, but we have to work beyond it' too many times. She won't know how 'difficult' it was, sitting in her nice office, soft relaxing colors, artwork from her patients. No, she won't know jack shit."

Joe backed away, hand up in defense. "I love you. I meant you've been through hell. You shouldn't have to bear the pain alone."

"Sorry," Weezy said, her tone softening from angry Weezy to loving Weezy.

Joe strained in the alternate universe feeling of never knowing which Weezy he was talking to. He loved both, though angry Weezy made that difficult.

In the end, Weezy went off to her assigned therapist, swearing she would do the minimum necessary to get cleared to go back to work.

When she returned that afternoon, the cloud that had hung over her before the meeting was a lighter shade of gray, maybe concealing a silver lining. "She didn't give me any sympathy at all," Weezy said.

A good thing, Joe recognized from her expression.

IT HAD BEEN two months since Weezy and Joe returned to her apartment. Weezy rose early, made coffee before Joe emerged from the bedroom, stretching. Sappho, also stretching, jumped down from the chair she had grudgingly made her sleeping spot when Joe took over her side of the queen-size bed.

Joe walked by the kitchen door as Weezy ate her toast. He nodded but didn't try to start a conversation. She felt a rush of affection for his understanding of her. In the weeks since her first therapy, he had been patient, not prodding her for answers. He waited for her to be ready for sex, and then held her in the quiet moments afterwards, when she shook and sobbed. He listened when she tried to tell him it wasn't his fault, that it had been, they had been, beautiful. She loved how he had chosen just the right time to give her a leather-bound notebook, which she filled with experiences and feelings. She loved how she slowly felt the tautness give way, how she fell in love with him all over again.

She went to the bedroom, opened her closet door, and evaluated several different outfits. She chose shorts, grabbed an MIT T-shirt, dropped it on the floor, and picked a dark blue polo shirt. Conservative for the first day back at work. In the kitchen, she poured coffee into an insulated cup, skritched Sappho, unfolded her e-pad and called an autocar. She passed the table where Joe was reading *realnews.ink* and gave him an honest-to-goodness kiss.

"I'm off," she said, making it sound bright and airy.

She wished she could ride her bike to work, as she had before the kidnapping. It was a gorgeous morning, urging her to enjoy the lush goodness of mid-summer Bethesda. The three-mile ride would have relaxed her and burned off some nervous energy. She sighed, took one last deep breath, and stepped into the waiting autocar.

Her pass key had disappeared early in her captivity, so she went to the main entrance, got clearance at the guard station, and turned down the hall that led to the tracking section. Normally, she would have gotten the DaveScan (a nod), but Dave came out from his station and wrapped her in a hug.

She stiffened at his touch. She knew he was only happy to see her, but fear and anger rose from deep, primitive places in her mind and almost won. She fought her impulse to pull away and returned his hug.

"Good to have you back. We missed you." She wanted to say thanks, she had missed him, too. But she managed a nod.

Freed from Dave's good wishes, she paused to let her breathing return to normal. She took tentative steps down the hall that led to the tracker section. She hesitated at the entry door, steeled herself and pushed through. For a moment, she stood quietly, taking in the thirty-plus workstations in the half-football field space, plus Keith Sanders's glassed-in office on her right. The big activity map on the wall to her left was spotted red-yellow with locations of potential hackers. Thirty heads down, the whisper of thirty keyboards.

Then, at the far end of the room, a young guy from Group Three stood, saw Weezy, and began to clap. Heads popped up, people stood, and the applause swelled.

Maddie strode across the floor. She enveloped Weezy in an embrace close to a linebacker's tackle. Laughing in Weezy's ear . . . well, crying a little. Maddie broke the hug, held Weezy at arm's length, a tear tracing down her cheek, studied Weezy's face, now mottled pink under the remaining burn scabs.

"You look like hell," Maddie said, still laughing.

"I'm okay. Glad to be back."

Keith Saunders had come to his door. "Say hello, take a few, then stop by my office."

The few minutes stretched into half an hour. People wanted to talk, wanted to connect with Weezy, wanted to say all the mundane things people say when they're happy to see you. It was almost too much for Weezy, like being parched and drinking the whole canteen. When they began drifting back toward workstations, Weezy returned to Keith's office.

"Have a seat," he said. "We have some hoops to jump through. Nothing major. Then we can get back to business."

Hoops? She raised an eyebrow. Keith often used business-babble when he was uncomfortable. Was this about the psych evaluation?

He cleared his throat. "There are some, that is to say, we have to clear up some issues raised by your recent . . . experience."

Fury clawed its way up from her gut. What she went through was an *experience?*

Keith ducked from her glare and picked up a single sheet of paper. "We're all relieved to have you back, Louise." The edge of the paper fluttered, magnifying a tremor in his hands.

"As you know, there were some irregularities in this process. We trackers know that protecting the IAC sometimes requires non-traditional methods, but"—he cleared his throat—"the larger world does not always understand this."

Where was he going?

Keith glanced from the paper to Weezy, then continued, "I have put together an action plan. I think it will help bring you back to normal operational capability and will satisfy the director's concerns."

"The director has concerns?"

"This whole process has been messy. You were abducted because of your membership in a group of hackers—"

"Not hackers, Keith . . . well, not *just* hackers."

"—In any case, a group of US and non-US citizens—"

"Yes, Keith, a group of highly sophisticated, generally friendly, computer experts. They include a non-US citizen who risked his life and that of his family to help the United States pinch off an attack on our power grid." Keith's expression had gone from nervous to defensive, but she couldn't hold back. "Oh, yes, and another one of those non-US hackers helped save my life."

Keith retreated behind a wall of formality.

"As I said, Louise, we are all grateful for your service. However, this man Puusepp stole part of the ransom money, and questions have been raised about our methods."

Keith's eyes dropped to the page. "For that reason, we . . . you and I . . . must be detailed and specific with respect to the execution of your duties."

"Uhh . . . Keith . . . you're reading that, right? So this is a review, and you're putting me on probation for helping prevent CyberWar Two? Have I got that right?"

Keith cleared his throat again. "I have put together an action plan that I think will help bring you back to full operational capability."

"How long?"

"Pardon?"

"Keith, let me help you out. You're putting me on probation. I get it. Which means monthly, weekly or daily reviews with you. At the end of some period, there'll be a huddle with the director to decide whether I can continue to have my GS rating and my job. How long?"

"Uhh. Just six weeks. Then a review."

"So go on. What are the conditions?"

"First, you must keep a daily list of resources you use in tracking. We should all do that anyway, right?" An encouraging smile.

"Second, you must not use non-government resources."

"By which you meant to say, 'Olegarten,' right?" Weezy said. It shouldn't have been a surprise, but it hit Weezy like a ton of bricks anyway.

"Well, really any non-approved resources, but . . ." Keith rushed the words and kept his eyes on the paper. "Third—"

His voice droned on through the third, fourth, fifth, sixth, seventh points. He punctuated each with a glance at Weezy, a hopeful look attesting to its fairness.

Weezy's anger cooled, like flames having consumed their fuel, and in the ashes lay sadness.

Keith was reciting the eighth point, the sheet of paper now motionless in his hand. In command. Firm but fair.

Weezy interrupted. "You don't have to read further, Keith."

Keith looked up, questioning, a hint of recognition in his eyes.

"Maddie is brilliant and capable," Weezy said. "Also a better manager than I am."

She stood.

"We haven't finished," Keith said, almost making it a question.

"Yes, Keith, we have."

CHAPTER FORTY-EIGHT

KALJU PUUSEPP SAT in the light of a window in the small room over a garage at Chicago Estonian House, the meeting place of the Estonian community. It was a gray day, and Puusepp was in a gray mood. He should have been happy. He had watched the explosion of data course through cyberspace, a sonar-like ping that returned an echo: three Sobaki gone. "Gone," of course, might mean many things.

The Estonian consul had offered the apartment at Estonian House as a safe place to stay while Puusepp's request for travel documents moved through channels. The Estonian police had found his passport and identity card in his Tallinn apartment and had delivered it to the consul. A fine and very expensive lawyer had helped him set up a trust and introduced him to a bank that would act as trustee. Then, the lawyer and his associates convinced the government that the fee he had asked for was extraordinarily fair, considering the risks Puusepp had undertaken, the substantial amount he had returned, and the reality that Puusepp could have taken the whole amount. In the end, Puusepp became a fee for service contractor for Homeland Security, and the $4.7 million stayed in his account. Tomorrow, he would leave for Tallinn.

He talked with Jake almost daily by video, and almost daily she told him he should come back to Solon Springs for a rest. But it made no sense to put her at risk. No matter how careful he was, he now had a footprint: the Estonian consul, the lawyer, his real name on the trust documents. The American intelligence services would have access to all of that. Despite the lawyer's assurance that the documents were confidential,

Puusepp had no doubt the Sobaki would find him if it survived.

He sighed. The window was north facing, toward Wisconsin and Jake. He realized he was lonely. His father had left the family long ago for a new woman somewhere in Russia. His mother was gone, too. Cancer. His sister had distanced herself and her family. For years, Olegarten had been his only family . . . good friends in cyberspace, but not the human touch.

He would write to Jake and to Louise Napolitani. More personal than a text. He had no way of finding Adeeb's physical address, so he would have to send a message to him through Olegarten.

He smiled and unfolded one of the handmade cards he had purchased at Estonian House's recent art show. Each had a brilliant blue cornflower in watercolor on the front, painted by a talented hand. The blue was Estonia's national color, and the flower had been a symbol of resistance against the Soviet invasion in his grandfather's time. Appropriate for the gift he was about to give.

He picked up his pen and copied the note he had composed on his e-pad so the grammar would be correct. He wished the algorithm could pick the right words to say how he felt. But that would be difficult in Estonian, much less English.

Dear Jake,

You have been a better friend than any person could ask for. Thank you for your help and letting me into your home. You must come to Estonia. Tallinn is a beautiful medieval city. Inland there are many lakes. My grandfather's house near Vorumaa is mine now, a place to enjoy the forest and the smoke sauna. It is built of logs, like yours.

A private message to you will appear on Olegarten five days from today. (Another fail-deadly. Ha Ha.) It is important.

Your good friend,
Kalju

He folded the card, slipped it into its envelope, sealed it, and reached for the second.

CHAPTER FORTY-NINE

JOE ALWAYS WOKE early in Panacea. Something about the air, maybe. He got up carefully. Weezy said "Mmmmpf," and rolled over.

Let her sleep, he thought. She deserves it.

He tiptoed to the kitchen and measured ground coffee into the basket of the ancient coffeemaker. Morning sun shafted through the kitchen window, touching his skin. A woodpecker began tap-tap-tapping on the live oak in front of the trailer. He had a sudden rush of happiness, of gratefulness for all that had been given back to him.

It had been over a month since she arrived home from the IAC, surprising him.

"You're early. Must've been a short meeting." He had glanced up from the spreadsheet he was working on. Her face was white, drawn.

"They put me on probation. I quit."

"You quit?" Joe repeated, feeling stupid.

She'd told him about the meeting, bottled up frustration pouring out as she listed the points in her performance review, the monumental stupidity of the bureaucracy. Finally, the names of the people she would miss, paid out like treasure.

Joe held her, feeling sad and a little jealous. He'd never had friends at work so close that leaving them hurt him the way it did Weezy. Of course, he hadn't worked with Maddie and the OddBalls.

The next week had been pandemonium . . . repeated entreaties from Keith Sanders for Weezy to think it over, come back. When that didn't work, the problem was elevated to the director. She switched from carrot to stick and reminded Weezy that it would be hard to get another government job with her "history." Which, of course, led Weezy to tell the Director where she could put the stick.

After the reality of Weezy's decision to quit IAC settled in, Joe watched her wind herself tighter and tighter, like a world-class athlete forced not to work out. The formidable logic machine in her head had to chew on something. She began outlining the possibility of other intrusions into the IAC. That led to anxiety about what she was going to do for money without a job. When Joe said he would support them, she said "You don't have a job either," her mouth tight. Worst of all, the Weezy who had begun to flourish—the funny, loving Weezy—went on hold.

Joe had suggested that maybe they should take some time in Panacea . . . unwind, go up to Wakulla Springs, paddle up the river, relax. To Joe's surprise, that computed in Weezy's tightly wound logic machine, and she agreed.

He'd flown to Miami and gone up to Boca to pick up his car, clear his apartment, and visit HelioCorp. He was to drive to Panacea, and Weezy was to follow in a week. He had been at his apartment transferring his few belongings to the back of the Subaru when his new implant tapped him.

"Joe, I may need to . . . well, I might have to . . . be a few days late."

Joe had exhaled. Too good to be true. The trip, turning over a new leaf. Too soon.

"I got a job."

"IAC?" Maybe they had come to their senses.

"Nope. FBI. Not a job, really. A contract. Henry Barber needs someone familiar with the kind of hack the Russians . . . well, HoHumJr . . . did. He called the IAC and asked for me. They jerked him around for a while, so he called me at home and found out I'm footloose and fancy free."

"So you can't come down," Joe said, not trying to cover his disappointment.

"Oh, I'm coming. It'll have to be later next week. But I'm going to be dragging a whole lot of computer equipment when you pick me up. In fact, we might be staying longer than we expected. If that's all right."

Joe had driven over to Panacea, lighthearted as he passed the spot where Kapoor's call had turned him back toward HelioCorp half a lifetime ago. He spent the next days in a flurry of activity, cleaning the old single-wide trailer, painting the master bedroom, installing a new shower head, setting in supplies. He checked the wired connection to the internet, signed a contract to bump the speed to the highest level the provider had, and waited.

Yesterday, he picked Weezy up at the Tallahassee station. He'd had that astonished feeling he always got when he first saw her after a separation. She was still tightly wound, but happy and excited too. Her luggage and the computer gear required the full capacity of the Subaru, and he briefly wondered how they would fit it all into the trailer. On the ride to Panacea, she'd been animated, describing the job she was working on for Barber. Joe had glanced over at her again and again, finally understanding it was happiness returning that was making her so beautiful.

"Can you put it on auto?" she'd asked about halfway home.

"On the main road, sure," Joe said, switching on the car's autopilot.

"I got this two days ago," Weezy said. She had pulled an envelope from her bag. The way she held it made Joe know it was important. She handed it to him, and he saw it was addressed to Louise Napolitani in precise European school script.

Joe drew out the card. A hand-painted blue flower. He opened it, read the text, then shouted, "Puusepp!" Then, "A private message on Olegarten?"

"Here, this explains it." She produced a thick legal-size mailing envelope. Puzzled, he withdrew the sheaf of paper. "A trust? . . . Olegarten, Jake, HoHumJr, Adeeb and you equal owners? . . . Four point seven million dollar consulting fee? . . . From Homeland Security?"

Her smile grew broader at each of Joe's questions. Finally, as they neared their turn onto the white sand track that led to the Panacea trailer, she said, "I guess we can afford to fix up the trailer, huh?"

They arrived at the trailer, Joe shaking his head in amazement at Puusepp's gift. When Joe deposited her suitcase in the newly painted master bedroom, she said, "Nice." She stuck her head into the smaller bedroom, where Joe had stacked his clothes on the bed. After quitting the IAC, Weezy had wanted to sleep alone. She scoped the room and said, "Let's push the bed against the wall and make this the computer room."

"But that will make it hard for me to . . ."

"Yeah, but you'll cope, right?"

Joe sighed inwardly. But when he turned to her, he saw a twinkle in her eye.

"We'll sleep together," she said. She had put a hand to his cheek and given him a gentle kiss. After setting up the computer gear, they had a long, relaxed dinner at Pelican's Roost, the best (and only) restaurant in town. They had returned last night to sit on the trailer steps and soak in the evening sounds. Later, they had made love, slowly and hesitantly savoring the taste of each other and the sweetness of the night.

The coffee maker hissed. Its last water gurgled over the grounds, and Joe poured himself a cup. A morning breeze from the Gulf carried the first hint of cooler weather coming. He heard Weezy stirring and called down the hall, "Bacon and eggs?"

"Sounds great." A minute or two later, the shower started. He dug a carton of eggs and a package of bacon out of the new compact refrigerator and sliced wheat bread from the Wakulla bakery. When the shower shut off, he dropped the slices in the toaster and lit the gas burner under the bacon.

"That offer still open?"

Weezy came into the kitchen, barefoot. He glanced at her, so lovely as she toweled her hair. He went back to concentrating on the bacon, turning each strip carefully to ensure even cooking.

"Sure. Scrambled or fried?"

She was at his shoulder then, her breath in his ear.

"No, dumbass. Marriage."

Joe, dangling bacon in mid-flip, spun toward Weezy open-mouthed. For a second he was off the high dive, in that glorious, scary moment of free fall before hitting the water.

"Quit gaping and turn off the bacon before you burn the place down."

Then he had her by the waist, spun her off her feet.

"Yes."

<The End>

Acknowledgements

So many have helped along my path to authorship. Arthur Dewing, my college creative writing teacher, conducted his classes with delicacy of judgment, instinctive tact, and a "keen discernment of the capacity of the student," as a colleague put it dryly. Much later, The Loft in the Twin Cities helped me learn technique, and my critique groups, Crème de la Crime and Minneapolis Writers Guild ironed out the wrinkles in my prose. My editor, Miranda Kopp gave valuable critique and precise correction. Finally, when the book was nearly ready, my sons and posse of Beta readers scoured the manuscript. Writing, at least for me, is not a solo art.

My main listener and critic is my wife, Beverly Boden Rogers. She is a fine writer and teacher in her own right, and her patience in listening and graciousness in giving me the freedom to write at any time, in any place has made all of this possible.

The Mayfield – Napolitani Thrillers

The series is built around Joe Mayfield and Louise (Weezy) Napolitani. Joe would tell you he's an ordinary guy; Weezy would tell you he's much more—steady, yes, but savvy and world-wise, too. He's the kick butt and take names part of the team. Weezy is the quirky, brilliant tracker for the IAC, USA's national firewall.

The stories are set a few years from now . . . not too different from today, except CyberWar I has led to the development of the IAC, and science/technology has moved forward predictably, putting most everyone on the grid.

In ***Fatal Score*** (2018), Joe is on the run from operatives of Phoenix, a project to skim billions in medical payments. Weezy catches up with him in a North Dakota diner just before Phoenix arrives to erase him. Skeptical of Joe's claims at first, Weezy ferrets out the truth and joins Joe in a singlewide trailer in Panacea, Florida—way off the grid, or so they think until Phoenix finds them and comes up with a whole new take on "burn the evidence."

In ***Skins and Bone*** (2021), Joe lands a dream job: Move to Manhattan, work for the respected investment bank ZCG, fly with the finance eagles—and be a short train ride away from Weezy. ZCG uses complex financial derivatives called 'Skins' to craft protection for firms working in politically unstable regions. Strangely, disaster seems to follow creation of each Skin, and someone is raking in millions. Joe and Weezy investigate. A financial conference in Vienna and a sumptuous cruise down the Danube to Budapest provide the opportunity for the man making the millions to eliminate his Joe and Weezy problem with help from a man called *Le Pic*.

In ***Fail Deadly*** (May 2023) When HelioCorp's connection to the power grid crashes, Joe has a hell of a problem. Maybe just a glitch, but it could crater the company's stock offering. Then lights go out up and down the East Coast. A ransom note draws Weezy and Joe into conflict with the Sobaki, Russian oligarchs intent on controlling the US power grid and incidentally scoring a couple of billion bucks. Weezy receives a fail-deadly from a fellow hacker. It's a ticking clock that threatens to spew data across the internet and expose the Sobaki, and it makes Weezy and Joe targets. They are captured and tortured in ways that test their relationship while their hacker friends rush to save them.

Upcoming in the series . . .

Fatal Cure: "Nothing that is vast enters into the life of mortals without a curse." Sophocles (Antigone) was prescient. Gene therapy is a wonderful thing. But wonderful things can be turned to evil purpose. Joe and Weezy uncover a terrifying gene manipulation.

CyberStorm: Putin has passed away, and Russia has splintered. Amid the chaos, hackers flourish. Joe and Weezy are falsely accused of cyber espionage, and Kalju Puusepp discovers his old enemy's plot to start the next cyberwar.

For news of upcoming books and events, subscribe to my bimonthly newsletter at my website, johnbairdrogers.com.

A sample of Mayfield-Napolitani #4

FATAL CURE

Scheduled for publication, Spring, 2024. To be an advance
reader, contact me at **jbr@johnbairdrogers.net**

CHAPTER ONE

THREE PEOPLE EMERGED from the Delta Sky Club into the scrum of the O'Hare concourse. Their leader, a middle-aged woman dressed in a conservative blue suit with a USA lapel pin, radiated assurance and power. Her aura was reinforced by two younger people, also professionally dressed, a woman to her left, a man to her right. Many who watched the group pass recognized her or thought they ought to.

The group cut through the slow-walkers, baby carriers, and Mobibags dutifully trailing their owners' Bluetooth signals.

The staffer on the left tapped her e-pad, answering a call. "The senator will be in DC this afternoon," she said. "Today is fully booked, but I have a slot at 10:45 tomorrow."

The man on the right flank moved forward to deflect a guy strolling toward the group, focused on his e-pad's screen and oblivious to their approach.

The senator swiped her nose absently, saw a red streak on her hand and hesitated. Both staffers kept on for several steps before they realized their boss was standing stock still in the flow of humanity, a puzzled expression on her face.

She held up a hand, as if formulating a question, coughed up a gout of blood, and collapsed.

CHAPTER TWO

WEEZY PUSHED BACK from her monitor bank, stretching her shoulders and neck. Three captures this morning, and one got away. Worry not, she told herself, hope springs eternal for hackers. They'll try again.

Joe had come down the stairs a few minutes ago. Clanking from the kitchen was followed by the luscious aroma of coffee. He stuck his head in the office.

"Good morning, sunshine. Can you take a break?"

"Sure. Just finishing up. Give me five."

His smile and the small gift of him waiting on her brought a warm shiver. Marriage had its challenges for a person used to living alone, but so many pleasures.

She added notes to the file and swiped, which opened her portal through the national firewall that protected the InterAgency Channel database. The IAC tracking section pinged back immediately, instructing her to send the tracking information to the FBI. She moved to stand. Sappho, their graceful black cat of the white socks, expressive tail, and voice indicating Siamese lineage, gave her a grumpy meow and uncurled herself.

Weezy stood and followed breakfast aromas to the living room. Joe had put a cup of coffee and a plate with a toasted bagel and melon chunks on an end table next to the gray, overstuffed sofa they called The Elephant. Joe was in an armchair that had survived from the prior decor, working his e-pad. They'd taken the house over fully furnished from Weezy's friend and former landlady and started to redecorate. The work had been interrupted by the higher priority of starting up their cybersecurity business, Mayfield-Napolitani CyberSecurity, which had become CyberSol. As a result, the room was a mishmash of pieces of the original formal furniture and the few they'd brought in.

Joe wore the button-down window-pane shirt Weezy's parents had given him for Christmas, slacks, and tan penny loafers that had become stylish after a generation in "too preppy" banishment. His dark hair was working its way toward a widow's peak, but his strong features and hazel eyes always gave Weezy a flutter she hoped would never go away.

"When do you have to leave?" she asked, folding herself onto the Elephant.

"An hour."

"Is that a Joe hour, or a real, wall-clock hour?"

"A real hour."

Weezy saw a flash of irritation and decided not to ping him any more about his fixation with allowing plenty of time for travel, which was a subset of his general orderliness.

"What are you going to say to the assembled multitudes in Florida?"

"I'll talk a little about how start-ups go about financing themselves. That's what the director asked for. I'm still not sure why a biotechnology incubator wants me on its advisory board."

"Uhhh . . . you're an alum of the university, and you're famous. You know about finance. And, of course, they hope you will be a wealthy donor at some point in the future."

Joe chuckled.

"Pretty far in the future, unless we develop more business," she continued and patted the sofa cushion next to her. "Come sit with me."

Joe put the pad aside and joined her on the Elephant and put his arm around her shoulders. She leaned into him, feeling his breathing quicken.

She planted a soft, slow kiss on his jawline, then another closer to his ear.

"Even on Joe time, we still have forty-five minutes."